I0823459

THE ANNOTATED

Mrs. Dalloway

OTHER ANNOTATED BOOKS FROM W. W. NORTON & COMPANY

• • •

The Annotated Alice
by Lewis Carroll, edited with an introduction
and notes by Martin Gardner

The Annotated Wizard of Oz
by L. Frank Baum, edited with an introduction
and notes by Michael Patrick Hearn

The Annotated Huckleberry Finn
by Mark Twain, edited with an introduction
and notes by Michael Patrick Hearn

The Annotated Christmas Carol
by Charles Dickens, edited with an introduction
and notes by Michael Patrick Hearn

The New Annotated Sherlock Holmes, Volumes I, II, and III
by Sir Arthur Conan Doyle, with an introduction by John LeCarré,
edited with a preface and notes by Leslie S. Klinger

The Annotated Classic Fairy Tales
edited with an introduction and notes by Maria Tatar

The Annotated Brothers Grimm
by Jacob and Wilhelm Grimm, with an introduction by A. S. Byatt,
edited with a preface and notes by Maria Tatar

The Annotated Hunting of the Snark
by Lewis Carroll, with an introduction by Adam Gopnik,
edited with notes by Martin Gardner

The Annotated Uncle Tom's Cabin
by Harriet Beecher Stowe, edited with an introduction
and notes by Henry Louis Gates Jr. and Hollis Robbins

The Annotated Hans Christian Andersen
translated by Maria Tatar and Julie Allen,
with an introduction and notes by Maria Tatar

The Annotated Secret Garden
by Frances Hodgson Burnett, edited with an introduction
and notes by Gretchen Holbrook Gerzina

The New Annotated Dracula
by Bram Stoker, with an introduction by Neil Gaiman,
edited with a preface and notes by Leslie S. Klinger

The Annotated Wind in the Willows
by Kenneth Grahame, with an introduction by Brian Jacques,
edited with a preface and notes by Annie Gauger

The Annotated Peter Pan
by J. M. Barrie, edited with an introduction
and notes by Maria Tatar

The New Annotated H. P. Lovecraft
with an introduction by Alan Moore,
edited with a foreword and notes by Leslie S. Klinger

The New Annotated Frankenstein
by Mary Shelley, with an introduction by Guillermo del Toro
and an afterword by Anne K. Mellor,
edited with a foreword and notes by Leslie S. Klinger

The Annotated African American Folktales
edited with a foreword, introduction, and notes by
Henry Louis Gates Jr. and Maria Tatar

The New Annotated H. P. Lovecraft: Beyond Arkham
with an introduction by Victor LaValle,
edited with a foreword and notes by Leslie S. Klinger

THE ANNOTATED

Mrs. Dalloway

VIRGINIA WOOLF

EDITED WITH AN INTRODUCTION AND NOTES BY

MERVE EMRE

LIVERIGHT PUBLISHING CORPORATION

A Division of W. W. Norton & Company

Independent Publishers Since 1923

NE W YORK || LONDON

Virginia Woolf outdoors at Garsington, smoking, June 1923. *(Virginia Woolf Monk's House photographs, MS Thr 564, [67]. Houghton Library, Harvard College Library.)*

Printed in the United States of America
First Edition

For information about permission to reproduce selections from this book, write to Permissions, Liveright Publishing Corporation, a division of W. W. Norton & Company, Inc., 500 Fifth Avenue, New York, NY 10110

For information about special discounts for bulk purchases, please contact W. W. Norton Special Sales at specialsales@wwnorton.com or 800-233-4830

Manufacturing by Versa Press
Book design by Marysarah Quinn
Production manager: Anna Oler

Library of Congress Cataloging-in-Publication Data

Names: Woolf, Virginia, 1882–1941, author. | Emre, Merve, editor.
Title: The annotated Mrs. Dalloway / Virginia Woolf ; edited with an introduction and notes by Merve Emre.
Other titles: Mrs. Dalloway | Mrs. Dalloway
Description: First edition. | New York : Liveright Publishing Corporation, [2021] | Includes bibliographical references.
Identifiers: LCCN 2021010616 | ISBN 9781631496769 (hardcover) | ISBN 9781631496776 (epub)
Subjects: LCSH: Triangles (Interpersonal relations)—Fiction. | Middle-aged women—Fiction. | Married women—Fiction. | Suicide victims—Fiction. | Psychological fiction. | Domestic fiction.
Classification: LCC PR6045.O72 M7 2021d | DDC 823/.912—dc23
LC record available at https://lccn.loc.gov/2021010616

Liveright Publishing Corporation, 500 Fifth Avenue, New York, N.Y. 10110
www.wwnorton.com

W. W. Norton & Company Ltd., 15 Carlisle Street, London W1D 3BS

1 2 3 4 5 6 7 8 9 0

To DD

Virginia Woolf, black-and-white photograph of portrait painted by Vanessa Bell, 1934.
(Monk's House photographs, MS Thr 564, [77]. Houghton Library, Harvard College Library)

CONTENTS

INTRODUCTION
xi

Mrs. Dalloway
1

ACKNOWLEDGMENTS
239

WORKS CONSULTED
241

Virginia Woolf, photographed by Man Ray, 1935.
(Granger Historical Picture Archive / Alamy)

INTRODUCTION

I.

Virginia Woolf's *Mrs. Dalloway*, first published in 1925, traces a single summer day in the lives of two people whose paths never cross: Clarissa Dalloway, just over fifty, elegant, charming, and self-possessed, the wife of Richard Dalloway, a Conservative member of Parliament; and Septimus Warren Smith, a solitary ex-soldier, a prophetic man haunted by visions he cannot explain to his anguished wife Lucrezia. Clarissa spends the day preparing for the party she will give later that night—buying flowers, managing servants, mending a dress, and receiving her old suitor, Peter Walsh, whose sudden reappearance in her life recalls her to the passion and freedom of their youth. While she and Peter reminisce, Septimus is in Regent's Park hallucinating. Given to thoughts of suicide, he visits an unsympathetic doctor at his wife's insistence. He throws himself from a window in the early evening, and several hours later, word that "a young man had killed himself" reaches Clarissa at her party.

Clarissa observes her guests and sees that they are oblivious to the disaster, the disgrace of death. She walks into an empty room, and in a moment of astonishing reverie, considers what her life has been—what any life must be: "the terror; the overwhelming incapacity, one's parents giving it into one's hands, this life, to be lived to the end, to be walked with serenely; there was in the depths of her heart an awful fear." Against this fear, her love of life rushes from her with a sense of triumph, with the rapture of existence—the sheer joy of being alive to experience all that the world still has to offer someone like her. She returns to her party, where Peter Walsh waits, eager to see her for the second time that day. "What is this terror? what is this ecstasy? he thought to himself. What is it that fills me with extraordinary excitement?" She enters the room. "It is Clarissa, he said. For there she was." The novel ends.

II.

I READ *Mrs. Dalloway* for the first time when I was maybe ten or eleven, too young to make much sense of it. It was summer. I was away from home, though I cannot recall where or why exactly—only that the mornings spread upon a countryside very green and bright, and that the days were hot, and longer than one felt they had any right to be. What I do remember, with a clarity that startles me, is a letter I received and opened with excitement, a letter I kept for many years. It was written on a sheet of paper torn from a composition notebook, with obvious care taken not to jag the edges. The writer was a friend from school, a boy to whom I had mailed my copy of *Mrs. Dalloway* after I finished so he could read it too. With the novel, I must have enclosed a letter of my own offering him some explanation, some insistence that he not only read *Mrs. Dalloway* but read my copy of it, and see something of us reflected in the pages I had annotated—most likely, the scenes about being young and half in love. Once he had read it, he was indignant and excited. "You were wrong," he wrote. "We're not Mrs. Dalloway and Peter Walsh. We are Jake Barnes and Lady Ashley from 'The Sun Also Rises' by one Ernest Hemingway. Don't jump to conclusions halfway through. Read the book to the end . . . the very end."

The self-seriousness of this exchange has been leveled by time, by the sheepishness and irony that this absurdly heady flirtation now summons. Reading the letter today, I feel embarrassed on behalf of our younger selves, for whatever childish misunderstanding had led us to believe that our relationship was well represented by either Clarissa and Peter, the repressed upper-class English wife and the dull, mawkish civil servant she refused to marry, or Lady Bret Ashley and Jake Barnes, the sexually liberated English divorcee and the impotent American journalist she loved too much to shake loose. Yet I confess to feeling some distant admiration for the readers we had been. I believe we had intuited something essential about novels, and about *Mrs. Dalloway* in particular, when we sought some continuity between our lives and the lives we read about in fiction. It must have seemed possible, even desirable to us, that her fictional characters would help us relieve "the pressure of an emotion" and feel the shape of a thought; would offer us a glimpse of the ever-deepening "colors, salts, tones of existence" that Woolf described in Clarissa's meditations on youth and its discoveries. In creating

Peter and Clarissa, she had laid a narrow spit of land between our lives and her art, on which she had scattered a procession of moods and postures, scraps of conversation that allowed us not just to endow her characters with the semblance of reality but to try on parts of it as our own.

Mrs. Dalloway let me sense what I would come to understand only later, that a fictional character is a marvelously and perplexingly hybrid creature. She is a piece of writing, and as such, is made up "of words, of images, of imaginings," writes John Frow. But she also requires the pretense of existence: the belief, however wide-eyed or fantastical, that from behind these words, or from within their vaporous trail, there rises a distinctly human shape. It is this shape who beckons to her readers, who swiftly and assuredly ushers them into her world as fellow travelers. It is she who extends the invitation to her party. So charmed are we by her presence—how is it that people can spring from nothing more than marks on a page?—that we are insensible to the fact that she is but the middleman, brokering a more far-flung relationship. Behind her stands our true hostess: the writer, exceptionally well-disguised.

This is, at least, how Woolf imagined the relationship between readers, writers, and characters in her 1924 essay "Mr. Bennett and Mrs. Brown," which she wrote at the same time as *Mrs. Dalloway*, and which gives expression to the same philosophy of character as the novel. Characters were to serve as a "common meeting-place" between the writer and her reader. "Mr. Bennett and Mrs. Brown" cast the writer and the reader as two strangers getting to know one another in a distant, impersonal way, learning through characters how to calibrate each other's sensibilities and thoughts. In Woolf's view, their fellowship was like the rapport that "the perfect hostess" (Peter's memorable description of Clarissa) cultivated with an unknown guest—the kind of guest who arrives at a party alone, unannounced and empty-handed, and must be coaxed into conversation with others, those whom the hostess can rely on to be courteous and entertaining, lest he begin to trail her from room to room. "Both in life and in literature, it is necessary to have some means of bridging the gulf between the hostess and her unknown guest on the one hand, the writer and his unknown reader on the other," Woolf wrote. "The writer must get into touch with his reader by putting before him something which he recognises, which therefore stimulates his imagination, and makes him willing to cooperate in the far more difficult business of intimacy."

So stimulated, the reader learns how to be the writer's accomplice in what

Woolf called the art of "character-reading": a practice of observing, of speculating about, people, both in life and in fiction. The adept character-reader was one who fixed people with a powerful, sympathetic, and searching gaze; who seized on their unobtrusive moments—their small habits, their humble memories, their incessant chatter—to grasp the full force of their spirit, their being. Character-reading was an everyday talent, imminently useful and even necessary. "Indeed, it would be impossible to live for a year without disaster unless one practiced character-reading and had some skill in the art," Woolf wrote. "Our marriages, our friendships depend on it; our business largely depends on it; everyday questions arise which can only be solved by its help." Though character-reading could smooth the social tribulations of adult life, Woolf held it to be, first and foremost, the art of the young. They drew on it for "friendships and other adventures and experiments" that were less frequently embarked on in middle or old age, when character-reading retreated from its inventiveness, its candid curiosity, and became a dutiful, pragmatic exercise, a way to avoid misunderstandings and arguments.

The novelist was distinct among adults. She was a perpetual youth, preoccupied with the lives of others long after it was either necessary or prudent. Character-reading clutched at her first as "an absorbing pursuit," then as an obsession. Like all obsessions, it demanded expression. To become a writer was to transform oneself from a reader of character, gazing at those around her with avid, gleaming eyes, to a creator of character, turning her observations into words, conjectures, fantasies. In life as in literature, she bathed ordinary people in the glow of her generous, affectionate imagination; remained attentive to the shadows and shades of their personalities. She did not seek to understand people completely, to master them. She knew all too well the disordered currents of emotion that ate away at the smooth and steady tracts of the mind, that no one, no matter how charming or successful or self-possessed, ever existed as a complete and wholly integrated self.

Suppose, then, that there was something supremely appropriate in my friend and I coming to *Mrs. Dalloway* in the dark, too ignorant to grasp its characters' relations fully, but capable of perceiving, with a sudden clap of recognition, that the possibilities and frustrations lighting their minds—excitement, defensiveness, fear; the inability to know another person with certainty—were also lighting ours. Suppose Woolf had created them with an eye to dissolving the boundary between fiction and life,

Virginia Woolf outdoors holding a walking stick, Cornwall, 1916. *(Virginia Woolf Monk's House photograph album, MH-2, MS Thr 559, [21]. Houghton Library, Harvard College Library)*

revealing to us that the patterns of thought and feeling arranged by the novel were already embedded in the trivial occurrences of our daily lives (though they may not have seemed trivial to us at the time). This was the explanation that Erich Auerbach ventured as to why Woolf's writing overflowed with such "good and genuine love but also, in its feminine way, with irony, amorphous sadness, and doubt in life." Her characters, for all the particularities of their nationality, their race and their class, offered an admirably collective and unifying vision of humankind. They modeled "nothing less than the wealth of reality and depth of life in every moment to which we surrender ourselves without prejudice," Auerbach wrote. "To be sure, what happens in that moment—be it outer or inner processes—concerns in a very personal way the individual who lives in it, but it also (and for that very reason) concerns the elementary things which men in general have in common": confusion, undoubtedly, but also the enigmatic beauty that could be dug out of minor, random, half-forgotten events.

I do not think that Auerbach is right in referring to this sense of shared life, in all its hope and all its melancholy, as a distinctly feminine way of seeing the world. But I do believe that only Woolf's characters could have shown us the common ground where life and fiction meet: not at fixed points in time and space, but in the recesses of our minds. Had we selected a novel by Flaubert, we might have been mesmerized by the scenes he set, every spoon in every tearoom polished, every grain of sand in the folds of Emma Bovary's dress discolored and rough. Had we selected a novel by Dickens, we might have flung ourselves into his grand, spirited plots, the action rising, falling, cresting and breaking, then carrying us, along with Pip and Estella, to the end of the book in the most orderly and satisfying manner. Woolf prided herself less on detail and plot than on the creation of characters, who, for all their physical indeterminacy and psychological inconstancy, their worldly insignificance, had minds that felt "real, true, and convincing," she wrote in "Mr. Bennett and Mrs. Brown." She burrowed deep into their processes of thought, and, so submerged, illuminated the astonishing perceptions and sensations concealed therein. From them, she extracted not just a stream of consciousness but an unlimited capacity for life—a vitality that could only have been hinted at by the lines of eyes and noses, by little speeches and long silences. One could scarcely imagine stepping into these depths of intimacy with Hemingway's terse, battered brood. (Though who knows what sort of intimacies my friend had imagined.)

It is perhaps too obvious to insist that *Mrs. Dalloway* is about a character—for there she is in the title, which Woolf changed from "At Home, or The Party" to "The Hours," before settling on "Mrs. Dalloway." (Woolf also considered "The Life of a Lady," "A Lady," "A Ladies Portrait," and "A Lady of Fashion"—titles that alluded to Henry James's *The Portrait of a Lady*, arguably the greatest novel of consciousness and character.) But *Mrs. Dalloway* is also a novel that thinks with extraordinary precision and virtuosity about what modern novelists mean when they talk about character: how characters are born; how they age and grow; how they navigate the world of the novel, bumping into the people and the objects that constitute it; how they reach for one another in moments of terror and joy, and, finding nothing solid to hold on to, shrink back, unfurling the dazzling intricacies of their thoughts like the petals of the flowers Clarissa Dalloway sees at the florist's shop, each burning in solitude, "softly, purely in the misty beds." The intimacy we are offered with her characters comes at the expense of the intimacy they cannot offer each other. So, in one of my favorite scenes in the novel (I must have asked my friend to attend to it closely), Peter and Clarissa sit in her drawing room, she with her sewing needle, he with his pocket knife, with all the recriminations of the past thirty years hanging between them, walling them off from each other, leaving each no choice but to turn inward, showing the reader, and the reader alone, the memories that still twinge and wound. So Septimus sits in the park, and the light of the sun dancing across the leaves overwhelms him—a feeling he can express to Lucrezia only in frightening, nonsensical murmur. But to the reader he offers an ode to truth and beauty.

Many years after my first reading, the great pleasure of annotating *Mrs. Dalloway* has been to follow the thread of character-reading through the novel, trying to impress its importance not on one or two readers in the past, but on many in the present. Looking beyond Peter and Clarissa, looking beyond the text to the history of its creation, we discover that the thread never slackens or snaps. We find it wound tightly around the novel's origins: Woolf's decision to turn Clarissa Dalloway, a minor character in her first novel, *The Voyage Out* (1915), into the main character of her story "Mrs. Dalloway in Bond Street" (1923)—and then, discovering that Clarissa clamored for more life, Woolf's slow and almost unwilling surrender to the novel. We find it stitched through her largest revision to the story: the creation of Septimus as Clarissa's double, so as to entwine the story of an aging, wealthy, vivacious woman with this story of the First World War and its deadly consequences. Her most famous diary entry about *Mrs. Dalloway* presents her two characters as representing the metaphysical and political extremes that most intrigued her: "I want to give life & death, sanity & insanity; I want to criticise the social system, & to show it at work, at its most intense." Yet as soon as she voiced this, she retracted it. "But here I may be posing," she wrote. There is no doubt her characters are shot with history: that, as

Alex Zwerdling observes, Woolf used her fiction to contemplate the death throes of the British Empire and to satirize its "hierarchies of class and sex, its complacency, its moral obtuseness." But the greatness of her novel comes from its refusal "to judge simply and divide the world into heroes and villains." Her characters remain irreducibly, unconventionally themselves, which means they remain eternally available to show us "the life of feeling in every human being."

The place to pick up the thread of character-reading is where Woolf tells us it originates: in life, with the early adventures and experiments that compelled her to attend to her family and friends with the same concentrated gaze she turned on the novels she read, and later, the novels she wrote. She mined her life for her fiction, though not in any obvious way. What she sought was not the crude, tangled stuff of gossip. She was after "the slipperiness of the soul." She wanted the novels to heave with deep, conflicted emotion, with love and with hate; with longing, irritation, regret, relief, madness, and the wonder of being alive to experience it all. At the same time, she believed the writer should absent herself, her person, from the scene of representation. "I think writing must be formal," she wrote in her diary while editing *Mrs. Dalloway* in the winter of 1924. "If one lets the mind run loose, it becomes egotistical: personal, which I detest." Yet she did not see how, if she were to play the hostess, she could avoid revealing some of herself, the idiosyncratic bent of her imagination. "The irregular fire must be there; & perhaps to loose it, one must begin by being chaotic, but not appear in public like that," she wrote. In creating her characters, she let her readers peep at her character, with all its passions and contradictions.

III.

Even a hasty glance at the life of Adeline Virginia Stephen will reveal that her beginning was irregular, at once enchanted and turbulent. Born on January 25, 1882, she was the second daughter to alight upon the union of Leslie Stephen, a historian and biographer, and Julia Duckworth, a woman far too charming, according to family friend Henry James, to have become "the receptacle" of Leslie Stephen's "ineffable and impossible taciturnity and dreariness." Both of Virginia's parents had been married and widowed

Julia Duckworth Stephen and Sir Leslie Stephen sitting on a couch reading; Virginia Woolf sitting behind the arm of the couch looking at her parents, Talland House, St Ives (Cornwall), 1893. *(Virginia Woolf Monk's House photograph album, MH-3, MS Thr 560, [2]. Houghton Library, Harvard College Library)*

once before. Both had brought older children with them to their new marriage. With Leslie came a daughter, Laura Makepeace Stephen; with Julia, two sons, George and Gerald Duckworth, and a daughter, Stella. To these four, Leslie and Julia added Vanessa in 1879, Thoby in 1880, Virginia in 1882, and Adrian in 1883. They grew their family mostly through carelessness and good fortune, at a time when violent coughs and raging fevers frequently cut short the lives of young children—and so, when they finished, judged themselves lucky not to have "lost" any of theirs along the way.

In a family cluttered with children, "Little 'Ginia" stood out from the start, a baby with red hair and large green eyes. She was an apprehensive character; intensely responsive and quick to anger; always pleading nervousness or fear; and refusing to submit to her parents' caresses, unless to get her way. Her knack for telling stories was apparent early on, in the

Top row, from left to right: Leslie Stephen, Lady Albutt, Julia Duckworth Stephen. Next to Gerald Duckworth is Sir Clifford Albutt. Bottom row, from left to right: Vanessa Bell, Virginia Woolf, Adrian Stephen. St Ives (Cornwall), 1892. *(Virginia Woolf Monk's House photograph album, MH-5, MS Thr 562, [5]. Houghton Library, Harvard College Library)*

Hayle from Lelant, Cornwall, Alfred East. Oil on panel, 1891–92. *(Birmingham Museums Trust)*

letter she wrote to her mother at age five or six "about an old man of 70 who got his legs caute in the weels of the train"; in the tale she told her father before bed, "a long rigmarole about a crow and a book." She could be comical, eccentric even. Her family nicknamed her "the Goat" for her bleating little laugh and accident-proneness. Photographs from her childhood show a small round girl with a high forehead and heavy eyes. Later, they depict an adolescent with a moody jaw and large thin ears. Hers was a face that needed time to grow into the supercilious elegance many would come to associate with it.

Virginia's winters were spent in the darkness and chill of London, at 22 Hyde Park Gate in Kensington. Summers were passed at Talland House, Leslie Stephen's "pocket-paradise" in Cornwall—a large, shabby, stucco house, with disorderly gardens that sloped to the shore and iron-railed

Facade of Talland House, St Ives (Cornwall), undated. *(Virginia Woolf Monk's House photograph album, MH-5, MS Thr 562, [1d]. Houghton Library, Harvard College Library)*

balconies that overlooked, first, St Ives Bay, and then, if one were to raise one's eyes to the horizon, the Celtic Sea. (The sound of the waves breaking, their powerful, rhythmic indifference to the human beings standing on the shore—Woolf would recall this scene and its sensations in all her novels.) For the Stephen children, as for Clarissa Dalloway, summer was a season of intense happiness. Carriage rides, moth hunts, fireworks, games of cricket, billiards and charades, swimming and boating competitions, putting on plays—all their joy and amusement was recorded in "The Hyde Park Gate News," the newspaper Virginia and Vanessa wrote and circulated to their neighbors. By the time Virginia was ten, she, Thoby, Vanessa, and Adrian had banded together as the family's "Explorers and revolutionists," casting off their half-siblings as the "consenting and approving Victorians."

From an early age, "the Victorian" would signify all that was dull, antiquated, and prim to her, in life as well as in the literature. Her half-siblings often appeared to her not as full-fleshed characters but as types—the musty and predictable figures one would find throughout all her fiction, and especially in *Mrs. Dalloway.* There was unctuous Gerald and loathsome, ignorant George, who, when Virginia turned seventeen, would start slipping into her room at night to fondle her. (One can see the two of them peeping out from behind "the admirable" Hugh Whitbread, Clarissa Dalloway's pompous, sexually abusive friend.) There was kind, dreamy Stella, whom one often found sitting in a corner, her golden head bent over her white dresses and doilies; and who, like Clarissa's sister Sylvia, would die young and tragically. There was Laura—a "little wretch," according to Leslie Stephen; "backward" and "wicked" and prone to "dreadful fits of passion." Cherished at first, she was afflicted by an unidentified mental illness and institutionalized when Virginia was eleven. When she created Septimus Smith nearly thirty years later, she insisted that, for all his delusions, he was no "degenerate." She had more sympathy for him than for her half-sister, the squealing, stammering, "vacant-eyed girl" she recalled in her memoirs.

Of all her siblings, it was Vanessa whom Virginia loved best. It was "Nessa" who took care of her—who bathed her and rubbed her back with scents to calm her nerves, and put her to bed in clean sheets; who guarded her, amused her, and encouraged her to read and to write. Their mother was often away, nursing sick and dying family members, or too unwell herself to rise from bed. Their father, a self-absorbed and resolutely tortured figure, spent most of his time fretting over work and money. Though Leslie read aloud to Virginia in the evenings, selecting his favorite passages from Shakespeare, Milton, Hawthorne, and Austen, the exact shape and substance of his daughters' intellectual development was left to them to decide.

Virginia Woolf and Vanessa Bell as young girls with cricket bat and ball at St Ives (Cornwall), c. 1893–94. *(Virginia Woolf Monk's House photographs, MS Thr 564, [50]. Houghton Library, Harvard College Library)*

The boys had their public schools, then Cambridge. Vanessa, who would become a painter and interior designer, took it upon herself to enroll in art classes at Sir Arthur Cope's Art School. Virginia's education was more haphazard: some courses in Greek and history at King's College, private Latin lessons with Clara Pater, the sister of the English essayist Walter Pater. Despite her schooling, and despite her family's "very communicative, literate, letter writing" life, Virginia sometimes presented herself as appallingly uneducated, ignorant even. All her life, she claimed, she was nothing more than "a common reader"—the title she would give to the essay collection she drafted while writing *Mrs. Dalloway*.

Still, it is true that most of the knowledge Virginia gleaned during her childhood came from the books she squirreled from her father's library. She turned their pages with a discipline so fierce, so relentless, that it concerned Leslie just as much as it astonished him. It was not unusual for her to read three or four books at once, "gobbling" her "beloved Macaulay," Lamb, Pepys, and Montaigne, savoring the novels of the Brontë sisters, Eliot, and Trollope as the purest and deepest pleasure she could imagine. If her autodidacticism had the effect of making her violently single-minded and contemptuous of authority—particularly when disguised as male benevolence or reason—then it also endowed her with a sense of intellectual self-sufficiency. She arrived in adolescence convinced that the curiosity that burned in her mind, the loving particularity of her imagination, would light her queer, crooked path through the world.

She was thirteen when, on May 5, 1895, her mother died of influenza. Some twenty-nine years later, while writing *Mrs. Dalloway*, she recalled Julia's death in her diary: "I think it happened early on a Sunday morning, & I looked out of the nursery window & saw old Dr Seton walking away with his hands behind his back, as if to say It is finished, & then the doves descending, to peck in the road, I suppose, with a fall & descent of infinite peace." After Julia's death, the remaining members of the Stephen family plunged into a period of oppressive mourning that stretched for nine unhappy years, from 1895 to 1904. Leslie turned theatrical. He took to wandering the house with his arms outstretched, proclaiming his undying love for Julia and demanding that his daughters care for him with the same selflessness their mother had shown. Embarrassed by their father's emotional excesses, the Stephen children learned to smother their own feel-

Virginia Woolf and Sir Leslie Stephen. *(Virginia Woolf Monk's House photograph album, MH-1, MS Thr 557, [180]. Houghton Library, Harvard College Library)*

ings of grief. Her mother's last words to her—"Hold yourself straight, little Goat"—lodged deep into Virginia's being, as did her fear of both sentimentality and stoicism. Shrinking from her father and her siblings, she never spoke of Julia if she could help it. "Used to sit up in my room raging—at father, at George. And read and read and read," she would later recall. She read to console and to distract herself. Books, she wrote, were "a mercy."

Virginia never stopped reading—not when Stella died in 1897 during an operation; nor when Leslie was diagnosed with bowel cancer in 1902; nor in the two excruciating years it took him to die. After his death, she set her books aside and had her first breakdown in the spring of 1904. "All that summer she was mad," her nephew Quentin Bell later recalled, in his infamous, bitterly contested account of her illness. Refusing food, refusing sleep, she started to hear voices. A chorus of birds chirped in Greek outside her bedroom window. (Twenty years later, the sparrows in Regent's Park would "sing freshly and piercingly in Greek words" to Septimus Smith.) She answered them in a thick stream of gibberish that frightened her siblings. The doctors who came exasperated her. She responded to their orders—sleep, rest, isolation from those she loved—with threats, behaving viciously toward her nurses. When she tried to commit suicide for the first time, she threw herself from a first-story window. Unlike "the large Bloomsbury lodging-house window" from which Septimus would plummet in *Mrs. Dalloway*, her window was too low for the fall to cause any lasting injuries.

"All the voices I used to hear telling me to do all kinds of wild things have gone—and Nessa says they were always only my imagination," Virginia wrote to her friend Violet Dickinson in September of 1904. By the autumn, when she had recovered enough to read and write again, it was in Bloomsbury, in the house her siblings had rented in Gordon Square after leaving their family home in Kensington. Orphaned, they adopted a new group of friends—the earnest, witty, liberated young men who had been at Cambridge with Thoby and now found themselves drawn to the Stephen family's "odd new Bloomsbury life." Outside the house were the great squares of London with their rows of pale, lamp-lit trees; Regent's Park and the London Zoo; and

Oxford Circus, c. 1920. *(UK Photo and Social History Archive)*

Piccadilly Circus, Jacques-Emile Blanche. Oil on panel, c. 1900. *(York Art Gallery)*

an old blind woman who had claimed a narrow strip of Oxford Street and stooped there all day long, singing above the sound of the omnibuses coming and going. (All this Woolf would memorialize in *Mrs. Dalloway*'s London.) Inside, on Thursday and Friday evenings, one could find an equally spirited gathering of painters, critics, novelists, aspiring politicians, and economists; for there, scattered about the sitting room, were Clive Bell, Roger Fry, Duncan Grant, Desmond MacCarthy, Lytton Strachey, John Maynard Keynes, and, before he left for Ceylon to do the bidding of the British Empire, Leonard Woolf. Virginia referred to them simply as her "group."

Both Virginia's admirers and her detractors would come to call her circle of friends "the Bloomsbury group." Over time, the freedom and creativity associated with Bloomsbury—its postimpressionist art, its socialist politics, its sexual liberties—would assume unreal proportions, eclipsing the very real tensions within it. Many have wondered what it must have been like for Virginia, to be one of the few women in the sitting room at Gordon Square, the only person who had neither attended Cambridge nor slept with anyone who had. Certainly, she admired the spontaneity of the group's talk, the burst of activity they brought to her life after years of grief had left her feeling raw and inert. But she also scorned these young men, whose chatter only skimmed the surface of life, who aped intelligence instead of embracing it fully, she felt. At times they struck her as perfect specimens of "the public school type": the term she used to describe a man whose path through life—a bedroom at Eton, a study at Oxford or Cambridge, a place in London society—betrayed an entitlement she found despicable. "No country but England could have produced him," proclaims Sally Seton, Clarissa Dalloway's girlhood friend and lover, of "the public school type." For Virginia, the roar and splendor of Bloomsbury concealed the social circumstances that made its genius, an overwhelmingly male genius, possible.

She returned to writing at twenty-three, partly out of pride, but mostly out of wonder at the struggles of modern fiction, working as a book critic for the *Guardian*, the *National Review*, and the *Times Literary Supplement*, eager to testify "to the great fun & pleasure my habit of reading has given me." She started to journey around the countryside, learning to train her eye on every stray sign of life, like a spaniel flushing the fields. In Norfolk, she threaded together impressions of "thatched cottages—sign posts—tiny villages—great waggons heaped with corn—sagacious dogs, farmers' carts." Peering down the white bluffs of Cornwall, she wondered why the sea seemed to her, as it did to so many others, "a symbol of their mother England." England intrigued her, with its strange, ancient, romantic ruins and faraway outposts in mysterious lands; its rigid, stony-hearted royals and its dingy, disagreeable servants. ("The fact is the lower classes *are* detestable," Woolf would write in her diary in 1920—a prejudice she harbored and took great care to ironize in *Mrs. Dalloway*.) Her fascination with the nation's character would shape all her work, tinging her portraits of the English with nostalgia and contempt, satire and snobbery. In 1905, she made her first attempt at novel writing with *Melymbrosia*, later pub-

Plowing in Norfolk, c. 1900. *(UK Photo and Social History Archive)*

The harbor at St Ives, c. 1920. *(UK Photo and Social History Archive)*

lished as *The Voyage Out*, and containing her earliest sketch of Clarissa and Richard Dalloway.

In her newfound state of happiness, Virginia was not prepared to lose two siblings almost at once: first Thoby, who died late in 1906, after contracting typhoid during a family holiday to Greece; then, in 1907, Vanessa, to marriage, to Clive Bell and their artistic union. The siblings who remained, Virginia and Adrian, moved to a house in Fitzroy Square and lived together for two uneasy years. Theirs was an unhappy relationship: Adrian found that his older sister was fussier and more demanding than he had anticipated. She judged him unambitious, lachrymose. In 1909, incapable of tolerating each other's company any longer, they moved to 38 Brunswick Square and acquired three tenants, or as Virginia called them, "inmates": Keynes and Grant (then lovers), and, a little later, Leonard Woolf, who had returned to England in June 1911 for a year of leave from his administrative duties in Ceylon. She served the inmates breakfast at 9 a.m., lunch at 1 p.m., tea at 4:30 p.m., and dinner at 8 p.m. "Trays will be placed in the halls punctually at these hours," Virginia wrote in the tenancy agreement she drew up for Leonard, who moved into one of the upstairs rooms and paid the Stephen family 35 shillings a week. "Inmates are requested to carry up their own trays; and to put the dirty plates on them and carry them down again *as soon as the meal is finished*."

None of Virginia's biographers presents a particularly compelling account of how and why the lodger fell in love with his landlord. Some accuse their mutual friend Lytton Strachey of meddling. In 1910, he wrote to Leonard, then still in Ceylon, informing him that the cool, virginal Virginia Stephen needed a man to come claim her: "If you came & proposed she'ld accept you. She really would." Others claim Vanessa went to great lengths to impress upon Leonard Virginia's vulnerability, her need for constant care. Primed to fall in love with her, he did so after only a handful of encounters: a weekend spent walking the Downs with her outside a friend's home in Firle, telling her about the seven years he spent in Ceylon "governing natives, inventing ploughs, shooting tigers"; a performance of Wagner's *Siegfried* in Covent Garden; a trip to the Russian ballet. "I see it will be the beginning of hopelessness," he wrote to Strachey on November 1, 1911. "To be in love with her—isn't that a danger?"

By Virginia's own admission, she could fall only half in love with him.

Leonard Woolf and Bella Sidney Woolf sitting outdoors in front of a tree, Sri Lanka. *(Virginia Woolf Monk's House photograph album, MH-1, MS Thr 557, [126a]. Houghton Library, Harvard College Library)*

The other half of herself she had pledged to her writing. Besides, she believed in maintaining some distance in the relations between husband and wife. Her letters to him express a need for privacy and self-preservation—the same language Clarissa Dalloway would reach for when describing her decision to marry Richard ("And there is a dignity in people; a solitude; even between husband and wife a gulf . . .") instead of Peter ("But with Peter everything had to be shared; everything gone into. And it was intolerable . . ."). She would later describe Leonard to her friends as a "penniless Jew," a foreigner to her English eyes; dark, thin, and tightly wound; fearfully caring and extraordinarily tender. That she found him sexually unappealing, that she felt nothing when he kissed her, would have surprised no one who knew her. Though she refused to call herself a "Sapphist"—the late Victorian term for a lesbian—all her life she had felt more attracted to women than to men, particularly women older than her. "She resented it, had a scruple picked up Heaven knows where, or, as she felt, sent by Nature (who is invariably wise); yet she could not resist sometimes yielding to the charm of a woman, not a girl," Clarissa would think, a thought that could have doubled as Woolf's confession of her own proclivities.

Their wedding on August 10, 1912, was unremarkable, attended by large thunderstorms and a few inattentive guests. The marriage, however, became the cause of much eager speculation. Her family and their friends gossiped about her need for constant nursing and the excessive control he exercised over her sleep, diet, and schedule. ("He would go on saying 'An hour's complete rest after luncheon' to the end of time," Clarissa Dalloway would think of Richard's caregiving.) Everyone from Clive Bell, Vanessa's husband, to Vita Sackville-West, the writer who would become Virginia's lover shortly after *Mrs. Dalloway* was published, shared stories about Virginia's sexual frigidity and Leonard's heroic restraint, a sacrifice he claimed to have made, according to their friends, because he believed "she was a genius." But alongside these vicious rumors was the London literary scene's quiet admiration for the Woolfs' partnership as editors and owners of the Hogarth Press, which they set up in 1917 "to publish at low prices short works of merit, in prose or poetry, which could not, because of their merits, appeal to a very large public." Whatever Leonard may or may not have been to her—and we can never know the precise nature of their relationship—he was her first and most exacting critic. Her "Mongoose," she called him, always bristling at her side with worry and affection. She would come to believe that his dependability was all that stood between her and madness.

For the first three years of their marriage, she veered in and out of illness. She exhausted herself finishing *The Voyage Out*, and found herself confined to her bed first in London, then at Asheham, the country home she and Leonard purchased near the old chalk quarry in Lewes. In March 1913, the novel was accepted for publication by Gerald Duckworth and Company, the publishing house her half-brother founded in 1898. Its release was delayed until March 1915, the year after the First World War began, the same month

Virginia Woolf and Leonard Woolf at Dalingridge Place, photographic postcard by George Duckworth, July 23, 1912. *(Virginia Woolf Monk's House photographs, MS Thr 564, [58]. Houghton Library, Harvard College Library)*

Jacket for *The Voyage Out*, Hogarth Press, seventh impression. Cover design by Vanessa Bell, 1947. *(© Estate of Vanessa Bell. All rights reserved, DACS 2021)*

An antiwar speech in Hyde Park, c. 1920. *(UK Photo and Social History Archive)*

the British army fought the Battle of Neuve Chapelle and the British navy joined the assault missions on the Dardanelles. Like all her friends, Virginia identified as a pacifist, and could not understand the madness and folly that drove men to slaughter one another—the "appalling crime" that ex-soldier Septimus Smith believes he has committed in *Mrs. Dalloway*, and for which he has "been condemned to death by human nature." She detested the fear that forced her to creep through the alleyways of London, hiding from the German airplanes circling overhead. The faces she met must have mirrored her own: pinched, frightened, hungry.

In 1914, Virginia, Leonard, and four nurses moved from London to Hogarth House in Richmond, where, in 1915, she had another breakdown. She spent weeks lying in bed and hallucinating scenes of immense beauty, "seeing the sunlight quivering like gold water, on the wall," and listening to "the voices of the dead." Again, the birds sang to her in Greek. Her recovery was slow. Weeks passed during which she was rumored to be "incoherent, excited and violent," with her diary suddenly breaking off in February 1915 and resuming only in August 1917. Everything that could have cheered her—the air in Richmond, her work with the Hogarth Press—was offset by the horror and senselessness of death. Reminders of it were everywhere: the German prisoners cutting wheat with hooks outside Asheham; English men without hands; the rationing of sugar and milk and yeast at the Co-op; the great many airplanes that droned over the house.

She worried that the rulers of England would encourage people to forget all about the war once it was over. "The fruits of our victory will grow as dusty as ornaments under glass cases in lodging house drawing rooms," she wrote just before Armistice Day in November 1918. But she resolved to remember, and to make the memory of death part of the life that awaited after the war. All she had endured—the visions, the voices, the feeling of "creeping about, like a rat struck on the head" during the madness of the war years—she would begin to impart to the imaginary men and women who crowded her head, demanding from her a new novel about the nation. The war left her determined to write "a historical disquisition on the return of peace," she plotted in her diary in February 1921. Though it was the first time she would articulate her plan so explicitly, she had felt it for a long time. *Mrs. Dalloway* was a novel she had started writing not knowing she was writing it. She committed to it only when she had pursued her characters too far to let them go.

IV.

THE CHARACTER of Clarissa Dalloway was born in 1912 or thereabouts. She started her life in Woolf's first novel, *The Voyage Out*, about a young English woman named Rachel Vinrace who boards a ship sailing to the fictitious South American colony of Santa Marina. *The Voyage Out* is an inexpert affair—prettily written, but confusingly plotted; garrulous yet dull. As Lytton Strachey told Woolf, the novel's most memorable feature was its satire of Rachel's fellow passengers, the Dalloways. Clarissa and her husband Richard embark at Lisbon after several weeks of roaming the continent "chiefly with a view to broadening Mr. Dalloway's mind." They make sure to tell everyone about their adventures—how they had toured factories in France, ridden mules in Spain, and photographed Henry Fielding's grave in Portugal, where Clarissa let loose a trapped bird, "because one hates to think of anything in a cage where English people lie buried," she confesses.

From her beginning, Clarissa Dalloway was tall, slight, and graying, with pink cheeks and very pale, very smooth skin. She wandered the ship's deck wrapped in furs and veils, and when she came down to dinner in a pure white gown, her diamond necklace glittering, she stood over the rest of the passengers "like an eighteenth-century masterpiece—a Reynolds or a Romney." She adored flowers; yearned to learn Greek so that she could read Plato in front of the fireplace; carried a copy of Jane Austen's *Persuasion* to read aloud to Richard ("Dick," she called him); plucked an aria from *Tristan und Isolde* on the piano while recalling her first time at Bayreuth. She confessed to Rachel that she used to sob over Shelley's "Adonais" in the garden. Inwardness would have been wasted on this Clarissa Dalloway. She was lovely, snobbish, and arch: a perfectly middle-aged philistine—a perfectly English type of woman. She disembarked from the ship never suspecting that Dick had kissed Rachel one night while, she, Mrs. Richard Dalloway, was lying in bed seasick.

Clarissa Dalloway was, at first, a freehand sketch of Woolf's childhood friend Kitty Maxse. She had been Kitty Lushington when they were girls. They had seen each other often then, along with Vanessa and Kitty's sister Margaret, and had all sat "screaming with laughter" at the Stephen family's latest foibles: Thoby and Adrian's scrapes, Stella's romances. And then Leo Maxse, soon to be appointed editor of the *National Review*, had proposed to Kitty one summer night at Talland House, the two of them kneeling in "the love corner, under the greenhouse; jackmanii grew there," Woolf recalled in her memoirs. Kitty was a dozen years older than Virginia and very charming—kind and cool and glamorous, but also "unsatisfactory." "She could see what she lacked. It was not beauty; it was not mind. It was something central which permeated," Woolf would write of Clarissa in *Mrs. Dalloway*. Kitty had failed her after her mother had died, tending only to her and Vanessa's social lives, not to their grief. Kitty had disapproved of the

Katharine Maxse, née Lushington, known as Kitty Maxse, wife of Leopold Maxse, thought to have been a model for Virginia Woolf's character Mrs. Dalloway. *(Mary Evans Picture Library)*

family's move to Bloomsbury, had feared Virginia might "marry an *author*," instead of the South Kensington public school type Kitty would have picked for her.

Still, she admired Kitty's love of life. Kitty spoke of life as a perfectly ordinary miracle, at once trivial and sublime, and always available for one's enjoyment if one only knew how to wring the fun out of it. In her story triptych "Friendship's Gallery," Woolf recalled how Kitty would look in the mirror every morning and make sure to think, "Gracious Heavens, I'm alive!" Then she would ask herself, "Now am I more alive or less alive?" and take her temperature to confirm her answer. "'The great thing in life, I'm sure (and so is Leo)' she went on as one sharing a secret of great importance, 'is to never lose your interest in things,'" Woolf wrote, caricaturing Kitty with affection and mockery. One glimpsed Kitty's love of life in the parties she threw, where her great gift for playing the piano washed over a swarm of smart people whom she neither cared for nor respected. Though caged by convention, Kitty did not struggle to escape it. But she was unwilling to cede her spirit to it entirely. To read her character was to allow for her contradictions, the many incompatible parts of her that could not be drawn together as a single self.

"Well, that's over," announces one of the ship's passengers after the Dalloways disembark. "We shall never see *them* again." Yet Clarissa Dalloway would stay with Woolf over the next several years—through the publication of her second novel, *Night and Day*, in 1919, and the drafting of her third, *Jacob's Room*, in 1922. "I always think it's *living*, not dying, that counts," Clarissa says to Rachel in *The Voyage Out*. One could imagine Clarissa's words lingering in Woolf's mind through the end of the war and her next serious illness. In April 1922, she lay in bed recovering from a long bout of influenza, her heart jigging so wildly that she had to consult a heart specialist for her "eccentric pulse," which "had passed the limits of reason and was insane," she wrote in her diary. Nine weeks of seclusion in London had led to the feeling of "being suspended between life & death in an unfamiliar way." She had the urge to "vault the wall, & pick a few flowers." She carried on reading (her diary lists *Moby-Dick*, *La Princesse de Clèves*, *Old Mortality*, *Small Talk at Wreyland*, and the first two volumes of the *Life of Robert, Marquis of Salisbury*), but she felt too woolly headed to write. "What a 12 months it has been for writing!—& I at the prime of life, with little creatures in my head which won't exist if I don't let them out," she lamented.

The most amusing visitor she received during her convalescence was the poet T. S. Eliot, whose second book of poetry, *Poems*, the Hogarth Press had published in 1919. Theirs was a guarded friendship. She was impressed by his poetry and eager for his pure praise, which he offered to her only sparingly and without the enthusiasm she expected. ("Unfortunately the living writers he admires are Wyndham Lewis & Pound.—Joyce too, but there's more to be said on this head," she wrote of Eliot's taste in her diary.) Now he had grown "supple as an eel," she observed, "positively familiar & jocular & friendly" when he asked her to submit a story to the magazine he was starting, *The Criterion*. By May 1922, she had recovered enough to travel from London to Monk's House, the cottage in Rodmell that she and Leonard had purchased in 1919—an unpretentious clapboard house, lying long and low on the Sussex meadows, that Virginia loved for the "size & shape & fertility & wildness of the garden." When she arrived, she wrote to Eliot and promised to send two stories she was just beginning: a long one, "Mrs. Dalloway in Bond Street," and a shorter one, "In the Orchard." "You will have to be sincere and severe," she instructed him. "I can never tell whether I'm good or bad; and I promise I shall respect you all the more for tearing me up and throwing me into the wastepaper basket." (One suspects she was lying; Eliot's eventual rejection of "Mrs. Dalloway in Bond Street" for *The Criterion* would bruise her badly.) In her diary, she vowed to write without distraction and send him her stories by the end of the summer.

Soon it was June. The Woolfs were back in London. No writing had gotten done at Monk's House. "*Disgraceful! disgraceful! disgraceful!*" Woolf upbraided herself in her diary, baffled and irritated by spring's irreversible passage into summer—"my season of doubts & ups & downs," as she described it. Along with her anxieties, her aspirations for "Mrs. Dalloway in Bond Street" had broadened. She thought she might use its setting, a single summer day, to fine-tune what she and Leonard had taken to calling her "method": the loose, jumpy style of storytelling she had started to experiment with in her short story "An Unwritten Novel" and her third novel, *Jacob's Room*. She claimed to have hit on her method by accident at first, dissatisfied with the tools she had inherited from her literary predecessors for creating character. She had little patience for nineteenth-century realism's fondness for linear plotlines and

Vivienne Eliot pointing her finger at T. S. Eliot, 1932. *(Virginia Woolf's Monk House photograph album, MS Thr 560 [184]. Houghton Library, Harvard College Library)*

psychological transparency; its accrual of the smallest and tritest historical detail, which encouraged one to read a character by noticing the cut of his clothes and the mud on his boots, by tracking his standing in polite English society. In retreat from realism's simplified relation of the social side of life to the life of the mind, Woolf sought for the modern novel a technique of narration that could "enclose everything, everything"—a style that would allow her to draw close to an individual character, to the slipperiness and mystery of his consciousness, "& yet keep form & speed," she wrote in her diary before starting *Jacob's Room*.

Jacob's Room offered its readers a genuinely new form for fiction. Published in the same year as *Ulysses* and *The Waste Land*, its fragmented, kaleidoscopic story concerned a young man named Jacob Flanders, born in Cornwall, educated at Cambridge, and soon to die in the First World War. The novel leaped through time, lurched in and out of the minds of many characters: Jacob's mother and brothers, his friends, his lovers. Its scenes were brief and sketched with intense sensory particularity. Exquisite descriptions of the Cornish seaside, the grounds of a Cambridge college, a trip to Greece, and a walk through London rose before the reader without warning, haphazardly. Characters moved in and out of the narrative without explanation, their thoughts unfinished, the precise nature of their relationships left inscrutable. "It is no use trying to sum people up. One must follow hints, not exactly what is said, nor entirely what is done," thinks the narrator of *Jacob's Room*. In writing this, Woolf was leading herself to the notion of character-reading she would articulate more forcefully in "Mr. Bennett and Mrs. Brown." But she was also clearing the ground for *Mrs. Dalloway*, which would improve upon her initial attempt at character-reading in *Jacob's Room* by providing not just a room, but a well-ordered "house" for her characters "to live in," as she would put it in her 1928 introduction to the novel.

As always, Leonard read *Jacob's Room* first. He judged it "amazingly well written" and "a work of genius." Still, he had his reservations. The novel had "no philosophy of life," he complained—nothing to explain why it flitted from one scene to the next. Her characters were like "ghosts," pallid and vaporous, impossible to cling to for too long. Plus, there were too many of them. The novel picked them up and put them down quickly, and the reader walked away from them without hesitation or afterthought, as one escapes

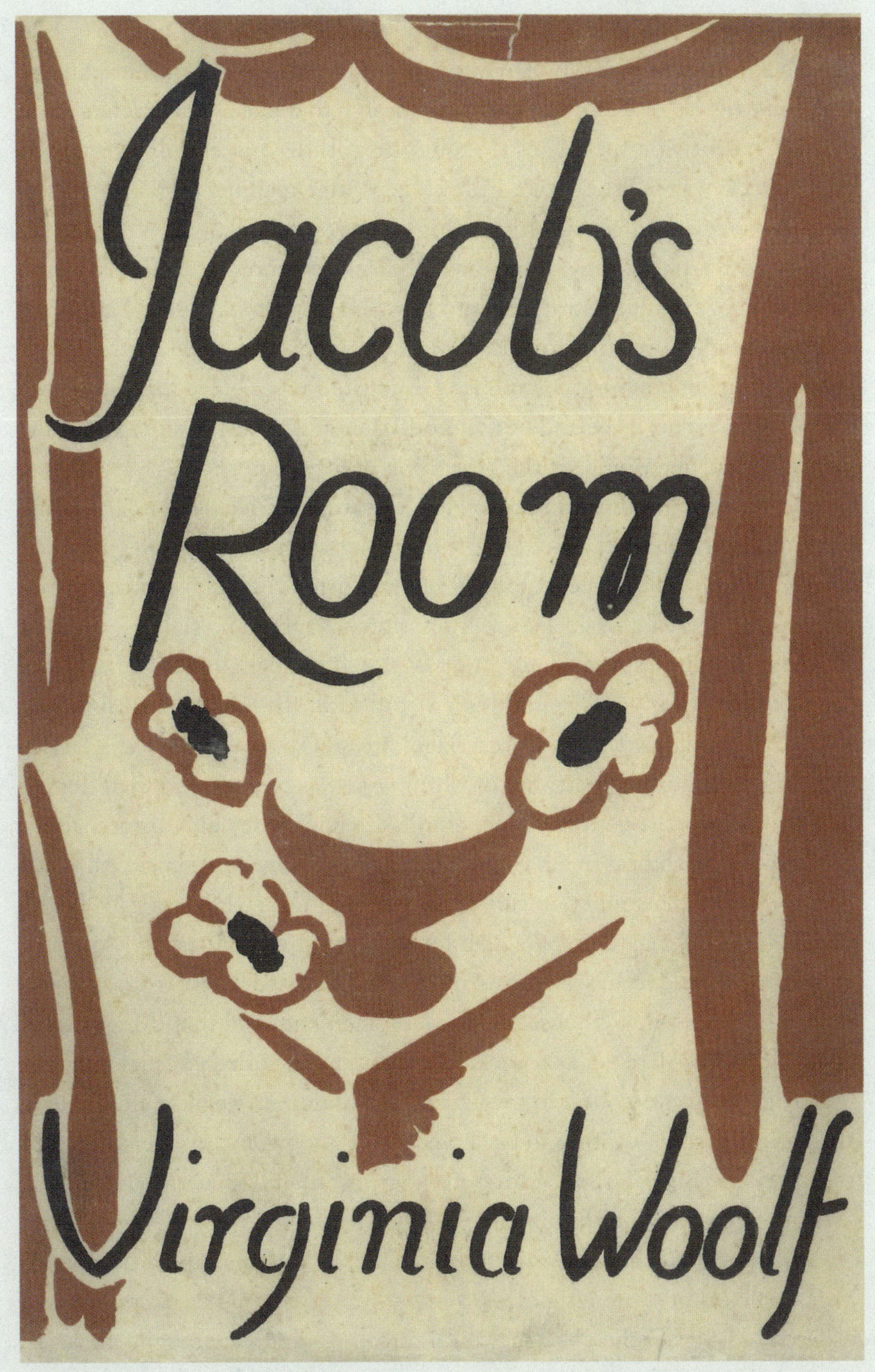

Jacket for *Jacob's Room*, Hogarth Press, Vanessa Bell, 1922.
(Washington State University, Rare Books and Special Collections)

dull party guests. Leonard "thinks I should use my 'method,' on one or two characters next time," Woolf wrote, thinking perhaps of a philosophy of life, some device or technique she could design to make her characters more vibrant, to entwine their fates. It could be nothing too cunning or tricky. "A first rate writer," she wrote in her diary after reading *Ulysses*, "respects writing too much to be tricky; startling; doing stunts."

But both a philosophy of life and the form to express it eluded her. The depression of early June stretched into July, and July into August. "I am laboriously dredging my mind for Mrs Dalloway and bringing up light buckets," she wrote in her diary in the middle of August. She scribbled away in a state of unhappiness until the end of the month, and finished the story when she had told Eliot she would, at the beginning of September 1922.

The results, Woolf would acknowledge, were imperfect. The story's opening line, "Mrs. Dalloway said she would buy the gloves herself," recalled how Kitty greeted her guests, extending one "fishy white glove to be clasped reverently." There followed a jerky procession of sounds and sights—Big Ben striking; omnibuses and motorcars passing; Buckingham Palace; a greeting from her "dear old" friend Hugh Whitbread; the lonely, regal figure of Lady Bexborough sitting in her carriage, dressed in mourning—as Clarissa walked down Bond Street, the sun shining just as brightly as it had during her girlhood in the country. Then she had read Shelley and argued about Shakespeare with passionate conviction, possessed by an intensity that she had no use for in her quiet, unruffled marriage to Dick. (He was still "Dick" here.) Nor could it have prepared her for the unsettling realization—it would come to her while trying on gloves and feeling irritated by the women working in the shop—that "thousands of young men had died that things might go on" for people like her and Dick. The story ended with a violent explosion that frightened everyone except Clarissa and another wealthy elderly lady sitting in the shop, waiting to be served. "The shopwomen cowered behind the counters. But Clarissa, sitting very up right, smiled at the other lady. 'Miss Anstruther!' she exclaimed."

Like the first Clarissa, this second Clarissa was born prim and priggish, an object of satire rather than sympathy. Yet, for all her faults, she had ushered "a host of others"—Hugh Whitbread, Lady Bexborough, the king, the queen, the girls working in the glove shop—into Woolf's mind. There she had left them, each clamoring for more attention. Woolf would spend the next year arranging men and women from all ranks of English society around her hostess. These were the characters she would depend on to make the story of Clarissa Dalloway's life less flimsy, less cosseted than it had been in "Mrs. Dalloway in Bond Street." She had too much to say, about the history of English society and the wreckage of the First World War, about Clarissa's life, its past and present, to fit it all in a single short story. She would need a series of linked short stories, she thought, or perhaps a novel, with each chapter offering a different character's perspective on war and peace, illuminating the distinct ways the memory of death haunted the squares and streets of London. "Shall I write the next chapter of Mrs. D.—if she is to have a next chapter; & shall it be The Prime Minister?" she asked herself on August 28, 1922.

Her melancholy summer had started to shade into a milder, more benignant autumn. She had returned in earnest to shaping what she called "her reading book," the essay collection that she would soon title *The Common Reader*. Writing criticism had always replenished her desire to write novels, and now that she was writing about Chaucer and trying to improve her Greek, she could marvel at her productivity. "Mrs. Dalloway & the Chaucer chapter are finished; I have read 5 books of the Odyssey; Ulysses; & now begin Proust. I also read Chaucer & the Pastons," she recorded on October 4, 1922. "I shall read Greek now steadily & begin 'The Prime Minister' on Friday morning." When Friday dawned, thunderous and forbidding, she sketched in a notebook labeled "Book of scraps of J's R & first version of The Hours" her initial plan for "a book to be called, perhaps, At Home: or The Party."

> This is to be a short book consisting of six or
> seven chapters, each complete separately,
> yet there must be some sort of fusion.
> And all must converge upon the party at the end
> My idea is to have some characters,
> like Mrs. Dalloway much in relief: then to have
> interludes of thought, or reflection, or short digressions
> (which must be related, logically, to the rest)
> all compact, yet not jerked.
> The Chapters might be,

> 1. Mrs. Dalloway in Bond Street.
> 2. The Prime Minister.
> 3. Ancestors.
> 4. A dialogue.
> 5. The old ladies.
> 6. Country house?
> 7. Cut flowers.
> 8. The Party.
>
> One, roughly, to be done in a month: but this
> plan is to allow of some very short ~~pages:~~
> intervals, not whole chapters.
> There should be some fun—

"The Prime Minister" began where "Mrs. Dalloway in Bond Street" left off: an explosion in the street outside the glove store; the sound of a motorcar backfiring as it begins to roll through London; a figure muffled inside, languid against the dove-gray upholstery; the glimpse of a hand drawing a blind. Was it "the Prince of Wales', the Prime Minister's, the Queen's?" the people watching the motorcar wondered. Trailing the motorcar was a character Woolf called "H. Z. Prentice," who would not make it into the final version of the novel. He was a conscientious man, a "homely, lonely" member of the "higher bourgeoisie" who stayed up all hours of the night groaning over politics with his university friends, "queer old fellows" who took the world's injustices to heart but believed there was nothing they could do about them. In one breath, H. Z. Prentice denounced the conservative prime minister who had brought the country "to the depths of degradation"—" 'unparalleled' said H. Z. Prentice 'in my experience' "—and in another, the working classes and their reverence for the English aristocracy. He left no doubt that this was a political book, an indictment of English insincerity and hypocrisy. "For old Virginia will be ashamed to think what a chatterbox she was, always talking about people, never about politics," she had written in her diary back in February 1921, when she had first planned to write about the return of peace.

Mrs. Dalloway might have been a different book entirely—perhaps not a novel at all—had Woolf's writing not been interrupted by news of the

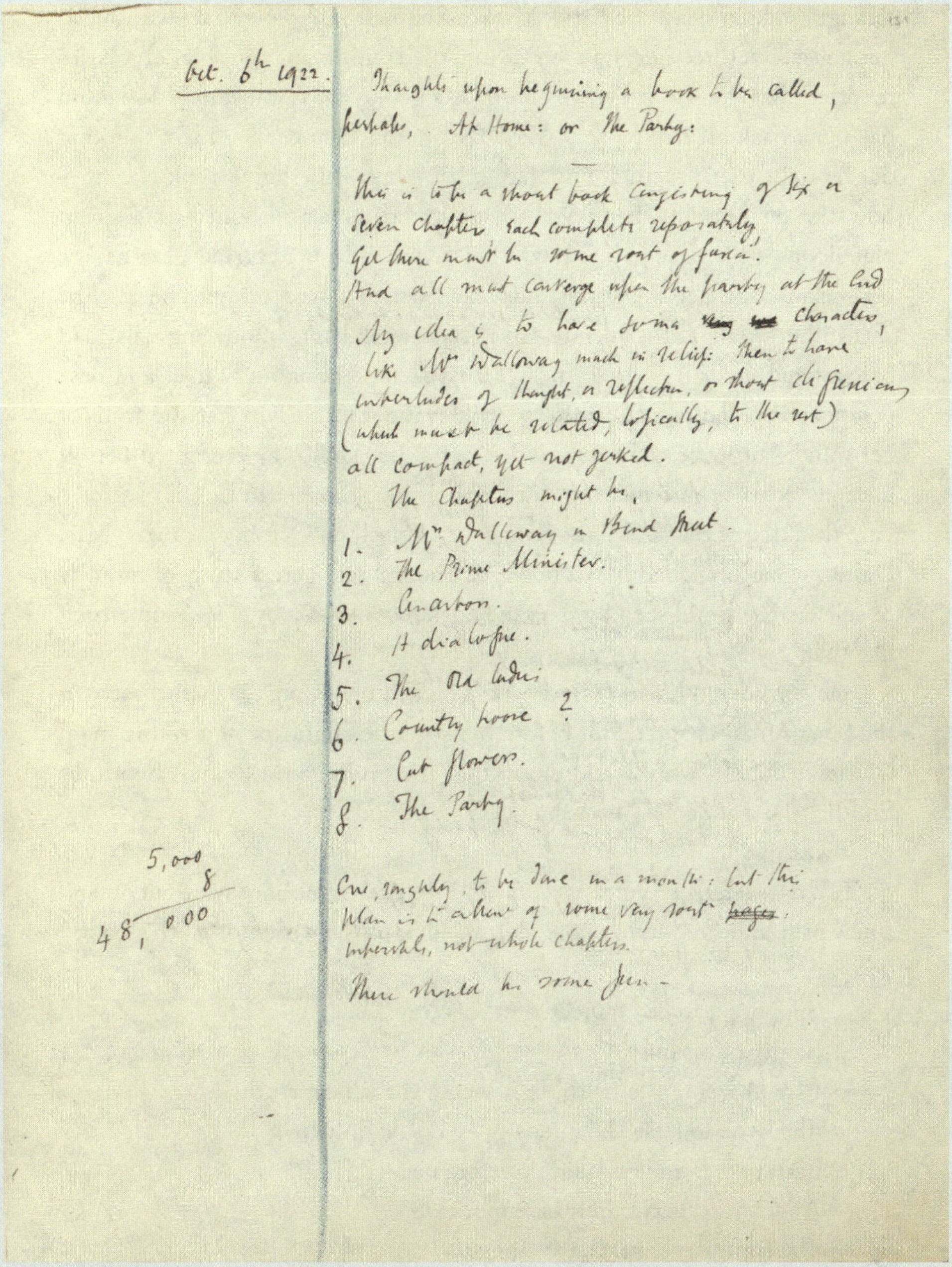

Oct. 6th 1922.

Thoughts upon beginning a book to be called, perhaps, At Home: or The Party:

This is to be a short book consisting of six or seven chapters each complete separately. Yet there must be some sort of fusion! And all must converge upon the party at the end. My idea is to have some ~~very~~ characters, like Mrs Dalloway much in relief: then to have interludes of thought, or reflection, or short digressions (which must be related, logically, to the rest) all compact, yet not jerked.

The chapters might be,

1. Mrs Dalloway in Bond Street.
2. The Prime Minister.
3. Ancestors.
4. A dialogue.
5. The Old ladies
6. Country house?
7. Cut flowers.
8. The Party.

5,000
8
48,000

One, roughly, to be done in a month: but this plan is to allow of some very short ~~pages~~ interludes, not whole chapters.

There should be some fun—

"Thoughts upon beginning a book to be called, perhaps, At Home: or The Party," Virginia Woolf, October 6, 1922. *(New York Public Library, Berg Collection)*

strange, sudden death of Kitty Maxse. She had fallen over the banister at her house, fractured her right femur, and died within an hour. Her obituaries reported that she was fifty-five and had "a genius for friendship." "My mind has gone back all day to her," Woolf wrote on October 8. "First thinking out how she died . . . Then visualizing her—her white hair—pink cheeks—how she sat upright—her voice—with its characteristic tones—her green blue floor—which she painted with her own hands; her earrings, her gaiety, yet melancholy; her smartness; her tears, which stayed on her cheek." She was still grasping at the memory of Kitty a week later, wondering what had precipitated her fall—carelessness perhaps, or some more willful and desperate action, too painful to name. She wanted to fix Kitty at the front of her mind, but in death, Kitty eluded her; Mrs. Dalloway presented herself instead. "Kitty is buried & mourned by half the grandees in London; & here I am thinking of my book," she reproached herself on October 14, 1922. "Mrs. Dalloway has branched into a book; & I adumbrate here a study of insanity & suicide: the world seen by the sane & the insane side by side—something like that."

She considered having Clarissa kill herself or simply die at the party in the book's final chapter. But before her rose the character of a young man, Clarissa's double, who would die so that she could go on living. "Septimus Smith?" she wondered. "Is that a good name?"

It was.

Two days later, on October 16, H. Z. Prentice's ramblings were cut off and a new page appeared in her notebook titled "a possible revision of this book."

> Suppose it to be connected in this way:
> Sanity & insanity.
> Mrs D seeing the truth. S.S. seeing the insane truth.
> The book to have the intensity of a play: only in
> narrative. Some revision therefore needed.
> At any rate; very careful composition.
> The contrast—must be arranged.
> Therefore how much detail — & digression?
> The pace is to be given by the gradual increase of S's
> insanity on the one side; by the approach of the party on the
> other.

> The design is extremely complicated.
> The balance must be very finely considered.
> Character must be indicated.
> All to take place in one day?
> There must be excitement to draw one on
> Also humour.
> The Question is whether the inside of the mind in
> both Mrs D. & S.S. can be made luminous—
> that is to say the stuff of the book—lights on it
> coming from external sources.

Did her reach exceed her grasp? Always she worried it did. Her plan willed her to work deliberately. She would attend to her book's composition with care, with a foresight belied by the apparent spontaneity of the novel's final form and its status as an exemplary work of "stream of consciousness." Behind her insistence on pacing, balance, and design lay her immense ambition to cover the entire range of human perception and cognition—the opposition of "sanity & insanity," "seeing the truth" and "seeing the insane truth." "The contrast must be arranged," she ordered. It required "detail & digression," as well as "intensity" and "excitement" and "humour." It would unfold not through outward speeches and gestures, but by making "the inside of the mind in both Mrs D. & S.S. . . . luminous." Their thoughts would be made to converge, drawn together in moments of astonishing beauty to illuminate truths divined by the sane and insane alike—about being young and growing old, about the cruelty of war and the complacency of peace. This would permit her to move from one character's mind to another's, this time with purpose she had lacked in *Jacob's Room*.

Woolf refused to puppet her characters into elaborate, overwrought performances of consciousness, an approach she associated with the excessive ingenuity of Henry James. She disliked melodrama, did not think love affairs and political scandals to be the proper stuff of fiction. She looked to "external sources" to light her characters' innermost minds. Sometimes her sources were simply other characters, long-ago friends or lovers who perceived how a character had transformed from a child into an adult, a grown woman holding her "whole life, a complete life" in her arms, Clarissa would think in *Mrs. Dalloway*. Other times her sources were everyday

Oct. 16th 1922.

a possible revision of this book

Suppose it to be connected in this way:
Sanity & insanity.
Mrs D. seeing the truth. S. S. seeing the insane truth.
The book to have the intensity of a play: only in narrative. Some revision therefore needed.
At anyrate, very careful composition.
The contrast must be arranged.
Therefore how much detail — & digression?
The pace is to be given by the gradual increase of S's insanity on the one side; by the approach of the party on the other.
The design is extremely complicated.
The balance must be very finely considered.
Character must be indicated.
All to take place in one day?
There must be excitement to draw one on.
Also humour.
The question is whether the inside of the mind in both Mrs D. & S.S. can be made luminous — that is to say the stuff of the book — lights on it coming from external sources.

"a possible revision of this book," Virginia Woolf, October 16, 1922.
(New York Public Library, Berg Collection)

objects: flowers, the trees in Regent's Park, the prime minister's motorcar rolling through the streets of London, an airplane writing letters in the sky. Observed by many characters all at once, these ordinary things would stir their emotions and concentrate their memories; send their minds reeling with excitement and unease and allow Woolf to plumb the depths of their thoughts. She would later describe this as her "tunneling process." "I dig out beautiful caves behind my characters; I think that gives exactly what I want; humanity, humor, depth," she would reflect. "The idea is that the caves shall connect, & each comes to daylight at the present moment."

Through the succession of short stories that would become *Mrs. Dalloway*, her theory of perception merged with her technique of creating character, yielding a depth and breadth of consciousness she believed no other modern writer had achieved. Eliot only "wants to describe externals. Joyce gives internals," she wrote in her diary, sizing up her modernist rivals. Her method had found a way to unite the two, showing the continuity between the world people shared and the sane and insane worlds they created in their minds. The mind "receives upon its surface a myriad impressions—trivial, fantastic, evanescent, or engraved with the sharpness of steel," she had written in her 1919 essay "Modern Novels," later republished in *The Common Reader* as "Modern Fiction." From nothing but the play of these impressions, she could catch the essence of a character and present it to the reader as a "whole life, a complete life." "Life is not a series of gig lamps symmetrically arranged; life is a luminous halo, a semi-transparent envelope surrounding us from the beginning of consciousness to the end," she wrote in "Modern Fiction."

What made *Mrs. Dalloway* a modern novel was its capacity to melt away the distinction between the inner and outer worlds, and leave hanging between them an extraordinary mist of beauty, a language whose radiance could be perceived by all. With this ambition in hand, she turned from Clarissa to Septimus and his view of her bright June day.

V.

THE CHARACTER of Septimus Smith, Clarissa's double, was born on Saturday, October 14, 1922, in the manuscript of "The Prime Minister." One might trace his origins to the death of Kitty Maxse, as Woolf's biographers have. Or one might go back further, to June 1920 and the strange death of a young man called Wright at a dance in Bloomsbury. Her sister, Vanessa, who had been at the dance along with their brother Adrian, told Virginia the story. Fascinated, she recorded it in her diary: "They sat out on the roof, protected by fairy lamps & chairs. He crossed, perhaps to light a cigarette, stepped over the edge, & fell 30 feet onto flagstones. Adrian alone saw the thing happen. He called a doctor sitting there, & very calmly & bravely, so Nessa felt, climbed the wall into the garden where the man had fallen, & helped the Dr over. But there was no hope. He died in the ambulance that fetched him." More upsetting than his death was the indifference of the partygoers to it. "No one was upset; some telephoned for news of other dances," Woolf wrote. "A strange event—to come to a dance among strangers & die—to come dressed in evening clothes, & then for it all to be over, instantly, so senselessly."

"Pale and freckled," with "eyes rather far apart" and "very white teeth," Septimus Smith began his life in a restaurant where H. Z. Prentice, not long for the world of the novel, was also dining. He stared at the "astonishing whiteness" of the tablecloth and laughed at nothing at all. In "The Prime Minister," Septimus was an eccentric, agitated and screwy. He was merely insane, as opposed to in *Mrs. Dalloway*, where he would emerge as a poetic, if not a prophetic, character, exquisitely attuned to the beauty and the suffering of the world, his mind filled with the sonnets of Shakespeare and the odes of Keats. Yet Woolf began by affording him only the most clichéd of delusions: "As he stood by the hat shop, he saw the sky full of birds, purple & red, descending. They fell through his body, giving him actually the sensation of gliding, swooping, alighting to the admiration of multitudes, who beheld him with terror (but he knew he was safe) & received him, as he bestowed upon them his extraordinary gift with a rapturous clamor of love. He was some sort of Christ, probably."

This Septimus makes the decision to kill himself immediately, lights a cigarette, and walks to Trafalgar Square, where strangers observe him staggering about, looking "awful queer." Here he pauses, and looking up, sees an airplane circling overhead. The airplane, a dreaded sight during the war, would become the most memorable external source Woolf used to light her characters' minds in *Mrs. Dalloway*. But here Woolf also paused, uncertain, at this point, about the novel's design and the significance of Septimus's character. "I shall try to sketch out Mrs. D. & consult L. & write the aeroplane chapter now," she wrote in her diary on November 7, 1922.

The next dozen pages or so of Woolf's notes, written from November 1922 to August 1923 in the back of a small book containing Greek exercises and her notes on Aeschylus, are stuffed with her commentary on individual characters and her plans for how to relate them to one another. She found innumerable faults with what she had scribbled so far, all of it "too jerky & minute" and lacking a general style that could hold her reader's attention. She reminded herself of the contrast she wished to draw between Clarissa's sane and Septimus's insane perceptions of the world. Only now, she discovered another contrast that intrigued her: the contrast between "life & death." She understood life and death not as physiological states but as psychological ones. To live was to take a great interest in the world, to welcome its possibilities and connections. It was to embrace the extremity of emotion. To die was to fear everything; to feel, or want to feel, nothing. "But life, life! How I long to take you in my arms & crush you out," Woolf would write in her diary in 1923. "What she liked was simply life," Clarissa thinks in *Mrs. Dalloway*, echoing Woolf, as does Septimus just before plunging to his death: "He did not want to die. Life was good." Paradoxically, only killing himself would allow Septimus to honor life as he believed it should be lived: with beauty, with freedom.

The most elemental contrast that would organize *Mrs. Dalloway* was not between Clarissa and Septimus, but between them and the other characters. Clarissa and Septimus on the side of life, and a menagerie of stiff, glittering characters, implicitly, on the side of death: Lady Bexborough and Lady Bruton, congenitally cold, militant women both; Hugh Whitbread, hypocritical and abusive; and Dr. Bradshaw and Dr. Holmes, the doctors who oppressed life's diversity and spoiled its excitement by abusing modern medical tools: prescriptions, hospitalization, birth control. It was no accident that these characters were members of the conservative governing class. They were the "public school types" responsible not just for the war but for exporting its horrors to the farthest reaches of the British Empire—to South Africa, India, even Canada. Instead of having H. Z. Prentice wander the streets of London, decrying English conservatism, Woolf would smuggle her critique of the social system into *Mrs. Dalloway* through the emotional inadequacies of her minor characters. Septimus would abhor and challenge them directly.

Clarissa, though a member of the ruling class herself, would never assimilate fully to their way of being.

The love of life that connected Clarissa and Septimus had "to have the effect of being incessant," Woolf wrote in her notebook in November 1922. She considered organizing the novel by hours, and calling it "The Hours":

> Fuller Plan: Hours: 10. 11. 12. 1. 2. 3. 4
> 5. 6. 7. 8. 9. 10. 11. 12. 1. 2.

Ten o'clock was to be the hour of Mrs. Dalloway's walk down Bond Street and the prime minister's drive; eleven o'clock, the "aeroplane hour"; twelve o'clock, the beginning of Septimus's appointment with the severe and arrogant Dr. Bradshaw. "All must bear finally upon the party at the end; which expresses life, in every variety & full of conviction; while S. dies," she plotted. "The human soul will be treated more seriously; one must emphasize character." Yet she feared smoothing her story with too firm a hand. "How far are breaks in the texture allowed?" she asked, already envisioning, perhaps, the novel's two beautiful, yet puzzling interludes: a dream vision of a solitary traveler riding through the woods and a mock-epic diatribe on psychiatry and its love of conformity. "Can one admit rhapsodies?" she asked.

Woolf meant to polish off the airplane chapter in early November 1922, first connecting Clarissa to Septimus, then leaping rapidly through the minds of the characters who would gather outside Buckingham Palace to watch the airplane overhead. But Septimus, who had grown along with her plan for the book, demanded more of her time and thought before she could continue. He needed to pass "through all extremes of feeling—happiness & unhappiness," she wrote in her notebook. His hallucinations would begin with the airplane, its trails of smoke bearing down on him with unbearable intensity. Then they would shift to the sunlight and the trees in Regent's Park, which she now decided to make a whole chapter. "The waving of the boughs; lights & shadows: voices. (real)," she wrote, perhaps recalling when, not so long ago, she had stared at the golden light on the wall and listened to the voices of the dead. There Septimus would sit; there he would stare. But he had to be seen by someone. "His wife?" Woolf asked on November 19, 1922. She answered by creating a wife for him: Lucrezia Warren Smith. She was Rezia for short—"simple, instinctive, childless," or as Woolf stressed, "a

Septimus (?) must be seen by someone. His wife? She to be founded on L? Simple, instinctive; childless.
They sit in Regents Park for example. But the interview with specialist must be in the middle.
She is to be a real character.
He only real insofar as she sees him. Otherwise to exist in his view of things: which is always to be contrasting with Mrs Dalloways.

Fuller plan.

Hours: 10. 11. 12. 1. 2. 3. 4
5. 6. 7. 8. 9. 10. 11. 12. 1. 2.

Eleven o'clock strikes
This is the aeroplane hour: wh. covers both Septimus & Rezia in Regents Park. & Clarissa reflections. ~~[illegible]~~ which lead to 12 o'clock: interview with specialist.

"Fuller plan," Virginia Woolf, November 9, 1922. *(New York Public Library, Berg Collection)*

real character." Woolf based her on Lydia Lopokova, a renowned Russian ballerina and wife of John Maynard Keynes. Rezia would love her husband but she would not understand him, and what she did not understand would amuse and pain her. Her passionate, indistinct perception of him would be the fulcrum on which their happiness and unhappiness would teeter. "This is to mean there is no reason in their happiness; or unhappiness; since the same things cause both," Woolf wrote. "R's character should be shown." Only through her character would his become legible.

Still, Septimus required not just a wife, but things to do and see, and through them, a finer characterization. As December approached, she cast about her friends to find models for him. "S's character founded on R?" she asked—"R" being Major Ralph Partridge, pale, stocky, and handsome, with amazingly wide-set blue eyes and a skittish manner. He had studied at

Lydia Lopokova: portrait taken for the British Broadcasting Company, c. 1938. *(Virginia Woolf Monk's House photograph album, MH-3, MS Thr 560, [20]. Houghton Library, Harvard College Library)*

Oxford with Lytton Strachey, then served in France, surviving the Somme and winning both a Military Cross and Bar and the Croix de Guerre. "His face. Eyes far apart—not degenerate," Woolf wrote. "Not wholly an intellectual. Had been in the war." But it was not enough to make Septimus a war hero. He should be a poet too. "Why not have something of G.B. in him?" she noted: Gerald Brennan, Ralph's fellow ex-officer, a novelist—dark-eyed, dark-haired, romantic, eccentric, and intense. In him, she glimpsed Septimus's prophetic bent. Brennan offered her a portrait of a young man "who takes life to heart: seeks truth—revelations—some reason; yet of course his insanity," she wrote in her notebook just before the new year. "His insensibility to other people's feelings—that is to say he must have the masculine feelings. Selfishness: egoism; but also has an extreme insight; & humility." His masculine features, however, cloaked the true inspiration for his madness. "Or founded on me?" she proposed. She would entrust a great deal of her past to Septimus's character—the precise nature of the visions she had seen and the voices she had heard, as well as her belief, as she put it in her diary, that the minds of all the people in the world were "threaded together" as one "common mind."

Writing about Septimus proved more depleting than she had anticipated. By the end of 1922, he had exhausted her. Once she had filled in his character, she would not return to him in earnest for nearly eight months. Blazing his way into the novel, he now forced Clarissa to move in tandem with him. "Mrs. D. must be seen by other people. As she sits in her drawing room," Woolf wrote in her notebook at the beginning of 1923. "Her chapter must correspond with his." Since Septimus had Rezia, she invented for Clarissa an "old buck": Peter Walsh, the outlines of his character largely cribbed from H. Z. Prentice. Shuffling between two notebooks, one old and one new, she labored all spring and into the start of summer on Peter, dragging his character into life at a slow and arduous pace. Peter would speak with Clarissa in her drawing room, she planned, reviving her "feeling about death youth." Around 11:30 a.m., he would walk away in a state of great agitation to the park, with the roar of their conversation still in his ear. His thoughts about her would mingle defensiveness with excitement, her past with his present. "Every scene should build up the idea of C's character. That will give unity as well as add to the final effect," Woolf wrote. Peter would encounter Rezia and Septimus in the park as they prepared to walk to the

Ralph Partridge, Dora de Houghton Carrington, and Lytton Strachey sitting on the porch with refreshments. Possibly Ham Spray House, Marlborough. *(Virginia Woolf Monk's House photograph album, MH-4, MS Thr 561, [8]. Houghton Library, Harvard College Library)*

doctor's office. Briefly, she would knot the two threads of her story together, then pull them apart when Big Ben struck noon.

When midsummer arrived, everything began to unravel at a quick and fierce pace. "I foresee, to return to The Hours, that is going to be the devil of a struggle," Woolf wrote in her diary in June. "The design is so queer & so masterful. I'm always having to wrench my substance to fit it." She had intended to return to Septimus's hallucinations, but could not. They proved too heated, too personal and agonizing for her to approach with any feeling of joyful abandon. "Am I writing The Hours from deep emotion?" she wondered. "Of course the mad part tries me so much, makes my mind squint so badly that I can hardly face spending the next weeks at it. Its a question though of these characters." The characters brought her only dread and despair when she reread what she had written in August: Peter's memories of being rejected by Clarissa, and Clarissa's memories of falling in love with her friend Sally Seaton. It was "sheer weak dribble," she proclaimed. "Parts are so bad, parts are so good." Twice she threatened to throw it into the fire, only it was still too uncomfortably hot at Monk's House to light one.

As the weather cooled, so did her mood. The autumn found her stranded in Regent's Park "in the thick of the mad scene"—Septimus's second hallucination, brought on by the sound of a boy playing a penny whistle and the honk of a motor horn. Its language borrowed from her dearest literary and artistic touchstones: the plays of Shakespeare, the poems of John Keats and T. S. Eliot, the operas of Wagner. She could eke out no more than fifty words a day, and suspected she would have to rewrite it all. Yet the depth and unity of Septimus's insane vision had started to cohere in a wonderful paean to beauty. "The doubtful point is I think the character of Mrs Dalloway," she wrote in her diary in November, worried that Clarissa had receded from her while she had attended to Septimus. "It may be too stiff, too glittering & tinsely—But then I can bring innumerable other characters to her support." By the beginning of December, she had in hand most of the other characters that would appear in *Mrs. Dalloway.* Its chapters included:

Mrs. Dalloway in Bond Street
The Prime Minister's Car
The Airplane / Septimus in Regent's Park I
Peter and Clarissa in the Drawing Room
Peter Walking to Regent's Park
Clarissa Recalling Sally Seaton
Septimus in Regent's Park II

Though she would shuffle this material in the final version of *Mrs. Dalloway*, Woolf believed that the design of the novel was finally satisfactory. Each chapter was linked to the one before it by an external source. She had refined her "tunneling process," boring into her characters' memories "to tell the past in instalments, as I have need of it. This is my prime discovery so far," she wrote in her diary. From Peter's mind, she had dug out Clarissa's radical, sensual youth, and from Clarissa's, her desire for Sally. From Septimus's mind, she had dug out his susceptibility to beauty, his resolute, uncolored honesty. Together, the sane and insane love of life created the frame for her novel.

Now that she had intermingled Clarissa's and Septimus's love of life, she turned to death. "There must be a reality which is not in human beings; at all," she had written back in August in her notebook. "What about death for instance? But where is death?" She would find it in the office of Sir William Bradshaw, the specialist whom Septimus would see at noon, in the longest section of the novel. She drafted the "Dr chapter," as she called it, steadily from December 1923 to April 1924, starting a new notebook and breaking off occasionally to lament "the cold raw edge of one's relinquished pages." In Sir William Bradshaw's presence, Septimus would find himself unable to speak about life:

> This is what he thinks at the drs.
> who goes on saying that he must
> weigh 11 stones. His cowardice
> is insisted upon. The sense that
> other people are engaged in living but
> that he is not. ~~His resolution~~
> He must somehow see through
> human nature—see its hypocrisy,
> & insincerity, its power to recover
> from every wound, incapable of
> taking any final impression.
> His sense that this is not worth
> having: that only the heat is
> worth while.

Against Bradshaw's cowardice and his clinical approach to human suffering, Septimus's sense that "only the heat is worth while" would begin to swell. "Fear no more the heat o' the sun," he and Clarissa would repeat throughout the novel, a line Woolf borrowed from Shakespeare's *Cymbeline*, her favorite of his plays. Septimus would realize that embracing life meant refusing to live in a world shaped by men like Bradshaw—protectors of life whose cruelty, ironically, would lead Septimus to his death. "I may have found my mine this time I think," she wrote in her diary on February 9, 1924, assuring

help finally. Then what remains? There is what he thinks at the Drs. who goes on saying that he must weigh 11 stones. His cowardice is insisted upon. The sense that other people are engaged in living but that he is not. ~~His resolution~~ He must somehow see through human nature—see its hypocrisy, & insincerity, its power to recover from every wound, incapable of taking any final impression. His sense that this is not worth having. That only the best is worth while.

Aug. 2nd) There must be a reality which is not in human beings at all. What about death for instance? But what is death? Strange if that were the reality—but in

"Then what remains," Virginia Woolf, July–August 1923. *(New York Public Library, Berg Collection)*

herself that Septimus's rejection of Bradshaw and his deadening conformity had gotten further into "the soul" than "any other novelist." "I may get all my gold out. . . . And my vein of gold lies so deep, in such bent channels. To get it out I must forge ahead, stoop & grope." She finished the "Dr chapter" at the beginning of April. Though she reported feeling assailed by the "usual depressions," she trusted that her "whimsical brain" would "pare away the ill fitting, till I have the shape exact."

The shape was, if not exact, very close to it. Suddenly, there was little need for her to stoop or grope. Her design had fallen into place. Her contrasts had been arranged. Her characters stood before her, closer than ever. She picked up her pace now; started to scribble at an amazing clip, seeing her way to the light glinting at the end of her tunnels. By May, the novel was reeling off her mind "fast & free now," she reported in her diary. Spring in London had driven away death with its brilliancy. People walked the streets freely and quickly, issuing invitations to parties, plays, dinners, and concerts. "But my mind is full of The Hours," she wrote, refusing all distractions as she mapped out her program for the next year.

> I am now saying that I will write at it for 4 months, June, July, August & September, & then it will be done, & I shall put it away for three months, during which I shall finish my essays, & then it will be—October, November, December—January; & I shall revise it January February March April, & in April my essays will come out, & in May my novel. . . . It is becoming more analytical & human I think; less lyrical; but I feel as if I had loosed the bonds pretty completely & could pour everything in.

The final third of the novel is less burdened by her planning and runs freer, though it is no less lyrical. In June, she listed in the notebook the last four or five scenes that remained for her to write: "Kilman & Elizabeth. The Warren Smiths. Peter. London. The party." She first attended to the characters of Clarissa's daughter Elizabeth and her tutor Miss Kilman, who took tea together, then parted, with Elizabeth boarding an omnibus and riding through London. In July, she opened a new notebook, the last one she would dedicate to *Mrs. Dalloway*, and turned to the tender parting scene between

Septimus and Rezia. August brought the "silver mist" of depression with the death of Septimus—"a low ebb," she reported in her diary, retreating from the incessant activity of London to Monk's House. "If only I could get into my vein & work it thoroughly deeply easily, instead of hacking out this miserable 200 words a day," she complained. "And then, as the manuscript grows, I have the old fear of it. I shall read it & find it pale. . . . Yet if this book proves anything, it proves that I can only write along those lines, & shall never desert them, but explore further & further, & shall, heaven be praised, never bore myself an instant." She willed herself to forget Septimus. She had bequeathed so much of herself to him that letting him go must have struck her as an exercise in self-forgetfulness, or perhaps a betrayal. It was "a very intense & ticklish business," she wrote.

With September came the party. "Now for the party!" she exclaimed in her notebook, and laid out all she wanted to offer her reader:

A general view of the world:

> The different groups:
> All sketched in.
> She makes her way gradually to the
> Bradshaw group.
> She is livid about Septimus. She
> Visualizes what happened.
> Goes into the little room. The clock striking her
> whole life
> Sees the old lady put her light out.
> Transition to Richard & Elizabeth, (They didn't enjoy
> themselves)
> Then to Peter & Sally on the stairs
> Sally loved plants: a mother.
> But we haven't seen Clarissa.

The party began in the kitchen, with Clarissa's servants, and moved through the crowd, the narrator interloping on conversations, landing briefly on important guests—Peter, Sally, Elizabeth—before Lady Bradshaw delivered the news of Septimus's death to Clarissa. Now Woolf's mind was so firmly screwed to *Mrs. Dalloway* that nothing could distract her from it, not even the stirrings of a flirtation with Vita Sackville-West on September 15: "Here I am, peering across at Vita at my blessed Mrs. Dalloway, & can't stop, of a night, thinking of the next scene, & how I'm to wind up." She wrote the party "sloppily," she confessed, "using nothing but present participles," repeating phrases and images from earlier chapters in her attempt to sum up everything in the novel. "It is to be a most complicated, spirited, solid piece, knitting together everything & ending on three notes," she planned in her diary. She wanted it to end with three people saying something to sum up Clarissa, and proposed Richard, Sally, and Peter for the task. But when the end came, she gave it entirely to Peter, who would spot Clarissa coming back into the room and think: "For there she was."

She wrote the novel's four final words on October 9, 1924, at 11:15 a.m., marking the time in the margins. She felt grateful, weary. Already, she started to misremember, or perhaps to fictionalize, how the novel had come about. She described it in her diary as "a feat," downplaying how long it had

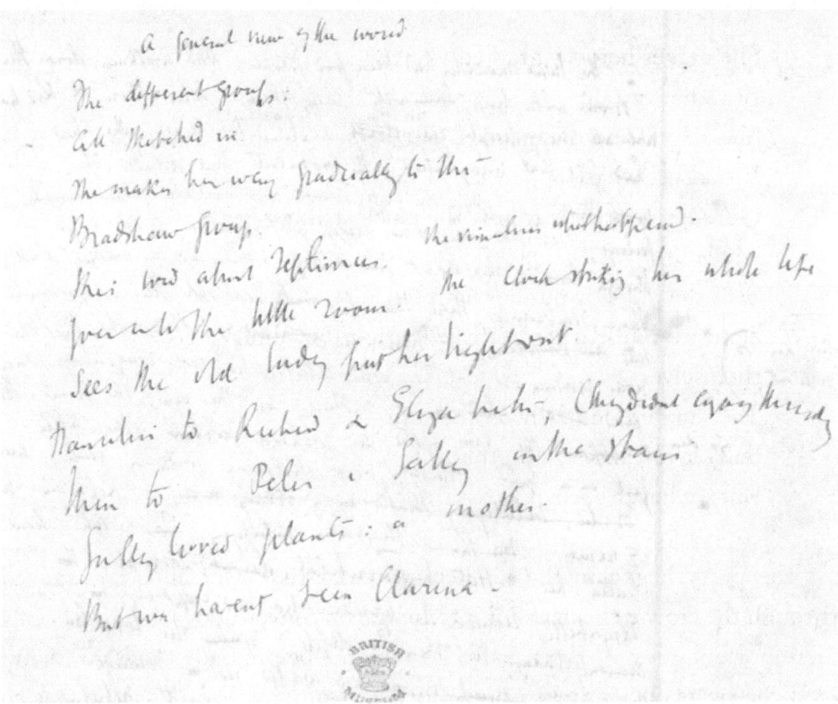
A general view of the world
The different groups:
She makes her way gradually to the
Bradshaw group.
the little room
Sees the old lady put her light out
Peter & Sally
mother
Sally loves plants
But we haven't seen Clarissa.

"A general view of the world," Virginia Woolf, September 1924. *(British Library)*

taken her to finish. It had been "written really, in one year; & finally, written from the end of March to the 8th of October without more than a few days break for writing journalism," she boasted. Riding high on her sense of triumph, she was ready to reacquaint herself with her characters, to mine them for more life than before, pulling their fates ever closer together. On October 20, she started to rewrite "Mrs. Dalloway in Bond Street" as the first chapter of the novel, beginning with a momentous change to the first line: "Mrs. Dalloway said she would buy the flowers herself." Briefly, when she edited the airplane chapter, she wondered if the book would have been better without Septimus's mad scenes, if Clarissa should have remained the focus of the novel. "But this is an afterthought," she wrote, "consequent upon learning how to deal with her. Always I think at the end, I see how the whole ought to have been written."

The end took her back to the beginning. She had handwritten the novel across two manuscripts and six notebooks, each littered with deletions, insertions, instructions to herself, numbers in the margins—rent, utilities bills, train times from Lewes to London—pages of Greek exercises, floorplans of her houses, and notes for other essays and books. It was time to type the novel herself. "I am now galloping over Mrs. Dalloway, re-typing it entirely from the start," she wrote in her diary on December 13, 1924. "A good method, I believe, as thus one works with a wet brush over the whole, & joins parts separately composed and gone dry." Typing the novel enlivened the act of writing. It made it purposive and gratifying, vanquished her doubts, allayed her fear of how critics would receive it. "The reviewers will say that it is disjoined because of the mad scenes not connecting with the Dalloway scenes. And I suppose there is some superficial glittery writing. But is it 'unreal'? Is it mere accomplishment? I think not," she concluded. "It seems to leave me plunged deep into the richest strata of my mind. I can write & write & write now: the happiest feeling in the world."

She could not have anticipated all that would come to pass after the novel was published on May 14, 1925. Some of it she may have guessed at: the mixed reviews, for instance, with some critics praising the beauty of her characters' minds, while others judged Clarissa uninteresting and Septimus "a huge piece of irrelevance." Some appreciated the novel's deliberate composition, while others found it artificial, "purely redundant, purely improbable, purely pointless." *Mrs. Dalloway* was compared to *Ulysses*, with Woolf described as "a sort of decorous James Joyce." It was compared to the postimpressionist paintings of Cézanne, to the modern ballet, to an orchestral composition. Likewise, she could not have known, when she sent a copy of *Mrs. Dalloway* to Vita Sackville-West, that Vita's life would become densely entwined with her own during the years she wrote *To the Lighthouse* (1927), *Orlando* (1928), and *The Waves* (1931). She could not have known that she would feel compelled to once again capture the apprehension of war in *The Years* (1937) and *Between the Acts* (1941), both written around the Second World War. She could not have known that her suicide in 1941 would make it impossible to read *Mrs. Dalloway* without a feeling of deep foreboding. And she could not have known that, after her death, in June of 1941, Leonard would send the last three notebooks of *Mrs. Dalloway* to Vita as a parting gift.

No—none of this would have occurred to her when, on December 21, 1924, she had "Mrs D. copied for L. to read at Rodmell." She planned to hand it to him over the Christmas holidays and to send the typescript to her publisher just after the new year. "Then I shall be free," she wrote.

VI.

I LAST READ *Mrs. Dalloway* several summers ago, though "read" may be a misleading term. When I first agreed to annotate the novel, the press offered to transcribe it for me. At the time I was feeling monkish, orderly and unencumbered and eager to dedicate myself to the novel with the punctiliousness Woolf had demonstrated in writing it. I was mindful of her contempt for readers who annotated books to argue with or correct their authors—though unable to repress my belief that, at times, critique was both necessary and truer to Woolf's approach to reading than fawning would have been. Indeed, as Woolf had written in her 1932 essay "How Should One Read a Book?" "Do not dictate to your author; try to become him."

So: I said I would type the manuscript myself.

Before I started typing, I drove from my home in Oxford to Monk's House, the Woolfs' cottage in Rodmell. It was June, the hottest June in forty years. A storm had come through southeast England the week before, and

Jacket for *Mrs. Dalloway*, Hogarth Press, Vanessa Bell, 1925. *(Washington State University, Rare Books and Special Collections)*

now the garden at Monk's House was all out: rows of cabbages with sweet-smelling wildflowers blooming between them; bees, their legs dusted with pollen, creeping in and out of the violet foxgloves, then whisking about the roses, irises, lilacs, and dahlias; a pale pink lily floating in the stone pond; a snail making its way down the garden path; not merely a bright sky, but a vaulting one. A cricket game was being played on the meadows just beyond the garden wall. I sat on it and spoke to a group of elderly English women who were admiring the great gray steeple of the church next door. They had found the listing for Monk's House in the National Heritage guide, they said. They confessed they had not heard of Virginia Woolf before—only Jane Austen. "Our beloved Jane," Clarissa says to Richard in *The Voyage Out*. "She is incomparably the greatest female writer we possess," he agrees, then falls asleep, twitching and snoring, as she begins to read *Persuasion* aloud to him.

From a set of stairs outside the house, I ascended to Woolf's bedroom. At the foot of her narrow bed, I found a docent, a young woman reading a novel, wearing a look of concentration so persistent and fierce that it seemed to demand interruption. She appeared to be one of those fresh, simply dressed students whose calculated attentiveness—every sigh measured, every flick of every page weighed—suggested more extreme self-consciousness than keeping quiet or fidgeting would have. There was something about her that made me feel protective—an earnestness, an anticipation, and besides that, she was very small. She had folded all of herself up in a folding chair, and there she managed to sit without touching anything beyond it. I felt she was lonely, that she hoped someone would speak to her, and, being the age she was, that she still believed a conversation with a stranger could touch some hidden spring in her mind, keeping her company long after their talk had ceased.

We spoke for some time about the city we both happened to be from; about the university she attended there and the novel she was reading, one I had long loved. When our polite conversation slowed, she asked if she could show me the objects in the room that she believed had been Woolf's favorites. I imagined she would turn to Woolf's complete set of the Arden Shakespeare, the only books she had actually owned in a house now cluttered with props and replicas. To stave off her migraines, Woolf had bound them by hand, in marbled paper whose red, brown, black, and silver-colored curves gave one the impression that their spines had been surrounded by the still-fluttering wings of hundreds, maybe thousands, of moths. But I was wrong. The docent guided me across the room to the mantel. From it, she lifted two things: a mirror, which she handed to me, and an iridescent blue shell: "Venus's ear," she said, holding it to hers.

She asked me what I thought. I sensed that what she wanted was a story, some way to make sense of these curious offerings and why they had imposed themselves on her with such immediacy. That they were enchanted objects, or that she wanted them to be, of that there was no doubt. Next to the shell, her face appeared elfin and restless. I looked into the mirror and was surprised to discover that it was a Claude glass, slightly convex and gray-tinted, a mirror that stretched the face and darkened the eyes. I asked her if she remembered the moment in *Mrs. Dalloway* when Clarissa appraises herself in the mirror: "That was her self—pointed; dartlike; definite. That was her self when some effort, some call on her to be her self, drew the parts together, she alone knew how different, how incompatible and composed so for the world only into one centre, one diamond, one woman." I told her I thought the mirror was for glimpsing things both as they were and as they were not: for seeing one's face at once absurdly elongated and arcing to a point, a shockingly incoherent portrait—yet one that came closer than any regular mirror to catching the essence of the self, of character, as Woolf understood it.

She came to my side, and we looked into the glass together. Our reflections wobbled in, then out of sight. From where I stood, my eyes remained focused and sharper than hers, which never lost their watery, wondering quality. And the shell? she asked, presenting it to the mirror. Instantly, it filled with blue.

The shell was for hearing voices that were not there, I said.

I suppose I must have added something else, something insubstantial and humorous, before leaving her there, still holding her treasures. I can recall little of our conversation. I have never been able to confirm that Woolf owned either the mirror or "Venus's ear"—a name so fanciful it is hard to believe Woolf did not conceive it herself—just as I have not been able to track down the docent, whom I occasionally worry I may have invented. The mood of our encounter as I remember it today was of two children playing a very serious game of make-believe, bestowing to these trinkets

Shelf of Shakespeare plays hand-bound by Virginia Woolf in her bedroom at Monk's House, Rodmell, Sussex.

an extraordinary, totemic power. It is a game in keeping with Woolf's theory of character, bringing people into a strange, intimate, and impersonal contact by flinging their thoughts outward together—to mirrors and shells, to airplanes and motorcars, to novels and the imaginary lives they contain.

What I am describing is nothing less than the possibility of connection, of beauty, that Septimus and Clarissa perceive in the shared matter of life. He sees it in the sun glinting through the trees. She sees it in her flowers, her party. We see it in the characters themselves, their minds made to kindle and glow before us. They are as exquisitely illuminated for me now as they were when I first lit upon them, many years ago, on a summer day in June.

Virginia Woolf seated in an armchair looking toward a window at Monk's House, undated. *(Virginia Woolf's Monk House photograph album, MS Thr 564 [76]. Houghton Library, Harvard College Library)*

REGENT'S PARK
THE BROAD WALK
EUSTON ROAD
TOTTENHAM COURT ROAD
BLOOMSBURY
MARYLEBONE ROAD
HARLEY STREET
PORTLAND PLACE
MARYLEBONE
NEW OXFORD STREET
OXFORD STREET
BROOK ST
CONDUIT ST
SOHO
SHAFTESBURY AVE
MAYFAIR
HYDE PARK
PICCADILLY
GREEN PARK
THE MALL
ST. JAMES'S PARK
ST. JAMES'S ST
VICTORIA ST
WESTMINSTER

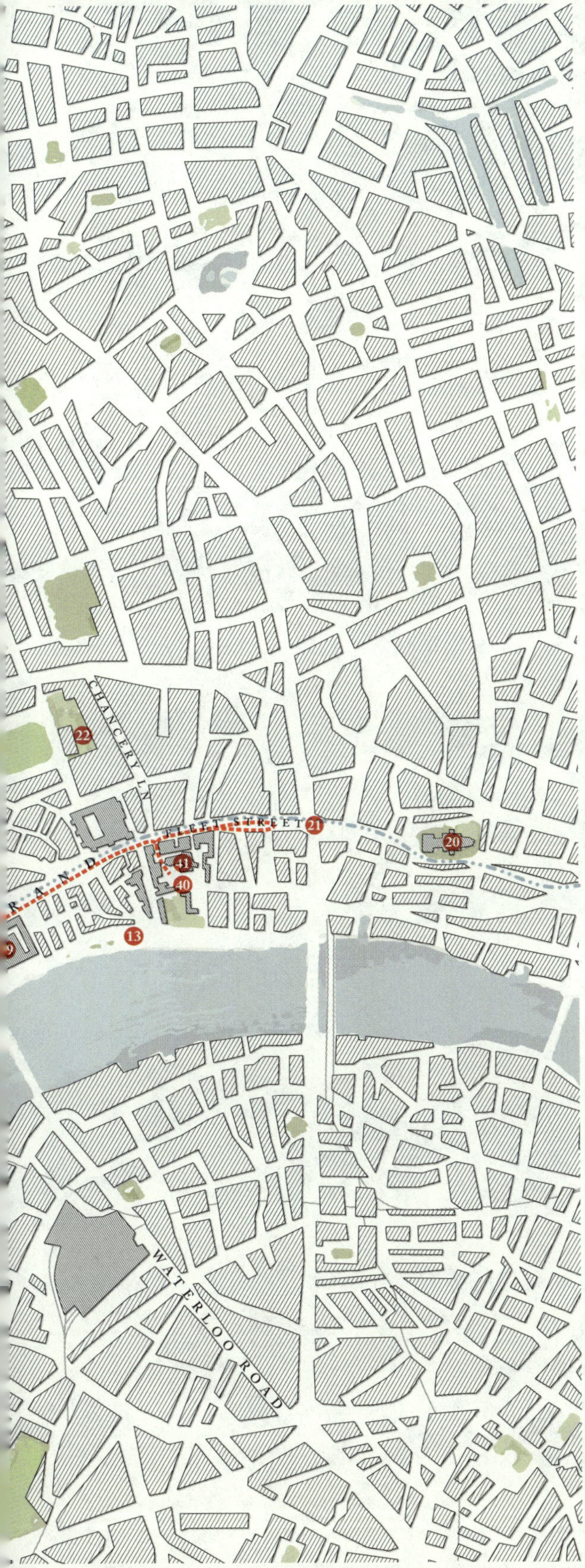

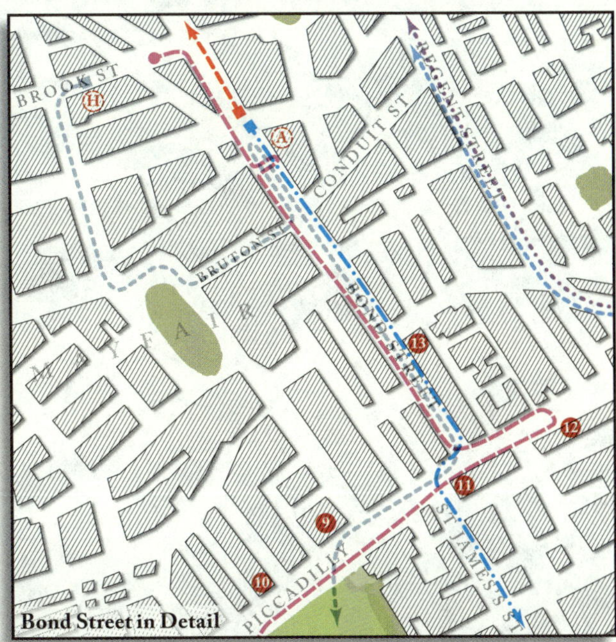

Bond Street in Detail

Historical Locations

1 Big Ben of Westminster
2 Buckingham Palace
3 Lord's Cricket Ground
4 Board of Trade
5 Foreign and India Offices
6 The Admiralty
7 Piccadilly Circus
8 Devonshire House
9 Bath House
10 The Serpentine
11 Hatchards Book Shop
12 Atkinson's Scent Shop
13 The Embankment
14 White's
15 St James's Palace
16 Queen Victoria Memorial
17 Ready Money Fountain
18 London Zoo
19 Regent's Park Tube Station
20 St Paul's Cathedral
21 Ludgate Circus
22 Lincoln's Inn
23 St Margaret's
24 The Duke of Cambridge
25 The Cenotaph
26 Nelson's Column
27 Trafalgar Square
28 E. Dent & Co.
29 Matilda Fountain
30 Euston Railway Station
31 Houses of Parliament
32 Bedford Square
33 Hyde Park Corner
34 Speakers' Corner
35 Dean's Yard
36 Army and Navy Stores
37 Westminster Cathedral
38 Westminster Abbey
39 Somerset House
40 Middle and Inner Temple
41 Temple Church
42 The British Museum
43 The Oriental Club
44 Russell Square

Fictional and Approximate Locations

A Mulberry's Florists
B Young Woman's Door
C Peter's Seat in the Park
D Septimus & Rezia's Seat
E Peter Steps into His Taxi
F Sir William's House
G Septimus & Rezia's House
H Lady Bruton's House
I Peter's Hotel
J Dalloway House

Approximate Paths of Travel

Clarissa Dalloway
The Motor Car
Septimus & Rezia
Peter Walsh
Marching Boys
Young Woman
Richard Dalloway
Elizabeth Dalloway
Doris Kilman

MRS. DALLOWAY'S LONDON *(Christian Nakarado)*

Mrs. Dalloway

MRS. DALLOWAY said she would buy the flowers herself.[1]

For Lucy had her work cut out for her. The doors would be taken off their hinges; Rumpelmayer's men were coming.[2] And then, thought Clarissa[3] Dalloway, what a morning—fresh as if issued to children on a beach.

Still Life on Corner of a Mantelpiece, Vanessa Bell. Oil on canvas, 1914. *(Tate, Estate of Vanessa Bell, courtesy Henrietta Garnett)*

1 Why did Virginia Woolf alter the opening of "Mrs. Dalloway in Bond Street" ("Mrs. Dalloway said she would buy the gloves herself")? What is the difference between gloves and flowers?

In a diary entry from January 2, 1923, Woolf linked her longing for flowers to her longing for life; for childhood, innocence, and the vitality of youth; "for the sense of flowers breaking all round me involuntarily," she wrote. "They make my life seem a little bare sometimes; & then my inveterate romanticism suggests an image of forging ahead, alone, through the night: of suffering inwardly, stoically; of blazing my way through to the end—& so forth." Flowers fascinate Clarissa Dalloway from her earliest appearance in *The Voyage Out* (1915), though she invokes them with a greater sense of whimsy than Woolf and no trace of melancholy. "What I find so tiresome about the sea is that there are no flowers in it. Imagine fields of hollyhocks and violets in mid-ocean! How divine!" Clarissa exclaims to the ship's owner Willoughby Vinrace.

In *Mrs. Dalloway*, the omniscient narrator opens with the promise and pleasure of shopping, one of the daily activities of life that Woolf celebrates throughout the novel. But the pleasure of life is always mingled with the inevitability of death; of "blazing my way through to the end," as she wrote in her diary. In the middle of London, the flowers Clarissa shops for are no longer rooted in nature. They are perishable and perishing goods, already cut and condemned to death. Buying them, arranging them, invites death into the house from the novel's first sentence.

2 No photographs remain of Anton Rumpelmayer (1832–1914), who changed his name to Antoine at thirty-eight years old, when he left his hometown of Pressburg, in Austria-Hungary, to seek his fortune as a world-renowned confectioner and caterer. Some believe he landed in Cannes or Nice, at the height of the 1870 summer season; others, that he arrived in Menton, where he started working as a candymaker for restaurant owner Viktor Sylvain Perrimond. Together, they opened Perrimond-Rumpelmayer's, followed by cafés in Aix and Baden-Baden, a chocolate factory in Dresden, and a tea house in Paris. "London has long wanted a Rumpelmayer's, and now it is to have one," announced *Putnam's Magazine*,

What a lark! What a plunge! For so it had always seemed to her when, with a little squeak of the hinges, which she could hear now, she had burst open the French windows and plunged at Bourton into the open air. How fresh, how calm, stiller than this of course, the air was in the early morning; like the flap of a wave; the kiss of a wave;[4] chill and sharp and yet (for a

Jacket for *The Waves*, Hogarth Press, Vanessa Bell, 1931. *(© Estate of Vanessa Bell. All rights reserved, DACS 2021)*

when a Rumpelmayer's franchise opened on St. James's Street in 1907. There one could gaze upon "the most tempting array imaginable of little individual, one-or-two mouthful tea cakes," wrote society columnist Frank Arnold in 1915. "All England and the English colonies may be visualized at that moment as one joy giving teapot." Rumpelmayer could not have commented on Arnold's imperialist appropriation of his tea cakes and teapots. He had died the year before, leaving his widow Angelina to see to his legacy.

3 "Lettice" was the name Woolf initially gave to Clarissa Dalloway in *The Voyage Out*, perhaps inspired by her friend and relation Lettice Fisher. Fisher was an Oxford-educated economist, historian, suffragette, and founder of the National Council for the Unmarried Mother and her Child, which provided support to single-parent families after the First World War. She was the wife of H. A. L. Fisher, a cousin of Woolf's and MP for the Combined English Universities, a university constituency represented in Parliament from 1918 to 1950. In February 1909, Woolf stayed with the Fishers in Oxford, a setting she despised for its chilly intellectualism but admired for its pastoral beauty. "Cabbages tap at the dining room windows," she wrote in her diary, an image that reappears on p. 6 of *Mrs. Dalloway* when Clarissa recalls Peter Walsh.

4 Among the most-quoted passages from Woolf's autobiography is her memory of waking up at Talland House, her family's summer home in St Ives, Cornwall, on the coast of the Celtic Sea. Lying in bed, "half asleep, half awake," she recalled "hearing the waves breaking, one, two, one, two, and sending a splash of water over the beach; and then breaking, one, two, one, two, behind a yellow blind." For Woolf, the feeling of childhood is inseparable from the "purest ecstasy" of hearing, through a slightly open window, the waves as they break, then relinquish the land and return to open water. Children listen to the waves first in *Jacob's Room* (1922), then in *Mrs. Dalloway*, *To the Lighthouse* (1927), and finally, *The Waves* (1931).

St Ives postcard. *(Virginia Woolf Monk's House photograph album, MH-5, MS Thr 562 [3], Houghton Library, Harvard College Library)*

Katharine Maxse, née Lushington. *(Mary Evans Picture Library)*

girl of eighteen as she then was) solemn, feeling as she did, standing there at the open window, that something awful was about to happen;[5] looking at the flowers, at the trees with the smoke winding off them and the rooks rising, falling; standing and looking until Peter Walsh said, "Musing among the vegetables?"—was that it?—"I prefer men to cauliflowers"—was that it? He must have said it at breakfast one morning when she had gone out on to the terrace—Peter Walsh. He would be back from India[6] one of these days, June or July, she forgot which, for

5 The squeak of the hinges, the opening of the windows, the plunge into the open air—these happy memories from Clarissa Dalloway's youth at Bourton, her family's country estate, double as omens of Septimus Smith's suicide later in the novel. Woolf revised the opening paragraphs of "Mrs. Dalloway in Bond Street" in October 1924, just after she finished the first full draft of the manuscript, so that Clarissa's rapturous abandonment of herself to life would parallel Septimus's violent fall to his death on p. 191: "the tiresome, the troublesome, and rather melodramatic business of opening the window and throwing himself out." (In the manuscript of "The Hours" Woolf tries, "What ~~an ecstasy! <a miracle~~>!" before deciding on "What a plunge!")

If buying flowers invites death into the novel, then the image of falling ushers it into the Dalloways' house. There it waits to announce its presence at the party later that night, when Clarissa will hear about Septimus's suicide and think, echoing her earlier thoughts: "But this young man who had killed himself—had he plunged holding his treasure?" The twining of life and death also appears in Woolf's descriptions of the day her mother had died. "I went to the open window & looked out," she wrote in her diary on May 4, 1937, remembering "the doves swooping" on May 5, 1885. "How that early morning picture has stayed with me!"

6 Peter Walsh, Clarissa's former "buck," works as a civil servant in British India. Just before Woolf started writing *Mrs. Dalloway*, India experienced another wave of uprisings against Britain's oppressive colonial rule. ("Ah, the news from India!" Lady Bruton will exclaim on p. 146.) The Indian National Congress had withdrawn support for British reforms in the colony following the Anarchical and Revolutionary Crimes Act of 1919, which authorized preventative detention and incarceration without trial to disable the activities of revolutionary nationalists. Mahatma Gandhi had started the non-cooperation movement on September 1, 1920, with the aim of securing full Indian independence through nonviolent means. The movement lasted until February 1922, when a group of protesters marched through a marketplace in the town of Chauri Chaura to protest high meat prices. When police publicly beat the leader of the march, the protesters circled the police station, throwing stones and shouting anti-government slurs. Police officers fired into the crowd, shooting three civilians to death. In retaliation, the

his letters were awfully dull; it was his sayings one remembered; his eyes, his pocket-knife, his smile, his grumpiness and, when millions of things had utterly vanished—how strange it was!—a few sayings like this about cabbages.

She stiffened a little on the kerb, waiting for Durtnall's van to pass.[7] A charming woman, Scrope Purvis thought her (knowing her as one does know people who live next door to one in Westminster);[8] a touch of the bird about her, of the jay, blue-green, light, vivacious, though she was over fifty, and grown very

Durtnall & Co. advertisement.
(Pelon's Illustrated Guide to Tunbridge Wells *[1896]*)

protesters set fire to the police station, killing all twenty-three policemen trapped inside. The British immediately declared martial law in Chauri Chaura, and one week later, the Indian National Congress halted the non-cooperation movement. Gandhi was arrested for sedition and sentenced to six years in prison. On April 20, 1923, nineteen of the Chauri Chaura protesters were sentenced to death, and 110 were sentenced to life in prison. The push for Indian independence against the "curse" of British rule would continue through the second half of the 1920s, 1930s, and 1940s, until August 15, 1947, the day when the provisions of the Indian Independence Act of 1947 went into effect.

7 Located at 4 Bartholomew Close in the City of London, Durtnall and Co. specialized in transportation, shipping, and furniture removal.

8 Scrope Purvis is unimportant in his own right: just one of many residents of Westminster, the wealthy neighborhood near Parliament and Buckingham Palace where the Dalloways reside. But he is significant as the first character Woolf introduces to shift narrative consciousness, focalizing Clarissa not as the eighteen-year-old girl of her memories but as a "charming woman" "over fifty" who has "grown very white since her illness." Despite the differences between the girl and the woman, there is a remarkable continuity of language between Clarissa's examination of her memory and Scrope's examination of Clarissa. Just as she stands in the street, recalling how she once looked at the rooks rising and falling, he stands in the street and looks at her, noting "a touch of the bird about her, of the jay, blue-green, light, vivacious." Just as the rooks do not see her, she does not see him.

As J. Hillis Miller has argued, the telepathic link between Clarissa and Scrope Purvis suggests that the minds of Woolf's characters, major and minor, are joined to one another. Together, their minds constitute "a general consciousness": a "social mind which rises into existence out of the collective mental experience of the individual human beings in the story." For Miller, it is this general consciousness that narrates *Mrs. Dalloway*. It moves in and out of the minds of the characters with wonderful subtlety, ferrying words and images from one paragraph to the next.

Miller's astute interpretation chimes with Woolf's pronouncement in "A Sketch of the Past" (1939) that the highest goal of fiction was to reveal the exquisite arrangement of thoughts and feelings that existed between conscious minds. "One's life is not confined to one's body and what one says and does; one is living all the time in relation to certain background rods or conceptions," she wrote. The "goodness" of individual existence was not to be discovered in the original features of one's personality or the unique

white since her illness.[9] There she perched, never seeing him, waiting to cross, very upright.

For having lived in Westminster—how many years now? over twenty,—one feels even in the midst of the traffic, or waking at night, Clarissa was positive, a particular hush, or solemnity; an indescribable pause; a suspense (but that might be her heart, affected, they said, by influenza)[10] before Big Ben strikes.[11] There! Out it boomed. First a warning, musical; then the hour, irrevocable. The leaden circles dissolved in the air. Such fools we are, she thought, crossing Victoria Street.[12] For Heaven only

incidents of one's biography. The essence of life was profoundly intersubjective. It was a state of "non-being"—an unconscious living "embedded in a kind of nondescript cotton wool" that kept its true nature hidden from the individual. "[T]here is a pattern hid behind the cotton wool," she declared. "And this conception affects me every day."

9 As noted in the Introduction, Clarissa Dalloway bears a striking resemblance to Woolf's childhood friend Kitty Maxse. "Almost Kitty verbatim," Woolf wrote to her sister Vanessa Bell while drafting *The Voyage Out*. "What would happen if she guessed?"

After Kitty died on October 4, 1922, Woolf memorialized her using the same language we see in Scrope Purvis's physical description of Clarissa. Yet

Pedestrians and traffic, Victoria Street, London, April 1912. Busy street scene with cars, horse-drawn vehicles, an open-topped omnibus on the left, and people crossing the road. Shop fronts are visible, including Hope Brothers, Bewlay, and Petter Oil Engines. *(Heritage Image Partnership Ltd / Alamy)*

knows why one loves it so, how one sees it so, making it up, building it round one, tumbling it, creating it every moment afresh; but the veriest frumps, the most dejected of miseries sitting on doorsteps (drink their downfall) do the same; can't be dealt with, she felt positive, by Acts of Parliament for that very reason: they love life. In people's eyes, in the swing, tramp, and trudge; in the bellow and the uproar; the carriages, motor cars, omnibuses, vans, sandwich men shuffling and swinging; brass bands; barrel organs; in the triumph and the jingle and the strange high singing of some aeroplane overhead was what she loved; life; London; this moment of June.[13]

For it was the middle of June.[14] The War was over, except for some one like Mrs. Foxcroft at the Embassy last night eating her heart out[15] because that nice boy was killed and now the old Manor House must go to a cousin; or Lady Bexborough who opened a bazaar, they said, with the telegram in her hand, John, her favourite, killed; but it was over; thank Heaven—over.[16] It was June. The King and Queen were at the Palace.[17]

King George V and Queen Mary arrive on the course at the Royal Ascot, June 14, 1921. *(PA Images / Alamy)*

Woolf did not attend Kitty's service. She wrote to Roger Fry to confess that too much time had passed since she and Kitty had been close: ". . . there's Kitty Maxse falling over the bannisters and killing herself . . . It seems a pity that Kitty did kill herself; but of course, she was an awful snob. No, one couldn't go on with people like that. One had to make a break somewhere." Woolf's relegation of Kitty to fiction, where she can be both satirized and memorialized, formalizes the break between the former friends.

10 The United Kingdom saw three pandemic waves of influenza (from the Italian word for "influence") during 1918–19, which affected over a quarter of the British population and resulted in the deaths of 228,000 people in Britain alone. In a letter written on September 29, 1918, Professor Roy Grist, a physician stationed at Camp Devens in Massachusetts, described his patients' violent speed of death: "When brought to the Hosp. they very rapidly develop the most viscious [*sic*] type of Pneumonia that has ever been seen. Two hours after admission they have the Mahogony [*sic*] spots over the cheek bones, and a few hours later you can begin to see the Cyanosis extending from their ears and spreading all over the face. . . . It is only a matter of a few hours then until death comes, and it is simply a struggle for air until they suffocate. It is horrible."

As Elizabeth Outka observes in *Viral Modernism: The Influenza Pandemic and Interwar Literature*, Woolf had intimate knowledge of influenza's devastating consequences. Her mother's sudden death on May 5, 1895, was linked to influenza. Her own frequent bouts of influenza were linked to her depression, which intensified when she found herself confined to bed, her temperature raging for weeks, her heart growing ever jumpier. "[M]y eccentric pulse had passed the limits of reason & was in fact insane," she wrote in her diary on February 14, 1922. Her doctors cautioned her against overexerting herself, as did Leonard. "L. on the telephone expressed displeasure," she wrote in a diary entry of January 2, 1923. "Late again. Very foolish. Your heart bad—& so my self reliance being sapped, I had no courage to venture against his will."

Influenza leaves its physical mark on Clarissa's face: her pink spotted cheeks; her pale coloring. But Woolf suggests that influenza's influence is strongest on Clarissa's heart. It is freshly susceptible to the terror and ecstasy of life after its brush with death.

11 Contrary to popular belief, Big Ben is the name not of the clock tower that sits at the north end of the Palace of Westminster but of the fifteen-ton Great Bell housed in the belfry. On the hour, every hour, it sounds an E natural. From 1916 to 1918, Big Ben and the four quarter bells in the belfry were silenced

And everywhere, though it was still so early, there was a beating, a stirring of galloping ponies, tapping of cricket bats; Lord's,[18] Ascot,[19] Ranelagh[20] and all the rest of it; wrapped the soft mesh of the grey-blue morning air, which, as the day wore on, would unwind them, and set down on their lawns and pitches the bouncing ponies, whose forefeet just struck the ground and up they sprung, the whirling young men, and laughing girls in their transparent muslins who, even now, after dancing all night, were taking their absurd woolly dogs for a run; and even now, at this hour, discreet old dowagers were shooting out in their motor cars on errands of mystery; and the shopkeepers were fidgeting in their windows with their paste and diamonds, their lovely old sea-green brooches in eighteenth-century settings to tempt Americans (but one must economise, not buy things rashly for Elizabeth), and she, too, loving it as she did with an absurd and faithful passion, being part of it, since her people were courtiers once in the time of the Georges,[21] she, too, was going that very night to kindle and illuminate; to give her party. But how

Royal Ascot fashions in 1921.
(Trinity Mirror / Mirrorpix / Alamy)

and the clock face kept dark so as not to illuminate the sky for German zeppelins dropping bombs on London. The suspense and thrill Clarissa feels hearing it registers the enduring trauma of this two-year silence, this fearful pause of the clock's striking and chiming during the First World War.

Big Ben of Westminster, 1873. (*The Reliquary: Depository for Precious Relics, Legendary Biographical, and Historical, Vol. 13)*

12 Once home to Charles Dickens's (1812–1870) "Devil's Acre" slum, Victoria Street opened for use in 1851. It runs on an east-west axis from Victoria Station to Broad Sanctuary at Westminster Abbey.

13 In her elegant reading of shopping in *Mrs. Dalloway*, Jennifer Wicke observes that Clarissa's "reverie on life is also a comment on consciousness"—on how consciousness is created by the social and economic world that one inhabits. Life is something one's eyes can see, one's ears can hear; something one's mind can take up, tumble down, build around, and make anew from one moment to the next. Here, Clarissa's perception of life is buttressed by sights and sounds of the market, from the "bellow and the uproar" of delivery vehicles driving past to the "shuffling and swinging" of people selling their wares.

In Woolf's modern consciousness, markets, like the minds that perceive their daily activities, are chaotic, dynamic, comprehensive, and hyper-receptive. As Wicke notes, the economist John Maynard Keynes, a Bloomsbury intimate of Woolf's, conceived of the market in similar terms in his polemical work *The Economic Consequences of the Peace* (1919). (*The Economic Consequences of the Peace* would sell its "15th thousand" copy by February 1920, Woolf noted in her diary.) For Keynes, the market was a "preternaturally sensitive organism ready to ramify the smallest shock throughout its limpid, limbic system," "resistant to representation, at least by traditional (realist, rationalist) means," Wicke writes. Bloomsbury's leading novelist and its leading economist both depicted a disorderly socioeconomic system and its "provisional, momentary, and intertwiningly intricate" nature.

"Maynard was our link with the great world of war and politics," wrote Woolf's nephew Quentin Bell in his memoir *Bloomsbury Recalled*. The "gross & stout" Keynes, as Woolf described him in 1923, was a man whose mind she admired greatly, more than she did his friendships with prime ministers or his presence at the Peace Conference in Versailles. Reading his writing, she proclaimed, "The process of mind there displayed is as far ahead of me as Shakespeare's." Keynes relished her praise, and was eager to reciprocate it. He judged her a wonderful creator of character, and particularly appreciated her satire of her half-brother George Duckworth in her 1920 memoir, *Moments of Being*. "The best thing you ever did, he said, was your Memoir on George," she wrote, recalling a conversation with Keynes on May 25, 1921. "You should pretend to write about real people & make it all up—I was dashed of course."

14 In 2018, after years of quibbling among academics and fans, the International Virginia Woolf Society and the Virginia Woolf Society of Great Britain settled on the third Wednesday in June as Dalloway Day.

But the day mattered less than the season to Woolf. Always, summer stretched before her as a season of "splintered disorder." Plans were made, then abandoned. People showed up to Monk's House and demanded their amusement and her attention. There was never enough time to write. June, July, and August made her think of "[a] broken china closet"—"so many smashes & tergivasations," she wrote in her diary. The bright clamor of Clarissa's June day catches the happy possibilities of summer's social life, all that Woolf could have enjoyed had she simply given in to the allure of flowers and parties and people.

15 Woolf slyly plays on the two meanings of "eat your heart out": to feel great anguish or grief (because Mrs. Foxcroft's son, "that nice boy was killed"); to suffer from envy or jealousy (because "now the old Manor House must go to a cousin").

16 As Paul Saint-Amour has observed, the repeated assertion that the war was "over" is "breached by the exceptions the narrator makes for those bereaved civilians whose grief recognizes no Armistice." Here exceptions are made for Mrs. Foxcroft and Lady Bexborough, though, as we will see later in the novel, none of Woolf's characters can escape the memories or the fears that the First World War has impressed upon their minds. The narrator "asserts closure as an ongoing psychic performance," Saint-Amour writes. It must be insisted on regularly and forcefully, rather than accepted as "an accomplished historical fact."

John Maynard Keynes, 1931. *(Virginia Woolf Monk's House photograph album, MH-3, MS Thr 560, [34]. Houghton Library, Harvard College Library)*

Angelica Garnett, Vanessa Bell, Clive Bell, Virginia Woolf, and Maynard Keynes seated on a patio, August 6, 1935. *(Virginia Woolf Monk's House photographs, MS Thr 564, [134]. Houghton Library, Harvard College Library)*

British royal family, King George and Queen Mary, 1914. *(Harris & Ewing)*

Lord's Cricket Ground, c. 1930. *(UK Photo and Social History Archive)*

17 In 1923, the king and queen of England were George V (1865–1936) and Queen Mary (1867–1953), formerly Princess Victoria Mary of Teck. Crowned on June 22, 1911, their reign coincided with, and helped usher in, a period of tremendous political change: the passage of the Parliament Act 1911, which effectively formalized the power of the House of Commons over the House of Lords; the First World War (1914–18); the Irish War of Independence (1919–21); the appointment of the first Labour Party prime minister, Ramsay MacDonald (1924); the nine-day General Strike (1926) to protest wage reductions for coal miners; the Great Depression (beginning in 1929). George V died on January 20, 1936.

18 Lord's Cricket Ground, the national headquarters of cricket, was founded in 1787 by Thomas Lord, a wine merchant, vestryman, and slow underhand bowler who had joined the White Conduit Club, but found it insufficiently exclusive. At the encouragement of his fellow members, the Earl of Winchilsea, "a great supporter of the noble game," and the Hon. Col. Charles Lennox, an eager wicketkeeper, Lord leased land on Dorset Fields and founded the Marylebone Cricket Club (MCC). The MCC, its weekend matches a loud, gleaming attraction for London's fashionable set, moved to its permanent home in the St John's Wood area of north London in 1811. There it has remained, known simply by the name of its founder, "Lord's."

Since childhood, Woolf counted cricket among the highest of amusements, more mature, more eventful, and more social than tea parties or picnics. "Cricket was played with enthusiasm, and Virginia was considered a formidable bowler," recalled Quentin Bell of his aunt in *Virginia Woolf: A Biography.*

19 The Ascot Racecourse is home to the Royal Ascot, five days of thoroughbred horse racing that takes place throughout the third week of June. Each day begins with the arrival of the royal family in horse-drawn carriages; then the opening of the Ascot's enclosures to over 300,000 guests: men in black top hats and gray waistcoats, planting and swinging walking sticks; women in gowns with boleros, shrugs, and pashminas, pearls and shells, topped with hats large enough to be visible, but not so cumbersome that they hamper kissing each other's powdered faces or obstruct the view. "Today is Cup day at Ascot; which I think marks the highest tide of the finest societies greatest season," Woolf wrote in her diary on July 17, 1920. "One must be young to feel the stir of it."

20 The eastern end of Ranelagh Gardens is home to the Hurlingham Club, a private members club on the north bank of the Thames.

21 The reign of "the Georges" spanned the eighteenth and early nineteenth centuries, beginning in 1714,

when George I became the first Hanoverian king of Great Britain and Ireland. He was followed by George II (r. 1727–1760), George III (r. 1760–1820), and George IV (r. 1820–1830).

22 Clarissa and Hugh meet near the eastern entrance to St. James's Park, the oldest Royal Park in the City of London. To the west lies St. James's Park Lake, with its "slow-swimming happy ducks." To the east is 10 Downing Street, the headquarters of the government of the United Kingdom.

23 Despatch boxes, custom-made by Barrow Hepburn & Gale, were, and continue to be, used by members of Parliament to carry official and sensitive documents into the Commons chamber. Before the Second World War, they were carved from slow-grown pine and encased in royal red leather. The royal cipher of the monarch and the title of the minister was and continues to be embossed in gold lettering. The box has a security lock and can only be opened by the minister or his private secretary.

Despatch box custom-made by Barrow Hepburn & Gale. *(Barrow Hepburn & Gale)*

24 The narrator of "Mrs. Dalloway in Bond Street" describes Hugh Whitbread as being "like a brother," then adds: "One would rather die than speak to one's brother." The manuscript of "The Hours" offers a more lascivious portrait of Hugh Whitbread, detailing his frank interest in the writings of "Dr. Freud" and his surveillance of the young girls who worked in his house. Reading Woolf's drafts of the novel, Christine Froula speculates that Whitbread is "a freehand portrait" of Woolf's half-brother ("like a brother," but not one) George Duckworth, the bullying, obsequious public servant who had sexually abused both Woolf and Vanessa when they were teenagers.

Virginia Woolf and Adrian Stephen as young children playing cricket at St Ives (Cornwall), c. 1888. *(Virginia Woolf Monk's House photographs, MS Thr 564, [49]. Houghton Library, Harvard College Library)*

strange, on entering the Park,[22] the silence; the mist; the hum; the slow-swimming happy ducks; the pouched birds waddling; and who should be coming along with his back against the Government buildings, most appropriately, carrying a despatch box stamped with the Royal Arms,[23] who but Hugh Whitbread; her old friend Hugh—the admirable Hugh!

"Good-morning to you, Clarissa!" said Hugh, rather extravagantly, for they had known each other as children. "Where are you off to?"[24]

"I love walking in London," said Mrs. Dalloway. "Really, it's better than walking in the country."

They had just come up—unfortunately—to see doctors. Other people came to see pictures; go to the opera; take their daughters out; the Whitbreads came "to see doctors". Times without number Clarissa had visited Evelyn Whitbread in a nursing home. Was Evelyn ill again? Evelyn was a good deal out of sorts, said Hugh, intimating by a kind of pout or swell of his very well-covered, manly, extremely handsome, perfectly upholstered body (he was almost too well dressed always, but presumably had to be, with his little job at Court) that his wife

The Lake, Regent's Park, c. 1930. *(UK Photo and Social History Archive)*

had some internal ailment, nothing serious, which, as an old friend, Clarissa Dalloway would quite understand without requiring him to specify.[25] Ah yes, she did of course; what a nuisance; and felt very sisterly and oddly conscious at the same time of her hat. Not the right hat for the early morning, was that it? For Hugh always made her feel, as he bustled on, raising his hat rather extravagantly and assuring her that she might be a girl of eighteen, and of course he was coming to her party to-night, Evelyn absolutely insisted, only a little late he might be after the party at the Palace to which he had to take one of Jim's boys,—she always felt a little skimpy beside Hugh; schoolgirlish; but attached to him, partly from having known him always, but she did think him a good sort in his own way, though Richard was nearly driven mad by him, and as for Peter Walsh, he had never to this day forgiven her for liking him.

She could remember scene after scene at Bourton—Peter furious; Hugh not, of course, his match in any way, but still not a positive imbecile as Peter made out; not a mere barber's block.[26] When his old mother wanted him to give up shooting or to take her to Bath[27] he did it, without a word; he was really unselfish,

Hermione Lee identifies as another model for Hugh Whitbread Sir Walter Lamb, one of Woolf's suitors. Though Lamb wrote her deeply emotional letters, Woolf disliked his wheedling demeanor, the "placatory manner" with which he "oiled the wheels of a large institution"—the Royal Academy, which appointed him its secretary from December 1913 to December 1951. "By the way, I met Walter Lamb at Dover Street station," she wrote in her diary on February 15, 1915. "A gentleman in frock coat, top hat, slip, umbrella &c. accosted me. I fairly laughed. It was old Wat. who had just been lunching with an M.P.'s wife, & seeing all the grandees. His satisfaction is amazing: it oozes out everywhere."

25 In "Mrs. Dalloway in Bond Street," Evelyn is named "Milly." She is "fifty—fifty-two," Clarissa thinks. "So it is probably *that*"—"*that*" being menopause, or as Woolf referred to it in her diaries, one's "time of life," or "t of l."

26 A barber's block was a hollow, rounded block on which expensive wigs were made and displayed. In satirical pamphlets from the nineteenth century, wig-wearing English aristocrats like Hugh were jeered at for being "in some essential respects, stupider than barbers' blocks" (from Thomas Carlyle's *Latter-Day Pamphlets*)

27 Bath, the largest city in the county of Somerset, became popular as a spa town in the Georgian era and remained so until it was bombed by the Germans during the Second World War. For Woolf, Bath signified aristocratic indulgence and chaos. Going to Bath was "a Meredithian expedition," she wrote in January 1907 of a trip she took there with Vanessa and Clive Bell. When she journeyed to Italy in 1908, she spied an elderly, affluent guest whom she imagined had been "taught French in Bath by an old gentleman who was page to Marie-Antoinette."

and as for saying, as Peter did, that he had no heart, no brain, nothing but the manners and breeding of an English gentleman, that was only her dear Peter at his worst; and he could be intolerable; he could be impossible; but adorable to walk with on a morning like this.

(June had drawn out every leaf on the trees. The mothers of Pimlico[28] gave suck to their young. Messages were passing from the Fleet to the Admiralty.[29] Arlington Street and Piccadilly[30] seemed to chafe the very air in the Park and lift its leaves hotly, brilliantly, on waves of that divine vitality which Clarissa loved. To dance, to ride, she had adored all that.)[31]

For they might be parted for hundreds of years, she and Peter; she never wrote a letter and his were dry sticks; but suddenly it would come over her, If he were with me now what

Northwest view of the Admiralty Citadel and the Old Admiralty Building. *(Tim Gage)*

28 At the turn of the nineteenth century, the neighborhood of Pimlico stretched from "The Neat Houses," a vast expanse of market gardens and public alehouses, across the canals built by the Chelsea Waterworks Company to the industrializing waterfront of the Thames. In 1839, city planner Thomas Cubitt started to design a grid of white stucco terraces that would connect the river's new docklands to the old Neat House gardens, creating a thriving residential area for the middle classes. Though the area was described at the turn of the twentieth century as "genteel" and "sacred to professional men . . . not rich enough to luxuriate in Belgravia proper," it declined rapidly in the lead-up to the First World War and was considered a slum by 1912. The women Clarissa sees breastfeeding their children in the park are most likely the poorer residents of Pimlico, described less sympathetically in "Mrs. Dalloway in Bond Street" as exposing their "mottled breasts" to onlookers.

29 The Admiralty was the government department responsible for commanding the Royal Navy, or "the Fleet." The Admiralty operated out of the Old Admiralty Building, a red-bricked, white-stoned, Queen Anne–style edifice, designed by Thomas Ripley in the early eighteenth century. In 1909, the Marconi Company installed a 200-foot-high wire antenna on the roof to help transmit messages from the Admiralty to the Fleet.

30 Arlington Street is a thoroughfare that runs perpendicular to Piccadilly. The manors along the street were inhabited by statesmen and aristocrats, dukes and lords, while Piccadilly itself was home to booksellers, artists, and hoteliers.

31 The "waves of that divine vitality" that lift the leaves on the trees will recur on p. 39 from the agitated, estranged, and poetically inspired perspective of Septimus Smith. As discussed in the Introduction, Woolf was fascinated by how describing a single object, like a tree, from multiple points of view could reveal both the convergences and divergences of individual minds. "For, simple in themselves, these objects can be made monstrous, strange, and indeed unrecognizable by the manner in which they are related to each other," she wrote in a review of Daniel Defoe's *Robinson Crusoe*, drafted shortly after *Mrs. Dalloway* was published. "People who live cheek by jowl and breathe the same air yet see trees very large and human beings very small, or the other way about, man vast and trees in miniature." These objects, the external sources that allow the minds of the characters to be "made luminous," get planted early on in *Mrs. Dalloway*, and reveal how the novel's freewheeling, ecstatic language sits atop its meticulous design.

Piccadilly Circus, c. 1900. *(UK Photo and Social History Archive)*

would he say?—some days, some sights bringing him back to her calmly, without the old bitterness; which perhaps was the reward of having cared for people; they came back in the middle of St. James's Park on a fine morning—indeed they did. But Peter—however beautiful the day might be, and the trees and the grass, and the little girl in pink—Peter never saw a thing of all that. He would put on his spectacles, if she told him to; he would look. It was the state of the world that interested him; Wagner,[32] Pope's poetry,[33] people's characters eternally, and the defects of her own soul. How he scolded her! How they argued! She would marry a Prime Minister and stand at the top of a staircase; the perfect hostess he called her (she had cried over it in her bedroom), she had the makings of the perfect hostess, he said.

So she would still find herself arguing in St. James's Park, still making out that she had been right—and she had too—not to marry him. For in marriage a little licence, a little independence there must be between people living together day in day out in the same house; which Richard gave her, and she him. (Where was he this morning, for instance? Some committee, she never asked what.) But with Peter everything had to be shared;

32 German composer Richard Wagner's (1813–1883) most famous works include *Parsifal*, *Die Meistersinger von Nürnberg*, and the four operas that comprise the *Ring* cycle. Like Clarissa Dalloway in *The Voyage Out*, Woolf had visited Bayreuth, the Bavarian town that to this day hosts an annual festival of Wagner performances. She had gone with her brother Adrian and their friend Saxon Sydney-Turner in August 1909 and published one of her earliest reviews, "Impressions at Bayreuth," for the *Times* later that month.

33 English poet Alexander Pope (1688–1744) was best known for his satirical poems, including *The Rape of the Lock* (1712) and *The Dunciad* (1728). Throughout Woolf's life, Pope was a figure of esteem, a nexus for debates about the English literary heritage and its elevation of political satire into a properly literary form. Her love of him was as personal as it was professional; in 1880, her father, Leslie Stephen, had published a reverential, well-received biography of Pope. The biography ended by prophesying that "the most abiding sentiment" readers of the future would feel for Pope would be "admiration for the exquisite skill which enabled him to discharge a function, not of the highest kind, with a perfection rare in any department of literature."

Yet Pope had fallen out of popular favor during the nineteenth century, a victim, according to Woolf and her Bloomsbury intimates, of Victorian high seriousness, pomposity, and bad taste in poetry. "[T]o these people, Pope is not one of the greatest of our poets, one of the most agreeable of men, but a man who was deformed in spirit as in body," wrote Edith Sitwell of the enthusiastic recovery of Pope's mischievous spirit by the British modernists. "This general blighting and withering of the poetic taste is the result of the public mind having been overshadowed by such Aberdeen-granite tombs and monuments as Matthew Arnold—is the result, also, of the substitution of scholar for poet, of school-inspector for artist." The disdain for the school-inspector's tastes is evident midway through *The Voyage Out*, when the elderly Miss Allan is reprimanded by Hughling Elliot, a ridiculous Oxford don, for wanting to read Pope instead of attending a party. "'Pope!' snorted Mr. Elliot. 'Who reads Pope, I should like to know? And as for reading about him—No, no, Miss Allan; be persuaded you will benefit the world much more by dancing than by writing.'"

A decade later, Lytton Strachey would deliver the 1925 Leslie Stephen Lecture at Cambridge, where he approvingly described Pope as "a fiendish monkey at an upstairs window" and celebrated his commitment to "civilization illuminated by animosity." One can sense a similar animosity coursing through *Mrs. Dalloway*, which repeatedly raises the banner of civilization (for instance, on pp. 75, 81, and 192) only to skewer it without mercy.

Piccadilly Circus and its noonday throngs. Photograph taken looking northeast up Shaftsbury Avenue, London, c. 1920. *(Library of Congress)*

everything gone into.[34] And it was intolerable, and when it came to that scene in the little garden by the fountain, she had to break with him or they would have been destroyed, both of them ruined, she was convinced; though she had borne about with her for years like an arrow sticking in her heart the grief, the anguish; and then the horror of the moment when some one told her at a concert that he had married a woman met on the boat going to India! Never should she forget all that! Cold, heartless, a prude, he called her. Never could she understand how he cared. But those Indian women[35] did presumably—silly, pretty, flimsy nincompoops. And she wasted her pity. For he was quite happy, he assured her—perfectly happy, though he had never done a thing that they talked of; his whole life had been a failure. It made her angry still.

34 Comparing Peter, the man who would have asked for "everything," to Richard, the man she chose to preserve "a little independence," Clarissa's thoughts on marriage map Woolf's evolving understanding of it through her life. In an extraordinary letter written on May 1, 1912, while she was still Virginia Stephen, to her suitor Leonard Woolf, she explained her hesitation to marry him. "I sometimes think that if I married you, I could have everything—and then—is it the sexual side of it that comes between us? As I told you brutally the other day, I feel no physical attraction in you. There are moments—when you kissed me the other day was one—when I feel no more than a rock. And yet your caring for me as you do almost overwhelms me. It is so real, and so strange. Why should you? What am I really except a pleasant attractive creature? But its just because you care so much that I feel I've got to care before I marry you. I feel I must give you everything; and that if I can't, well, marriage would only be second-best for you as well as for me. If you can still go on, as before, letting me find my own way, as that is what would please me best; and then we must both take the risks. But you have made me very happy too. We both of us want a marriage that is a tremendous living thing, always alive, always hot, not dead and easy in parts as most marriages are. We ask a great deal of life, don't we? Perhaps we shall get it; then, how splendid!"

35 By "Indian women," Clarissa means the women of India, who will reappear on p. 214 in the letters Peter Walsh receives from Hugh Whitbread, associating India with "baboons chatter[ing] and coolies beat[ing] their wives." Woolf's invocation of "Indian women" has prompted a fascinating debate among critics on the limitations of Woolf's feminist and anti-imperialist thought. Is the narrator insufficiently attentive to the subjecthood of nonwhite, non-English women—those "silly, pretty, flimsy nincompoops"? Or does the narrator criticize the snobbery of the English by pointing out that, for governing-class men and women, the women of India only signify as objects of desire? Is Woolf's representation of otherness a "failure" of imagination or does it raise the "possibility" of critique?

In her excellent essay "Reading Woolf in India," Supriya Chaudhuri introduces some crucial biographical context to the debate, showing how Woolf's diaries make it "impossible to ignore the racial and intellectual prejudices" she expresses repeatedly against "coolies," "darkies," and Jews. Chaudhuri argues that Woolf's resentment toward the colonies is what makes her exceptionally agile at "transforming racial prejudice into anti-colonial critique." She represents prejudice from the intimate position of one who feels it, who inhabits it constantly. We see this first in *Mrs. Dalloway*, then

She had reached the Park gates. She stood for a moment, looking at the omnibuses in Piccadilly.[36]

She would not say of any one in the world now that they were this or were that. She felt very young; at the same time unspeakably aged. She sliced like a knife through everything; at the same time was outside, looking on. She had a perpetual sense, as she watched the taxi cabs, of being out, out, far out to sea and alone; she always had the feeling that it was very, very dangerous to live even one day.[37] Not that she thought herself clever, or much out of the ordinary. How she had got through life on the few twigs of knowledge Fräulein Daniels gave them she could not think. She knew nothing; no language, no history; she scarcely read a book now, except memoirs in bed; and yet to her it was absolutely absorbing; all this; the cabs passing; and she would not say of Peter, she would not say of herself, I am this, I am that.

Her only gift was knowing people almost by instinct, she thought, walking on. If you put her in a room with some one, up went her back like a cat's; or she purred. Devonshire House,[38]

Devon House, artist unknown. Engraving, c. 1800.

in *The Waves*, when Bernard has a vision of India as a colony whose exploitation has led to its decay: "'I see India,' said Bernard. 'I see the low, long shore; I see the tortuous lanes of stamped mud that lead in and out among ramshackle pagodas; I see the gilt and crenellated buildings which have an air of fragility and decay as if they were temporarily run up buildings in some Oriental exhibition.'" According to Chaudhuri, Woolf is critiquing what she knows best: her failure to transcend her own racism and xenophobia, as well as the impossibility of separating her individual prejudices from the institutions of the British Empire, whose doom she foreshadows in both *Mrs. Dalloway* and *The Waves*.

36 When Woolf and Leonard contemplated moving from Fitzroy Square to 52 Tavistock Square during the winter of 1924, one of their major considerations was the noise from the omnibuses. "Fitzroy Sqre rubbed a nerve bare which will never sleep again while an omnibus is in the neighborhood," Woolf wrote in her diary on February 9, 1924. As Anne Fernald observes, omnibuses jammed London traffic all the time, not only because there were so many of them, but also because their routes were not regulated until Parliament passed the London Traffic Act of 1924.

37 As Hermione Lee has observed, Woolf's characters often think of life as a narrow tract of land, a space of "extreme reality" threatened by hostile forces—an "invisible giant" or "two great grindstones," as Woolf wrote in her essay "Sketch of the Past," where she attributed her violent imagination of life to Thoby's sudden death. Clarissa's "plunge" into life at the beginning of the novel draws its ecstatic quality from her belief that life is "very, very dangerous" to live. In *To the Lighthouse*, Mrs. Ramsay fears life as "terrible, hostile, and quick to pounce on you if you gave it a chance," while in *The Waves*, Bernard explains that mankind is engaged in a "daily battle," a "perpetual warfare" waged on two violent fronts: one against life, and one against death. As noted in the Introduction, this contrast is the "philosophy of life" that Woolf intended to draw out in *Mrs. Dalloway*.

38 The house of William Cavendish, 3rd Duke of Devonshire. In 1919, the house had been abandoned by the 9th Duke of Devonshire, Victor Christian William Cavendish (1868–1938), secretary of state for the colonies and former governor general of Canada: an imperialist whom Woolf criticized in her essay "Thunder at Wembley," a review of the British Empire Exhibition held at Wembley Park from April 1924 to October 1925. In the exhibition's exposure to the elements—it was held outside, under a windy, tempestuous English sky—Woolf saw omens of the empire's end. "It is whirling water-spouts of clouds

into the air; of dust in the Exhibition," she wrote. "Dust swirls down the avenues, hisses and hurries like erected cobras round the corners. Pagodas are dissolving in dust. Ferro-concrete is fallible. Colonies are perishing and dispersing in spray of inconceivable beauty and terror which some malignant power illuminates. . . . The Empire is perishing; the bands are playing; the Exhibition is in ruins."

Devonshire House was demolished in 1924, and Woolf wrote about peering into its ruins in the *Nation and Athenaeum*: "At the price of a penny fare, anyone can now sit on the top of an omnibus and see into the very saloons—or the angles and corners of the very saloons—in which the lovely Duchess received Fox and Burke and Sheridan."

39 No longer extant, Bath House was built by the Earl of Bath in the eighteenth century. In 1923, it was occupied by Lady Ludlow, previously Alice Sedgwick Mankiewicz, dark-haired, stern-gazed, and bulbous-nosed. She was the first wife and widow of Julius Charles Wernher, who made his fortune from South African diamond mines, and the second wife and widow of Henry Ludlow Lopes, with whom she lived rather unhappily until his death in a horseback riding accident in 1922. She was a benefactress of wartime headquarters and hospitals, and, during the First World War, she converted her country house, Luton Hoo, into a hospital for officers.

Alice Wernher. John Singer Sargent. Oil painting, 1902. *(English Heritage)*

Devonshire House, Piccadilly, Westminster. Devonshire House viewed from the southwest during demolition with the Berkeley Hotel partially visible in the background, c. 1924. *(Heritage Image Partnership Ltd / Alamy)*

Bath House,[39] the house with the china cockatoo,[40] she had seen them all lit up once; and remembered Sylvia, Fred, Sally Seton—such hosts of people; and dancing all night; and the waggons plodding past to market; and driving home across the Park. She remembered once throwing a shilling into the Serpentine.[41] But every one remembered; what she loved was this, here, now, in front of her; the fat lady in the cab. Did it matter then, she asked herself, walking towards Bond Street,[42] did it matter that she must inevitably cease completely; all this must go on without her; did she resent it; or did it not become consoling to believe that death ended absolutely? but that somehow in the streets of London, on the ebb and flow of things, here, there, she survived, Peter survived, lived in each other, she being part, she was positive, of the trees at home; of the house there, ugly, rambling all to bits and pieces as it was; part of people she had never met; being laid out like a mist between the people she knew best, who lifted her on their branches as she had seen the trees lift the mist, but it spread ever so far, her life, herself.[43] But what was she dreaming as she looked into Hatchards'[44] shop window? What was she trying to recover? What image of white dawn in the country, as she read in the book spread open:

> *Fear no more the heat o' the sun*
> *Nor the furious winter's rages.*[45]

This late age of the world's experience had bred in them all, all men and women, a well of tears. Tears and sorrows; courage and endurance; a perfectly upright and stoical bearing. Think,

Angela Burdett-Coutts, seated on the right in white, Piccadilly, undated. *(English Heritage)*

Hatchards Bookshop, Piccadilly, Westminster, undated. *(The London Picture Archive)*

40 The home of Angela Georgina Burdett-Coutts (1814–1906), baroness, heiress, and philanthropist. She was "after my mother, the most remarkable woman in the Kingdom," wrote Edward VII; "the noblest spirit we can ever know," wrote her friend Charles Dickens, with whom she worked on many charitable projects, including homeless shelters for former prostitutes and schools in West London slums. After the death of her longtime companion Hannah Brown, she proposed marriage, at sixty-six, to a twenty-nine-year-old American named William Ashmead Bartlett. They met when he was a child being cared for by his widowed mother. He said yes to her proposal and took her last name. Until her death, she had a fondness for placing porcelain cockatoos in the front window of her house at 1 Stratton Street, Mayfair, to indicate that she was at home and willing to receive callers.

41 The Serpentine is a gently curving, forty-acre lake that separates Kensington Gardens from Hyde Park.

42 Bond Street is the only street connecting Piccadilly to Oxford Street. Since the nineteenth century, it has enjoyed a reputation as the premier street for luxury shopping, home to London's finest jewelers, gallery owners, and clothing designers.

43 Clarissa's imagination of individual being is as something dispersed, extended, and communal, capable of spanning all manner of people and species. The space of the self, as Maria DiBattista has suggested in her reading of *Mrs. Dalloway*, is "unseated from its confining locality of 'here, here, here'" that

makes dying the end of being. Rather, Clarissa's self is rambling, unbounded; woven through the spirits of friends and strangers alike; twined with the material of trees and houses. This persists even, or especially, in the face of death. The philosophy of life *Mrs. Dalloway* offers, then, is a powerful vision of life and death not as complete contrasts, but as dependent and dialectical states of being.

44 Hatchards Bookshop, located at 187 Piccadilly, is London's oldest bookshop, established in 1797 by publisher John Hatchard.

45 The beginning of a dirge sung by Guiderius and Arviragus, sons of King Cymbeline, in Act 4, Scene 2, of William Shakespeare's *Cymbeline.*

> Fear no more the heat o' th' sun,
> Nor the furious winter's rages,
> Thou thy worldly task hast done,
> Home art gone, and ta'en thy wages.
> Golden lads and girls all must,
> As chimney-sweepers, come to dust.

They sing it over the body of two men they believe to be dead: Cloten, whom Guiderius has killed in combat; and Fidele, who is alive, drugged, and only disguised as a man, when she is, in fact, their long-lost sister Imogen. The dirge encourages its listener to face death without fear; reassures her that death marks the end of worldly hardship; and shows her through the resurrection of Fidele/Imogen how life may continue in death.

In a letter to her brother Thoby, written when she was nineteen, Virginia Stephen reported that *Cymbeline* was the play that had converted her early skepticism about Shakespeare's genius into a deep, envious admiration. "I read Cymbeline just to see if there mightnt be more in the great William than I supposed," she wrote to him. "And I was quite upset! Really and truly I am now let in to [the] company of worshippers—though I still feel a little oppressed by his—greatness I suppose." Yet she still had reservations about his characters. "Why aren't they more human?" she wondered. "Really they might have been cut out with a pair of scissors—as far as mere humanity goes."

46 This marks the second appearance of Lady Bexborough, now described to us as the woman Clarissa "admired most" for converting her "tears and sorrows" into a "perfectly upright and stoical bearing." As Alex Zwerdling argues in "Mrs. Dalloway and the Social System," stoicism is an "ideal of conduct" embraced by all of *Mrs. Dalloway*'s governing-class characters, who are determined to deny the lasting pain and importance of the war. Their denial makes a mockery of the hope for a new society and the

for example, of the woman she admired most, Lady Bexborough, opening the bazaar.[46]

There were Jorrocks' *Jaunts and Jollities*;[47] there were *Soapy Sponge*[48] and Mrs. Asquith's *Memoirs*[49] and *Big Game Shooting in Nigeria*,[50] all spread open. Ever so many books there were; but

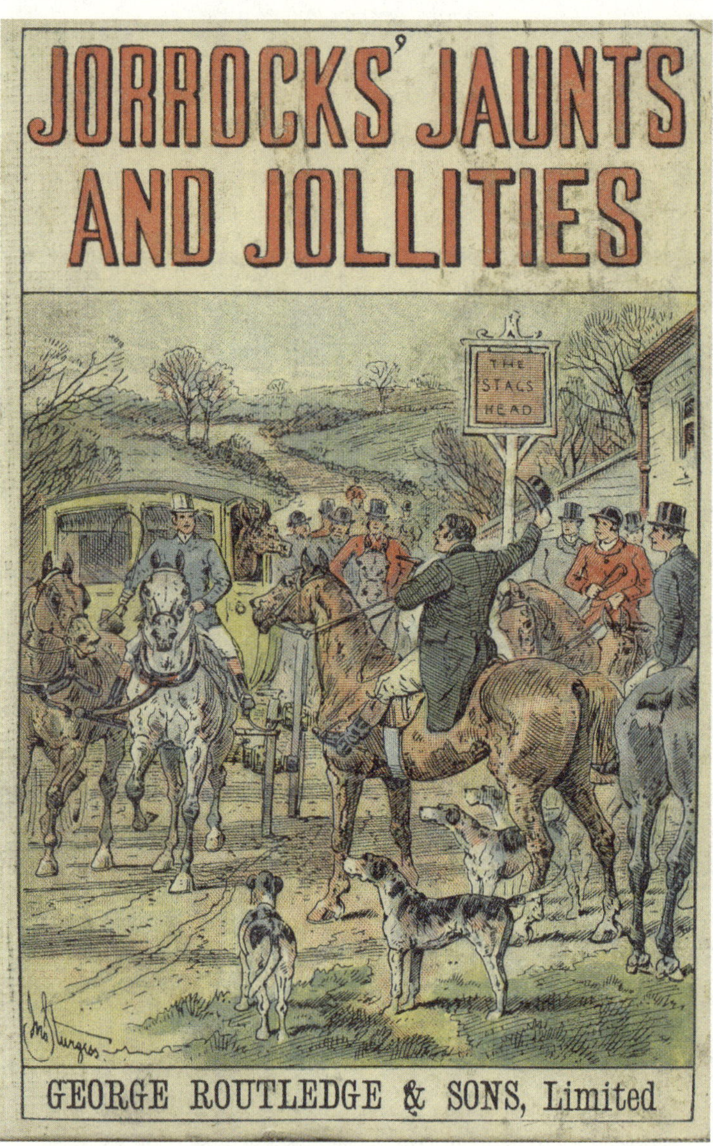

Cover design for *Jorrocks' Jaunts and Jollities. (Yellowback Cover Art)*

"Mr. Sponge completely scatters his Lordship," *Mr. Sponge's Sporting Tour. (John Leech and Robert Smith / Biodiversity Heritage Library)*

none that seemed exactly right to take to Evelyn Whitbread in her nursing home. Nothing that would serve to amuse her and make that indescribably dried-up little woman look, as Clarissa came in, just for a moment cordial; before they settled down for the usual interminable talk of women's ailments. How much she wanted it—that people should look pleased as she came in, Clarissa thought and turned and walked back towards Bond Street, annoyed, because it was silly to have other reasons for doing things. Much rather would she have been one of those people like Richard who did things for themselves, whereas, she thought, waiting to cross, half the time she did things not simply, not for themselves; but to make people think this or that; perfect idiocy she knew (and now the policeman held up his hand) for no one was ever for a second taken in. Oh if she could have had her life over again! she thought, stepping on to the pavement, could have looked even differently!

She would have been, in the first place, dark like Lady Bexborough, with a skin of crumpled leather and beautiful eyes. She would have been, like Lady Bexborough, slow and stately; rather

liberation from old social and political relations that might, in some disproportionate way, redeem the dreadful human cost of the trenches. "Thousands of young men had died that things might go on," thinks Clarissa in "Mrs. Dalloway in Bond Street." But, as Zwerdling points out, it also "makes the governing class in *Mrs. Dalloway* seem hopelessly out of step with its time": "Woolf gives us a picture of a class impervious to change in a society that desperately needs or demands it, a class that worships tradition and settled order but cannot accommodate the new and disturbing."

Of course, it was impossible for Woolf to disentangle herself from the ruling class, whose patronage she cultivated and whose country estates she liked nothing more than to frequent, spending hours and sometimes entire weekends admiring their "endless treasures—chairs that Shakespeare might have sat on—tapestries, pictures, floors made of the halves of oaks." Her nostalgic attraction to wealth and history was, in part, what seems to have motivated her love affair with Vita Sackville-West (1892–1962), whose family home, Knole, had been given to her ancestor Thomas Sackville, 1st Earl of Dorset, by Queen Elizabeth I. "All these ancestors & centuries, & silver & gold, have bred a perfect body," Woolf wrote of Vita, whom she called "my aristocrat" and deemed "stag like, or race horse like, save for the face, which pouts, & has no very sharp brain." "We motored down through Kent, which Vita loves; all very free & easy, supple jointed as the aristocrat is . . . but as usual, that fatal simplicity or rigidity of mind which makes it seem all a little unshaded, & empty." Her fascination with the aristocracy forced Woolf to separate her "human values" from her "aesthetic values." *Mrs. Dalloway* remains firmly on the side of the former, while Woolf's mock biography of Vita, *Orlando*, would revel in the beauty and grandeur of Vita's lineage.

47 *Jorrocks' Jaunts and Jollities; or, The Hunting, Shooting, Racing, Driving, Sailing, Eating, Eccentric and Extravagant Exploits of that Renowned Sporting Citizen, Mr. John Jorrocks, of St. Botolph Lane and Great Coram Street* was a popular series of comic stories by Robert Smith Surtees about a vulgar, clever, sporting Cockney grocer. The stories first appeared in Surtees's *New Sporting Magazine* from July 1831 to September 1834, then were collected in book form in 1838. Clarissa most likely sees the 1911 edition in Hatchards, though one can assume the stories would have been familiar to her from her childhood.

48 *Mr. Sponge's Sporting Tour*, also written by Surtees and published in 1852, told the story of the "characterless character" Soapy Sponge, a Victorian trickster who liked to swindle country gentlemen by challenging them to preposterous fox hunting competitions.

large; interested in politics like a man; with a country house; very dignified, very sincere. Instead of which she had a narrow pea-stick figure; a ridiculous little face, beaked like a bird's.[51] That she held herself well was true; and had nice hands and feet; and dressed well, considering that she spent little. But often now this body she wore (she stopped to look at a Dutch picture), this body, with all its capacities, seemed nothing—nothing at all. She had the oddest sense of being herself invisible; unseen; unknown; there being no more marrying; no more having of children now, but only this astonishing and rather solemn progress with the rest of them, up Bond Street, this being Mrs. Dalloway; not even Clarissa any more; this being Mrs. Richard Dalloway.[52]

Bond Street fascinated her; Bond Street early in the morning in the season; its flags flying; its shops; no splash; no glitter; one roll of tweed in the shop where her father had bought his suits for fifty years; a few pearls; salmon on an iceblock.

"That is all," she said, looking at the fishmonger's. "That is all," she repeated, pausing for a moment at the window of a glove shop where, before the War, you could buy almost perfect gloves.[53] And her old Uncle William used to say a lady is known by her shoes and her gloves. He had turned on his bed one morning in the middle of the War. He had said, "I have had enough." Gloves and shoes; she had a passion for gloves; but her own daughter, her Elizabeth, cared not a straw for either of them.

Not a straw, she thought, going on up Bond Street to a shop where they kept flowers for her when she gave a party. Elizabeth really cared for her dog most of all. The whole house this morning smelt of tar. Still, better poor Grizzle[54] than Miss Kilman; better distemper and tar and all the rest of it than sitting mewed in a stuffy bedroom with a prayer book! Better anything, she was inclined to say. But it might be only a phase, as Richard said, such as all girls go through. It might be falling in love. But why with Miss Kilman? who had been badly treated of course; one must make allowances for that, and Richard said she was very able, had a really historical mind. Anyhow they were inseparable, and

49 Margot Asquith, Countess of Oxford and Asquith (1864–1945) and wife to Prime Minister H. H. Asquith, published *An Autobiography: Volumes I & II* in 1920, and *My Impressions of America* in 1922. Woolf declared them full of inaccuracies in her diaries and offered a half-admiring, half-vicious sketch of Asquith the next time she met her at Ottoline Morrell's country estate, Garsington. "She is stone white: with the brown veiled eyes of an aged falcon; & in them more depth & scrutiny than I expected; a character, with her friendliness, & ease, & decision. . . . [S]he is a rigid frigid puritan; & in spite of spending thousands on dress. She rides life, if you like; & has picked up a thing or two, which I should like to plunder & never shall."

Margot Asquith, Philip de László. Oil on canvas, 1909. *(Parliamentary Art Collection)*

50 There is no publication record of a book called *Big Game Shooting in Nigeria*. It is a fictional example of the travel writing inspired by big-game hunting safaris in Africa and South America, popular among wealthy British and American tourists.

51 On p. 26, Woolf also describes Septimus as bird-like and "beaknosed," the only obvious physical point of convergence between the characters.

52 Running alongside Clarissa's vision of dispersed being is her fear of bodily atrophy: that her body seems to be, and will soon become, "nothing—nothing at all"—as discardable as the dress she will wear and tear, then mend on p. 62. The fear is distinctly feminized, invoking the fear of aging as the absolute end of one's childbearing years; the menopause she alludes to through Evelyn first on p. 12–13,

Elizabeth, her own daughter, went to Communion; and how she dressed, how she treated people who came to lunch she did not care a bit, it being her experience that the religious ecstasy made people callous (so did causes); dulled their feelings, for Miss Kilman would do anything for the Russians, starved herself for the Austrians,[55] but in private inflicted positive torture, so insensitive was she, dressed in a green mackintosh coat.[56] Year in year out she wore that coat; she perspired; she was never in the room five minutes without making you feel her superiority, your inferiority; how poor she was; how rich you were; how she lived in a slum without a cushion or a bed or a rug or whatever it might be, all her soul rusted with that grievance sticking in it, her dismissal from school during the War—poor embittered unfortunate creature! For it was not her one hated but the idea of her, which undoubtedly had gathered in to itself a great deal that was not Miss Kilman; had become one of those spectres with which one battles in the night; one of those spectres who stand astride us and suck up half our life-blood,[57] dominators

Vintage postcard of Bond Street, undated.
(Mark's Vintage Topographical Postcards)

then on p. 21. It then turns to the existential fear that accompanies her enduring and conventionally heterosexual marriage: the complete erasure of the womanly self that was Clarissa and the ascendance of "Mrs. Richard Dalloway" in her place.

53 In "Mrs. Dalloway in Bond Street," Clarissa enters the glove shop to look for white French gloves with pearl buttons. Much of what has taken place in the novel's previous paragraphs—the admiration of Lady Bexborough; the wistful desire to live her life again; the anxious meditations on aging—is, in the short story, interspersed with Mrs. Dalloway's talk with the salesgirl and her appraisal of the dowdier customers. Here, Woolf allows these thoughts to stand on their own and expands them, drawing out the contrast between life and death that will structure the novel.

54 Woolf borrowed the name "Grizzle" from her own mongrel terrier, who was euthanized after suffering from eczema in 1926. In Woolf's letters to Vita Sackville-West, Grizzle often appeared as Woolf's sexual double, a creature tempted, fondled, and seduced by Sackville-West. "Remember your dog Grizzle and your Virginia, waiting for you; both rather mangy but what of that?" she wrote to Sackville-West on April 13, 1926. "These shabby mongrels are always the most loving, warmhearted creatures. Grizzle and Virginia will rush down to meet you—they will lick you all over."

55 The decade-long transformation of the Russian Empire into the Soviet Union (1917–27) saw economic failure, rebellion, mass starvation, and political persecution. The creation of the First Austrian Republic after the First World War (1919) similarly involved violent political clashes and rampant food shortages.

56 The inventor Charles Macintosh caused a great sensation in nineteenth-century fashion when he patented the world's first waterproof overcoat in 1823. Made from "Indian rubber cloth," its seams sealed with rubberized glue, the mackintosh was not an especially attractive coat. It fell to the ankle, billowed absurdly, and emitted such a hot, rotten odor that mackintosh wearers often were not "admitted to an omnibus on account of the offensive stench." Prior to the First World War, the mackintosh was worn mainly by army men and industrial workers, a symbol of war and poverty that would have repelled an upper-class woman like Clarissa.

57 Why should Clarissa hate the "idea" of Miss Kilman, portrayed in rapid succession as a ghost, a vampire, a dominator, and a tyrant? Yet the list ends with a curious proposition, a counterfactual: "for no doubt with another throw of the dice, had the black been uppermost and not the white, she would have

loved Miss Kilman!" Many critics have read Clarissa's outburst of hatred for Doris Kilman as a projection of Clarissa's own ferociously suppressed lesbianism. Others have treated it as Clarissa's acknowledgment of her desires for women, but a refusal to recognize a similar desire in her daughter. For Kathryn Bond Stockton, Clarissa's "epic catalogue of the older woman who steals your daughter" rejects Elizabeth's reproduction of her mother's own queerness.

As Hermione Lee has shown, Woolf's sexual preference for women had been an accepted fact of her childhood and adolescence. Yet the thought of identifying as a "Sapphist" rasped at her. She felt uneasy in the "2ndrate schoolgirl atmosphere" of lesbian groups. Though she had cultivated flirtations with women all her life, the first long love affair she had was with Vita Sackville-West: a writer with an aristocratic lineage, married but "violently Sapphic," full breasted and voluptuous. Woolf called her "donkey West" and initially judged her and her husband, Harold Nicholson, rich and stupid. But after Woolf and Vita visited Vita's father, Lord Sackville, at his country estate at Knole in the summer of 1925, the women grew increasingly intimate. They spent much of 1926 and 1927 writing to each other—sly, sexy, heady letters about their love and their writing; letters that troubled their husbands, with Harold worrying that Vita would cause irreparable damage to the Woolfs' marriage, and Leonard blaming Vita for his wife's frequent bouts of exhaustion during these years. Yet the exhaustion, and the relationship it testified to, would inspire *Orlando* (1928). As Woolf admitted to Vita, "It is all about you and the lusts of your flesh and the lure of your mind."

58 The hatred projected onto Doris Kilman in the previous paragraph boomerangs back to Clarissa in the next, when she acknowledges that the brutality thundering through "the depths of that leaf-encumbered forest, the soul," may be "nothing but self love." In the early twentieth century, lesbianism was pathologized by Freudian psychoanalysts and sexologists as a woman's inability to make the transition from self-love to object-love.

59 No flower shop by the name of "Mulberry's" existed on Bond Street at the time.

60 Miss Pym is the second character Woolf introduces to shift consciousness. Again, the minor character is used to emphasize Clarissa's aging. We see Clarissa briefly through Miss Pym's eyes ("but she looked older, this year"), before the point of view shifts back to Clarissa, "opening her eyes" to see only the freshness of the roses and imagine, once more, the girls in muslin frocks. Like Scrope Purvis, Miss Pym has nothing more to offer us. She and her thoughts are buried among Woolf's rapid, thrilling descriptions of the flowers and never reappear.

and tyrants; for no doubt with another throw of the dice, had the black been uppermost and not the white, she would have loved Miss Kilman! But not in this world. No.

It rasped her, though, to have stirring about in her this brutal monster! to hear twigs cracking and feel hooves planted down in the depths of that leaf-encumbered forest, the soul; never to be content quite, or quite secure, for at any moment the brute would be stirring, this hatred, which, especially since her illness, had power to make her feel scraped, hurt in her spine; gave her physical pain, and made all pleasure in beauty, in friendship, in being well, in being loved and making her home delightful rock, quiver, and bend as if indeed there were a monster grubbing at the roots, as if the whole panoply of content were nothing but self love! this hatred![58]

Nonsense, nonsense! she cried to herself, pushing through the swing doors of Mulberry's the florists.[59]

She advanced, light, tall, very upright, to be greeted at once by button-faced Miss Pym, whose hands were always bright red, as if they had been stood in cold water with the flowers.

There were flowers: delphiniums, sweet peas, bunches of lilac; and carnations, masses of carnations. There were roses; there were irises. Ah yes—so she breathed in the earthy garden sweet smell as she stood talking to Miss Pym who owed her help, and thought her kind, for kind she had been years ago; very kind, but she looked older, this year, turning her head from side to side among the irises and roses and nodding tufts of lilac with her eyes half closed, snuffing in, after the street uproar, the delicious scent, the exquisite coolness.[60] And then, opening her eyes, how fresh, like frilled linen clean from a laundry laid in wicker trays, the roses looked; and dark and prim the red carnations, holding their heads up; and all the sweet peas spreading in their bowls, tinged violet, snow white, pale—as if it were the evening and girls in muslin frocks came out to pick sweet peas and roses after the superb summer's day, with its almost blue-black sky, its delphiniums, its carnations, its arum lilies was over; and it was the moment between six and seven when every flower—roses, carnations, irises, lilac—glows; white, violet, red, deep orange; every flower seems to burn by itself, softly, purely in the misty beds; and how she loved the grey white moths spinning in and out, over the cherry pie, over the evening primroses!

And as she began to go with Miss Pym from jar to jar, choosing, nonsense, nonsense, she said to herself, more and more gently, as if this beauty, this scent, this colour, and Miss Pym liking her, trusting her, were a wave which she let flow over her and surmount that hatred, that monster, surmount it all; and it lifted her up and up when—oh! a pistol shot in the street outside!

"Dear, those motor cars," said Miss Pym, going to the window to look, and coming back and smiling apologetically with her hands full of sweet peas, as if those motor cars, those tyres of motor cars, were all *her* fault.

THE VIOLENT EXPLOSION which made Mrs. Dalloway jump and Miss Pym go to the window and apologise came from a motor car which had drawn to the side of the pavement precisely opposite Mulberry's shop window.[61] Passers-by who, of course, stopped and stared, had just time to see a face of the very greatest importance against the dove-grey upholstery, before a male hand drew the blind and there was nothing to be seen except a square of dove grey.

Yet rumours were at once in circulation from the middle of Bond Street to Oxford Street[62] on one side, to Atkinson's scent shop[63] on the other, passing invisibly, inaudibly, like a cloud, swift, veil-like upon hills, falling indeed with something of a cloud's sudden sobriety and stillness upon faces which a second before had been utterly disorderly.[64] But now mystery had brushed them with her wing; they had heard the voice of authority; the spirit of religion was abroad with her eyes bandaged tight and her lips gaping wide. But nobody knew whose face had

61 While shopping in London on February 1, 1915, Woolf experienced the explosion that would inspire the novel's second section, which is bookended by the motorcar backfiring in the street and the airplane flying overheard. "In St James Street there was a terrific explosion; people came running out of Clubs; stopped still & gazed about them," she wrote in her diary. "But there was no Zeppelin or aeroplane—only, I suppose, a very large tyre burst. But it is really an instinct with me, & most people, I suppose, to turn any sudden noise, or dark object in the sky into an explosion, or a German aeroplane. And it always seems utterly impossible that one should be hurt." Both technologies presented themselves to her at once, and as opposites: the motorcar, an ordinary feature of life; the airplane, an instrument of death.

The section of *Mrs. Dalloway* that opens with the backfiring of the motorcar was first drafted as the short story "The Prime Minister," which Woolf started writing in October of 1922. Her aim was to "give 2 points of view at once: authority vs irresponsibility" in the opposed figures of the prime minister, whose car would go "prancing through the streets sending uneasiness to Gerard Street," and "H. Z.," one of London's "Scullywags," a homely, lonely, educated man who railed against the governing class. She drafted the story, but judged H. Z. "dull." "Oh dear!" she sighed in the margins of the manuscript. When she returned to the second section in November, she replaced H. Z. with the freshly formed character of Septimus Smith. "My feeling is that Chapter 2 should be calm & well written: . . . Gradually increasing in tension all through the day. But the continuous style? Must have the effect of being incessant. texture unbroken," she instructed herself.

62 Said to be the busiest shopping street in Europe, Oxford Street runs from Tottenham Court Road to Marble Arch. Its transformation into a middle-class retail center took place in the nineteenth century, with the arrival of drapers, cobblers, and furniture salesmen, prostitutes, and street traders, all of whom made Oxford Street decidedly less glamorous than Bond Street. Woolf liked to frequent its "old book shops," particularly "Mudies," a circulating library famous in the nineteenth century for its low annual subscription rate of one guinea.

63 Atkinson's of London was founded by James Atkinson, perfumer to the Court of St. James's, and was housed at 24 Old Bond Street. The shop's logo, a quizzical-looking bear, with either its legs chained to each other or a pageant sash dangling from his teeth—"Atkinson's Bear Grease," the sash read—testified to Atkinson's successful use of bear grease

(made from the fat of the brown bear mixed with beef marrow) in his pomades, perfumes, and balms.

Trademark of Atkinson & Co., c. 1830. *(Atkinson & Co.)*

64 The spirit of gossip is invisible and inaudible, an atmospheric disturbance that ushers Woolf's narrator out of the flower shop, where Clarissa remains, and through the crowd that watches first the motorcar, then the airplane. Gossip alights on the "innumerable other characters" Woolf brings to Clarissa's aid, counterbalancing her "stiff," "glittering & tinsley" nature with the variety and clamor of British social life. In the novel's second interlude, the narrator plunges into the minds of working-class man Edgar J. Watkiss; ex-soldier Septimus Warren Smith and his wife Rezia; old Judge Sir John Buckhurst; Irish flower lady Moll Pratt; well-to-do Mr. Bowley; the two poor mothers of Pimlico, Sarah Bletchley and Emily Coates; young Maisie Johnson, down from Edinburgh, fascinated by London's queer cast of characters; old, self-pitying Mrs. Dempster; educated Mr. Bentley; and the "seedy-looking nondescript man" on the steps of St Paul's Cathedral.

65 In 1923, the Prince of Wales was Edward VIII (1894–1972). He would shock the country in 1936,

Mrs. Dalloway's walk. *(Christian Nakarado)*

been seen. Was it the Prince of Wales's,[65] the Queen's, the Prime Minister's?[66] Whose face was it? Nobody knew.

Edgar J. Watkiss, with his roll of lead piping round his arm, said audibly, humorously of course: "The Proime Minister's kyar."

Septimus Warren Smith, who found himself unable to pass, heard him.

Septimus Warren Smith, aged about thirty, pale-faced, beak-nosed, wearing brown shoes and a shabby overcoat, with hazel

Oxford Street, looking toward Oxford Circus. c. 1920–30. *(Library of Congress)*

New Oxford Street, Joseph Pennell. Etching, c. 1900. *(Library of Congress)*

eyes which had that look of apprehension in them which makes complete strangers apprehensive too.[67] The world has raised its whip; where will it descend?

"Let us go on, Septimus," said his wife, a little woman, with large eyes in a sallow pointed face; an Italian girl.[68]

But Lucrezia herself could not help looking at the motor car and the tree pattern on the blinds. Was it the Queen in there—the Queen going shopping?

The chauffeur, who had been opening something, turning something, shutting something, got on to the box.

"Come on," said Lucrezia.

But her husband, for they had been married four, five years now, jumped, started, and said, "All right!" angrily, as if she had interrupted him.

People must notice; people must see.[69] People, she thought, looking at the crowd staring at the motor car; the English people, with their children and their horses and their clothes, which she admired in a way; but they were "people" now, because Septimus had said, "I will kill myself"; an awful thing to say. Suppose they had heard him? She looked at the crowd. Help, help! she wanted to cry out to butchers' boys and women. Help! Only last autumn she and Septimus had stood on the Embankment[70] wrapped in the same cloak and, Septimus reading a paper instead of talking, she had snatched it from him and laughed in the old man's face who saw them! But failure one conceals. She must take him away into some park.

"Now we will cross," she said.

She had a right to his arm, though it was without feeling. He would give her, who was so simple, so impulsive, only twenty-four, without friends in England, who had left Italy for his sake, a piece of bone.

The motor car with its blinds drawn and an air of inscrutable reserve proceeded towards Piccadilly, still gazed at, still ruffling the faces on both sides of the street with the same dark breath of veneration whether for Queen, Prince, or Prime Minister nobody knew. The face itself had been seen only once by three

when he abdicated the crown to marry twice-divorced American socialite Wallis Warfield Simpson. Fascinated by the country's reactions to Edward's renunciation of the throne, Woolf observed with agitated and derisive enthusiasm how the English gossiped about the fate of the Crown. "Meanwhile 'the people' have swung round to a kind of sneering contempt," she wrote in her diary in December 1936. "'Ought to be ashamed of himself' the tobacconists young woman said."

66 During the writing of *Mrs. Dalloway*, the office of the prime minister churned through four men. David Lloyd George (1863–1945), the last Liberal to hold the post, served from December 1916 to October 1922, and is likely the figure Woolf had in mind when writing the first draft of "The Prime Minister." He was followed by Conservative statesman Bonar Law (1858–1923), who announced that he had terminal cancer in May 1923 and retired immediately. King George V appointed another Conservative politician, Stanley Baldwin (1867–1947), to succeed Law in May 1923, and it is likely a fictionalized Baldwin who shows up at Clarissa Dalloway's party at the end of the novel. Baldwin occupied the position until January 1924, when he was replaced by Ramsay MacDonald (1866–1937), the first Labour Party politician to become prime minister. After presiding over a minority Labour government for nine months, he was replaced by a reappointed Baldwin in November 1924.

67 "Apprehensive" is the word Woolf used in her diaries to describe the onset of her depressive states. Recalling the deaths of her mother and her half-sister Stella Duckworth, she recalled feeling "extraordinarily unprotected, unformed, unshielded, apprehensive, receptive, anticipatory. . . . All this had toned my mind and made it apprehensive." The same feeling haunted her while waiting for reviews of her novels to appear. "Very apprehensive," she wrote just after the publication of *The Years*. "As if something cold & horrible—a roar of laughter at my expense were about to happen. And I am powerless to ward it off: I have no protection."

Apprehension is a state of suspension, the condition of waiting for some undefined time for something "cold & horrible" to happen: a shock, a lashing, something crushing and unreal. To the apprehensive mind, time seems to slow, to swell with the anticipation of a terror that is as inevitable as it is unintelligible, impossible to deflect or to overcome. "The world has raised its whip; where will it descend?" asks the narrator. The question does not belong to Septimus alone. Rather, it is addressed to a novel peopled with many apprehensive characters.

68 In her notebook, Woolf stresses the importance of Rezia's "Southernness" and "passionateness" for

Thames Embankment, London, c. 1890–1900. *(Library of Congress)*

people for a few seconds. Even the sex was now in dispute. But there could be no doubt that greatness was seated within; greatness was passing, hidden, down Bond Street, removed only by a hand's-breadth from ordinary people who might now, for the first and last time, be within speaking distance of the majesty of England, of the enduring symbol of the state which will be known to curious antiquaries, sifting the ruins of time, when London is a grass-grown path and all those hurrying along the pavement this Wednesday morning are but bones with a few wedding rings mixed up in their dust and the gold stoppings of innumerable decayed teeth. The face in the motor car will then be known.

It is probably the Queen, thought Mrs. Dalloway, coming out of Mulberry's with her flowers; the Queen. And for a second she wore a look of extreme dignity standing by the flower shop in the sunlight while the car passed at a foot's pace, with its blinds drawn. The Queen going to some hospital; the Queen opening some bazaar, thought Clarissa.

making her a "real character." In *Modernism and Eugenics: Woolf, Eliot, Yeats, and the Culture of Degeneration*, Donald Childs suggests that Woolf may have derived her ideas about Rezia's character from biologist Thomas Huxley's description of "the Mediterranean race: 'short of stature, dark of complexion and hair, long skulled, vivacious, gregarious, and, one may perhaps add, at once restless and easy going—the typical Italian.'" Huxley was an acquaintance of Leslie Stephen whose writings Virginia Stephen surely would have known, at least well enough to write on p. 111 of *Mrs. Dalloway* that he was young Clarissa's favorite writer.

69 "Septimus (?) must be seen by some one. His wife?" Woolf planned in the manuscript. Through Rezia's point of view, we see Septimus paralyzed and frightened, muttering to himself, incapable of articulating the thoughts that crowd him. These thoughts are more intense, less controlled versions of the thoughts that preoccupy Clarissa on her walk on p. 7–12.

70 The Thames Embankment is the river road that runs along the north bank of the River Thames, between Westminster Bridge and Blackfriar's Bridge.

The crush was terrific for the time of day. Lord's, Ascot, Hurlingham, what was it? she wondered, for the street was blocked. The British middle classes sitting sideways on the tops of omnibuses with parcels and umbrellas, yes, even furs on a day like this, were, she thought, more ridiculous, more unlike anything there has ever been than one could conceive; and the Queen herself held up; the Queen herself unable to pass. Clarissa was suspended on one side of Brook Street; Sir John Buckhurst, the old Judge on the other, with the car between them (Sir John had laid down the law for years and liked a well-dressed woman) when the chauffeur, leaning ever so slightly, said or showed something to the policeman, who saluted and raised his arm and jerked his head and moved the omnibus to the side and the car passed through. Slowly and very silently it took its way.

Clarissa guessed; Clarissa knew of course; she had seen something white, magical, circular, in the footman's hand, a disc inscribed with a name,—the Queen's, the Prince of Wales's, the Prime Minister's?—which, by force of its own lustre, burnt its way through (Clarissa saw the car diminishing, disappearing), to blaze among candelabras, glittering stars, breasts stiff with oak leaves,[71] Hugh Whitbread and all his colleagues, the gentlemen of England, that night in Buckingham Palace. And Clarissa, too, gave a party. She stiffened a little; so she would stand at the top of her stairs.

The car had gone, but it had left a slight ripple which flowed through glove shops and hat shops and tailors' shops on both sides of Bond Street. For thirty seconds all heads were inclined the same way—to the window. Choosing a pair of gloves—should they be to the elbow or above it, lemon or pale grey?—ladies stopped; when the sentence was finished something had happened. Something so trifling in single instances that no mathematical instrument, though capable of transmitting shocks in China, could register the vibration;[72] yet in its fulness rather formidable and in its common appeal emotional; for in all the hat shops and tailors' shops strangers looked at each other and

71 After his defeat at the Battle of Worcester (1651), twenty-one-year-old Charles II was stripped of his coat and breeches, outfitted in a hemp shirt and an old gray hat, and escorted to Boscobel House in Shropshire, where he and some fellow fugitives were hidden in the trunk of a great oak that had been lopped three or four years prior and had grown very bushy. Charles's birthday was observed as a day of thanksgiving, when people wore sprigs of oak with gilded apple leaves to honor the restoration of the monarchy.

72 The modern seismograph was invented by a team of British geologists working in Yokohama, Japan, in 1880. Modernist writers were mesmerized by the seismograph—not only Woolf, but also Wyndham Lewis ("Enemy of the Stars"), Ezra Pound ("Mauberley"), and F. Scott Fitzgerald (*The Great Gatsby*), who compares his most famous character, Jay Gatsby, to "one of those intricate machines that register earthquakes ten thousand miles away." In *Mrs. Dalloway*, the comparison between the seismograph and the crowd favors the perceptual apparatuses of human beings, capable of assessing the smallest shifts in one another's moods across great distances, more acute than any "mathematical instrument." No matter how advanced our devices, none can replicate the sensitivity of the human mind, Woolf suggests—save for the novel, the only technology capable of catching and containing the mind's "fulness."

thought of the dead; of the flag; of Empire. In a public house in a back street a Colonial insulted the House of Windsor[73] which led to words, broken beer glasses, and a general shindy,[74] which echoed strangely across the way in the ears of girls buying white underlinen threaded with pure white ribbon for their weddings. For the surface agitation of the passing car as it sunk grazed something very profound.

Gliding across Piccadilly, the car turned down St. James's Street.[75] Tall men, men of robust physique, well-dressed men with their tail-coats and their white slips and their hair raked back who, for reasons difficult to discriminate, were standing in the bow window of White's[76] with their hands behind the tails of their coats, looking out, perceived instinctively that greatness was passing, and the pale light of the immortal presence fell upon them as it had fallen upon Clarissa Dalloway. At once they stood even straighter, and removed their hands, and seemed ready to attend their Sovereign, if need be, to the cannon's mouth, as their ancestors had done before them. The white busts and the little tables in the background covered with copies of the

73 "The House of Windsor" is the name for the royal family.

74 Slang for a noisy disturbance or quarrel.

75 Running downhill from Piccadilly to Pall Mall, St. James's Street was known for its coffeehouses and gentlemen's clubs, including White's, Ozinda's, the Cocoa Tree, the Smyrna, the Thatched House Tavern, and the St. James's Coffee House.

76 Located at 37–38 St. James's Street, White's is the oldest and most distinguished gentlemen's club in London. Founded by Francesco Bianchi in 1693, White's opened its doors as an eighteenth-century chocolate-house society, before its more aristocratic members began to demand elections, rules, and dues to ensure that all the men they gambled with were wealthy enough to pay off their debts. White's first rule book was issued in 1736, and since then, it has served as a gathering place for the most prominent landowners and politicians of England. In the first British edition of *Mrs. Dalloway*, Woolf misidentifies the club as "Brooks's," then corrects it in the 1929 British Uniform Edition.

White's facade, St. James's Street, *Survey of London: Vol. 29 & 30*, ed. F. H. W. Sheppard (London: London County Council, 1960). *(London Metropolitan Archives)*

Tatler[77] and syphons of soda water seemed to approve; seemed to indicate the flowing corn and the manor houses of England; and to return the frail hum of the motor wheels as the walls of a whispering gallery return a single voice expanded and made sonorous by the might of a whole cathedral. Shawled Moll Pratt with her flowers on the pavement wished the dear boy well (it was the Prince of Wales for certain) and would have tossed the price of a pot of beer—a bunch of roses—into St. James's Street out of sheer light-heartedness and contempt of poverty had she not seen the constable's eye upon her, discouraging an old Irish-

The Medical Cold Baths, and Fenton's Hotel, St. James's Street, London, attributed to T. C. Bibdin. Watercolor, undated. Watercolor. *(Wellcome Collection)*

White's interior, St. James's Street, *Survey of London: Vol. 29 & 30*, ed. F. H. W. Sheppard (London: London County Council, 1960). *(London Metropolitan Archives)*

The *Tatler*, volume IV, number 4, May 1922. *(*Tatler*)*

woman's loyalty. The sentries at St. James's saluted; Queen Alexandra's[78] policeman approved.

A small crowd meanwhile had gathered at the gates of Buckingham Palace. Listlessly, yet confidently, poor people all of them, they waited; looked at the Palace itself with the flag flying; at Victoria, billowing on her mound, admired her shelves of running water, her geraniums;[79] singled out from the motor cars

77 The *Tatler* was an outgrowth of two eighteenth-century papers, the *Tatler* and the *Spectator.* Published by Richard Steele and Joseph Addison from 1709 to 1714, the *Tatler*'s aim was to capture "coffee house gossip" among the new middle class. In 1901, journalist and critic Clement King Shorter bought and relaunched the *Tatler* as a glossy society magazine, featuring photographs of social events, country sport, and celebrities.

78 Queen Alexandra (1844–1925) was the wife of Edward VII, Queen of the United Kingdom and Empress consort of India from 1901 to 1910. Formerly Princess Alexandra of Denmark, she was fashionable, politically uncontroversial, and left largely unmolested by the press during her lifetime, spending her days tending to her children and pets.

79 Located opposite the main entrance to Buckingham Palace, the Queen Victoria Memorial was unveiled on May 16, 1911, at a ceremony presided over by King George V and Winston Churchill. Designed by Sir Thomas Brock and standing more than eighty feet high, the monument is topped by three bronze figures: Winged Victory, wreathed and robed, stretches her arms upward while the figures of Constancy and Courage sit penitently beneath her. Below them are four statues carved from white Carrara marble: Truth, Justice, Motherhood, and an enthroned Queen Victoria, absently frowning in the direction of the Mall, an orb in one hand, a scepter in the other. Mermaids and mermen sit with their arms in the fountains that surround her. At the monument's four corners stand the bronze figures of Peace, Progress, Agriculture, and Manufacture, each grasping a lion by the mane. Richard Dalloway admires Victoria's "billowing motherliness" when on p. 153 he retreads the route the narrator lays out here.

80 In 1921, Princess Marie Louise commissioned Sir Edwin Lutyens, considered by many to be the greatest English architect of the early twentieth century, to build her childhood friend Queen Mary a dollhouse. To make a dollhouse worthy of the queen, who loved all things miniature and delicate, Lutyens formed a committee that consisted of 250 craftsmen, 60 interior decorators, and 700 artists. Designed as an Edwardian town house instead of a palace, the house had running water, electric lights, working elevators, and a facade that opened to expose the interior: dozens of chambers with beds, thrones, silverware, ceramics, soaps, textiles, real items of food, a set of crown jewels, over 1,000 works of art, and exactly 588 tiny leather-bound books, from the Bible to a new Sherlock Holmes story written by Sir Arthur Conan Doyle specifically for the dollhouse. Woolf had been asked to contribute miniaturized versions of her novels, but illness interfered and Leonard disapproved.

Wounded American soldiers in front of the memorial to Queen Victoria, London, February 4, 1919. *(Library of Congress)*

in the Mall first this one, then that; bestowed emotion, vainly, upon commoners out for a drive; recalled their tribute to keep it unspent while this car passed and that; and all the time let rumour accumulate in their veins and thrill the nerves in their thighs at the thought of Royalty looking at them; the Queen bowing; the Prince saluting; at the thought of the heavenly life divinely bestowed upon Kings; of the equerries and deep curtsies; of the Queen's old doll's house;[80] of Princess Mary married to an Englishman,[81] and the Prince—ah! the Prince! who took wonderfully, they said, after old King Edward,[82] but was ever so much slimmer. The Prince lived at St. James's; but he might come along in the morning to visit his mother.

So Sarah Bletchley said with her baby in her arms, tipping her foot up and down as though she were by her own fender in Pimlico, but keeping her eyes on the Mall,[83] while Emily Coates ranged over the Palace windows and thought of the housemaids, the innumerable housemaids, the bedrooms, the innumerable

81 Princess Mary (1897–1965), the only daughter of Queen Mary and King George V, married the 6th Earl of Harewood in 1922.

82 The reference is to Edward VII (1841–1910).

83 The Mall, the rust-red boulevard that runs from Buckingham Palace to Trafalgar Square, was once a field for playing pall-mall, the sixteenth-century precursor to croquet. Charles II transformed it into a place of fashionable promenade in the seventeenth

Victory parade passing through Admiralty Arch and down the Mall, July 19, 1919. *(The Print Collector / Alamy)*

bedrooms. Joined by an elderly gentleman with an Aberdeen terrier, by men without occupation, the crowd increased. Little Mr. Bowley, who had rooms in the Albany[84] and was sealed with wax over the deeper sources of life but could be unsealed suddenly, inappropriately, sentimentally, by this sort of thing—poor women waiting to see the Queen go past—poor women, nice little children, orphans, widows, the War—tut-tut—actually had tears in his eyes.[85] A breeze flaunting ever so warmly down the Mall through the thin trees, past the bronze heroes,[86] lifted some flag flying in the British breast of Mr. Bowley and he raised his hat as the car turned into the Mall and held it high as the car approached; and let the poor mothers of Pimlico press close to him, and stood very upright. The car came on.

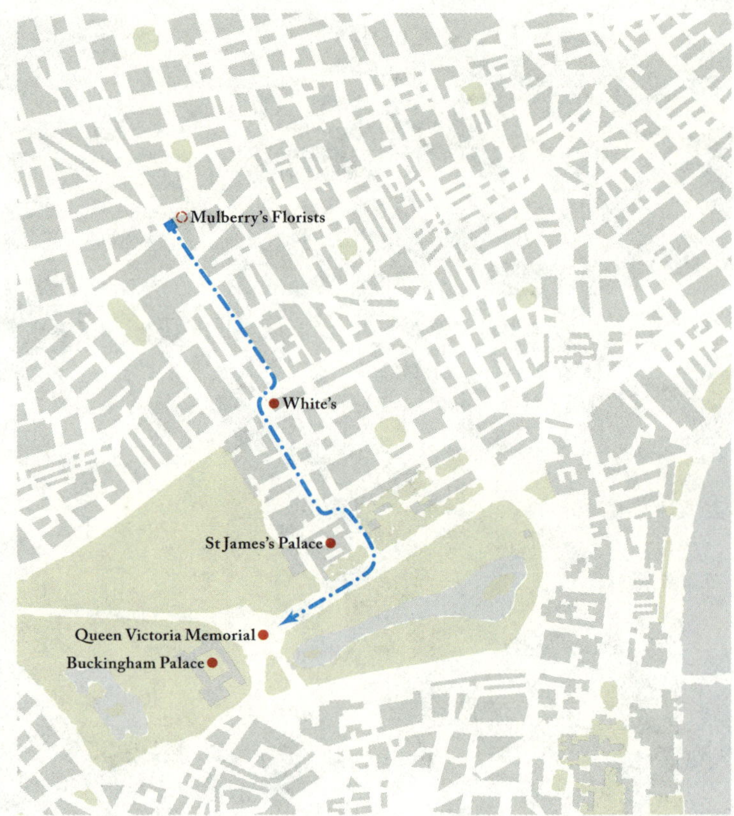

The motor car's path. *(Christian Nakarado)*

century, which encouraged wealthy landowners and politicians in the eighteenth to build their mansions behind the large elm trees that lined its north side. In the nineteenth century, the Mall emerged as the carriage road for royal processions. By the early twentieth century, the construction of the Victoria monument in the west and Admiralty Arch in the east had transformed it into a ceremonial route.

84 The Albany was an eighteenth-century mansion, converted into a prestigious set of bachelor apartments in 1802. At different times, it was home to Lord Byron (1788–1824) and Prime Minister William Gladstone (1809–1898).

85 "Little Mr. Bowley . . . sealed with wax over the deeper sources of life" offers one of the most explicit examples of what Alex Zwerdling describes as the "petrifaction" of the upper classes in *Mrs. Dalloway.* Mr. Bowley is not only incapable of perceiving the deep suffering of others—the orphans and widows of the war whom he dismisses with an inadequate "tut-tut"—but also susceptible to shallow emotional responses. He finds himself moved to tears by ceremonial displays of patriotism, by the idea of the women before him as supplicants "waiting to see the Queen go past," but not by their status as "poor mothers of Pimlico."

86 The bronze heroes refers to the two figures on the Royal Marines National Memorial near Admiralty Arch: a marine who rests on a rock, wounded, his rifle slipping from his hand, and the marine who stands guard over him. The monument was sculpted by Adrian Jones in 1903 to honor the marines "who were killed in action or died of wounds or disease in South Africa and China." The Second Boer War in Africa, triggered by the discovery of diamonds and gold in the Boer states, began in October 1899 and ended in May 1902, after the British implementation of a "scorched earth" policy. The British army destroyed crops, burned farms, raped women and children, and opened concentration camps in South Africa, until the Boers were forced to surrender. The Boxer Rebellion in China also began in 1899, as an anti-imperialist uprising against Western colonizers and Christian missionaries, supported by Empress Dowager Cixi. It ended in 1901, when the Eight-Nation Alliance (including British troops) defeated the Imperial Chinese Army and executed government officials who had supported the Boxers.

Suddenly Mrs. Coates looked up into the sky. The sound of an aeroplane bored ominously into the ears of the crowd. There it was coming over the trees, letting out white smoke from behind, which curled and twisted, actually writing something![87] making letters in the sky! Every one looked up.

Skywriting, photograph, 1922.
(Chronicle / Alamy)

Dropping dead down the aeroplane soared straight up, curved in a loop, raced, sank, rose, and whatever it did, wherever it went, out fluttered behind it a thick ruffled bar of white smoke which curled and wreathed upon the sky in letters. But what letters? A C was it? an E, then an L? Only for a moment did they

87 Some claim that skywriting was invented during the First World War by the British Royal Air Force (RAF), whose pilots realized they could create smoke screens for ships or send messages to people on the ground by running paraffin oil through the plane's exhaust system. Others believe it was started after the war as a commercial enterprise by one Major Jack Savage, a daring and business-savvy RAF officer. "The world first saw sky-writing in England," explained veteran skywriter Captain O. C. LeBoutillier in the March 1929 issue of *Popular Science*. "Some years previous—before the World War—Major Savage had conceived the idea that a skilled aerial acrobat might be able to write smoke letters. But it was not until after the War that he perfected the smoke-producing mechanism to do it, and formed a company to exploit his invention. The company was about broke with no takers, when Lord Northcliffe, British publishers, signed the first order to write the name of his London newspaper, the *Daily Mail*, in the sky as an advertising stunt." The name of the *Daily Mail* appeared in the sky in May 1922 during the historic races at Epsom Downs, the Derby course, over the heads of two million spectators who "loosed a spontaneous cheer," claimed LeBoutillier. The easiest letters for a sky-writer to write were "X," "O," and "I"; the hardest were "M" and "E." Each letter required flying about fifteen miles to make, and the pilot always wanted to write into the wind; otherwise, the already fragile letters would expand and disperse.

Though Woolf had planned to use the airplane as one of her "external sources" from a very early stage in the writing of the novel, it was only in revising the full manuscript in October 1924 that she decided to portray it as skywriting.

lie still; then they moved and melted and were rubbed out up in the sky, and the aeroplane shot further away and again, in a fresh space of sky, began writing a K, an E, a Y perhaps?

"Glaxo,"[88] said Mrs. Coates in a strained, awe-stricken voice, gazing straight up, and her baby, lying stiff and white in her arms, gazed straight up.

"Kreemo," murmured Mrs. Bletchley, like a sleep-walker. With his hat held out perfectly still in his hand, Mr. Bowley gazed straight up. All down the Mall people were standing and looking up into the sky. As they looked the whole world became perfectly silent, and a flight of gulls crossed the sky, first one gull leading, then another, and in this extraordinary silence and peace, in this pallor, in this purity, bells struck eleven times, the sound fading up there among the gulls.

The aeroplane turned and raced and swooped exactly where it liked, swiftly, freely, like a skater—

"That's an E," said Mrs. Bletchley—

or a dancer—

"It's toffee," murmured Mr. Bowley—

(and the car went in at the gates and nobody looked at it), and shutting off the smoke, away and away it rushed, and the smoke faded and assembled itself round the broad white shapes of the clouds.

It had gone; it was behind the clouds. There was no sound. The clouds to which the letters E, G, or L had attached themselves moved freely, as if destined to cross from West to East on a mission of the greatest importance which would never be revealed, and yet certainly so it was—a mission of the greatest importance. Then suddenly, as a train comes out of a tunnel, the aeroplane rushed out of the clouds again, the sound boring into the ears of all people in the Mall, in the Green Park, in Piccadilly, in Regent Street, in Regent's Park, and the bar of smoke curved behind and it dropped down, and it soared up and wrote one letter after another—but what word was it writing?[89]

Lucrezia Warren Smith, sitting by her husband's side on a seat in Regent's Park in the Broad Walk,[90] looked up.

88 With her baby "lying stiff and white in her arms," Mrs. Coates believes the plane has spelled "Glaxo," a New Zealand dried-milk powder company. Glaxo had become a household name during the First World War when contracts from municipalities and the Ministry of Food boosted its sales. In the manuscript of "The Hours," the narrator makes it clear that the plane is advertising a brand of toffee.

89 Perhaps no single passage in *Mrs. Dalloway* has been subject to as many rich and contradictory interpretations as the skywriting of the airplane, which is almost always juxtaposed to the motorcar that precedes it. If the motorcar is a symbol of the governing class and its authority, then the airplane appears more civic-minded, its writing open to readings by characters that, however different, coexist peaceably with one another. "The aeroplane is sybaritic, novel, and commercial," writes Gillian Beer, comparing the playful interpretive openness of the airplane favorably to the skewering social comedy of the motorcade. Jennifer Wicke similarly sees the airplane as a "feature of modernity capable of hieroglyphic play," stressing that its commercial mission distinguishes it from the wartime bombers, making it a less threatening aerial presence. Vincent Sherry disagrees, offering a more ominous take on the plane's timing, its descent on the crowd precisely at the stroke of eleven: "The recent war, which ended officially on the eleventh hour of the eleventh day of the eleventh month, still owns this number by rights of association."

Shifting from the point of view of the onlookers to the point of view of the plane, Paul Saint-Amour argues that the airplane represents the unsettling convergence of novel writing and wartime technologies of surveillance. What Septimus perceives as the "exquisite beauty" of the airplane as it swoops and soars over the characters recalls the narrator's "extraordinary powers of mobility, penetration, observation, and juxtaposition," Saint-Amour writes. "The narrator seems to admit the aeroplane into her own airspace in order either to imitate it or to outperform it in the registers of sympathetic and high-resolution seeing." By this reading, the narrator's acts of reconnaissance are willfully, even violently intrusive, plunging in and out of the frightened minds of the crowd to reveal that Septimus is not the only character who continues to inhabit a wartime mentality.

90 An ornamental avenue in Regent's Park, lined with horse-chestnut and lime trees, statuary, and Italianate urns.

"Look, look, Septimus!" she cried. For Dr. Holmes had told her to make her husband (who had nothing whatever seriously the matter with him but was a little out of sorts) take an interest in things outside himself.

So, thought Septimus, looking up, they are signalling to me. Not indeed in actual words; that is, he could not read the language yet; but it was plain enough, this beauty, this exquisite beauty, and tears filled his eyes as he looked at the smoke words languishing and melting in the sky and bestowing upon him in their inexhaustible charity and laughing goodness one shape after another of unimaginable beauty and signalling their intention to provide him, for nothing, for ever, for looking merely, with beauty, more beauty! Tears ran down his cheeks.

It was toffee; they were advertising toffee, a nursemaid told Rezia. Together they began to spell t . . . o . . . f . . .

"K . . . R . . ." said the nursemaid, and Septimus heard her say "Kay Arr" close to his ear, deeply, softly, like a mellow organ, but with a roughness in her voice like a grasshopper's, which rasped his spine deliciously and sent running up into his brain waves of sound which, concussing, broke. A marvellous discovery indeed—that the human voice in certain atmospheric conditions (for one must be scientific, above all scientific) can quicken trees into life! Happily Rezia put her hand with a tremendous weight on his knee so that he was weighted down, transfixed, or the excitement of the elm trees rising and falling, rising and falling with all their leaves alight and the colour thinning and thickening from blue to the green of a hollow wave, like plumes on horses' heads, feathers on ladies', so proudly they rose and fell, so superbly, would have sent him mad. But he would not go mad. He would shut his eyes; he would see no more.

But they beckoned; leaves were alive; trees were alive. And the leaves being connected by millions of fibres with his own body, there on the seat, fanned it up and down; when the branch stretched he, too, made that statement.[91] The sparrows fluttering, rising, and falling in jagged fountains were part of the pattern; the white and blue, barred with black branches. Sounds made

91 Recall the "waves" of "divine vitality" that lift the trees when Clarissa walks through the park on p. 14, imagining the trees as an extension of her spirit. Compare her thoughts to the simple statements of fact that issue from Septimus's mind: "But they beckoned; leaves were alive; trees were alive."

Just as the opening of *Mrs. Dalloway* was revised in October 1924 after Woolf finished the first full draft of the manuscript, so too was Septimus's response to the skywriting rewritten to make the parallels between her two main characters clearer. Clarissa's reactive, unbound self gives us a glimpse of "the truth," of how imperceptibly individual being can extend into and saturate the social world. Septimus's consciousness overwhelms both him and the reader with the "insane truth." The leaves, the sparrows, the fountains, the branches, the child, and the horn are all "part of the pattern" of his being; a being scattered so far and wide that his mind must work with great intensity to concentrate it, to charge it with beauty. The world as he perceives it is both intensely, personally responsive—the human voice can "quicken trees into life"—and utterly impersonal and indifferent to him. The sounds he hears form a "premeditat[ed]" "pattern" that absorbs his being.

Septimus's insane point of view amplifies Woolf's understanding of the connectivity afforded by literature. "I think I see for a moment how our minds are all threaded together—how any live mind today is of the very same stuff as Plato's & Euripides," she wrote in her early journals. "It is only a continuation & development of the same thing. It is this common mind that binds the whole world together; & all the world is mind."

harmonies with premeditation; the spaces between them were as significant as the sounds. A child cried. Rightly far away a horn sounded. All taken together meant the birth of a new religion—

"Septimus!" said Rezia. He started violently. People must notice.

"I am going to walk to the fountain and back," she said.

For she could stand it no longer. Dr. Holmes might say there was nothing the matter. Far rather would she that he were dead! She could not sit beside him when he stared so and did not see her and made everything terrible; sky and tree, children playing, dragging carts, blowing whistles, falling down; all were terrible. And he would not kill himself; and she could tell no one. "Septimus has been working too hard"—that was all she could say, to her own mother. To love makes one solitary, she thought. She could tell nobody, not even Septimus now, and looking back, she saw him sitting in his shabby overcoat alone, on the seat, hunched up, staring. And it was cowardly for a man to say he would kill himself, but Septimus had fought; he was brave; he was not Septimus now. She put on her lace collar. She put on her new hat and he never noticed; and he was happy without her. Nothing could make her happy without him! Nothing![92] He was selfish. So men are. For he was not ill. Dr. Holmes said there was nothing the matter with him. She spread her hand before her. Look! Her wedding ring slipped—she had grown so thin. It was she who suffered—but she had nobody to tell.

Far was Italy and the white houses and the room where her sisters sat making hats, and the streets crowded every evening with people walking, laughing out loud, not half alive like people here, huddled up in Bath chairs, looking at a few ugly flowers stuck in pots!

"For you should see the Milan gardens," she said aloud. But to whom?

There was nobody. Her words faded. So a rocket fades. Its sparks, having grazed their way into the night, surrender to it, dark descends, pours over the outlines of houses and towers; bleak hill-sides soften and fall in. But though they are gone,

92 The character of Rezia was a study of John Maynard Keynes's wife Lydia Lopokova (1892–1981), a charming Russian ballerina, dark-haired and large-eyed, "gay" and "peripatetic," but "without two solid ideas to rub together," recalled Quentin Bell in his biography of his aunt. Though Keynes and Lopokova met in 1921, they did not marry until 1925. "The marriage of the most brilliant of English economists with the most popular of Russian dancers makes a delightful symbol of the mutual dependence upon each other of art and science," reported the announcement in *Vogue*. As Woolf plunged deeper into the novel, Lydia became a more explicit model for Rezia. "I wanted to observe Lydia as a type for Rezia; & did observe one or two facts," Woolf noted in her diary on September 11, 1923. Her later entries suggest she made a closer study of Lydia than she had intended. "Lydia (I called her Rezia by mistake) leaves crumbs sticking to her face," she wrote on August 15, 1924, after Keynes and Lopokova visited their home.

the night is full of them; robbed of colour, blank of windows, they exist more ponderously, give out what the frank daylight fails to transmit—the trouble and suspense of things conglomerated there in the darkness; huddled together in the darkness; reft of the relief which dawn brings when, washing the walls white and grey, spotting each window-pane, lifting the mist from the fields, showing the red-brown cows peacefully grazing, all is once more decked out to the eye; exists again. I am alone; I am alone! she cried, by the fountain in Regent's Park (staring at the Indian and his cross),[93] as perhaps at midnight, when all boundaries are lost, the country reverts to its ancient shape, as the Romans saw it, lying cloudy, when they landed, and the hills had no names and rivers wound they knew not where—such was

93 The Ready Money Drinking Fountain in Regent's Park is an awkward, bulging, four-sided Gothic drinking fountain in the style of a market cross. Constructed from white Sicilian marble and red Aberdeen granite, the fountain was a gift to Princess Mary of Teck from Sir Cowasji Jehangir Readymoney, a wealthy Parsi industrialist from Bombay who was grateful for the protection he and his fellow Parsis received under British rule in India. "Readymoney" was a nickname given to Cowasji and his brother when they worked as bankers; they later adopted it as a surname.

Ready Money Drinking Fountain, Regent's Park. *(Richard George)*

her darkness; when suddenly, as if a shelf were shot forth and she stood on it, she said how she was his wife, married years ago in Milan, his wife, and would never, never tell that he was mad! Turning, the shelf fell; down, down she dropped. For he was gone, she thought—gone, as he threatened, to kill himself—to throw himself under a cart! But no; there he was; still sitting alone on the seat, in his shabby overcoat, his legs crossed, staring, talking aloud.[94]

Men must not cut down trees. There is a God. (He noted such revelations on the backs of envelopes.) Change the world. No one kills from hatred. Make it known (he wrote it down). He waited. He listened. A sparrow perched on the railing opposite chirped Septimus, Septimus, four or five times over and went on, drawing its notes out, to sing freshly and piercingly in Greek words[95] how there is no crime and, joined by another sparrow, they sang in voices prolonged and piercing in Greek words, from trees in the meadow of life beyond a river where the dead walk, how there is no death.

There was his hand; there the dead. White things were assembling behind the railings opposite. But he dared not look. Evans was behind the railings!

"What are you saying?" said Rezia suddenly, sitting down by him.

Interrupted again! She was always interrupting.

Away from people—they must get away from people, he said (jumping up), right away over there, where there were chairs beneath a tree and the long slope of the park dipped like a length of green stuff with a ceiling cloth of blue and pink smoke high above, and there was a rampart of far irregular houses, hazed in smoke, the traffic hummed in a circle, and on the right, dun-coloured animals stretched long necks over the Zoo[96] palings, barking, howling. There they sat down under a tree.

"Look," she implored him, pointing at a little troop of boys carrying cricket stumps, and one shuffled, spun round on his heel and shuffled, as if he were acting a clown at the music hall.

"Look," she implored him, for Dr. Holmes had told her to

94 In planning this section in the *Mrs. Dalloway* manuscript, Woolf plotted the narrative shift "to Ready money" very carefully in the spring of 1923. She would begin with Rezia, who would gaze upon Septimus and feel him "alternately far & near." "Might he be left vague—as a mad person is—not so much character as an idea—This is what is painful to her, becomes generalized—universalized. So can be partly R; partly me," she wrote, planning to use both Ralph Partridge and herself as models for Septimus. Then she outlined the layout of the place in the park where he would hallucinate: "The long slope of grass, tables where people have tea."

95 When Woolf had her first breakdown in 1904, she lay in bed "thinking that the birds were singing Greek choruses." Her hallucination was neither paranoid nor grandiose. Rather, it was supremely Romantic in its imagination of how an artist might commune with nature. Yet neither her breakdowns, which she experienced in 1904, 1913, and 1915, nor her moods of despair, which descended on her more frequently through the 1920s and 1930s, were conducive to actual artistic production. "I know the feeling now, when I can't spin a sentence, & sit mumbling & turning; & nothing flits by my brain which is as blank as a window," she wrote in her diary on February 11, 1928.

After her breakdown of 1915, when she had had time to reflect on what she had seen, or thought she had seen, she used the memory of her hallucinations to create Septimus's madness. While writing this scene, she was also teaching herself Greek for an essay to be published in *The Common Reader* called "On Not Knowing Greek." (Her Greek exercises can be found scattered throughout the manuscript of *Mrs. Dalloway*.) She read Homer: "5 books of the Odyssey," she reported in her diary. She also read "one Greek play," "some Plato," Alfred Zimmern's *The Greek Commonwealth* (1911), and J. T. Sheppard's *Greek Tragedy* (1911). Her studies gave her a stronger sense for the structure and the importance of the Greek chorus.

"On Not Knowing Greek" discusses the impersonality of the Greek chorus, "the undifferentiated voices who sing like birds in the pauses of the wind." One can sense Woolf grappling in the essay with the same paradox of personal receptivity and impersonal beauty that confronts Septimus as he sits among the trees, going mad. She would stress the distinctively poetic quality of his madness throughout the novel, but particularly on p. 39, when the beckoning, fluttering trees in Regent's Park once again overwhelm him with their natural magnificence. Yet she also noted in the manuscript that he had to be "logical enough to make the comparison between the two worlds"—the sane world and the insane one.

make him notice real things, go to a music hall, play cricket—that was the very game, Dr. Holmes said, a nice out-of-door game, the very game for her husband.

"Look," she repeated.

Look the unseen bade him, the voice which now communicated with him who was the greatest of mankind, Septimus, lately taken from life to death, the Lord who had come to renew society, who lay like a coverlet, a snow blanket smitten only by the sun, for ever unwasted, suffering for ever, the scapegoat, the eternal sufferer, but he did not want it, he moaned, putting from him with a wave of his hand that eternal suffering, that eternal loneliness.

"Look," she repeated, for he must not talk aloud to himself out of doors.

96 Located in Regent's Park, the collection of the Zoological Society of London opened to members in 1828, then to the public two decades later. When people started to come by the thousands in the mid-nineteenth century, they saw such rarities as the Sumatran rhinoceros, the Arabian oryx, the greater kudu, the now-extinct quagga, a docile, squat little zebra, and the equally extinct thylacine, a wolflike marsupial.

Among the zoo's most enthusiastic visitors was Charles Darwin (1809–1882), whose ideas recur in Septimus's hallucinations and who, we learn on p. 221, had a personal relationship with Clarissa's aunt, Miss Parry. After returning from the voyage of the *Beagle* in October 1836, Darwin developed a fascination with Jenny, the zoo's first orangutan, for her childlike behavior. He narrated her activities with delight in an 1838 letter to his grandmother Susan: "I saw also the Ourang-outang in great perfection: the keeper showed her an apple, but would not give it her, whereupon she threw herself on her back, kicked

Riding on an elephant at the London Zoo, 1902. *(UK Photo and Social History Archive)*

"Oh look," she implored him. But what was there to look at? A few sheep. That was all.

The way to Regent's Park Tube station—could they tell her the way to Regent's Park Tube station—Maisie Johnson wanted to know. She was only up from Edinburgh two days ago.

"Not this way—over there!" Rezia exclaimed, waving her aside, lest she should see Septimus.

Both seemed queer, Maisie Johnson thought. Everything seemed very queer. In London for the first time, come to take up a post at her uncle's in Leadenhall Street,[97] and now walking through Regent's Park in the morning, this couple on the chairs gave her quite a turn; the young woman seeming foreign, the man looking queer; so that should she be very old she would still remember and make it jangle again among her memories how she had walked through Regent's Park on a fine summer's morning fifty years ago. For she was only nineteen and had got her way at last, to come to London; and now how queer it was, this couple she had asked the way of, and the girl started and jerked her hand, and the man—he seemed awfully odd; quarrelling, perhaps; parting for ever, perhaps; something was up, she knew; and now all these people (for she returned to the Broad Walk), the stone basins, the prim flowers, the old men and women, invalids most of them in Bath chairs[98]—all seemed, after Edinburgh, so queer. And Maisie Johnson, as she joined that gently trudging, vaguely gazing, breeze-kissed company—squirrels perching and preening, sparrow fountains fluttering for crumbs, dogs busy with the railings, busy with each other, while the soft warm air washed over them and lent to the fixed unsurprised gaze with which they received life something whimsical and mollified—Maisie Johnson positively felt she must cry Oh! (for that young man on the seat had given her quite a turn. Something was up, she knew).

Horror! horror! she wanted to cry. (She had left her people; they had warned her what would happen.)

Why hadn't she stayed at home? she cried, twisting the knob of the iron railing.

& cried, precisely like a naughty child.— She then looked very sulky & after two or three fits of pashion [*sic*], the keeper said, 'Jenny if you will stop bawling & be a good girl, I will give you the apple.'— She certainly understood every word of this, &, though like a child, she had great work to stop whining, she at last succeeded, & then got the apple, with which she jumped into an arm chair & began eating it, with the most contented countenance imaginable."

Darwin's metamorphosis of human beings into animals and animals into human beings recurs in the imaginations of Septimus (p. 100) and Peter (p. 108). But the first transformation is a sly grammatical one enacted at the end of the paragraph, when the "dun-coloured animals" of the zoo, howling and barking, seem to be the subjects who sit under the tree.

97 Leadenhall Street, a short road in London's financial district, was home to Lloyds Bank and adjacent to Leadenhall Market.

98 Bath chairs were wheeled chairs with folding hoods, which could be opened or closed by the invalids who used them. Invented in Bath, the chairs could be attached to ponies or donkeys or pushed by an attendant to pump rooms, or through spa resorts like Buxton and Tunbridge Wells.

Regent's Park, Duncan Grant. Oil on canvas, 1935. *(Somerville College, University of Oxford, Courtesy of the Estate of Duncan Grant)*

St Paul's Cathedral, west front, c. 1890–1900. *(Library of Congress)*

That girl, thought Mrs. Dempster (who saved crusts for the squirrels and often ate her lunch in Regent's Park), don't know a thing yet; and really it seemed to her better to be a little stout, a little slack, a little moderate in one's expectations. Percy drank. Well, better to have a son, thought Mrs. Dempster. She had had a hard time of it, and couldn't help smiling at a girl like that. You'll get married, for you're pretty enough, thought Mrs. Dempster. Get married, she thought, and then you'll know. Oh, the cooks, and so on. Every man has his ways. But whether I'd have chosen quite like that if I could have known, thought Mrs. Dempster, and could not help wishing to whisper a word to Maisie Johnson; to feel on the creased pouch of her worn old face the kiss of pity. For it's been a hard life, thought Mrs. Dempster. What hadn't she given to it? Roses; figure; her feet too. (She drew the knobbed lumps beneath her skirt.)

Roses, she thought sardonically. All trash, m'dear. For really, what with eating, drinking, and mating, the bad days and good, life had been no mere matter of roses, and what was more, let me tell you, Carrie Dempster had no wish to change her lot with any woman's in Kentish Town![99] But, she implored, pity. Pity, for the loss of roses. Pity she asked of Maisie Johnson, standing by the hyacinth beds.

Ah, but that aeroplane! Hadn't Mrs. Dempster always longed to see foreign parts? She had a nephew, a missionary. It soared and shot. She always went on the sea at Margate,[100] not out o' sight of land, but she had no patience with women who were afraid of water. It swept and fell. Her stomach was in her mouth. Up again. There's a fine young feller aboard of it, Mrs. Dempster wagered, and away and away it went, fast and fading, away and away the aeroplane shot; soaring over Greenwich and all the masts;[101] over the little island of grey churches, St. Paul's and the rest,[102] till, on either side of London, fields spread out and dark brown woods where adventurous thrushes, hopping boldly, glancing quickly, snatched the snail and tapped him on a stone, once, twice, thrice.

Away and away the aeroplane shot, till it was nothing but

99 Kentish Town, located to the north of London, was described in 1901 as a "healthful suburb," known for its piano and organ makers, street markets, and schools. It grew poorer and overcrowded after the war, when local manufacturing declined.

100 Margate, a seaside town in the county of Kent, in the southeast of England, was a popular resort for London tourists.

101 Many masted ships would have floated and bobbed near the docks of Greenwich, located on the south bank of the Thames and home to both the Royal Observatory and the Royal Naval College.

102 Designed by Christopher Wren and completed in 1711, St Paul's Cathedral is the second-largest church in England and has served as the site of royal weddings, funerals, jubilee celebrations, and birthdays. It sits atop Ludgate Hill, where its dome and spires cut deep into the London skyline, and its facade appears "all gilt & spangled with light & glittering mosaics," Woolf wrote in a 1905 journal entry. In her 1927 essay "Abbeys and Cathedrals," St Paul's impressed her as "august in the extreme; but not in the least mysterious," a sanctuary where "civic virtue and civic greatness are ensconced securely."

London Bridge, with St. Paul's Cathedral in the distance, William Anderson. Oil on panel, 1815. *(Paul Mellon Collection, Yale Center for British Art)*

a bright spark; an aspiration; a concentration; a symbol (so it seemed to Mr. Bentley, vigorously rolling his strip of turf at Greenwich) of man's soul; of his determination, thought Mr. Bentley, sweeping round the cedar tree, to get outside his body, beyond his house, by means of thought, Einstein,[103] speculation, mathematics, the Mendelian theory[104]—away the aeroplane shot.

Then, while a seedy-looking nondescript man carrying a leather bag stood on the steps of St. Paul's Cathedral, and hesitated, for within was what balm, how great a welcome, how many tombs with banners waving over them, tokens of victories not over armies, but over, he thought, that plaguy spirit of truth seeking which leaves me at present without a situation, and more than that, the cathedral offers company, he thought, invites you to membership of a society; great men belong to it; martyrs have died for it; why not enter in, he thought, put this leather bag stuffed with pamphlets before an altar, a cross, the symbol of something which has soared beyond seeking and questing and

103 German-born physicist Albert Einstein (1879–1955) won the 1921 Nobel Prize in Physics "for his services to Theoretical Physics, and especially for his discovery of the law of the photoelectric effect." "Woolf, like most educated people of the 1920s, was well aware of Einstein as an intellectual presence," reports Gillian Beer. His paper on the special theory of relativity, translated into English in 1920, posited that space and time were interwoven into a single continuum known as space-time, and that the speed of light was a universal constant, regardless of the velocity of the observer. His general theory of relativity showed that massive objects distort the space-time continuum, creating the effect of gravity. While there is little evidence to show how much of Einstein's theories Woolf absorbed, or how intimately she understood them, critics like Mark Husey have claimed that Woolf's fiction is "clearly post-Einsteinian: from the direct references to Einstein in *Mrs. Dalloway*, to the image of the world spinning in the trackless wastes of the universe in *The Waves*, to the leitmotif of eternal recurrence in *The Years*, to the blue 'that had escaped registration' imagined by Lucy Swithin in *Between the Acts* as she gazes in the sky."

104 From 1856 to 1863, Augustinian monk Gregor Mendel (1822–1884) cultivated more than 10,000 pea plants in his garden. By staging experiments in

Somerset House Terrace from Waterloo Bridge, John Constable. Oil on canvas, c. 1819. *(Paul Mellon Collection, Yale Center for British Art)*

knocking of words together and has become all spirit, disembodied, ghostly—why not enter in? he thought and while he hesitated out flew the aeroplane over Ludgate Circus.[105]

It was strange; it was still.[106] Not a sound was to be heard above the traffic. Unguided it seemed; sped of its own free will. And now, curving up and up, straight up, like something mounting in ecstasy, in pure delight, out from behind poured white smoke looping, writing a T, an O, an F.

"WHAT ARE THEY looking at?" said Clarissa Dalloway to the maid who opened her door.[107]

The hall of the house was cool as a vault. Mrs. Dalloway raised her hand to her eyes, and, as the maid shut the door to, and she heard the swish of Lucy's skirts, she felt like a nun who has left the world and feels fold round her the familiar veils and the response to old devotions.[108] The cook whistled in the kitchen. She heard the click of the typewriter. It was her life, and, bending her head over the hall table, she bowed beneath the influence, felt blessed and purified, saying to herself, as she took the pad with the telephone message on it, how moments like this are buds on the tree of life, flowers of darkness they are, she thought (as if some lovely rose had blossomed for her eyes only); not for a moment did she believe in God; but all the more, she thought, taking up the pad, must one repay in daily life to servants, yes, to dogs and canaries, above all to Richard her husband, who was the foundation of it—of the gay sounds, of the green lights, of the cook even whistling, for Mrs. Walker was Irish and whistled all day long—one must pay back from this secret deposit of exquisite moments, she thought, lifting the pad, while Lucy stood by her, trying to explain how[109]

"Mr. Dalloway, ma'am—"

Clarissa read on the telephone pad, "Lady Bruton wishes to know if Mr. Dalloway will lunch with her to-day."

self-fertilization (allowing the plants to pollinate themselves) and cross-pollination (helping plants to pollinate other plants, including those of different varieties), he hypothesized that variations among species could be explained by alternative forms of hereditary factors—what we now refer to as "genes." Mendel's theory of biological inheritance would serve as the basis for classical genetics in the early twentieth century. An earlier reference to Mendel comes in *Night and Day*, when Cassandra expresses her interest in laws governing "the recurrence of blue eyes and brown."

105 Ludgate Circus, or "Farringdon-circus" when it was built in 1864, is formed by the intersection of Farringdon Street to the north, New Bridge Street to the south, Fleet Street to the west, and Ludgate Hill to the east.

106 The final paragraphs of the section connect four characters—Maisie Johnson, Mrs. Dempster, Mr. Bentley, and the unnamed man on the steps of St Paul's—with amazing precision and subtlety, often with the repetition of a single, small word or phrase whose meaning is dramatically revised by the shift from one character to another. "Oh!" thinks Maisie Johnson silently, horrified by the scene between Septimus and Rezia. "Oh," thinks Mrs. Dempster matter-of-factly, unperturbed by the spectacle of marital unhappiness. The plane seems to the earthbound Mr. Bentley "a symbol" of "man's soul," freed from his body by modern knowledge. The plane seems to the unnamed man a "symbol" of spirituality, of mysticism, of knowledge that soars beyond the human truth-seeking that Mr. Bentley worships, becoming "all spirit, disembodied, ghostly."

Recall the seismograph from earlier in this section, and its inability to match the perceptual and communicative sensitivity of the human mind. Here, as the plane swoops, curves, and mounts the sky, forming its smoky white letters with unthinking "ecstasy," Woolf seems to end the section by suggesting that language is the only impersonal device capable of matching—or even outdoing—the human mind in its capacity to forge connections between human beings.

107 In her notebooks, Woolf indicated that the third section of the novel would take place simultaneous to Septimus and Rezia watching the airplane soar above Regent's Park. She did not intend for Clarissa to see the airplane or its skywriting; did not mean for her to get caught up in the swell of narrative consciousness that would carry Septimus, Rezia, and the others through London. Clarissa was set apart. Though she can see people looking ("What are they looking at?" she asks her maid), she remains far from the crowd, unavailable for surveillance by either the airplane or the narrator.

"Mr. Dalloway, ma'am, told me to tell you he would be lunching out."

"Dear!" said Clarissa, and Lucy shared as she meant her to her disappointment (but not the pang); felt the concord between them; took the hint; thought how the gentry love; gilded her own future with calm; and, taking Mrs. Dalloway's parasol, handled it like a sacred weapon which a Goddess, having acquitted herself honourably in the field of battle, sheds, and placed it in the umbrella stand.[110]

"Fear no more," said Clarissa. Fear no more the heat o' the sun;[111] for the shock of Lady Bruton asking Richard to lunch without her made the moment in which she had stood shiver, as a plant on the river-bed feels the shock of a passing oar and shivers: so she rocked: so she shivered.

Millicent Bruton, whose lunch parties were said to be extraordinarily amusing, had not asked her. No vulgar jealousy could separate her from Richard. But she feared time itself, and read on Lady Bruton's face, as if it had been a dial cut in impassive stone, the dwindling of life; how year by year her share was sliced; how little the margin that remained was capable any longer of stretching, of absorbing, as in the youthful years, the colours, salts, tones of existence, so that she filled the room she entered, and felt often as she stood hesitating one moment on the threshold of her drawing-room, an exquisite suspense, such as might stay a diver before plunging while the sea darkens and brightens beneath him, and the waves which threaten to break, but only gently split their surface, roll and conceal and encrust as they just turn over the weeds with pearl.

She put the pad on the hall table. She began to go slowly upstairs, with her hand on the banisters, as if she had left a party, where now this friend now that had flashed back her face, her voice; had shut the door and gone out and stood alone, a single figure against the appalling night, or rather, to be accurate, against the stare of this matter-of-fact June morning; soft with the glow of rose petals for some, she knew, and felt it, as she paused by the open staircase window which let in blinds flapping,

108 Departing the steps of St Paul's Cathedral, mystical, companionate, and consoling, we are suddenly ushered into the hall of the Dalloway house, "cool as a vault," and spiritualized by the narrator, who cannot fly from St Paul's to Westminster without the language and images of the latter tailing it like the contrails of an airplane. Clarissa feels like a "nun," devoted, cloistered, and pure—the first of several gently ironizing references in the section to her virginity, the spirit of girlishness that attends to her, even as she contemplates her aging body.

109 The "exquisite moment" recalls one of Woolf's most luminous sketches, "The Moment: Summer's Night," from the posthumous collection *The Moment and Other Essays* (1947). The essay opens with an airplane humming overhead "like a piece of plucked wire" and, somewhere down the road, "the distant explosion of a motor cycle, shooting further and further away"—a reversal of *Mrs. Dalloway*'s shift from the streets to the skies. As these disturbances fade, what emerges from the silence trailing them is "the moment," an opportunity to catch hold of life's vitality. The moment "is largely composed of visual and of sense impressions," Woolf wrote. "[T]he surface of the body is opened, as if all the pores were open and everything lay exposed, not sealed and contracted." The moment is a state of supreme receptivity, when one's mind and body brim with sensual feelings, when time transforms into a presence whose weight one can almost feel. "If one does not lie back & sum up & say to the moment, this very moment, stay you are so fair, what will be one's gain, dying? No: stay, this moment. No one ever says that enough," Woolf wrote in her diary on December 31, 1932. Unlike apprehension, which aligns the suspension of time with the feeling of dysphoria, the moment is "exquisite"—and, as we will see on p. 53, erotic and often queer.

110 The first intimation of a connection between Clarissa and another woman, her maid Lucy, is delivered with a playful, mythologized mockery. At first, the intimacy Lucy offers seems woefully partial; she will share Clarissa's "disappointment," "but not the pang" of it. But a respectful, distant sympathy was precisely what an upper-class woman like Clarissa would have expected of her employees: that Lucy would receive her as untouchable, otherworldly, just as a mere mortal might receive a goddess. Like "the gay sounds" and "green lights" of social life, the intimacy performed by the working class is itself a commodity, a form of labor procured by Richard Dalloway's wealth and paid for by Clarissa from her "secret deposit of exquisite moments."

111 An echo from p. 19.

dogs barking, let in, she thought, feeling herself suddenly shrivelled, aged, breastless, the grinding, blowing, flowering of the day, out of doors, out of the window, out of her body and brain which now failed, since Lady Bruton, whose lunch parties were said to be extraordinarily amusing, had not asked her.

Like a nun withdrawing, or a child exploring a tower, she went, upstairs, paused at the window, came to the bathroom.[112] There was the green linoleum and a tap dripping. There was an emptiness about the heart of life; an attic room. Women must put off their rich apparel. At midday they must disrobe. She pierced the pincushion and laid her feathered yellow hat on the bed. The sheets were clean, tight stretched in a broad white band from side to side. Narrower and narrower would her bed be. The candle was half burnt down and she had read deep in Baron Marbot's *Memoirs*.[113] She had read late at night of the retreat from Moscow. For the House sat so long that Richard insisted, after her illness, that she must sleep undisturbed. And really she preferred to read of the retreat from Moscow. He knew it. So the room was an attic; the bed narrow; and lying there reading, for she slept badly, she could not dispel a virginity preserved through childbirth which clung to her like a sheet. Lovely in girlhood, suddenly there came a moment—for example on the river beneath the woods at Clieveden[114]—when, through some contraction of this cold spirit, she had failed him. And then at Constantinople,[115] and again and again. She could see what she lacked. It was not beauty; it was not mind. It was something central which permeated; something warm which broke up surfaces and rippled the cold contact of man and woman, or of women together. For *that* she could dimly perceive. She resented it, had a scruple picked up Heaven knows where, or, as she felt, sent by Nature (who is invariably wise); yet she could not resist sometimes yielding to the charm of a woman, not a girl, of a woman confessing, as to her they often did, some scrape, some folly. And whether it was pity, or their beauty, or that she was older, or some accident—like a faint scent, or a violin next door (so strange is the power of sounds

112 The vulnerability Clarissa feels when confronted with the memory of Lady Bruton darkens the exalted vision that opens the section. No longer is she "blessed and purified," immune to time's marking of the flesh, but "shrivelled, aged, breastless." She retreats, mounts the stairs, and as she does, the nun suddenly withdraws, turning into "a child exploring a tower." This child will light the way back in time to Clarissa's recollections of her girlhood.

113 Jean-Baptiste Antoine Marcelin, Baron de Marbot, known as Marcellin Marbot (1782–1854), was a general of the French cavalry whose military adventures included participating in the invasion of Russia in 1812 and fighting alongside Napoleon I at the Battle of Waterloo in 1815. His memoirs were published in 1891 in Paris and translated into English in 1892. In her essay "A Talk About Memoirs," Woolf designated memoir reading an acceptable diversion for ladies in "the morning when it was wet and the hours between tea and dinner when it was dark."

114 There is no town or country home in England called Clieveden. Woolf is likely thinking of Cliveden House, a lavish country estate northwest of London, just beyond the town of Maidenhead. It was the home of Lady Nancy Astor (1879–1964), a beautiful, scandalous American heiress who had taken the American-born English aristocrat Waldorf Astor, 2nd Viscount Astor, as her second husband. Openly anti-Semitic, anti-Catholic, and anticommunist, she was the second woman to be elected to a seat in Parliament in 1919 and the first to take her seat. (Irish Republican Constance Markievicz, the first woman to be elected, did not take her seat, as it was against Sinn Féin's abstentionist policy.)

115 Constantinople was the capital first of the Byzantine Empire, then of the Ottoman Empire until its defeat by the Allied powers in 1922. The newly established Republic of Turkey officially changed the city's name to Istanbul in 1930, though Turks had called it Istanbul since at least the fifteenth century. Woolf visited Constantinople in 1906 and described it as "a place of live nerves, & taut muscles." "It was not ten years ago that the Turks & Armenians massacred each other in the streets," she wrote. "So perhaps if it were your lot to spend your life here you might think your station one of some happy risk—as a resting place beneath a volcano."

People walking on a street in Istanbul, Turkey, with the watchtower in the distance. *(Frank and Frances Carpenter Collection, Library of Congress)*

at certain moments), she did undoubtedly then feel what men felt. Only for a moment; but it was enough. It was a sudden revelation, a tinge like a blush which one tried to check and then, as it spread, one yielded to its expansion, and rushed to the farthest verge and there quivered and felt the world come closer, swollen with some astonishing significance, some pressure of rapture, which split its thin skin and gushed and poured with an extraordinary alleviation over the cracks and sores! Then, for that moment, she had seen an illumination; a match burning in a crocus; an inner meaning almost expressed. But the close withdrew; the hard softened. It was over—the moment.[116] Against such moments (with women too) there contrasted (as she laid her hat down) the bed and Baron Marbot and the candle half-burnt. Lying awake, the floor creaked; the lit house was suddenly darkened, and if she raised her head she could just hear the click of the handle released as gently as possible by Richard, who slipped upstairs in his socks and then, as often as not, dropped his hot-water bottle and swore! How she laughed!

But this question of love (she thought, putting her coat away), this falling in love with women. Take Sally Seton; her relation in the old days with Sally Seton. Had not that, after all, been love?[117]

She sat on the floor—that was her first impression of Sally—she sat on the floor with her arms round her knees, smoking a cigarette. Where could it have been? The Mannings'? The Kinloch-Jones's? At some party (where, she could not be certain), for she had a distinct recollection of saying to the man she was with, "Who is *that*?" And he had told her, and said that Sally's parents did not get on (how that shocked her—that one's parents should quarrel!). But all that evening she could not take her eyes off Sally. It was an extraordinary beauty of the kind she most admired, dark, large-eyed, with that quality which, since she hadn't got it herself, she always envied—a sort of abandonment, as if she could say anything, do anything; a quality much commoner in foreigners than in Englishwomen. Sally always said she had French blood in her veins, an ancestor had been with Marie Antoinette, had his head cut off, left a ruby ring.[118] Perhaps that summer she came to stay at Bourton, walking in quite unexpectedly without a penny in her pocket, one night after dinner, and upsetting poor Aunt Helena to such an extent that she never forgave her. There had been some awful quarrel at home. She literally hadn't a penny that night when she came to them—had pawned a brooch to come down. She had rushed off in a passion. They sat up till all hours of the night talking. Sally it was who made her feel, for the first time, how sheltered

116 Critics have read Woolf's description of the moment as either an orgasmic rush or, as she suggested in her 1924 essay "The Patron and the Crocus," a sudden surge of artistic inspiration. Yet the moment here is curiously pestilent. Consider the cracks and the sores; the thin skin splitting and the relief that comes from the expulsion of fluid, more pus-like than anything else. The alliance of sexual ecstasy with disease, the imagination of sexuality as a wound or a rupture—this mingling of attraction and repulsion makes a great deal of sense in a novel where, as we will see, many characters suppress or repress their queer desires: Clarissa's love for Sally Seton, Miss Kilman's love for Elizabeth (p. 168), and Septimus's love for his commanding officer Evans (p. 120).

117 In the manuscript of "The Hours," Clarissa's reminiscences about Sally came when Rezia and Septimus encountered little Elise Mitchel in the park. In the initial draft, Woolf played up the surprise of Clarissa's attraction to Sally: "[S]he had a distant recollection ~~of being shocked &~~ saying to the man she was with Who is that? ~~girl? The next thing was very~~ She was rather shocked, but ~~still~~ could not take her eyes off her." The shock of same-sex desire, however, was tempered and perhaps ironized by Woolf's insistence on the women as opposites: "~~In every way they were completely the opposite. Sally was the kind of person that she often wanted to be. She was the type most unlike her own—the one she most admired.~~In every way they were completely opposite." The language of shock and of opposites attracting was cut from the final draft of *Mrs. Dalloway.*

118 Woolf liked to boast of her own descent from Marie Antoinette (1755–1793), the last queen of France before the French Revolution. She was famous for her poise and her voice, her lavish spending on frocks and jewelry, her wild gambling during a serious financial crisis. "If you want to know where I get my (ahem!) charm, read Herbert Fisher's autobiography," Woolf wrote to Ethel Smyth, referencing the family history written by one of her cousins. "Marie Antoinette loved my ancestor; hence he was exiled; hence the Pattles, the barrel that burst, and finally Virginia." As Hermione Lee disentangles this apocryphal romantic story, Woolf's maternal great-grandfather James Pattle had married a French aristocrat named Adeline de l'Etang, who was the daughter of the Chevalier de l'Etang, a page to Marie Antoinette and very possibly her lover.

Marie Antoinette in Court Dress, Elisabeth Louise Vigée Le Brun. Oil painting, 1778. *(Paris 16(16)*

the life at Bourton was. She knew nothing about sex—nothing about social problems. She had once seen an old man who had dropped dead in a field—she had seen cows just after their calves were born. But Aunt Helena never liked discussion of anything (when Sally gave her William Morris,[119] it had to be wrapped in brown paper). There they sat, hour after hour, talking in her bedroom at the top of the house, talking about life, how they were to reform the world. They meant to found a society to abolish private property, and actually had a letter written, though not sent out. The ideas were Sally's, of course—but very soon she was just as excited—read Plato[120] in bed before breakfast; read Morris; read Shelley[121] by the hour.

Sally's power was amazing, her gift, her personality. There was her way with flowers, for instance. At Bourton they always had stiff little vases all the way down the table. Sally went out, picked hollyhocks, dahlias—all sorts of flowers that had never

119 The socialist visionary William Morris (1834–1896) was a textile designer, bookbinder, printer, poet, novelist, and activist. One of the leaders of the Arts and Crafts movement, he espoused an anti-industrial school of thought that urged the return to traditional handicraft methods in the arts. In 1884, he founded the Socialist League and published several utopian works, including *The Well at the World's End* (1896), *A Dream of John Ball* (1888), and *News from Nowhere* (1890). Morris's politics had earned him sufficient notoriety among the upper classes by the turn of the century to warrant Sally wrapping a book by him in brown paper so that "poor Aunt Helena" would not see the name of its author.

120 The Athenian philosopher Plato (ca. 427–ca. 347 BCE) was the author of the *Phaedrus* (370 BCE), *Euthyphro* (380 BCE), and the *Symposium* (ca. 385–370 BCE), which Woolf read while drafting *Mrs. Dalloway* and "On Not Knowing Greek." As Emily Dalgarno observes from her careful examination of Woolf's notes on the *Symposium*, Woolf was primarily concerned with Plato's meditations on beauty. She summarized Plato's aesthetic philosophy as: "[Man] should learn to love the beauty in one form first; then he will perceive that all beauty is related, and he will love the beauty in all forms equally. Then he will love the beauty of the mind above all others. Personal beauty is only a trifle. Then he will see the beauty of the sciences—he will contemplate the whole sea of beauty."

The notion of beauty spilling from one beloved form to another animates Clarissa's recollections of Sally. "Sally's power was amazing," Clarissa recalls, and her mind leaps from images of Sally reading to Sally bicycling, from Sally's political disquisitions to her flower arrangements. The appreciation of Sally's beauty in all its distinct but contiguous forms lends to Clarissa's memory of her its swift, seamless movement.

121 The Romantic poet Percy Bysshe Shelley (1792–1822) championed the socialist politics of his friend William Godwin in his poems *Queen Mab; A Philosophical Poem; with Notes* (1813) and *Prometheus Unbound* (1820). The Clarissa Dalloway of *The Voyage Out* and "Mrs. Dalloway in Bond Street" adores Shelley, recalls reading "Adonais" (1821) as a girl and weeping over its beauty. Woolf admired Shelley's poems not for their political philosophy or expressive perfection but for their capacity to capture what she called "a state of being"—a feeling of life, simple and unalloyed. "We come through skeins of clouds and gusts of whirlwind out into a space of pure calm, of intense and windless serenity," she wrote in a 1927 review of his work.

"Trellis," William Morris wallpaper, designed in 1862, first produced in 1864. *(Purchase, Edward C. Moore Jr. Gift, Drawings and Prints, Metropolitan Museum of Art, 1923)*

been seen together—cut their heads off, and made them swim on the top of water in bowls. The effect was extraordinary—coming in to dinner in the sunset. (Of course Aunt Helena thought it wicked to treat flowers like that.) Then she forgot her sponge, and ran along the passage naked. That grim old housemaid, Ellen Atkins, went about grumbling—"Suppose any of the gentlemen had seen?" Indeed she did shock people. She was untidy, Papa said.

The strange thing, on looking back, was the purity, the integrity, of her feeling for Sally. It was not like one's feeling for a man. It was completely disinterested, and besides, it had a quality which could only exist between women, between women just grown up. It was protective, on her side; sprang from a sense of being in league together, a presentiment of something that was bound to part them (they spoke of marriage always as a catastrophe), which led to this chivalry, this protective feeling which was much more on her side than Sally's. For in those days she was completely reckless; did the most idiotic things out of bravado; bicycled round the parapet on the terrace; smoked cigars. Absurd, she was—very absurd. But the charm was overpowering, to her at least, so that she could remember standing in her bedroom at the top of the house holding the hot-water can in her hands and saying aloud, "She is beneath this roof. . . . She is beneath this roof!"

No, the words meant absolutely nothing to her now. She could not even get an echo of her old emotion. But she could remember going cold with excitement, and doing her hair in a kind of ecstasy (now the old feeling began to come back to her, as she took out her hairpins, laid them on the dressing-table, began to do her hair), with the rooks flaunting up and down in the pink evening light, and dressing, and going downstairs, and feeling as she crossed the hall "if it were now to die 'twere now to be most happy".[122] That was her feeling—Othello's feeling, and she felt it, she was convinced, as strongly as Shakespeare meant Othello to feel it, all because she was coming down to dinner in a white frock to meet Sally Seton!

She was wearing pink gauze—was that possible? She *seemed*, anyhow, all light, glowing, like some bird or air ball that has flown in, attached itself for a moment to a bramble. But nothing is so strange when one is in love (and what was this except being in love?) as the complete indifference of other people. Aunt Helena just wandered off after dinner; Papa read the paper. Peter Walsh might have been there, and old Miss Cummings; Joseph Breitkopf certainly was, for he came every summer, poor old man, for weeks and weeks, and pretended to read German with her, but really played the piano and sang Brahms[123] without any voice.

122 These lines are spoken by Othello to Desdemona in Act 2, Scene 1 of *Othello*, after Othello has returned from battle. It is a disquieting declaration of happiness given how it foreshadows the unhappiness soon to come: Othello's suspicions of Desdemona; and, in a more minor key, Clarissa's marriage to Richard and the foreclosure of desire's intensities. As a teenager, Clarissa borrows the line for its romantic sentiments, not its prophecy of domestic humdrumness. She does not realize, as Woolf did in her 1909 reading notes on *Othello*, that these were "lovely words" that "presage sorrow." Woolf would echo these words in reflecting on her own marriage, in a diary entry written shortly after she had corrected the proofs of *Mrs. Dalloway*: "But L. & I were too too happy, as they say; if it were now to die &c. Nobody shall say of me that I have not known perfect happiness, but few could put their finger on the moment, or say what made it."

Mr. W. J. Hammond and Miss Daly as Othello and Desdemona at the New Strand Theatre, print made by John W. Gear, printed by Charles J. Hullmandel, lithograph. *(Paul Mellon Collection, Yale Center for British Art)*

123 German composer Johannes Brahms (1833–1897), an "old brute," according to Woolf, composed patriotic works like *Lieder* (Op. 41, 1861) and the *Triumphlied* (Op. 55, 1871), which celebrated German victory in the Franco-Prussian war. Along with Clarissa's governess Fräulein Daniels and the detested Miss Kilman (herself a lover of violin music, we are informed on p. 161), Breitkopf is one of three Anglo-German characters Woolf creates to hint at the strained relationship between the English and the Germans after the war. As Emma Sutton notes in her excellent study of Woolf's relationship to music, *Virginia Woolf and Classical Music*, public performances of German music were banned in Britain during the war, making the voiceless Breitkopf's love of Brahms all the more politically resonant.

All this was only a background for Sally. She stood by the fireplace talking, in that beautiful voice which made everything she said sound like a caress, to Papa, who had begun to be attracted rather against his will (he never got over lending her one of his books and finding it soaked on the terrace), when suddenly she said, "What a shame to sit indoors!" and they all went out on to the terrace and walked up and down. Peter Walsh and Joseph Breitkopf went on about Wagner. She and Sally fell a little behind. Then came the most exquisite moment of her whole life passing a stone urn with flowers in it. Sally stopped; picked a flower; kissed her on the lips.[124] The whole world might have turned upside down! The others disappeared; there she was alone with Sally. And she felt that she had been given a present, wrapped up, and told just to keep it, not to look at it—a diamond, something infinitely precious, wrapped up, which, as they walked (up and down, up and down), she uncovered, or the radiance burnt through, the revelation, the religious feeling![125]—when old Joseph and Peter faced them:

"Star-gazing?" said Peter.

It was like running one's face against a granite wall in the darkness! It was shocking; it was horrible!

Not for herself. She felt only how Sally was being mauled already, maltreated; she felt his hostility; his jealousy; his determination to break into their companionship. All this she saw as one sees a landscape in a flash of lightning—and Sally (never had she admired her so much!) gallantly taking her way unvanquished. She laughed. She made old Joseph tell her the names of the stars, which he liked doing very seriously. She stood there: she listened. She heard the names of the stars.

"Oh this horror!" she said to herself, as if she had known all along that something would interrupt, would embitter her moment of happiness.

Yet, after all, how much she owed to him later. Always when she thought of him she thought of their quarrels for some reason—because she wanted his good opinion so much, perhaps. She owed him words: "sentimental", "civilised"; they started up

124 The thrill Clarissa derives from Sally's kiss is presented in stark contrast to the disgust and indignation Sally feels at Hugh's nonconsensual kiss on p. 232. Hugh's kiss, according to Hermione Lee, replays "the first and last graphically described heterosexual kiss in all Virginia Woolf's writing": the kiss between Rachel Vinrace and Richard Dalloway in *The Voyage Out*. That kiss takes place during a storm at sea and goes undetected by Clarissa. In *Mrs. Dalloway*, however, Clarissa's mind refuses to give up the memory of the kiss from Sally, fixing as "the most exquisite moment of her whole life." As Kate Haffey has observed, the queer kiss recurs throughout the novel, repeatedly pulling Clarissa back into the past, into her adolescence, and refusing to commit her fully to the heterosexual compromises of her present.

125 Woolf's first attempt at writing Clarissa's memory of the kiss in "The Hours" focused more on its physical sensations than its spiritual quality: "The body must be a finer instrument than people know. ~~For~~ The physical change was so extraordinary. From being exalted, hot, cold, all spasms & starts, she became ~~now~~ instantly ~~soothed very~~ soothed ~~into a~~ & yet stimulated, as if myriads of bells ~~had begun to~~ chimed . . . . the <this> sense of entire & absolute trust, ~~delight, in another human being. Nothing could have been purer, than her at the same time more penetrating, than her feeling that she knew Sally to the depths, & It was the~~ so moving, so strangely exciting, & yet—to use an odd word religious~~—as~~ of being able to care, with out ~~any~~ <any> reservation, ~~but without blindness~~ <a properly [ ]> for another person." The bodily delights of the kiss were excised from the final draft of *Mrs. Dalloway* and replaced with the metaphor of the kiss as "a present," a gift—an offering made from Clarissa's past to her present.

every day of her life as if he guarded her. A book was sentimental; an attitude to life sentimental. "Sentimental", perhaps she was to be thinking of the past.[126] What would he think, she wondered, when he came back?

That she had grown older? Would he say that, or would she see him thinking when he came back, that she had grown older? It was true. Since her illness she had turned almost white.

Laying her brooch on the table, she had a sudden spasm, as if, while she mused, the icy claws had had the chance to fix in her. She was not old yet. She had just broken into her fifty-second year. Months and months of it were still untouched. June, July, August! Each still remained almost whole, and, as if to catch the falling drop, Clarissa (crossing to the dressing-table) plunged into the very heart of the moment, transfixed it, there—the moment of this June morning on which was the pressure of all the other mornings, seeing the glass, the dressing-table, and all the bottles afresh, collecting the whole of her at one point (as she looked into the glass), seeing the delicate pink face of the woman who was that very night to give a party; of Clarissa Dalloway; of herself.

How many million times she had seen her face, and always with the same imperceptible contraction! She pursed her lips when she looked in the glass. It was to give her face point. That was her self—pointed; dartlike; definite.[127] That was her self when some effort, some call on her to be her self, drew the parts together, she alone knew how different, how incompatible and composed so for the world only into one centre, one diamond, one woman who sat in her drawing-room and made a meeting-point, a radiancy no doubt in some dull lives, a refuge for the lonely to come to, perhaps; she had helped young people, who were grateful to her; had tried to be the same always, never showing a sign of all the other sides of her—faults, jealousies, vanities, suspicions, like this of Lady Bruton not asking her to lunch; which, she thought (combing her hair finally), is utterly base! Now, where was her dress?

Her evening dresses hung in the cupboard. Clarissa, plung-

126 Woolf's fear of sentimentality derived from her father's deep antipathy to anything fanciful, "sham," "humbug," or "sentimental," in either life or fiction. In *History of English Thought in the Eighteenth Century*, Leslie Stephen reviled sentimentalism as "a kind of mildew which spreads over the surface of literature at this period to indicate a sickly constitution." He scorned those who made "a luxury of grief" and regarded "sympathetic emotion as an end rather than a means—a need rightly despised by men of masculine nature."

Yet he frequently proved the greatest offender of his own sensibilities. He was a needy man, who demanded constant emotional outpourings from Julia Stephen and his children. Woolf resented her father's hypocrisy, just as she did his equation of feeling with femininity and weakness, charges that made her feel vulnerable. Peter Walsh comes bearing Leslie's emotional dishonesty, which Woolf made more explicit in "The Hours": "~~Peter would say it~~ was 'sentimentally' ~~dear to her~~. that was one of his <~~or Peters words one of his~~> favourite words. ~~But~~ And though her heart ~~was only~~ He ~~would~~ used it ~~or~~ practically of ~~any~~ everyone. A book was sentimental, a person was sentimental; ~~to think of the past was sentimental; & when, as sometimes happened now, since <she knew that her> her heart had b was damanged, she often caught herself~~." And later in the manuscript: "Peter would ~~call that~~ <say it was> sentimental feeling—but who was more sentimental than Peter, <himself> sobbing~~, over his love affairs~~?

127 Woolf had a lifelong mistrust of mirrors. She was never particularly vain or proud of her appearance. She did not fear the physical signs of aging, the lines and wrinkles etched into her face. Rather, she worried that mirrors imparted a false coherence to one's sense of self, that they contracted a person's being to a single fine and illusory point. The image Clarissa sees in the mirror is "her self" but only "when some effort, some call on her to be her self, drew the parts together." It is not the "different" and "incompatible" woman she knows herself to be.

The suspicion of mirrors repeats in Woolf's exquisite short story about aging, "The Lady in the Looking Glass: A Reflection," published in *Harper's* in December 1929. The main character, Isabella Tyson, a little older than Clarissa Dalloway, has no trouble believing in the wonder and variety of her life, the ineffable mystery of her thoughts—that is, until she looks in the looking glass. "At once the looking-glass began to pour over her a light that seemed to fix her; that seemed like some acid to bite off the unessential and superficial and to leave only the truth. It was an enthralling spectacle. Everything dropped from her—clouds, dress, basket, diamond—all that one had called the creeper and convolvulus. Here was the hard wall beneath. Here was the woman herself. She stood naked in that pitiless light. And there was nothing. Isabella was perfectly empty. She had no thoughts. She had no friends. She cared for nobody." The story begins and ends with a chilling warning: "People should not leave looking-glasses hanging in their rooms."

Katharine Maxse, née Lushington. *(Mary Evans Picture Library)*

ing her hand into the softness, gently detached the green dress and carried it to the window. She had torn it. Some one had trod on the skirt. She had felt it give at the Embassy party at the top among the folds. By artificial light the green shone, but lost its colour now in the sun. She would mend it. Her maids had too much to do. She would wear it tonight. She would take her silks, her scissors, her—what was it?—her thimble, of course, down into the drawing-room, for she must also write, and see that things generally were more or less in order.

Strange, she thought, pausing on the landing, and assembling that diamond shape, that single person, strange how a mistress knows the very moment, the very temper of her house! Faint sounds rose in spirals up the well of the stairs; the swish of a mop; tapping; knocking; a loudness when the front door opened; a voice repeating a message in the basement; the chink of silver on a tray; clean silver for the party. All was for the party.

(And Lucy, coming into the drawing-room with her tray held out, put the giant candlesticks on the mantelpiece, the silver casket in the middle, turned the crystal dolphin towards the clock. They would come; they would stand; they would talk in the mincing tones which she could imitate, ladies and gentlemen. Of all, her mistress was loveliest—mistress of silver, of linen, of china, for the sun, the silver, doors off their hinges, Rumpelmayer's men, gave her a sense, as she laid the paper-knife on the inlaid table, of something achieved. Behold! Behold! she said, speaking to her old friends in the baker's shop, where she had first seen service at Caterham,[128] prying into the glass. She was Lady Angela,[129] attending Princess Mary, when in came Mrs. Dalloway.)

"Oh Lucy," she said, "the silver does look nice!"

"And how," she said, turning the crystal dolphin to stand straight, "how did you enjoy the play last night?" "Oh, they had to go before the end!" she said. "They had to be back at ten!" she said. "So they don't know what happened," she said. "That does seem hard luck," she said (for her servants stayed later, if they asked her). "That does seem rather a shame," she said, taking the old bald-looking cushion in the middle of the sofa and putting it in Lucy's arms, and giving her a little push, and crying:

"Take it away! Give it to Mrs. Walker with my compliments! Take it away!" she cried.

And Lucy stopped at the drawing-room door, holding the

128 Caterham is a small, hilly town in the county of Surrey, south of London.

129 There exists no historical figure by the name of Lady Angela who served as a courtier to Princess Mary. Like the first interaction between Lucy and Clarissa on p. 50, the mock epic quality of the parenthetical extends Woolf's parody of the worshipful servitude demanded by, and bestowed upon, the upper classes. Seen from Lucy's point of view, Clarissa is not only the loveliest mistress but "mistress of silver, of linen, of china," commander of all the pristine inanimate objects that throng her and, as we will see on p. 207 at the beginning of the party, all the hyper-animated people rushing around to please her.

cushion, and said, very shyly, turning a little pink, Couldn't she help to mend that dress?

But, said Mrs. Dalloway, she had enough on her hands already, quite enough of her own to do without that.

"But, thank you, Lucy, oh, thank you," said Mrs. Dalloway, and thank you, thank you, she went on saying (sitting down on the sofa with her dress over her knees, her scissors, her silks), thank you, thank you, she went on saying in gratitude to her servants generally for helping her to be like this, to be what she wanted, gentle, generous-hearted. Her servants liked her.[130] And then this dress of hers—where was the tear? and now her needle to be threaded. This was a favourite dress, one of Sally Parker's, the last almost she ever made, alas, for Sally had now retired, lived at Ealing,[131] and if ever I have a moment, thought Clarissa (but never would she have a moment any more), I shall go and see her at Ealing. For she was a character, thought Clarissa, a real artist. She thought of little out-of-the-way things; yet her dresses were never queer. You could wear them at Hatfield;[132] at Buckingham Palace. She had worn them at Hatfield; at Buckingham Palace.

Quiet descended on her, calm, content, as her needle, drawing the silk smoothly to its gentle pause, collected the green folds together and attached them, very lightly, to the belt. So on a summer's day waves collect, overbalance, and fall; collect and fall; and the whole world seems to be saying "that is all" more and more ponderously, until even the heart in the body which lies in the sun on the beach says too, That is all. Fear no more,[133] says the heart. Fear no more, says the heart, committing its burden to some sea, which sighs collectively for all sorrows, and renews, begins, collects, lets fall. And the body alone listens to the passing bee; the wave breaking; the dog barking, far away barking and barking.

"Heavens, the front-door bell!" exclaimed Clarissa, staying her needle. Roused, she listened.

"Mrs. Dalloway will see me," said the elderly man in the hall. "Oh yes, she will see *me*,"[134] he repeated, putting Lucy aside very

130 Compare the mild self-involvement of Clarissa's attitude toward her servants, as well as how quickly her thoughts about them arrive and depart, to Lucy's long, mythological paeans to Clarissa. The disparity in the language each uses to describe the other measures the disparity between their social and economic positions—a ridiculous disparity, Woolf suggests here, as well as in her diaries and letters. "It is an absurdity, how much time L. & I have wasted in talking about servants," Woolf wrote in April 1929. "And it can never be done with because the fault lies in the system. How can an uneducated woman let herself in, alone, into our lives? What happens is that she becomes a mongrel; & has no roots any where."

Though Woolf's style in *Mrs. Dalloway* encodes her criticism of an unjust social system, in life she was just as dependent on her servants as Clarissa, though more impatient and abusive toward them. She had a particularly vicious relationship with her cook of eighteen years, Nellie Boxall, whom she and Leonard kept in their employ despite Woolf's antipathy toward Nellie's "dependence and defencelessness." As Alison Light observes in her incisive study of class in modernist fiction, *Mrs. Woolf and the Servants*, "Virginia's public sympathy with the lives of poor women was always at odds with private recoil." Woolf's fiction is as much a public front as her essays and speeches.

131 Ealing is a district of West London, known in the early twentieth century as the "Queen of the Suburbs."

132 Built in 1611, Hatfield House was the grand Jacobean home of the Marquess and Marchioness of Salisbury. Hatfield House was later used as a filming location for the 1992 film version of *Orlando* with Tilda Swinton.

133 An echo from p. 19.

134 Since Woolf wanted Septimus and Clarissa to move in tandem, it was necessary for someone to see her just as Rezia had seen him. "Mrs. D. must be seen by other people," Woolf planned in her notebook. "As she sits in her drawing room. But there must be a general idea—one must not get lost in detail: her chapter must correspond with his." In February 1922, she entertained the idea of creating a Greek "chorus" to comment on Clarissa, but by May 1923, she had judged it "not convincing." "One wants the effect of real life," she wrote. "There shd. now be a long talk between Mrs. D. & some old buck. Hurry over. His view of her. Her substitutions of feeling about death youth the past."

So the character of Peter Walsh was born, and there is a delightful irony to his opening dialogue: his benevolent insistence to Lucy that "Mrs. Dalloway

benevolently, and running upstairs ever so quickly. "Yes, yes, yes," he muttered as he ran upstairs. "She will see me. After five years in India, Clarissa will see me."

"Who can—what can," asked Mrs. Dalloway (thinking it was outrageous to be interrupted at eleven o'clock on the morning of the day she was giving a party), hearing a step on the stairs. She heard a hand upon the door. She made to hide her dress, like a virgin protecting chastity, respecting privacy. Now the brass knob slipped. Now the door opened, and in came—for a single second she could not remember what he was called! so surprised she was to see him, so glad, so shy, so utterly taken aback to have Peter Walsh come to her unexpectedly in the morning! (She had not read his letter.)

"And how are you?" said Peter Walsh, positively trembling; taking both her hands; kissing both her hands. She's grown older, he thought, sitting down. I shan't tell her anything about it, he thought, for she's grown older. She's looking at me, he thought, a sudden embarrassment coming over him, though he had kissed her hands. Putting his hand into his pocket, he took out a large pocket-knife and half opened the blade.[135]

Exactly the same, thought Clarissa; the same queer look; the same check suit; a little out of the straight his face is, a little thinner, dryer, perhaps, but he looks awfully well, and just the same.

"How heavenly it is to see you again!" she exclaimed. He had his knife out. That's so like him, she thought.[136]

He had only reached town last night, he said; would have to go down into the country at once; and how was everything, how was everybody—Richard? Elizabeth?

"And what's all this?" he said, tilting his pen-knife towards her green dress.

He's very well dressed, thought Clarissa; yet he always criticizes *me.*

Here she is mending her dress; mending her dress as usual, he thought; here she's been sitting all the time I've been in India; mending her dress; playing about; going to parties; run-

will see me," when, in fact, his purpose in the novel is to see her.

135 It is gripping to read this scene, where Peter sits across from Clarissa, the two of them observing each other, and observing each other observing, alongside the scene of Clarissa looking at herself in front of the mirror. Note the symmetrical setup of Peter and Clarissa's encounter. She thinks about him in one paragraph; he thinks about her in the next. She holds her scissors; he plays with his pocketknife. The objects in their hands threaten violence. But the violence is the violence of unresolved feelings, of memory and misunderstanding. Together, they whittle and prick at the past. He is instantly irritated by the life she has made; she is enchanted to see him sitting amid her silver and chairs. He is enchanted by the specter of his grief; she is wounded and irritated by his foolishness. She draws "up to the surface something which positively hurt him as it rose"; he confesses that he is in love with someone who is not her.

The mirror's inhuman gaze presents too tidy a portrait of the self. In the mirror, subjectivity is contained, safe. Confronting another person, however, and confronting yourself through that other person's searching gaze, makes any stable representation of the self impossible to sustain. What the mirror contracts to a single point in space and time, a human being threatens with dispersal and disorder.

136 Hermione Lee suggests that Peter Walsh is based on Woolf's cousin, Harry Stephen, son of Woolf's father's brother and husband to a cousin of Florence Nightingale (1820–1910), whose feminist writings Woolf admired and would quote from in *A Room of One's Own*: "Women never have an half hour . . . that they can call their own." In a diary entry dated November 21, 1918, Woolf describes Harry playing with his pocketknife much as she has Peter do here. "Harry Stephen who sat like a frog with his legs akimbo, opening & shutting his large knife, & asserting with an egoism proper to all Stephens, that he knew how to behave himself, & how other people ought to behave. . . . The impenetrable wall of the middle class conservative was never more stolid."

ning to the House and back and all that, he thought, growing more and more irritated, more and more agitated, for there's nothing in the world so bad for some women as marriage, he thought; and politics; and having a Conservative husband, like the admirable Richard. So it is, so it is, he thought, shutting his knife with a snap.

"Richard's very well. Richard's at a Committee," said Clarissa.

And she opened her scissors, and said, did he mind her just finishing what she was doing to her dress, for they had a party that night?

"Which I shan't ask you to," she said. "My dear Peter!" she said.

But it was delicious to hear her say that—my dear Peter! Indeed, it was all so delicious—the silver, the chairs; all so delicious!

Why wouldn't she ask him to her party? he asked.

Now of course, thought Clarissa, he's enchanting! perfectly enchanting! Now I remember how impossible it was ever to make up my mind—and why did I make up my mind—not to marry him, she wondered, that awful summer?

"But it's so extraordinary that you should have come this morning!" she cried, putting her hands, one on top of another, down on her dress.

"Do you remember," she said, "how the blinds used to flap at Bourton?"

"They did," he said; and he remembered breakfasting alone, very awkwardly, with her father; who had died; and he had not written to Clarissa. But he had never got on well with old Parry, that querulous, weak-kneed old man, Clarissa's father, Justin Parry.

"I often wish I'd got on better with your father," he said.

"But he never liked any one who—our friends," said Clarissa; and could have bitten her tongue for thus reminding Peter that he had wanted to marry her.

Of course I did, thought Peter; it almost broke my heart too, he thought; and was overcome with his own grief, which rose like a moon looked at from a terrace, ghastly beautiful with light from the sunken day. I was more unhappy than I've ever been since, he thought. And as if in truth he were sitting there on the terrace he edged a little towards Clarissa; put his hand out; raised it; let it fall. There above them it hung, that moon. She too seemed to be sitting with him on the terrace, in the moonlight.

"Herbert has it now," she said. "I never go there now," she said.

Then, just as happens on a terrace in the moonlight, when one person begins to feel ashamed that he is already bored, and yet as the other sits silent, very quiet, sadly looking at the moon, does not like to speak, moves his foot, clears his throat, notices some iron scroll on a table leg, stirs a leaf, but says nothing—so Peter Walsh did now. For why go back like this to the past? he thought. Why make him think of it again? Why make him suffer, when she had tortured him so infernally? Why?

"Do you remember the lake?" she said, in an abrupt voice, under the pressure of an emotion which caught her heart, made the muscles of her throat stiff, and contracted her lips in a spasm as she said "lake". For she was a child, throwing bread to the ducks, between her parents, and at the same time a grown woman coming to her parents who stood by the lake, holding her life in her arms which, as she neared them, grew larger and larger in her arms, until it became a whole life, a complete life, which she put down by them and said, "This is what I have made of it! This!" And what had she made of it? What, indeed? sitting there sewing this morning with Peter.

She looked at Peter Walsh; her look, passing through all that time and that emotion, reached him doubtfully; settled on him tearfully; and rose and fluttered away, as a bird touches a branch and rises and flutters away. Quite simply she wiped her eyes.

"Yes," said Peter. "Yes, yes, yes," he said, as if she drew up to the surface something which positively hurt him as it rose. Stop! Stop! he wanted to cry. For he was not old; his life was not over; not by any means. He was only just past fifty. Shall I tell her, he thought, or not? He would like to make a clean breast of it all. But she is too cold, he thought; sewing, with her scissors; Daisy would look ordinary beside Clarissa. And she would think me a failure, which I am in their sense, he thought; in the Dalloways sense. Oh yes, he had no doubt about that; he was a failure, compared with all this—the inlaid table, the mounted paper-knife, the dolphin and the candlesticks, the chair-covers and the old valuable English tinted prints—he was a failure! I detest the smugness of the whole affair, he thought; Richard's doing, not Clarissa's; save that she married him. (Here Lucy came into the room, carrying silver, more silver, but charming, slender, graceful she looked, he thought, as she stooped to put it down.) And this has been going on all the time! he thought; week after week; Clarissa's life; while I—he thought; and at once everything seemed to radiate from him; journeys; rides; quarrels; adventures; bridge parties; love affairs; work; work, work! and he took out his knife quite openly—his old horn-handled knife which Clarissa could swear he had had these thirty years—and clenched his fist upon it.

What an extraordinary habit that was, Clarissa thought; always playing with a knife. Always making one feel, too, frivolous; empty-minded; a mere silly chatterbox, as he used. But I too, she thought, and, taking up her needle, summoned, like a Queen whose guards have fallen asleep and left her unprotected (she had been quite taken aback by this visit—it had upset her) so that any one can stroll in and have a look at her where she lies with the brambles curving over her, summoned to her help the things she did; the things she liked; her husband; Elizabeth; her self, in short, which Peter hardly knew now, all to come about her and beat off the enemy.[137]

"Well, and what's happened to you?" she said. So before a battle begins, the horses paw the ground; toss their heads; the light shines on their flanks; their necks curve. So Peter Walsh and Clarissa, sitting side by side on the blue sofa, challenged each other. His powers chafed and tossed in him. He assembled from different quarters all sorts of things; praise; his career at

137 The violence of emotion between Peter and Clarissa, first hinted at by the scissors and the knife, now emerges as a fairy-tale battle. There is a perceptible shift in the tone of the narrative once it allows the characters to indulge the grandiosity of their feelings. What was once touching becomes comic, ridiculous: Peter with his scrawny neck; his red hands; his dry, officious manner of speaking; Clarissa with her aged and "indomitable egotism." They try to revive the feelings of youth, desire and jealousy tuned to the highest pitch. Yet Woolf's narrator does not let them resurrect these feelings without a sense of irony.

As Anne Fernald has observed, Woolf's notebook featured an extended analogy to the fable of Sleeping Beauty, with Clarissa sewing, certain to prick her finger and fall asleep, and to be awakened a hundred years later by Peter the prince, battling through the thorns to climb her tower and kiss her. But in the published version of the novel, the metaphor becomes confused. Or rather, Clarissa rejects it as inappropriate to the occasion. Instead of the brambles challenging Peter while she sleeps, she challenges him. Wielding her sewing needle against his knife, she insists that her marriage has not been some slumbering interlude, but the making of a happy life in his absence.

Oxford; his marriage, which she knew nothing whatever about; how he had loved; and altogether done his job.

"Millions of things!" he exclaimed, and, urged by the assembly of powers which were now charging this way and that and giving him the feeling at once frightening and extremely exhilarating of being rushed through the air on the shoulders of people he could no longer see, he raised his hands to his forehead.

Clarissa sat very upright; drew in her breath.

"I am in love," he said, not to her however, but to some one raised up in the dark so that you could not touch her but must lay your garland down on the grass in the dark.

"In love," he repeated, now speaking rather dryly to Clarissa Dalloway; "in love with a girl in India." He had deposited his garland. Clarissa could make what she would of it.

"In love!" she said. That he at his age should be sucked under in his little bow-tie by that monster! And there's no flesh on his neck; his hands are red; and he's six months older than I am! her eye flashed back to her; but in her heart she felt, all the same; he is in love. He has that, she felt; he is in love.

But the indomitable egotism which for ever rides down the hosts opposed to it, the river which says on, on, on; even though, it admits, there may be no goal for us whatever, still on, on; this indomitable egotism charged her cheeks with colour; made her look very young; very pink; very bright-eyed as she sat with her dress upon her knee, and her needle held to the end of green silk, trembling a little. He was in love! Not with her. With some younger woman, of course.

"And who is she?" she asked.

Now this statue must be brought from its height and set down between them.

"A married woman, unfortunately," he said; "the wife of a Major in the Indian Army."

And with a curious ironical sweetness he smiled as he placed her in this ridiculous way before Clarissa.

(All the same, he is in love, thought Clarissa.)

"She has," he continued, very reasonably, "two small children;

a boy and a girl; and I have come over to see my lawyers about the divorce."

There they are! he thought. Do what you like with them, Clarissa! There they are! And second by second it seemed to him that the wife of the Major in the Indian Army (his Daisy) and her two small children became more and more lovely as Clarissa looked at them; as if he had set light to a grey pellet on a plate[138] and there had risen up a lovely tree in the brisk sea-salted air of their intimacy (for in some ways no one understood him, felt with him, as Clarissa did)—their exquisite intimacy.

She flattered him; she fooled him, thought Clarissa; shaping the woman, the wife of the Major in the Indian Army; with three strokes of a knife. What a waste! What a folly! All his life long Peter had been fooled like that; first getting sent down from Oxford;[139] next marrying the girl on the boat going out to India; now the wife of a Major—thank Heaven she had refused to marry him! Still, he was in love; her old friend, her dear Peter, he was in love.

"But what are you going to do?" she asked him. Oh the lawyers and solicitors, Messrs. Hooper and Grateley of Lincoln's Inn,[140] they were going to do it, he said. And he actually pared his nails with his pocket-knife.

For Heaven's sake, leave your knife alone! she cried to herself in irrepressible irritation; it was his silly unconventionality, his weakness; his lack of the ghost of a notion what any one else was feeling that annoyed her, had always annoyed her; and now at his age, how silly!

I know all that, Peter thought; I know what I'm up against, he thought, running his finger along the blade of his knife, Clarissa and Dalloway and all the rest of them; but I'll show Clarissa—and then to his utter surprise, suddenly thrown by those uncontrollable forces thrown through the air, he burst into tears; wept; wept without the least shame, sitting on the sofa, the tears running down his cheeks.

And Clarissa had leant forward, taken his hand, drawn him

138 Fireworks are usually black or gray pellets shaped into small spheres. When ignited, they smoke and hiss for a moment before exploding into light and color.

139 "Getting sent down from Oxford" means to be expelled from an Oxford college, either permanently or temporarily.

140 Lincoln's Inn, one of the oldest Inns of Court in London, was founded in the early fifteenth century and remains one of the most prestigious professional bodies of judges and lawyers in England. In *Night and Day*, Messrs. Hooper and Grateley are the lawyers for whom Ralph Denham clerks.

Lincoln's Inn Fields, artist unknown. Watercolor painting, c. 1835. *(Wellcome Collection)*

to her, kissed him,—actually had felt his face on hers before she could down the brandishing of silver-flashing plumes like pampas grass in a tropic gale in her breast, which, subsiding, left her holding his hand, patting his knee, and feeling as she sat back extraordinarily at her ease with him and light-hearted, all in a clap it came over her, If I had married him, this gaiety would have been mine all day!

It was all over for her. The sheet was stretched and the bed narrow. She had gone up into the tower alone and left them blackberrying in the sun. The door had shut, and there among the dust of fallen plaster and the litter of birds' nests how distant the view had looked, and the sounds came thin and chill (once on Leith Hill,[141] she remembered), and Richard, Richard! she

141 Leith Hill is a wooded hill in the southwest Surrey Hills, the second-highest hill in southeast England. At the top stands Leith Hill Tower, an eighteenth-century Gothic tower built from dark yellow stone, with a spiral staircase inside and telescopes at the top. Through the telescope's eye, one can see the clock tower of the Palace of Westminster in London.

cried, as a sleeper in the night starts and stretches a hand in the dark for help. Lunching with Lady Bruton, it came back to her. He has left me; I am alone for ever, she thought, folding her hands upon her knee.

Peter Walsh had got up and crossed to the window and stood with his back to her, flicking a bandanna handkerchief from side to side. Masterly and dry and desolate he looked, his thin shoulder-blades lifting his coat slightly; blowing his nose violently. Take me with you, Clarissa thought impulsively, as if he were starting directly upon some great voyage; and then, next moment, it was as if the five acts of a play that had been very exciting and moving were now over and she had lived a lifetime in them and had run away, had lived with Peter, and it was now over.

Now it was time to move, and, as a woman gathers her things together, her cloak, her gloves, her opera-glasses, and gets up to go out of the theatre into the street, she rose from the sofa and went to Peter.

And it was awfully strange, he thought, how she still had the power, as she came tinkling, rustling, still had the power as she came across the room, to make the moon, which he detested, rise at Bourton on the terrace in the summer sky.

"Tell me," he said, seizing her by the shoulders. "Are you happy, Clarissa? Does Richard—"

The door opened.

"Here is my Elizabeth," said Clarissa, emotionally, histrionically, perhaps.

"How d'y do?" said Elizabeth coming forward.

The sound of Big Ben striking the half-hour struck out between them with extraordinary vigour, as if a young man, strong, indifferent, inconsiderate, were swinging dumb-bells this way and that.

"Hullo, Elizabeth!" cried Peter, stuffing his handkerchief into his pocket, going quickly to her, saying "Good-bye Clarissa" without looking at her, leaving the room quickly, and running downstairs and opening the hall door.

"Peter! Peter!" cried Clarissa, following him out on to the landing. "My party to-night! Remember my party to-night!" she cried, having to raise her voice against the roar of the open air, and, overwhelmed by the traffic and the sound of all the clocks striking, her voice crying "Remember my party to-night!" sounded frail and thin and very far away as Peter Walsh shut the door.[142]

Remember my party, remember my party, said Peter Walsh as he stepped down the street, speaking to himself rhythmically, in time with the flow of the sound, the direct downright sound of Big Ben striking the half-hour.[143] (The leaden circles dissolved in the air.)[144] Oh these parties, he thought; Clarissa's parties. Why does she give these parties, he thought. Not that he blamed her or this effigy of a man in a tail-coat with a carnation in his button-hole coming towards him. Only one person in the world could be as he was, in love. And there he was, this fortunate man, himself, reflected in the plate-glass window[145] of a motor-car manufacturer in Victoria Street. All India lay behind him; plains, mountains; epidemics of cholera; a district twice as big as Ireland; decisions he had come to alone—he, Peter Walsh; who was now really for the first time in his life, in love. Clarissa had grown hard, he thought; and a trifle sentimental into the bargain, he suspected, looking at the great motorcars capable of doing—how many miles on how many gallons? For he had a turn for mechanics; had invented a plough in his district, had ordered wheel-barrows from England, but the coolies[146] wouldn't use them, all of which Clarissa knew nothing whatever about.

The way she said "Here is my Elizabeth!"—that annoyed him. Why not "Here's Elizabeth" simply? It was insincere. And Elizabeth didn't like it either. (Still the last tremors of the great booming voice shook the air round him; the half-hour; still early; only half-past eleven still.) For he understood young

142 "Must now go on to make Peter walk away through the Green Park with the sound of the roar in his ear," Woolf wrote in her notebook on June 18, 1923, concluding the conversation between Clarissa and Peter. On rereading, she judged it "too thin & unreal somehow." "The merit of this book so far lies in its design, wh. is original—very difficult," she scribbled, then crossed out her next unhelpful thought: "~~Really the truth is that~~." Instead, she planned what she would do with Peter now that she had left Clarissa: "P.W. should now walk in a great state of excitement to Green Park, as if on the waves of the sound: which should die out & leave him somewhere in the Green Park: He should dislike the thought of Clarissa: yet be excited by her: should all the time be on the defensive against people who think him old. That was why he ran away from Elizabeth. But he must think: not merely see." The next section, which she started writing in the first notebook of "The Hours," would intertwine Peter's thoughts about Clarissa, aging, and the political and cultural changes that had taken place in England since he had last seen her.

143 Big Ben is striking half past eleven.

144 The parenthetical is a precise echo from p. 7, when Clarissa crosses Victoria Street.

145 Recall the mirror Clarissa gazes at in the previous section, as well as the mirroring of each other that Clarissa and Peter enact in her drawing room. Here we have the final panel of the triptych: Peter greeting the image of "this fortunate man," the only person in the world who could be in love as he is in love. He calls on love to draw himself together, to affirm his singularity after Clarissa's gaze and his memories of her have torn him asunder. Though, as we will soon see on p. 87, his defensive protest that he "was now really for the first time in his life in love" does not hold true for long.

146 A racist term for a laborer in India, and a term Woolf used liberally in her diaries. On Woolf's racism toward the colonies, see n. 35 on p. 16.

Duncan Grant in front of a Mirror, Vanessa Bell. Oil on plywood, 1915–17. *(Peter Horree / Alamy)*

people; he liked them. There was always something cold in Clarissa, he thought. She had always, even as a girl, a sort of timidity, which in middle age becomes conventionality, and then it's all up, it's all up, he thought, looking rather drearily into the glassy depths, and wondering whether by calling at that hour he had annoyed her; overcome with shame suddenly at having been a fool; wept; been emotional; told her everything, as usual, as usual.

As a cloud crosses the sun, silence falls on London; and falls on the mind. Effort ceases. Time flaps on the mast. There we stop; there we stand.[147] Rigid, the skeleton of habit alone upholds the human frame. Where there is nothing, Peter Walsh said to himself; feeling hollowed out, utterly empty within. Clarissa refused me, he thought. He stood there thinking, Clarissa refused me.

Ah, said St Margaret's,[148] like a hostess who comes into her drawing-room on the very stroke of the hour and finds her guests there already.[149] I am not late. No, it is precisely half-past eleven, she says. Yet, though she is perfectly right, her voice, being the voice of the hostess, is reluctant to inflict its individuality. Some grief for the past holds it back; some concern for the present. It is half-past eleven, she says, and the sound of St. Margaret's glides into the recesses of the heart and buries itself in ring after ring of sound, like something alive which wants to confide itself, to disperse itself, to be, with a tremor of delight, at rest—like Clarissa herself, thought Peter Walsh, coming downstairs on the stroke of the hour in white. It is Clarissa herself, he thought, with a deep emotion, and an extraordinarily clear, yet puzzling, recollection of her, as if this bell had come into the room years ago, where they sat at some moment of great intimacy, and had gone from one to the other and had left, like a bee with honey, laden with the moment. But what room? What moment? And why had he been so profoundly happy when the clock was striking? Then, as the sound of St. Margaret's languished, he thought, She has been ill, and the sound expressed languor and suffering. It was her heart, he remembered; and the sudden loudness of the

147 From the previous paragraph to this one, the shift from the third person to the first-person plural, and from the past to the present tense, is striking, particularly given that Woolf's subject is time. The feeling that time has stopped is transformed into a collective experience: "There we stop; there we stand." In a novel preoccupied with individual perceptions of time, as well as the division of time into individual moments, the universal stillness experienced by all—by Peter; by London; by Woolf's narrator; by her readers left lingering in the present tense—offers a spectacularly concentrated moment of shared sensation and thought.

148 St Margaret's, known as "the church on Parliament Square," is a twelfth-century church adjacent to Westminster Abbey. The church was built by the Benedictine monks of Westminster Abbey, then a Benedictine abbey, at the end of the eleventh century. The monks, disturbed from their worship by the swells of people who came to hear mass in the abbey, built St Margaret's to absorb the crowds.

149 Though the metaphor of St Margaret as a hostess belongs first to Woolf's narrator, it is passed on to Peter later in the passage, a wonderful dispersal of voice that mirrors the sound of the bells, their ringing also spreading and dissolving in the air. Woolf ruminated on the gendering of the clock of St Margaret's in the manuscript of "The Hours": "But her voice was a womans <voice>, since it is impossible to have anything to do with inanimate objects without giving them sex, & the very stair rods have character, & should fate sent them to the old furniture shop & their owners pass by their voices would be heard in their own accents bringing back countless passages up & down stairs, moments ~~to~~ of happiness, of despair, moments not otherwise communicable, for there has attached itself even to the stair rod, something that lies below words."

The interior of St Margaret's, 1809. *(Dean & Chapter of Westminster)*

final stroke tolled for death that surprised in the midst of life, Clarissa falling where she stood, in her drawing-room. No! No! he cried. She is not dead! I am not old, he cried, and marched up Whitehall,[150] as if there rolled down to him, vigorous, unending, his future.[151]

He was not old, or set, or dried in the least. As for caring what they said of him—the Dalloways, the Whitbreads, and their set, he cared not a straw—not a straw (though it was true he would have, some time or other, to see whether Richard couldn't help him to some job). Striding, staring, he glared at the statue of the Duke of Cambridge.[152] He had been sent down from Oxford—true. He had been a Socialist, in some sense a failure—true. Still the future of civilisation lies, he thought, in the hands of young men like that; of young men such as he was, thirty years ago; with their love of abstract principles; getting books sent out to them all the way from London to a peak in the Himalayas; reading science; reading philosophy. The future lies in the hands of young men like that, he thought.

A patter like the patter of leaves in a wood came from behind, and with it a rustling, regular thudding sound, which as it overtook him drummed his thoughts, strict in step, up Whitehall, without his doing. Boys in uniform, carrying guns, marched with their eyes ahead of them, marched, their arms stiff, and on their faces an expression like the letters of a legend written round the base of a statue praising duty, gratitude, fidelity, love of England.

It is, thought Peter Walsh, beginning to keep step with them, a very fine training. But they did not look robust. They were weedy for the most part, boys of sixteen, who might, to-morrow, stand behind bowls of rice, cakes of soap on counters. Now they wore on them unmixed with sensual pleasure or daily preoccupations the solemnity of the wreath which they had fetched from Finsbury Pavement to the empty tomb.[153] They had taken their vow. The traffic respected it; vans were stopped.

I can't keep up with them, Peter Walsh thought, as they marched up Whitehall, and sure enough, on they marched, past

150 Whitehall runs south from Trafalgar Square toward Parliament Square. Named after the Palace of Whitehall, which burned down in 1698, the street is the center of government operations, including the Ministry of Defence, Richmond House, the former headquarters of the Department of Health, the Cabinet Office, the Foreign and Commonwealth Office, and HM Treasury.

151 Peter's and Clarissa's respective meditations on aging, desire, and "the moment" diverge in fascinating, humorous, and somewhat stereotypical ways. What remains a memory of youthful ecstasy for her ("an illumination; a match burning in a crocus; an inner meaning almost expressed") is a reminder of mortality for him ("What moment? . . . No! No! he cried. She is not dead! I am not old, he cried.") Peter's fear that the past can never be retrieved spurs his retreat from death, his bumbling quest throughout this section for the passion of his youth and the innocence of his childhood. Watching the marching teenage boys, he examines how British civilization has deadened the feelings of others, but not his feelings, he tells himself. Life "had been laid under a pavement of monuments and wreaths and drugged into a stiff yet staring corpse by discipline," but he refuses to adopt the "marble stare" of other men. Then, in a funny, poignant, and pathetic turn, he follows an attractive young woman to her house; plays the "romantic buccaneer" in his mind; imagines a "fling"; "makes up the better part of life." Exhausted by the affair he does not have, he sits on a bench in Regent's Park and falls asleep next to a baby in its stroller.

152 Prince George, Duke of Cambridge (1819–1904), a heavy, kindly, and energetic sportsman, served as

Prince George, Duke of Cambridge statue, Whitehall, 2015. *(Man Vyi)*

commander-in-chief of the forces (the military head of the British army) from 1856 to 1895. He gained control of the troops serving in India when the European troops of the East India Company merged with the army of the Crown in 1862. A staunch defender of the virtues of the old army and the privileging of social status over merit, his archconservativism irritated many of his fellow officers and government ministers, who persuaded him to retire in October 1895. A bronze equestrian statue commemorating his service was erected outside the new War Office building on Whitehall in 1907.

153 Finsbury Pavement is a short promenade that connects the City of London to the old drained moors of Moorfield, described by Walter Thornbury in *Old and New London* (1873) as "a place for cudgel-players and train-band musters," "wrestlers, pedestrians, bookstall-keepers, and balladsellers." The "empty tomb" is the Cenotaph, a war memorial made of Portland stone whose name derives from the Greek word *kenotaphion*, or "empty tomb." The Cenotaph was designed by Edwin Lutyens and was unveiled in 1920 to honor "the Glorious Dead" of the First World War.

154 A word first invented by Woolf in *Night and Day* to indicate the condition of being irreticent, or unreserved: "On the other hand, unless he checked him, Rodney might begin to talk about his feelings, and irreticence is apt to be extremely painful, at any rate in prospect."

155 Nelson's Column stands in the middle of Trafalgar Square. it is an imperious 150-foot granite column topped by a sandstone statue of Vice-Admiral Horatio Nelson (1758–1805). Nelson places one hand on his breast, while the other leans on his sword, a thick pile of nautical rope coiled behind him. Four bronze Barbary lions, irresistible to the naughty children who want to climb them, guard the column's base. Designed by the English architect William Railton in 1840, the column commemorates Nelson's last great victory and death during the Battle of Trafalgar in 1805.

156 Major General Charles George Gordon (1833–1885), also known as "Chinese Gordon," was famous for dying nobly, or so his supporters claimed, during the Siege of Khartoum (1884–85) while defending the city against the forces of Muhammad Ahmad, the self-proclaimed Mahdi. A statue of Gordon was erected in Trafalgar Square and moved to the Victoria Embankment Gardens in 1953. There the bronze general stands, or rather slouches, with a Bible and cane under his left arm, his right hand tucked under his chin, and his left foot atop a cannon.

The members of the Bloomsbury group disliked Gordon, whom they believed had spent his life preaching Christian compassion while brutalizing the

Unveiling of the Cenotaph, November 11, 1920.
(Queensland State Archives)

him, past every one, in their steady way, as if one will worked legs and arms uniformly, and life, with its varieties, its irreticences,[154] had been laid under a pavement of monuments and wreaths and drugged into a stiff yet staring corpse by discipline. One had to respect it; one might laugh; but one had to respect it, he thought. There they go, thought Peter Walsh, pausing at the edge of the pavement; and all the exalted statues, Nelson,[155] Gordon,[156] Havelock,[157] the black, the spectacular images of great soldiers stood looking ahead of them, as if they too had made the same renunciation (Peter Walsh felt he, too, had made it, the great renunciation), trampled under the same temptations, and achieved at length a marble stare. But the stare Peter Walsh did not want for himself in the least; though he could respect it in others. He could respect it in boys. They don't know the troubles of the flesh yet, he thought, as the marching boys disappeared in the direction of

Nelson's Column, Trafalgar Square, c. 1908. *(United Photograph Company, Library of Congress)*

the Strand[158]—all that I've been through, he thought, crossing the road, and standing under Gordon's statue, Gordon whom as a boy he had worshipped; Gordon standing lonely with one leg raised and his arms crossed,—poor Gordon, he thought.[159]

And just because nobody yet knew he was in London, except Clarissa, and the earth, after the voyage, still seemed an island to him, the strangeness of standing alone, alive, unknown, at half-past eleven in Trafalgar Square overcame him. What is it? Where am I? And why, after all, does one do it? he thought, the divorce seeming all moonshine. And down his mind went flat as a marsh, and three great emotions bowled over him; understanding; a vast philanthropy; and finally, as if the result of the others, an irrepressible, exquisite delight; as if inside his brain by another hand strings were pulled, shutters moved, and he, having nothing to do with it, yet stood at the opening of endless

people he had helped colonize. What Victorian politicians and papers once celebrated as Gordon's religion and patriotism, Lytton Strachey savaged as Gordon's disdain for the oppressed, his thirst for foreign blood. "It is only fitting that the last moments of one whose whole life was passed in contradiction should be involved in mystery and doubt," Strachey wrote in *Eminent Victorians* (1918), expressing his skepticism about the circumstances of Gordon's death. Gordon's supporters claimed he had submitted to the followers of the Mahdi unarmed and Christ-like, passively yielding to death at the hands of men more wicked than he. "Other witnesses told a very different story," Strachey wrote. "The man whom they saw die was not a saint but a warrior. With intrepidity, with skill, with desperation, he flew at his enemies."

General Charles George Gordon, Embankment, 2012. *(Eluveitie)*

157 Major General Sir Henry Havelock (1795–1857) served in the First Anglo-Burmese War (1824–26), the First Afghan War (1839–42), and the Sikh Wars (1845–46). He died of dysentery after failing to secure Lucknow during the Indian Rebellion of 1857

(1857–58). His bronze-cast statue stands to the east of Nelson's Column in Trafalgar Square.

Major General Henry Havelock, Whitehall, 2016. *(Luke McKernan)*

158 Running east from Trafalgar Square into the City of London, the Strand was one of Woolf's favorite streets to walk in London. In a diary entry on March 29, 1940, she wrote, "What shall I think of that['s] liberating & freshening? [. . .] Say the Thames at London bridge; & buying a notebook; & then walking along the Strand & letting each face give me a buffet."

159 Note the extraordinary concentration of statues commemorating imperial politics in this section of the novel. The streets of London are at once buzzing and blooming with life and shadowed by death: by tombs and effigies and the hard, frozen faces of men responsible for oppressing and killing people in lands too distant for the average British man on the street to care. Peter, looking up at the statue of Gordon, can only think of Gordon—"poor Gordon," he thought—not of the people he slew.

Trafalgar Square and its statues, early twentieth century. *(UK Photo and Social History Archive)*

avenues, down which if he chose he might wander. He had not felt so young for years.

He had escaped! was utterly free—as happens in the downfall of habit when the mind, like an unguarded flame, bows and bends and seems about to blow from its holding. I haven't felt so young for years! thought Peter, escaping (only of course for an hour or so) from being precisely what he was, and feeling like a

"Street Scene, The Strand, London," Léon & Lévy No. 81 Postcard, c. 1910. *(Léon & Lévy)*

child who runs out of doors, and sees, as he runs, his old nurse waving at the wrong window. But she's extraordinarily attractive, he thought, as, walking across Trafalgar Square in the direction of the Haymarket, came a young woman who, as she passed Gordon's statue, seemed, Peter Walsh thought (susceptible as he was), to shed veil after veil, until she became the very woman he had always had in mind; young, but stately; merry, but discreet; black, but enchanting.[160]

Straightening himself and stealthily fingering his pocket-knife he started after her to follow this woman, this excitement, which seemed even with its back turned to shed on him a light which connected them, which singled him out, as if the random uproar of the traffic had whispered through hollowed hands his name, not Peter, but his private name which he called himself in his own thoughts. "You," she said, only "you", saying it with her white gloves and her shoulders. Then the thin long cloak which the wind stirred as she walked past Dent's shop in Cockspur Street[161] blew out with an enveloping kindness, a mournful tenderness, as of arms that would open and take the tired—

E. Dent & Co. advertisement, 1931.
(Lett's Office Diary)

But she's not married; she's young; quite young, thought Peter, the red carnation he had seen her wear as she came across Trafalgar Square burning again in his eyes and making her lips red. But she waited at the kerbstone. There was a dignity about her. She was not worldly, like Clarissa; not rich, like Clarissa. Was she, he wondered as she moved, respectable? Witty, with a lizard's flickering tongue, he thought (for one must invent, must

160 In the manuscript of "The Hours," Woolf emphasized not this mysterious woman's youth and merriment, but her maternal anguish: "Peter, the lady called to him, . . . ~~& how maternal as she was with an exquisite maternally; for there was a mournfulness in the flow of the black expressed the mournful tenderness of a mother, a young mother, to whom her child comes crying, at the end of the day~~ . . ."

161 Edward John Dent (1790–1853) was an English watchmaker renowned for the chronometers he created for Britain's maritime conquests. The grandson of a candlemaker, he had no passion for tallow or wicks and was apprenticed at fourteen to his cousin, a watchmaker named Richard Rippon. Dent soon surpassed Rippon as a maker of beautiful, reliable, and precise timepieces; he opened his own practice in 1814. His clocks kept time for the empire as it expanded through the nineteenth century. His designs included the Great Clock of Westminster (better known as Big Ben) for the Houses of Parliament; chronometer no. 633, which accompanied Charles Darwin aboard the HMS *Beagle*; and the Standard Clock at the Royal Observatory in Greenwich, which kept Greenwich Mean Time (GMT), the time to which all other times were synchronized and on which all time zones were based.

allow oneself a little diversion), a cool waiting wit, a darting wit; not noisy.

She moved; she crossed; he followed her. To embarrass her was the last thing he wished. Still if she stopped he would say "Come and have an ice," he would say, and she would answer, perfectly simply, "Oh yes."

But other people got between them in the street, obstructing him, blotting her out. He pursued; she changed. There was colour in her cheeks; mockery in her eyes; he was an adventurer, reckless, he thought, swift, daring, indeed (landed as he was last night from India) a romantic buccaneer, careless of all these damned proprieties, yellow dressing-gowns, pipes, fishing-rods, in the shop windows; and respectability and evening parties and spruce old men wearing white slips beneath their waistcoats. He was a buccaneer. On and on she went, across Piccadilly, and up Regent Street, ahead of him, her cloak, her gloves, her shoulders combining with the fringes and the laces and the feather boas in the windows to make the spirit of finery and whimsy which dwindled out of the shops on to the pavement, as the light of a lamp goes wavering at night over hedges in the darkness.

Laughing and delightful, she had crossed Oxford Street and Great Portland Street and turned down one of the little streets, and now, and now, the great moment was approaching, for now she slackened, opened her bag, and with one look in his direction, but not at him, one look that bade farewell, summed up the whole situation and dismissed it triumphantly, for ever, had fitted her key, opened the door, and gone! Clarissa's voice saying, Remember my party, Remember my party, sang in his ears. The house was one of those flat red houses with hanging flower-baskets of vague impropriety. It was over.

Well, I've had my fun; I've had it, he thought, looking up at the swinging baskets of pale geraniums. And it was smashed to atoms—his fun, for it was half made up, as he knew very well; invented, this escapade with the girl; made up, as one makes up the better part of life, he thought—making oneself up; making her up; creating an exquisite amusement, and something more.[162] But odd it was, and quite true; all this one could never share—it smashed to atoms.

He turned; went up the street, thinking to find somewhere to sit, till it was time for Lincoln's Inn—for Messrs. Hooper and Grateley. Where should he go? No matter. Up the street, then, towards Regent's Park. His boots on the pavement struck out "no matter"; for it was early, still very early.

It was a splendid morning too. Like the pulse of a perfect heart, life struck straight through the streets. There was no fumbling—no hesitation. Sweeping and swerving, accurately, punctually, noiselessly, there, precisely at the right instant, the motor-car stopped at the door. The girl, silk-stockinged, feathered, evanescent, but not to him particularly attractive (for he had had his fling), alighted. Admirable butlers, tawny chow dogs, halls laid in black and white lozenges with white blinds blowing, Peter saw through the opened door and approved of. A splendid achievement in its own way, after all, London; the season; civilisation.[163] Coming as he did from a respectable Anglo-Indian family which for at least three generations had administered the affairs of a continent (it's strange, he thought, what a sentiment I have about that, disliking India, and empire, and army as he did),[164] there were moments when civilisation, even of this sort, seemed dear to him as a personal possession; moments of pride in England; in butlers; chow dogs; girls in their security. Ridiculous enough, still there it is, he thought. And the doctors and men of business and capable women all going about their business, punctual, alert, robust, seemed to him wholly admirable, good fellows, to whom one would entrust one's life, companions in the art of living, who would see one through. What with one thing and another, the show was really very tolerable; and he would sit down in the shade and smoke.

There was Regent's Park. Yes. As a child he had walked in Regent's Park—odd, he thought, how the thought of childhood keeps coming back to me—the result of seeing Clarissa,

162 While one could read Peter's pursuit of this strange woman as his foray into "character-reading," there is something seedy, something vain, suspicious, possessive, and unwanted, about how he practices it—following a woman to her home, imagining himself a colonizing "buccaneer" "landed as he was last night from India." The manuscript of "The Hours" makes Peter out to be more obviously entitled than he appears in the final draft. "[H]e was ruffled," Woolf wrote, "angry with himself, & the sense of unity was snapped, & he felt like a pursuer, who has been checked— So she went on For, ~~as A,~~ <as> other people in the street now got between them, blotting her out, giving him a ~~most irritating~~ sense of wilful obstruction, ~~as if they obscured her maliciously, he~~ his eagerness increased . . . . ~~She walked provokingly, conscious of his pursuit.~~"

Character-reading has its politics. Not everyone pursues it sympathetically, respectfully, or with Woolf's commitment to lighting the extraordinary spirit of ordinary people's lives. "For he controlled her," Peter thinks of his mystery woman in the manuscript of "The Hours." His version of character-reading is uneasy and exploitative, a practice of surveillance, stalking, and imaginative domination more akin to his service in India than to the creation of fiction as Woolf theorized it.

163 Turning away from the statues and their celebration of imperial victories, Peter's thoughts on "civilisation" begin to mirror Woolf's begrudging admiration of its daily activities. In a diary entry dated August 26, 1922, she recalled a trip she and Leonard took to Charleston, riding a bus through the city for the first time and seeing the people stepping out on the streets, frantic with activity. "After all, one must respect civilisation," she wrote. "This thought came to me standing in a Brighton street the other day from which one sees the downs. Mankind was fuming & fretting & shouldering each other about; the down was smoothly sublime. But I thought this street frenzy is really the better of the two—the more courageous. One must put up a fight against passive turf, with an occasional snail, & a swell in the ground which it takes 2,000 years to produce."

164 Compare Peter's love of "civilisation" with his dislike of "India, and empire, and army." England must be cleansed of its affiliation with its colonies before he can take pride in its people: "the doctors and men of business"; the rich, showy woman whose hall he glimpses and approves. Peter's semi-acknowledgment of the racism that animates his sentimentality makes him a shade more self-conscious than a character like Mr. Bowley. But this awareness is relegated to a parenthetical here. It yields no

thought or feeling strong enough to trouble Peter just before he falls asleep.

165 David Bradshaw suggests that this is "almost certainly the *Matilda* fountain" opposite the Gloucester Gate of Regent's Park. A milkmaid in bronze shields her eyes from the sun at the top while, below her and right next to the statue's edge, her pail teeters. The inscription on the bottom identifies the figure as Matilda, wife of Richard Kent Jr., a local churchwarden, and the sculptor as Joseph Durham.

Matilda Fountain, Regent's Park, 2014. *(Eden Pictures)*

perhaps; for women live much more in the past than we do, he thought. They attach themselves to places; and their fathers—a woman's always proud of her father. Bourton was a nice place, a very nice place, but I could never get on with the old man, he thought. There was quite a scene one night—an argument about something or other, what, he could not remember. Politics presumably.

Yes, he remembered Regent's Park; the long straight walk; the little house where one bought air-balls to the left; an absurd statue with an inscription somewhere or other.[165] He looked for an empty seat. He did not want to be bothered (feeling a little drowsy as he did) by people asking him the time. An elderly grey nurse, with a baby asleep in its perambulator—that was the best he could do for himself; sit down at the far end of the seat by that nurse.

She's a queer-looking girl, he thought, suddenly remembering Elizabeth as she came into the room and stood by her mother. Grown big; quite grown-up; not exactly pretty; handsome rather; and she can't be more than eighteen. Probably she doesn't get on with Clarissa. "There's my Elizabeth"—that sort of thing—why not "Here's Elizabeth" simply?—trying to make out, like most mothers, that things are what they're not. She trusts to her charm too much, he thought. She overdoes it.

The rich benignant cigar smoke eddied coolly down his throat; he puffed it out again in rings which breasted the air bravely for a moment; blue, circular—I shall try and get a word alone with Elizabeth to-night, he thought—then began to wobble into hour-glass shapes and taper away; odd shapes they take, he thought. Suddenly he closed his eyes, raised his hand with an effort, and threw away the heavy end of his cigar. A great brush swept smooth across his mind, sweeping across it moving branches, children's voices, the shuffle of feet, and people passing, and humming traffic, rising and falling traffic. Down, down he sank into the plumes and feathers of sleep, sank, and was muffled over.

THE GREY NURSE resumed her knitting as Peter Walsh, on the hot seat beside her, began snoring. In her grey dress, moving her hands indefatigably yet quietly, she seemed like the champion of the rights of sleepers, like one of those spectral presences which rise in twilight in woods made of sky and branches. The solitary traveller, haunter of lanes, disturber of ferns, and devastator of great hemlock plants, looking up suddenly, sees the giant figure at the end of the ride.[166]

By conviction an atheist perhaps, he[167] is taken by surprise with moments of extraordinary exaltation. Nothing exists outside us

166 "There is something helpless, ridiculous—about him as well as terrifying: this abandonment to sleep," Woolf scribbled on July 22, 1922, wondering what to do with Peter now that he was snoring on the park bench. She decided to leave him there and create around him a dream state, a vision of life and death. "There should now be a chorus, half of calm & security, the nursemaid & the ~~fo~~ sleeping baby; half of fear & apprehension," she planned in her notebook. "These feelings should be treated however generally: as poetry, not psychology." It took her another year to begin sketching the interlude many would come to call "The Solitary Traveller," the most beautiful and inscrutable narrative interruption in *Mrs. Dalloway.*

167 "He" should not necessarily be read as referring back to Peter. Rather "he" refers back to "the solitary traveller," an indistinct figure, occasionally taking on Peter's character, but then shedding it to assume the more abstract and universal position of man in the modern world.

Main Walk, London Zoo, c. 1940. *(UK Photo and Social History Archive)*

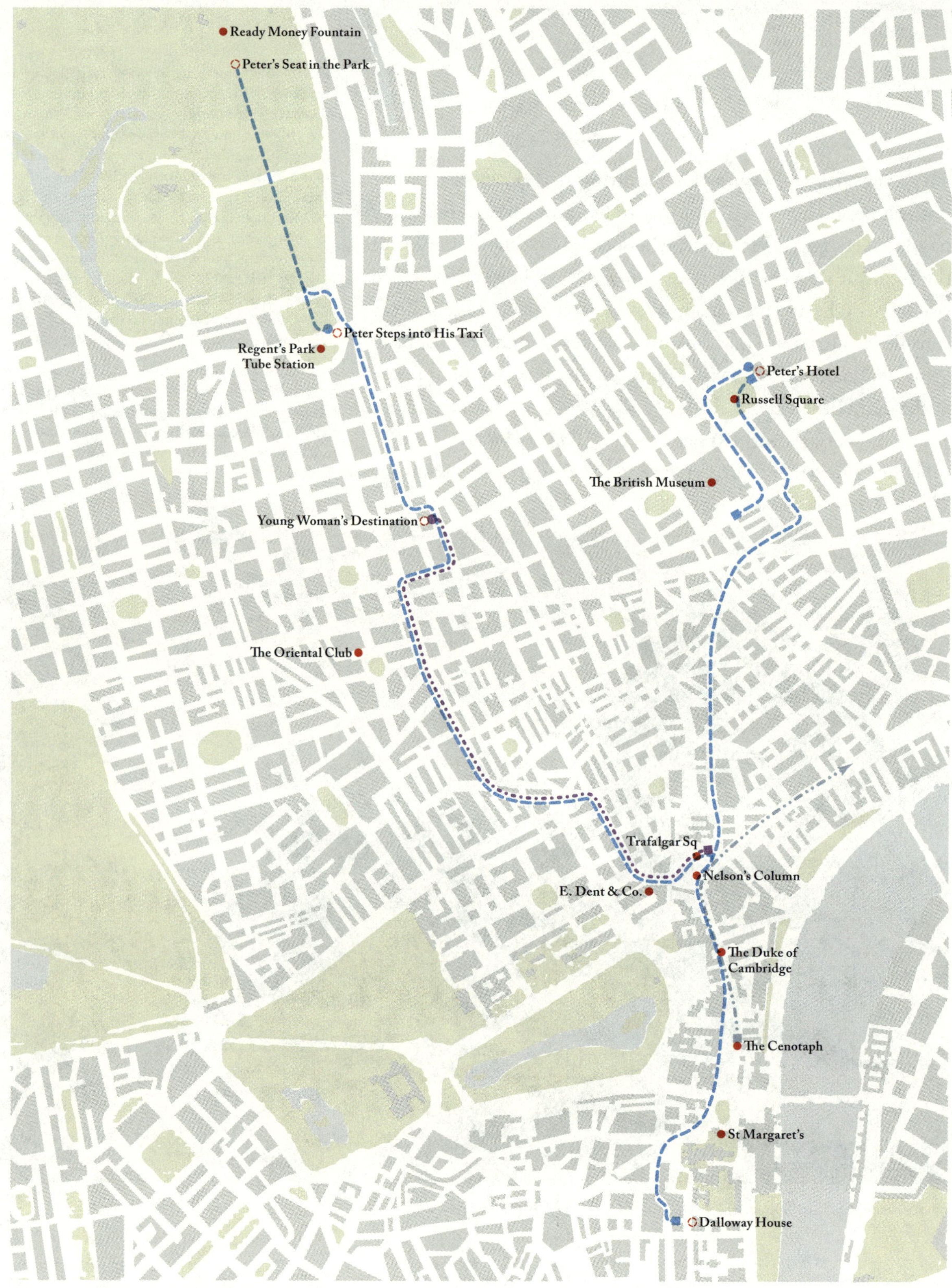

Peter's walk. *(Christian Nakarado)*

except a state of mind, he thinks; a desire for solace, for relief, for something outside these miserable pigmies, these feeble, these ugly, these craven men and women. But if he can conceive of her, then in some sort she exists, he thinks, and advancing down the path with his eyes upon sky and branches he rapidly endows them with womanhood; sees with amazement how grave they become; how majestically, as the breeze stirs them, they dispense with a dark flutter of the leaves charity, comprehension, absolution, and then, flinging themselves suddenly aloft, confound the piety of their aspect with a wild carouse.[168]

168 Though the solitary traveler is not synonymous with Peter, he shares Peter's tendency to create fantasies about women out of nothing more than "sky and branches," endowing the vast, incomprehensible natural world with not only "womanhood" but also grace—with "charity, comprehension, absolution," as well as a wild and enticing sense of impiety.

The Lark at Heaven's Gate Sings, Francis Seymour Haden. Etching and drypoint, 1859. *(Paul Mellon Collection, Yale Center for British Art)*

Such are the visions which proffer great cornucopias full of fruit to the solitary traveller, or murmur in his ear like sirens lolloping away on the green sea waves, or are dashed in his face like bunches of roses, or rise to the surface like pale faces which fishermen flounder through floods to embrace.

Such are the visions which ceaselessly float up, pace beside, put their faces in front of, the actual thing; often overpowering the solitary traveller and taking away from him the sense of the earth, the wish to return, and giving him for substitute a general peace, as if (so he thinks as he advances down the forest ride) all this fever of living were simplicity itself; and myriads of things merged in one thing; and this figure, made of sky and branches as it is, had risen from the troubled sea (he is elderly, past fifty now) as a shape might be sucked up out of the waves to shower down from her magnificent hands compassion, comprehension, absolution. So, he thinks, may I never go back to the lamplight; to the sitting room; never finish my book;[169] never knock out my pipe; never ring for Mrs. Turner to clear away; rather let me walk straight on to this great figure, who will, with a toss of her head, mount me on her streamers and let me blow to nothingness with the rest.

Such are the visions. The solitary traveller is soon beyond the wood; and there, coming to the door with shaded eyes, possibly to look for his return, with hands raised, with white apron blowing, is an elderly woman who seems (so powerful is this infirmity) to seek, over the desert, a lost son; to search for a rider destroyed; to be the figure of the mother whose sons have been killed in the battles of the world. So, as the solitary traveller advances down the village street where the women stand knitting and the men dig in the garden, the evening seems ominous; the figures still; as if some august fate, known to them, awaited without fear, were about to sweep them into complete annihilation.[170]

Indoors among ordinary things, the cupboard, the table, the window-sill with its geraniums, suddenly the outline of the landlady, bending to remove the cloth, becomes soft with light, an adorable emblem which only the recollection of cold human contacts forbids us to embrace. She takes the marmalade; she shuts it in the cupboard.

"There is nothing more to-night, sir?" But to whom does the solitary traveller make reply?

So THE ELDERLY NURSE knitted over the sleeping baby in Regent's Park. So Peter Walsh snored. He woke with extreme suddenness, saying to himself, "The death of the soul."

"Lord, Lord!" he said to himself out loud, stretching and opening his eyes. "The death of the soul." The words attached

169 While "finish my book" could refer to anyone reading a book, we later learn on p. 230 that Peter had once planned to write a book and, as he confesses to Sally Seton, has written "not a word."

170 Is the "Solitary Traveller" interlude, as Reuben Brower claims, a "beautiful passage . . . which could be detached with little loss?" Is it Peter's dream, an enchanted version of the fantasies he creates about women in his waking life?

Against both these readings, Elizabeth Abel suggests that the solitary traveler's vision only loosely attaches to Peter's private thoughts. (Recall Woolf stipulating that the interlude should be "poetry, not psychology.") Rather, the narrator expresses nostalgia for a pastoral world reminiscent of Clarissa's youth at Bourton—a "sylvan feminine apotheosis," as Christine Froula describes it. The solitary traveler's journey is overseen by a cosmic maternal presence, a figure of beauty and grace. But in the novel's modernized present, the generous, seductive powers of the goddess shrink to two elderly women: the mother who waits for the sons who will never come home from war and the nurse knitting next to Peter Walsh as she watches over him and the sleeping baby.

themselves to some scene, to some room, to some past he had been dreaming of. It became clearer; the scene, the room, the past he had been dreaming of.[171]

It was at Bourton that summer, early in the 'nineties, when he was so passionately in love with Clarissa. There were a great many people there, laughing and talking, sitting round a table after tea, and the room was bathed in yellow light and full of cigarette smoke. They were talking about a man who had married his housemaid, one of the neighboring squires, he had forgotten his name. He had married his housemaid, and she had been brought to Bourton to call—an awful visit it had been. She was absurdly overdressed, "like a cockatoo," Clarissa had said, imitating her, and she never stopped talking. On and on she went, on and on. Clarissa imitated her. Then somebody said—Sally

171 Woolf allocated this short section to Peter's memory to help make the character of Clarissa more real—to give her a history; to show feelings more complicated than any she would display in the present. "Every scene should build up the idea of C's character," Woolf wrote in the manuscript of *Mrs. Dalloway*. "That will give continuity as well as add to the final effect."

The town of Bourton-on-the-Water, c. 1920. *(UK Photo and Social History Archive)*

172 The wonderful irony, of course, is that immediately after describing Sally Seton ("flushed, wanting to talk," and then, in the parenthetical, "an attractive creature, handsome, dark"), Peter still cannot imagine that Clarissa's performance may have been for Sally, not for him.

Seton it was—did it make any real difference to one's feelings to know that before they'd married she had had a baby? (In those days, in mixed company, it was a bold thing to say.) He could see Clarissa now, turning bright pink; somehow contracting; and saying, "Oh, I shall never be able to speak to her again!" Whereupon the whole party sitting round the tea-table seemed to wobble. It was very uncomfortable.

He hadn't blamed her for minding the fact, since in those days a girl brought up as she was, knew nothing, but it was her manner that annoyed him; timid; hard; arrogant; prudish. "The death of the soul." He had said that instinctively, ticketing the moment as he used to do—the death of her soul.

Every one wobbled; every one seemed to bow, as she spoke, and then to stand up different. He could see Sally Seton, like a child who has been in mischief, leaning forward, rather flushed, wanting to talk, but afraid, and Clarissa did frighten people. (She was Clarissa's greatest friend, always about the place, an attractive creature, handsome, dark, with the reputation in those days of great daring, and he used to give her cigars, which she smoked in her bedroom, and she had either been engaged to somebody or quarrelled with her family, and old Parry disliked them both equally, which was a great bond.) Then Clarissa, still with an air of being offended with them all, got up, made some excuse, and went off, alone. As she opened the door, in came that great shaggy dog which ran after sheep. She flung herself upon him, went into raptures. It was as if she said to Peter—it was all aimed at him, he knew[172]—"I know you thought me absurd about that woman just now; but see how extraordinarily sympathetic I am; see how I love my Rob!"

They had always this queer power of communicating without words. She knew directly he criticised her. Then she would do something quite obvious to defend herself, like this fuss with the dog—but it never took him in, he always saw through Clarissa. Not that he said anything, of course; just sat looking glum. It was the way their quarrels often began.

She shut the door. At once he became extremely depressed.

Vita Sackville-West with Virginia Woolf, August 1933. *(Virginia Woolf Monk's House photographs, MS Thr 564, [92]. Houghton Library, Harvard College Library)*

It all seemed useless—going on being in love; going on quarrelling; going on making it up, and he wandered off alone, among outhouses, stables, looking at the horses. (The place was quite a humble one; the Parrys were never very well off; but there were always grooms and stable-boys about—Clarissa loved riding—and an old coachman—what was his name?—an old nurse, old Moody, old Goody, some such name they called her, whom one was taken to visit in a little room with lots of photographs, lots of bird-cages.)

It was an awful evening! He grew more and more gloomy, not about that only; about everything. And he couldn't see her; couldn't explain to her; couldn't have it out. There were always people about—she'd go on as if nothing had happened. That was the devilish part of her—this coldness, this woodenness, something very profound in her, which he had felt again this morning talking to her; an impenetrability. Yet Heaven knows he loved her. She had some queer power of fiddling on one's nerves, turning one's nerves to fiddle-strings, yes.

He had gone into dinner rather late, from some idiotic idea of making himself felt, and had sat down by old Miss Parry—Aunt Helena—Mr. Parry's sister, who was supposed to preside. There she sat in her white Cashmere shawl, with her head against the window—a formidable old lady, but kind to him, for he had found her some rare flower, and she was a great botanist, marching off in thick boots with a black tin collecting-box slung between her shoulders. He sat down beside her, and couldn't speak. Everything seemed to race past him; he just sat there, eating. And then half-way through dinner he made himself look across at Clarissa for the first time. She was talking to a young man on her right. He had a sudden revelation. "She will marry that man," he said to himself. He didn't even know his name.

For of course it was that afternoon, that very afternoon, that Dalloway had come over; and Clarissa called him "Wickham"; that was the beginning of it all. Somebody had brought him over; and Clarissa got his name wrong. She introduced him to everybody as Wickham. At last he said "My name is Dalloway!"—that was his first view of Richard—a fair young man, rather awkward, sitting on a deck-chair, and blurting out "My name is Dalloway!" Sally got hold of it; always after that she called him "My name is Dalloway!"

He was a prey to revelations at that time. This one—that she would marry Dalloway—was blinding—overwhelming at the moment. There was a sort of—how could he put it?—a sort of ease in her manner to him; something maternal; something gentle. They were talking about politics. All through dinner he tried to hear what they were saying.

Afterwards he could remember standing by old Miss Parry's chair in the drawing-room. Clarissa came up, with her perfect manners, like a real hostess, and wanted to introduce him to some one—spoke as if they had never met before, which enraged him. Yet even then he admired her for it. He admired her courage; her social instinct; he admired her power of carrying things through. "The perfect hostess," he said to her, whereupon she winced all over. But he meant her to feel it. He would have done anything to hurt her, after seeing her with Dalloway. So she left him. And he had a feeling that they were all gathered together in a conspiracy against him—laughing and talking—behind his back. There he stood by Miss Parry's chair as though he had been cut out of wood, talking about wild flowers. Never, never had he suffered so infernally! He must have forgotten even to pretend to listen; at last he woke up; he saw Miss Parry looking rather disturbed, rather indignant, with her prominent eyes fixed. He almost cried out that he couldn't attend because he was in Hell! People began going out of the room. He heard them talking about fetching cloaks; about its being cold on the water, and so on. They were going boating on the lake by moonlight—

A Rowing Boat at Twickenham, John Linnell. Black chalk, white chalk, paper, undated. *(Paul Mellon Collection, Yale Center for British Art)*

one of Sally's mad ideas. He could hear her describing the moon. And they all went out. He was left quite alone.

"Don't you want to go with them?" said Aunt Helena—poor old lady!—she had guessed. And he turned round and there was Clarissa again. She had come back to fetch him. He was overcome by her generosity—her goodness.

"Come along," she said. "They're waiting."

He had never felt so happy in the whole of his life! Without a word they made it up. They walked down to the lake. He had twenty minutes of perfect happiness. Her voice, her laugh, her dress (something floating, white, crimson), her spirit, her adventurousness; she made them all disembark and explore the island; she startled a hen; she laughed; she sang. And all the time, he knew perfectly well, Dalloway was falling in love with her; she was falling in love with Dalloway; but it didn't seem to matter. Nothing mattered. They sat on the ground and talked—he and Clarissa. They went in and out of each other's minds without any effort. And then in a second it was over. He said to himself as they were getting into the boat, "She will marry that man," dully, without any resentment; but it was an obvious thing. Dalloway would marry Clarissa.

Dalloway rowed them in. He said nothing. But somehow as they watched him start, jumping on to his bicycle to ride twenty miles through the woods, wobbling off down the drive, waving his hand and disappearing, he obviously did feel, instinctively, tremendously, strongly, all that; the night; the romance; Clarissa. He deserved to have her.

For himself, he was absurd. His demands upon Clarissa (he could see it now) were absurd. He asked impossible things. He made terrible scenes. She would have accepted him still, perhaps, if he had been less absurd. Sally thought so. She wrote him all that summer long letters; how they had talked of him; how she had praised him, how Clarissa burst into tears! It was an extraordinary summer—all letters, scenes, telegrams—arriving at Bourton early in the morning, hanging about till the servants were up; appalling *tête-à-têtes* with old Mr. Parry at breakfast;

Aunt Helena formidable but kind; Sally sweeping him off for talks in the vegetable garden; Clarissa in bed with headaches.

The final scene, the terrible scene which he believed had mattered more than anything in the whole of his life (it might be an exaggeration—but still, so it did seem now), happened at three o'clock in the afternoon of a very hot day. It was a trifle that led up to it—Sally at lunch saying something about Dalloway, and calling him "My name is Dalloway"; whereupon Clarissa suddenly stiffened, coloured, in a way she had, and rapped out sharply, "We've had enough of that feeble joke." That was all; but for him it was as if she had said, "I'm only amusing myself with you; I've an understanding with Richard Dalloway." So he took it. He had not slept for nights. "It's got to be finished one way or the other," he said to himself. He sent a note to her by Sally asking her to meet him by the fountain at three. "Something very important has happened," he scribbled at the end of it.

The fountain was in the middle of a little shrubbery, far from the house, with shrubs and trees all round it. There she came, even before the time, and they stood with the fountain between them, the spout (it was broken) dribbling water incessantly. How sights fix themselves upon the mind! For example, the vivid green moss.

She did not move. "Tell me the truth, tell me the truth," he kept on saying. He felt as if his forehead would burst. She seemed contracted, petrified. She did not move. "Tell me the truth," he repeated, when suddenly that old man Breitkopf popped his head in carrying the *Times*; stared at them; gaped; and went away. They neither of them moved. "Tell me the truth," he repeated. He felt that he was grinding against something physically hard; she was unyielding. She was like iron, like flint, rigid up the backbone. And when she said, "It's no use. It's no use. This is the end"[173]—after he had spoken for hours, it seemed, with the tears running down his cheeks—it was as if she had hit him in the face. She turned, she left him, she went away.

"Clarissa!" he cried. "Clarissa!" But she never came back. It was over. He went away that night. He never saw her again.

173 The manuscript of "The Hours" makes it clear that Clarissa actively tries to squash Peter's interest in her: "[I]t was physically ~~startling when she said "No, I don['] t care for you. I can[']t care for you~~ . . . It was as if she were determined to kill; to exterminate." The final draft makes her seem at once more unyielding and more passive, as if her inability to commit to him were not an act of volition but a fact of her nature.

174 "The child turns away frightened toward Rezia," Woolf wrote in her notebook on July 22, 1923, when she created the minor character of Elise Mitchell to link Peter to Rezia and Septimus. She then plotted Rezia and Septimus's interaction through the next section of the novel: "However, R & S (or whatever they are called) must be reached. He is still exalted. She is bored, yet apprehensive. They must go to the dr."

175 A pocket watch Peter presents to Elise Mitchell, telling her to blow on the cover while he releases the catch, creating the illusion that her little breath alone has caused it to open.

It was awful, he cried, awful, awful!

Still, the sun was hot. Still, one got over things. Still, life had a way of adding day to day. Still, he thought, yawning and beginning to take notice—Regent's Park had changed very little since he was a boy, except for the squirrels—still, presumably there were compensations—when little Elise Mitchell, who had been picking up pebbles to add to the pebble collection which she and her brother were making on the nursery mantelpiece, plumped her handful down on the nurse's knee and scudded off again full tilt into a lady's legs. Peter Walsh laughed out.

But Lucrezia Warren Smith was saying to herself, It's wicked; why should I suffer? she was asking, as she walked down the broad path. No; I can't stand it any longer, she was saying, having left Septimus, who wasn't Septimus any longer, to say hard, cruel, wicked things, to talk to himself, to talk to a dead man, on the seat over there; when the child ran full tilt into her, fell flat, and burst out crying.[174]

That was comforting rather. She stood her upright, dusted her frock, kissed her.

But for herself she had done nothing wrong; she had loved Septimus; she had been happy; she had had a beautiful home, and there her sisters lived still, making hats. Why should *she* suffer?

The child ran straight back to its nurse, and Rezia saw her scolded, comforted, taken up by the nurse who put down her knitting, and the kind-looking man gave her his watch to blow open[175] to comfort her—but why should *she* be exposed? Why not left in Milan? Why tortured? Why?

Slightly waved by tears the broad path, the nurse, the man in grey, the perambulator, rose and fell before her eyes. To be rocked by this malignant torturer was her lot. But why? She was like a bird sheltering under the thin hollow of a leaf, who blinks at the sun when the leaf moves; starts at the crack of a dry twig. She was exposed; she was surrounded by the enormous trees,

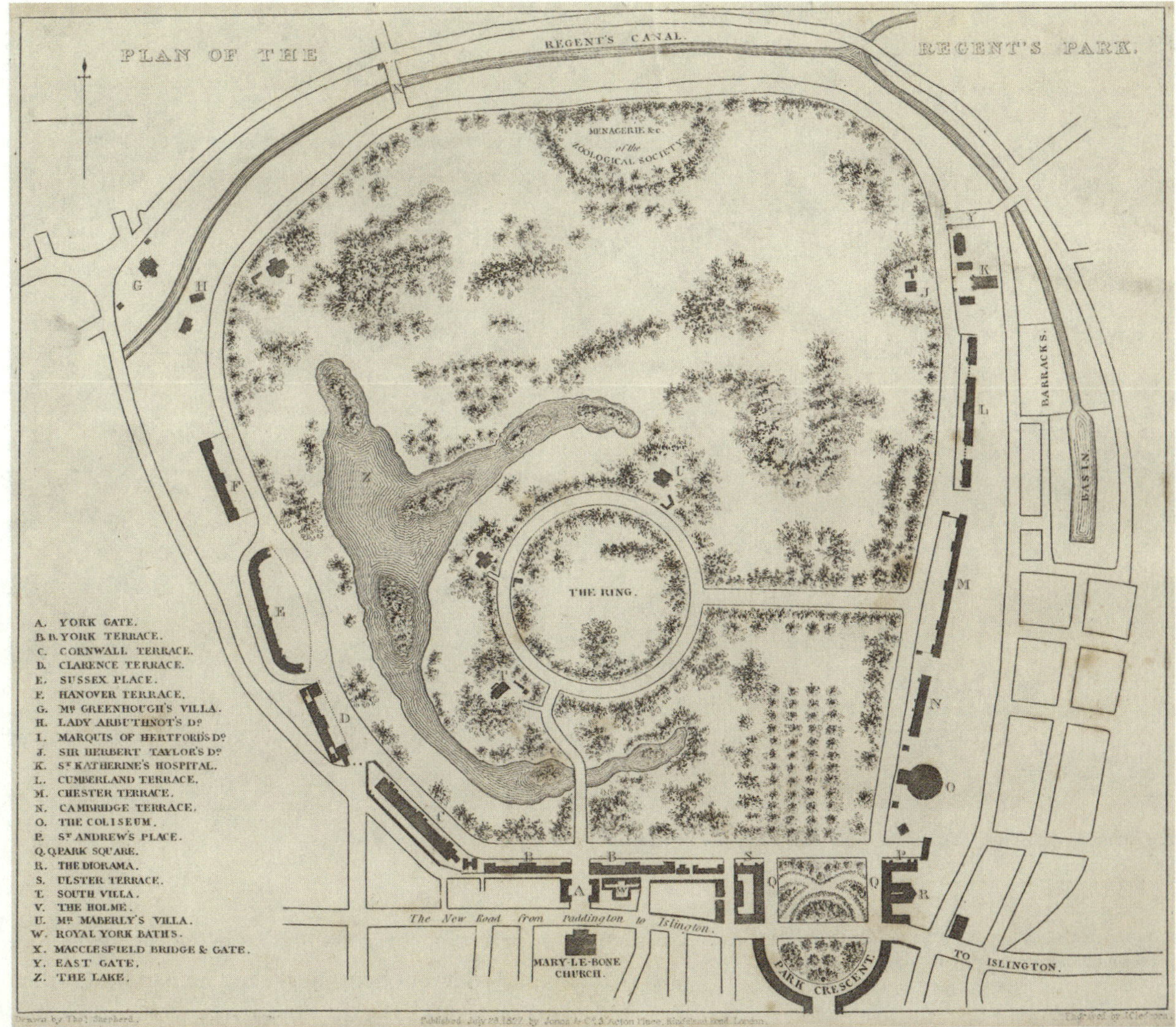

Plan of the Regent's Park, John Cleghorn. Etching on paper, 1827. *(Yale Center for British Art, Paul Mellon Collection)*

vast clouds of an indifferent world, exposed; tortured; and why should she suffer? Why?

She frowned; she stamped her foot.[176] She must go back again to Septimus since it was almost time for them to be going to Sir William Bradshaw. She must go back and tell him, go back to him sitting there on the green chair under the tree, talking to himself, or to that dead man Evans, whom she had

176 One of the narrator's slyest comedic flourishes is the transformation of men and women into children: Clarissa ascending the staircase like "a child exploring a tower"; Peter sleeping next to a baby as a nurse watches over them both; Rezia stamping her foot like a toddler after colliding with little Elise Mitchell. "Suddenly she got cross, frowned, complained of the heat, seemed about to cry, precisely like a child of six," wrote Woolf of Lydia Lopokova, her model for Rezia, after spending the afternoon with her

Children playing in Regent's Park, c. 1920. *(UK Photo and Social History Archive)*

and John Maynard Keynes in September 1923. The novel's metamorphoses vary in sophistication. Some are merely gestural, others more dramatically psychological. But whether as an infant, a child, or an adolescent, the regression to youth seems to protest the intrusion of death into the present, turning back human time.

177 Located in Richmond upon Thames, Hampton Court Palace was built in the early sixteenth century for Cardinal Thomas Wolsey, one of King Henry VIII's favorite advisers. When Wolsey fell from favor in 1529, he felt pressure to "gift" the palace to the king to get back in his good graces—an unsuccessful gambit, for Wolsey was subsequently stripped of his office and retreated in fear and shame to Yorkshire, where he died within the next year.

Henry VIII expanded the original structure, a Renaissance cardinal's palace built from Tudor brick,

only seen once for a moment in the shop. He had seemed a nice quiet man; a great friend of Septimus's, and he had been killed in the War. But such things happen to every one. Every one has friends who were killed in the War. Every one gives up something when they marry. She had given up her home. She had come to live here, in this awful city. But Septimus let himself think about horrible things, as she could too, if she tried. He had grown stranger and stranger. He said people were talking behind the bedroom walls. Mrs. Filmer thought it odd. He saw things too—he had seen an old woman's head in the middle of a fern. Yet he could be happy when he chose. They went to Hampton Court[177] on top of a bus, and they were perfectly happy. All the little red and yellow flowers were out on the grass, like floating lamps he said, and talked and chattered and laughed, making up stories. Suddenly he said, "Now we will kill ourselves," when they were standing by the river, and he looked at it with a look which she had seen in his eyes when a train went by, or an omnibus—a look as if something fascinated him; and she felt he was going from her and she caught him by the arm. But going home he was perfectly quiet—perfectly reasonable. He would argue with her about killing themselves; and explain how wicked people were; how he could see them making up lies as they passed in the street. He knew all their thoughts, he said; he knew everything. He knew the meaning of the world, he said.

Then when they got back he could hardly walk. He lay on the sofa and made her hold his hand to prevent him from falling down, down, he cried, into the flames! and saw faces laughing at him, calling him horrible disgusting names, from the walls, and hands pointing round the screen. Yet they were quite alone. But he began to talk aloud, answering people, arguing, laughing, crying, getting very excited and making her write things

to include the great hall and more elaborate galleries. The gatehouse in the inner court was adorned with the Hampton Court astronomical clock, whose three copper dials showed the hour, the month, the phases of the moon, the age of the moon, the sign of the zodiac, and high water at London Bridge. In 1689, William III had half the Tudor palace demolished and hired the architect Christopher Wren to replace it with a Baroque palace reminiscent of Versailles. George I and George II were the last monarchs to live at Hampton Court, after which Queen Victoria opened it to the public, making it one of England's most popular tourist destinations.

Woolf visited Hampton Court for the first time as a child in 1893 and recalled little of it. Her second visit took place on a chilly, idle summer afternoon in July 1903. "My one visit ten years ago, had not left in my mind any adequate picture of the beauty & space of this old garden," she wrote in her diary. "I had forgotten too the richness of the dark red palace itself. At first I felt simply inclined to pace slowly up & down the terrace & let my eye rest first on the smooth turf lit by brilliant flowers, then on the perfectly satisfying shape of the palace. But it was cold, & we were hungry, & somewhat to our surprise, half London apparently had the same idea of visiting Hampton Court at the same day & hour as we had. The terraces & the turf which I felt ought only to have been peopled by ladies in brocade & gentlemen in knee breeches & swords, swarmed with a very different class of person—perhaps more moral than their ancestors of Charles 2nds time, but in penalty for it far less ornamental. I could not help regretting the improvement in morality." Wandering through the galleries, bedrooms, and antechambers, through once-resplendent rooms now transformed into instructive tourist attractions, her nostalgia for the English aristocracy swelled into something "absurd," she wrote—an implacable longing for "a less machine driven, & sunnier age than ours."

The luster of Hampton Court would fade in her later fiction, particularly *The Waves*. Then Hampton Court would evoke a jadedness of spirit, the loss of youthful excitement. "'Hampton Court,' said Bernard. 'Hampton Court. This is our meeting-place. Behold the red chimneys, the square battlements of Hampton Court. The tone of my voice as I say "Hampton Court" proves that I am middle-aged. Ten years, fifteen years ago, I should have said "Hampton Court?" with interrogation—what will it be like? Will there be lakes, mazes? Or with anticipation, What is going to happen to me here? Whom shall I meet? Now, Hampton Court—Hampton Court—the

Hampton Court astronomical clock, London, 2009. *(The Royal Parks / Man Vyi)*

Hampton Court Palace, England, artist unknown. Oil on canvas, c. 1900.. *(Library of Congress)*

down.[178] Perfect nonsense it was; about death; about Miss Isabel Pole. She could stand it no longer. She would go back.

She was close to him now, could see him staring at the sky, muttering, clasping his hands. Yet Dr. Holmes said there was nothing the matter with him. What, then, had happened—why had he gone, then, why, when she sat by him, did he start, frown at her, move away, and point at her hand, take her hand, look at it terrified?

Was it that she had taken off her wedding ring? "My hand has grown so thin," she said; "I have put it in my purse," she told him.

He dropped her hand. Their marriage was over, he thought,

words beat a gong in the space which I have so laboriously cleared with half a dozen telephone messages and postcards, give off ring after ring of sound, booming, sonorous.'"

178 In an article published in the *Lancet* on February 13, 1915, Dr. Charles S. Myers, a captain in the Royal Army Medical Corps (RAMC), offered the first detailed medical account of what others had started to call "shell shock." He observed three "nervy" patients, all combat veterans who had suffered injuries from an exploding shell. The three men each complained of reduced vision, reduced acuity of taste and smell, constipation, and amnesia. Some suffered from sleeplessness, others from tremors. Of his most affected patient, Myers wrote, "Distant vision, he says, is affected, and objects and type become blurred when long looked at. He has slept very little the last two nights. . . . Abdomen, general

Chapel at Hampton Court Palace, from *A Summer's Day at Hampton Court*, Edward Jesse, 1839.

with agony, with relief. The rope was cut; he mounted; he was free, as it was decreed that he, Septimus, the lord of men, should be free; alone (since his wife had thrown away her wedding ring; since she had left him), he, Septimus, was alone, called forth in advance of the mass of men to hear the truth, to learn the meaning, which now at last, after all the toils of civilisation—Greeks, Romans, Shakespeare, Darwin, and now himself—was to be given whole to . . . . "To whom?" he asked aloud, "To the Prime Minister," the voices which rustled above his head replied. The supreme secret must be told to the Cabinet; first, that trees are alive; next, there is no crime; next, love, universal love, he mut-

spasm of muscles of wall on being touched. Hands tremulous."

Over the next four years, "shell shock" would become a commonly discussed ailment, though there was little agreement over the nature of its cause. Many doctors believed that it resulted from a physical disruption to the brain—a concussion, a slow poisoning, or a vacuum that had opened in the patient's skull when the shell had exploded. Others understood it to be a psychological condition, but found themselves baffled by its wide and contradictory range of symptoms. Writing in the *British Medical Journal* on April 13, 1918, Dr. Ernest W. White, honorary lieutenant colonel in the RAMC, described the psychological state of his shell-shocked patient as alternately "confusional, melancholic, delusional, stuporose, and maniacal," though he noted "relatively few cases of mania to melancholia." Still others insisted that shell shock could not be distinguished from cowardice, a failure to govern one's mind in the face of death, more prominent among the working class than the middle class. Shell-shocked ex-servicemen were thought to be weak, degenerate, undisciplined, and uneducated. The diagnosis "shell shock," with its pejorative implications of unmanly hysteria, was more often applied to soldiers than to officers, who were diagnosed with "neurasthenia" or depression.

By 1920, 65,000 British veterans were drawing disability benefits for neurasthenia and 900 remained hospitalized. That same year, in the House of Lords, Lord Southborough proposed a committee to investigate shell shock. "All would desire to forget it—to forget . . . the roll of insanity, suicide, and death," he proclaimed. "But, my Lords, we cannot do this, because a great number of cases of those who suffer from shell-shock and its allied disorders are still upon our hands and they deserve our sympathy and care." Published in 1922, the report of the War Office committee included over fifty pages of interviews with shell-shocked soldiers and the doctors who treated them. Urging sympathy over skepticism, the committee unanimously agreed that shell shock was "a gross and costly misnomer, and that the term should be eliminated from our nomenclature." They differentiated between three different cases of shell shock: (1) "Genuine concussion without visible wound as a result of shell explosion"; (2) "Emotional shock, either acute in men with a neuropathic predisposition, or developing slowly as a result of prolonged strain and terrifying experience"; and (3) "Nervous and mental exhaustion, the result of prolonged strain and hardship." Recommended treatments ranged from bed rest with a strictly controlled diet to psychotherapy, to admission to a base hospital.

Like any British citizen at the time, Woolf would have been familiar with shell shock. But Septimus's symptoms, his voices, visions, and sudden attacks of what she called the "fidgets," drew as much on her breakdowns as they did on the popular perception of shell shock. Septimus should not be "founded on me," but "might be left vague," she wrote in her notes on the manuscript of *Mrs. Dalloway*. In a diary entry dated June 19, 1923, she was more explicit about the personal dimension of "the mad part." "Am I writing The Hours from deep emotion?" she asked. "Of course the mad part tries me so much, makes my mind squint so badly that I can hardly face spending the next weeks at it."

Septimus's "insane" vision of the world's connectivity sits closer to the creative vision of a novelist or a poet than it does to the medical literature on shell shock. Convinced of his genius and grandeur, Septimus anoints himself a truth-teller whose artistic consciousness assimilates and transforms the writing of his predecessors: the sonnets of William Shakespeare, the odes of John Keats, and the lyrics of T. S. Eliot. From the scene in Regent's Park to his suicide, the arc of his madness literalizes Eliot's argument in his 1919 essay "Tradition and the Individual Talent" about the poet's submission to artistic truth: "What happens is a continual surrender of himself as he is at the moment to something which is more valuable. The progress of an artist is a continual self-sacrifice, a continual extinction of personality."

179 "On a Faithful Friend," the first piece Woolf produced for publication in 1905, was an obituary of her childhood family dog Shag, a mongrel with the head and body of a collie and "terribly Skye-terrier legs." Septimus's insane belief that the animal is turning into a man reverses Woolf's sane transformation of men into animals throughout the novel.

180 In her notebook, Woolf insisted that Septimus not be a "degenerate" type. Even amid his insanity, he had to have access to rational thought and to a sense of irony, however faint. Here his will to rationality—he repeats his mocking command from p. 39 that "one must be scientific"—attaches itself to the language of Darwin's theory of evolution. "<At> ~~a certain pitch of evolution~~," Woolf crossed out in the manuscript of "The Hours." Several paragraphs later, when Septimus imagines himself a drowned sailor, she wrote, and then cut from the final version: "[B]ut I go and come through these waters . . . only a green mist. ~~at last our~~ because of Darwin, evolution, (A.D. stands for Anno Darwini in future he ~~th said~~ muttered)."

tered, gasping, trembling, painfully drawing out these profound truths which needed, so deep were they, so difficult, an immense effort to speak out, but the world was entirely changed by them for ever.

No crime; love; he repeated, fumbling for his card and pencil, when a Skye terrier snuffed his trousers and he started in an agony of fear. It was turning into a man! He could not watch it happen! It was horrible, terrible to see a dog become a man![179] At once the dog trotted away.

Heaven was divinely merciful, infinitely benignant. It spared him, pardoned his weakness. But what was the scientific explanation (for one must be scientific above all things)?[180] Why could he see through bodies, see into the future, when dogs will become men? It was the heat wave presumably, operating upon a brain made sensitive by eons of evolution. Scientifically speaking, the flesh was melted off the world.[181] His body was macerated until only the nerve fibres were left. It was spread like a veil upon a rock.[182]

He lay back in his chair, exhausted but upheld. He lay resting, waiting, before he again interpreted, with effort, with agony, to mankind. He lay very high, on the back of the world. The earth thrilled beneath him. Red flowers grew through his flesh; their stiff leaves rustled by his head. Music began clanging against the rocks up here. It is a motor horn down in the street, he muttered; but up here it cannoned from rock to rock, divided, met in shocks of sound which rose in smooth columns (that music should be visible was a discovery) and became an anthem, an anthem twined round now by a shepherd boy's piping (That's an old man playing a penny whistle[183] by the public-house, he muttered) which, as the boy stood still, came bubbling from his pipe, and then, as he climbed higher, made its exquisite plaint while the traffic passed beneath. The boy's elegy is played among the traffic, thought Septimus.[184] Now he withdraws up into the snows, and roses hang about him—the thick red roses which grow on my bedroom wall, he reminded himself. The music stopped. He has his penny, he reasoned it out, and has gone on to the next public-house.

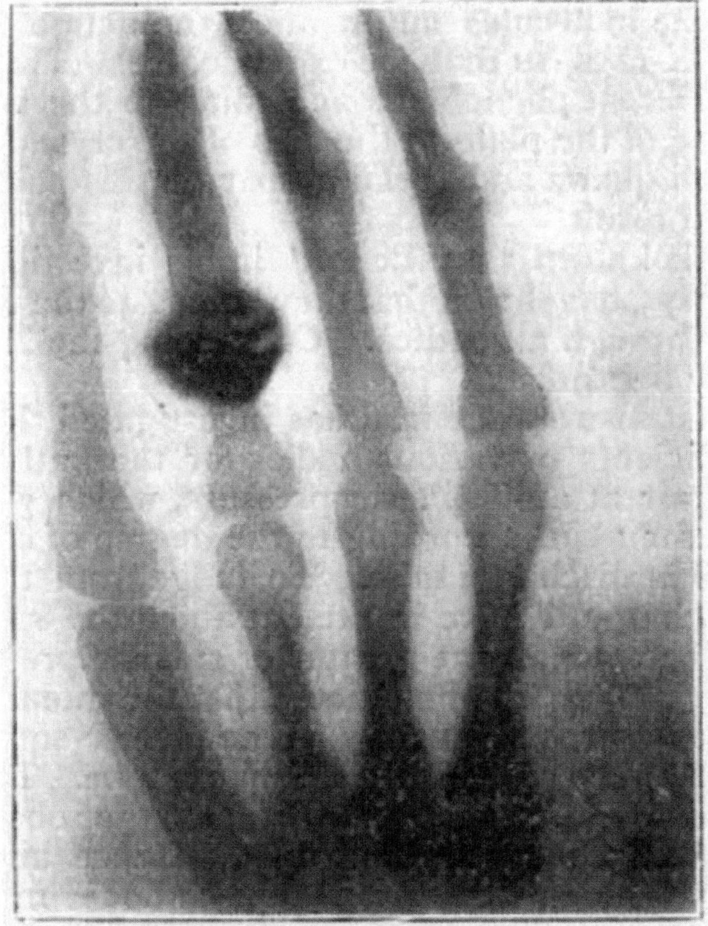

Fig. 1.—Photograph of the bones in the fingers of a living human hand. The third finger has a ring upon it.

W. C. Röntgen, "On a New Kind of Rays." *Nature* 53 (January 23, 1896), 276, fig. 1. *(Reprinted by permission from Springer Nature:* Nature. *Röntgen, W. C. "On a New Kind of Rays."* Nature, *vol. 53, 23 Jan. 1896, p. 276, fig. 1. Copyright 1896 Nature Publishing Group)*

181 Septimus's belief that he can "see through bodies" recalls Woolf's fascination with X-rays, which she encountered for the first time when she was fourteen years old. In her diary entry of January 9, 1897, she wrote of a trip to the Polytechnic Young Men's Christian Institute in London with Vanessa and Adrian: "We went to see the Animatographs, but by some mistake were hustled in to the wrong room, and had a lecture on the Rontgen Rays instead. We were shown photographs of normal hands and diseased hands, a baby, and a puppy—and a lady and gentleman from the audience had their hands photographed—the gent. declared that a piece of needle was in his hand, but the photograph did not discover it." For Michael Whitworth, Woolf's fascination with the X-ray invites us to question "the idea of solidity": the ease with which the flesh, the outer covering of the body, melts away and becomes supremely receptive to the world in Septimus's imagination.

182 Among the many books that Woolf read while writing *Mrs. Dalloway*, *The Odyssey* stands out for its description of how Odysseus, battered by Poseidon's angry waves, receives a magic veil from the goddess Ino, allowing him to land on the rocky shore of Phaecia with his skin torn, but his bones unbroken. As Anne Fernald observes, the language Woolf uses to describe Septimus echoes her notes on Odysseus's body: "At last he was dashed against rocks; a very odd image comes—his skin was torn off by the rocks."

183 "The Barrel organ?" wondered Woolf in her notebook on July 22, 1923, as she listed all the sounds Septimus would hear and the beauty he would find in them. "Beauty of an impersonal kind is still real. But human beings betray each other," she concluded, cryptically.

184 Recall the interlude of the solitary traveler, his retreat from urban modernity into a pastoral dream world. We hear echoes of it in Septimus's hallucination of the motor horn and the penny whistle carrying the tune of a shepherd boy's elegy, the sound of his pipe mingling with the sounds of the traffic below. Emma Sutton suggests that the shepherd boy alludes to Richard Wagner's opera *Tristan und Isolde*. (Woolf had gone to the annual Wagner festival in Bayreuth with Adrian in 1909 and had seen *Siegfried* with Leonard in 1911.) The third act of *Tristan und Isolde* opens with a young shepherd playing a mournful refrain on his pipe as Tristan waits for Isolde to arrive. The melody reminds

But he himself remained high on his rock, like a drowned sailor on a rock.[185] I leant over the edge of the boat and fell down, he thought. I went under the sea. I have been dead, and yet am now alive, but let me rest still, he begged (he was talking to himself again—it was awful, awful!);[186] and as, before waking, the voices of birds and the sound of wheels chime and chatter in a queer harmony, grow louder and louder, and the sleeper feels himself drawing to the shores of life, so he felt himself drawing towards life, the sun growing hotter, cries sounding louder, something tremendous about to happen.

He had only to open his eyes; but a weight was on them; a fear. He strained; he pushed; he looked; he saw Regent's Park before him.[187] Long streamers of sunlight fawned at his feet. The trees waved, brandished. We welcome, the world seemed to say; we accept; we create. Beauty, the world seemed to say. And as if to prove it (scientifically) wherever he looked, at the houses, at the railings, at the antelopes stretching over the palings, beauty sprang instantly. To watch a leaf quivering in the rush of air was an exquisite joy. Up in the sky swallows swooping, swerving, flinging themselves in and out, round and round, yet always with perfect control as if elastics held them; and the flies rising and falling; and the sun spotting now this leaf, now that, in mockery, dazzling it with soft gold in pure good temper; and now and again some chime (it might be a motor horn) tinkling divinely on the grass stalks—all of this, calm and reasonable as it was, made out of ordinary things as it was, was the truth now; beauty, that was the truth now. Beauty was everywhere.[188]

"It is time," said Rezia.

The word "time" split its husk; poured its riches over him;[189] and from his lips fell like shells, like shavings from a plane,[190] without his making them, hard, white, imperishable, words, and flew to attach themselves to their places in an ode to Time; an immortal ode to Time. He sang. Evans answered from behind the tree. The dead were in Thessaly,[191] Evans sang, among the orchids.[192] There they waited till the War was over, and now the dead, now Evans himself—

Tristan of the death of his parents and his own fate to "yearn and die": "*Sehnen! Sehnen! Im Sterben mich zu sehnen, vor Sehnsucht nicht zu sterben!*" ("Longing! Longing! In death longing, for longing not to die!")

185 The "drowned sailor on a rock" chimes with T. S. Eliot's description of a pack of Tarot cards in his poem *The Waste Land* (1922): "Is your card, the drowned Phoenician Sailor, / (Those are pearls that were his eyes. Look!) / Here is Belladonna, the Lady of the Rocks." Woolf first heard Eliot recite *The Waste Land* when he dined with her and Leonard on June 18, 1922. "He sang it & chanted it rhythmed it," she wrote in her diary the following week. "It has great beauty & force of phrase: symmetry; & tensity. What connects it together, I'm not so sure." The Hogarth Press published the first 460 English copies of *The Waste Land* the next year, with Woolf handsetting the poem herself. "I have just finished setting up the whole of Mr Eliots poem with my own hands: you see how my hand trembles," she wrote in a letter on July 8, 1923. "Don't blame your eyes. It is my writing."

186 "It was awful, awful!" echoes Peter's cry from p. 94. It is unclear from whose mind the cry issues. The parenthetical suggests that it may be Rezia watching Septimus, but it also could be the narrator's interjection, a collective recognition of the awful despair of Septimus's condition. Whoever the cry belongs to, it explicitly draws a parallel between Peter and Septimus that we can trace through the end of this paragraph and into the next. Peter, the sleeper, feels his spirit "drawing to the shores of life" as he wakes from his dream in Regent's Park. Septimus, the dead man, feels himself "drawing towards life" as his mind rushes toward an ecstatic communion with nature.

187 "I am now in the thick of the mad scene in Regents Park," Woolf wrote in her diary on October 15, 1923. "I find I write it by clinging as tight to fact as I can, & write perhaps 50 words a morning. This I must re-write some day. I think the design is more remarkable than in any of my books. I daresay I shan't be able to carry it out. I am stuffed with ideas for it. I feel I can use up everything I've ever thought." Septimus's desire for all the poetry he has read and all the ideas he has held in his mind, for the world in all its terror and glory to converge in a single, exquisite moment of beauty cannot be spoken out loud. The more his excesses of thought run up against his limits of expression the more he begins to resemble Woolf as she wrote him into existence, struggling to eke out "perhaps 50 words a morning" when she felt "stuffed with ideas."

"For God's sake don't come!" Septimus cried out. For he could not look upon the dead.

But the branches parted. A man in grey was actually walking towards them. It was Evans! But no mud was on him; no wounds; he was not changed. I must tell the whole world, Septimus cried, raising his hand (as the dead man in the grey suit came nearer), raising his hand like some colossal figure who has lamented the fate of man for ages in the desert alone with his hands pressed to his forehead, furrows of despair on his cheeks, and now sees light on the desert's edge which broadens and strikes the iron-black figure (and Septimus half rose from his chair), and with legions of men prostrate behind him he, the giant mourner, receives for one moment on his face the whole—

Regents Park, George Harvey. Watercolor, c. 1875. *(Paul Mellon Collection, Yale Center for British Art)*

188 "Was he not like Keats," asks Isabel Pole, the woman whom Septimus once loved, on p. 118. Septimus's reverie in Regent's Park refashions Keats's "Ode on a Grecian Urn" (1819), a "flowery tale" about a long-lost pastoral world, glimpsed through the melodies of "soft pipes." The last sentences of Septimus's reverie (". . . beauty, that was the truth now. Beauty was everywhere") echo the last lines of Keats's poem: "'Beauty is truth, truth beauty,'—that is all / Ye know on earth, and all ye need to know." The reference to Keats is made more explicit in the manuscript of "The Hours," where Woolf writes: "~~This ode to Time will lives, forever~~. saw it join the rest of the ode ~~to Time~~ this, immortal, ode to Time. This poem which was ~~faultless~~ <flawless> from its birth."

The Waste Land, exterior cover.
(Frances Hooper Collection of Virginia Woolf Books and Manuscripts, Smith College Special Collections)

189 The idea that the word "time" could "split its husk" recalls Clarissa's description of revelation on p. 53: the moment when one "felt the world come closer, swollen with some astonishing significance, some pressure of rapture, which split its thin skin and gushed and poured with an extraordinary alleviation over the cracks and sores." Yet "time," when it splits its husk, exposes its contamination by history, by the "shells, like shavings from a plane" that have attached themselves to the word and annihilated Septimus's attempt to speak of beauty in a language anyone can comprehend. The idea of revelation is suddenly transfigured from its earlier use. No longer is it a crocus burning behind the walled-in garden of memory—the revelation of war is an open, weeping sore. The human body has been cracked, made filthy with death, infected by history, and set to walk

"But I am so unhappy, Septimus," said Rezia, trying to make him sit down.

The millions lamented; for ages they had sorrowed. He would turn round, he would tell them in a few moments, only a few moments more, of this relief, of this joy, of this astonishing revelation—

"The time, Septimus," Rezia repeated. "What is the time?"

He was talking, he was starting, this man must notice him. He was looking at them.

"I will tell you the time," said Septimus, very slowly, very drowsily, smiling mysteriously at the dead man in the grey suit. As he sat smiling, the quarter struck—the quarter to twelve.

And that is being young, Peter Walsh thought as he passed them.[193] To be having an awful scene—the poor girl looked absolutely desperate—in the middle of the morning. But what was it about, he wondered; what had the young man in the overcoat been saying to her to make her look like that; what awful fix had they got themselves into, both to look so desperate as that on a fine summer morning? The amusing thing about coming back to England, after five years, was the way it made, anyhow the first days, things stand out as if one had never seen them before; lovers squabbling under a tree; the domestic family life of the parks. Never had he seen London look so enchanting—the softness of the distances; the richness; the greenness; the civilisation, after India, he thought, strolling across the grass.

This susceptibility to impressions had been his undoing, no doubt. Still at his age he had, like a boy or a girl even, these alternations of mood; good days, bad days, for no reason whatever, happiness from a pretty face, downright misery at the sight of a frump. After India of course one fell in love with every woman one met. There was a freshness about them; even the poorest dressed better than five years ago surely; and to his eye the fashions had never been so becoming; the long black cloaks; the slimness; the elegance; and then the delicious and

around London as if nothing at all has changed. All this Septimus sees in the figure of Evans.

190 The simile also appears in Woolf's diary entry of June 13, 1923, to describe a lunch she had with Lady Sibyl Colefax, an English socialite, interior decorator, and salonnière who would not stop speaking of trivial things: "That was Derby Day & it rained, & all the light was brown & cold, & she went on talking talking, in consecutive sentences like the shavings that come from planes, artificial, but unbroken."

191 Thessaly is a region in northern Greece. It appears in Homer's *Odyssey* as Aeolia, the kingdom of Aeolus, keeper of storm winds strong enough to wreak devastation on mankind.

192 In the manuscript of "The Hours," Septimus imagines Evans as "a Greek nightingale" who sings the ode Septimus imagines before joining the dead poets in Thessaly. The reference is to Keats's "Ode to a Nightingale," whose speaker, numbed by his knowledge of death, hears the bird, the "light-winged Dryad of the trees," sing of an eternal summer amid the branches and leaves.

193 Septimus's confusion of Peter for Evans, "the dead man in the grey suit," seems to confirm Peter's fear of death, of becoming "old, or set, or dried." While Peter misreads the situation between Septimus and Rezia, dismissing them as "lovers squabbling under a tree," turning them into backdrop for his feelings of enchantment, Septimus correctly, though inadvertently, identifies Peter's slow amble toward death as the truth of his being.

apparently universal habit of paint. Every woman, even the most respectable, had roses blooming under glass; lips cut with a knife; curls of Indian ink; there was design, art, everywhere; a change of some sort had undoubtedly taken place. What did the young people think about? Peter Walsh asked himself.

Those five years—1918 to 1923—had been, he suspected, somehow very important.[194] People looked different. Newspapers seemed different. Now, for instance, there was a man writing quite openly in one of the respectable weeklies about water-closets.[195] That you couldn't have done ten years ago—written quite openly about water-closets in a respectable weekly. And then this taking out a stick of rouge, or a powder-puff, and making up in public. On board ship coming home there were lots of young men and girls—Betty and Bertie he remembered in particular—carrying on quite openly; the old mother sitting and watching them with her knitting, cool as a cucumber. The girl would stand still and powder her nose in front of every one. And they weren't engaged; just having a good time; no feelings hurt on either side. As hard as nails she was—Betty Whatshername—but a thorough good sort. She would make a very good wife at thirty—she would marry when it suited her to marry; marry some rich man and live in a large house near Manchester.

Who was it now who had done that? Peter Walsh asked himself, turning into the Broad Walk—married a rich man and lived in a large house near Manchester? Somebody who had written him a long, gushing letter quite lately about "blue hydrangeas." It was seeing blue hydrangeas that made her think of him and the old days—Sally Seton, of course! It was Sally Seton—the last person in the world one would have expected to marry a rich man and live in a large house near Manchester, the wild, the daring, the romantic Sally!

But of all that ancient lot, Clarissa's friends—Whitbreads, Kindersleys, Cunninghams, Kinloch-Jones's—Sally was probably the best. She tried to get hold of things by the right end

194 As Alex Zwerdling argues, Peter's significance arises from his status as an outsider, returning to England after five years abroad. He is the only character in *Mrs. Dalloway* who can appreciate the dramatic transformation of society after the First World War. Though fixated as he is on young women and their sexual promise, he largely misses the point of what he observes. "Water-closets," and "powder-puffs" have no importance in and of themselves. They are symptoms of the decline of the conservative governing class. "The early 1920s brought to an end the Conservative-Liberal coalition in British politics; the elections of 1922 and 1923 marked the eclipse of the Liberals and the rise of Labour," Zwerdling writes. "For the first time the Labour Party became the official government opposition. It was only a matter of time before this 'socialist' power, with its putative threat to the governing classes examined in the novel, would be in office."

195 Flush toilets. "If the British spoke openly about W.C.'s, & copulation, then they might be stirred by universal emotions," Woolf wrote in her diary on January 3, 1915.

anyhow. She saw through Hugh Whitbread anyhow—the admirable Hugh—when Clarissa and the rest were at his feet.

"The Whitbreads?" he could hear her saying. "Who are the Whitbreads? Coal merchants. Respectable tradespeople."

Hugh she detested for some reason. He thought of nothing but his own appearance, she said. He ought to have been a Duke. He would be certain to marry one of the Royal Princesses. And of course Hugh had the most extraordinary, the most natural, the most sublime respect for the British aristocracy of any human being he had ever come across. Even Clarissa had to own that. Oh, but he was such a dear, so unselfish, gave up shooting to please his old mother—remember his aunts' birthdays, and so on.

Sally, to do her justice, saw through all that. One of the things he remembered best was an argument one Sunday morning at Bourton about women's rights (that antediluvian topic),[196] when Sally suddenly lost her temper, flared up, and told Hugh that he represented all that was most detestable in British middle-class life. She told him that she considered him responsible for the state of "those poor girls in Piccadilly"[197]—Hugh, the perfect gentleman, poor Hugh!—never did a man look more horrified! She did it on purpose, she said afterwards (for they used to get together in the vegetable garden and compare notes). "He's read nothing, thought nothing, felt nothing," he could hear her saying in that very emphatic voice which carried so much farther than she knew. The stable boys had more life in them than Hugh, she said. He was a perfect specimen of the public school type,[198] she said. No country but England could have produced him. She was really spiteful, for some reason; had some grudge against him. Something had happened—he forgot what—in the smoking-room. He had insulted her—kissed her? Incredible! Nobody believed a word against Hugh, of course. Who could? Kissing Sally in the smoking-room! If it had been some Honourable Edith or Lady Violet, perhaps; but not that ragamuffin Sally without a penny to her name, and a father or a mother gambling at Monte Carlo. For of all the people he had ever met Hugh was the greatest snob—the most obsequious—no, he didn't cringe exactly. He

196 Woolf's attitude toward "women's rights" and, more broadly, feminist struggle remains a richly controversial subject. In her fascinating study *Virginia Woolf as Feminist*, Naomi Black traces Woolf's involvement with women's activism, beginning in January 1910, when Virginia Stephen addressed envelopes for the People's Suffrage Federation (PSF). Initially, her participation was scattered, slipshod: two suffrage meetings just before Christmas later that year and a suffrage bazaar with Leonard in 1912. "My time has been wasted a good deal upon Suffrage," she complained in a letter to Violet Dickinson in 1910. Her feelings on winning "the vote" in 1918 were tepid. The ineloquence of the speakers at the victory rally she and Leonard attended "seemed to beat the waves in vain." She treated suffrage as if it offered confirmation of her value as an individual political actor; as if it were something to be taken personally, rather than politically; and, taking it personally, she judged herself unimpressed by what it had to offer. "I don't feel much more important—perhaps slightly so," she wrote. "It's like a knighthood; might be useful to impress people one despises. But there are other aspects of it naturally."

But if she remained indifferent to the explicitly political activities of the women's movement, she became deeply invested in its literary activities. In 1913, she accompanied Leonard to Manchester, Liverpool, Leeds, Glasgow, Leicester, and Newcastle for the annual congresses of the Women's Co-operative Guild (WCG). While recovering from her suicide attempt in 1914, she read the letters that would become the WCG publication *Maternity: Letters from Working Women*, which she urged Margaret Llewelyn Davies, general secretary of the WCG, to publish in 1915. She developed a close friendship with Davies, and when Davies edited *Life as We Have Known It*, a collection of testimonials from British working-class women, Woolf wrote an introduction for it in 1929 and published it at the Hogarth Press in 1931.

The two most markedly feminist of Woolf's writings are her book-length essays *A Room of One's Own* (1929) and *Three Guineas* (1938). *A Room of One's Own* agitates for economic independence and privacy, as well as for equality of education within families. (Woolf's brothers, Thoby and Adrian, had both attended public schools and Cambridge, unlike Woolf, who had little formal education.) As Black notes, Woolf echoed the language of the WCG when she demanded for working women "reformed divorce laws, minimum wages, and the modernization of household equipment." *Three Guineas* extends the argument from *A Room of One's Own* to include in its list of long-term demands "a women's party in electoral politics, progressive education . . . and state subsidies for underpaid or unemployed single

was too much of a prig for that. A first-rate valet was the obvious comparison—somebody who walked behind carrying suit cases; could be trusted to send telegrams—indispensable to hostesses. And he'd found his job—married his Honourable Evelyn; got some little post at Court, looked after the King's cellars, polished the Imperial shoe-buckles, went about in knee-breeches and lace ruffles. How remorseless life is! A little job at Court!

He had married this lady, the Honourable Evelyn, and they lived hereabouts, so he thought (looking at the pompous houses overlooking the Park), for he had lunched there once in a house which had, like all Hugh's possessions, something that no other house could possibly have—linen cupboards it might have been. You had to go and look at them—you had to spend a great deal of time always admiring whatever it was—linen cupboards, pillow-cases, old oak furniture, pictures, which Hugh had picked up for an old song. But Mrs. Hugh sometimes gave the show away. She was one of those obscure mouse-like little women who admire big men. She was almost negligible. Then suddenly she would say something quite unexpected—something sharp. She had the relics of the grand manner, perhaps. The steam coal was a little too strong for her—it made the atmosphere thick. And so there they lived, with their linen cupboards and their old masters and their pillow-cases fringed with real lace, at the rate of five or ten thousand a year presumably, while he, who was two years older than Hugh, cadged for a job.

At fifty-three he had to come and ask them to put him into some secretary's office, to find him some usher's job teaching little boys Latin, at the beck and call of some mandarin in an office, something that brought in five hundred a year; for if he married Daisy, even with his pension, they could never do on less. Whitbread could do it presumably; or Dalloway. He didn't mind what he asked Dalloway. He was a thorough good sort; a bit limited; a bit thick in the head; yes; but a thorough good sort. Whatever he took up he did in the same matter-of-fact sensible way; without a touch of imagination, without a spark of brilliancy, but with the inexplicable niceness of his type. He ought

women as well as for wives and mothers." In the short term, Woolf advocated for anesthesia during childbirth, equal citizenship, and equal access for women to all male-dominated institutions.

Despite her writing, Woolf harbored an antipathy toward anything identifiably feminist. Partially this was for strategic reasons. She believed feminism tempted backlash. As she proposed in *A Room of One's Own*, "the Suffrage campaign" is "no doubt to blame" for the sex-consciousness of the age. "And when one is challenged, even by a few women in black bonnets, one retaliates, if one has never been challenged before, rather excessively," Woolf wrote. Yet, as Black argues, Woolf believed that the most powerful manifestation of her feminist activism was her writing. "Societies seem wrong for me," she observed in a 1936 letter. "What can I do but Write?"

197 "Those poor girls in Piccadilly" refers to the prostitutes of Piccadilly Circus, whom Woolf first mentioned in *The Voyage Out*. "'Tell me,'" Rachel Vinrace says to Helen Ambrose. "'What are those women in Piccadilly?' 'In Piccadilly? They are prostitutes,' said Helen." More pointedly than *The Voyage Out*, *Mrs. Dalloway* uses the "poor girls in Piccadilly" to make a larger point about where responsibility lies in the social system. As Jeremy Hawthorn has argued, Sally Seton's suggestion that conservative hypocrisy, emblematized by the secretly lustful but outwardly civilized Hugh, has led to the rise of prostitution is hardly as far-fetched as Hugh believes it to be. Both Richard Dalloway and Peter Walsh acknowledge prostitution as a social problem exacerbated by conservative indifference to structural inequality, with Peter claiming on p. 214, "God knows, the rascals who get hanged for battering the brains of a girl out in a train do less harm on the whole than Hugh Whitbread and his kindness!"

198 The "public school type" (or "private school type" in the United States) would have referred in 1923 to a man who attended one of the seven private all-male boarding schools regulated by the Public Schools Act 1868: Charterhouse School, Eton College, Harrow School, Rugby School, Shrewsbury School, Westminster School, and Winchester College. With their intimate ties to Parliament, the Cabinet, and the military, these schools were essential to the reproduction of the British ruling classes. The manuscript of "The Hours" offers a more spirited sketch of the student these schools produced: "~~They're always the same—these beautiful young men who go to Eton & Oxford~~ . . . . And of course Hugh had the most extraordinary, the most natural respect for the British aristocracy of any human being he'd ever come across. To be a snob on such a scale was almost sublime."

In her diary on June 4, 1923, Woolf recalled a

to have been a country gentleman—he was wasted on politics. He was at his best out of doors, with horses and dogs—how good he was, for instance, when that great shaggy dog of Clarissa's got caught in a trap and had its paw half torn off, and Clarissa turned faint and Dalloway did the whole thing; bandaged, made splints; told Clarissa not to be a fool. That was what she liked him for, perhaps—that was what she needed. "Now, my dear, don't be a fool. Hold this—fetch that," all the time talking to the dog as if it were a human being.

But how could she swallow all that stuff about poetry? How could she let him hold forth about Shakespeare? Seriously and solemnly Richard Dalloway got on his hind legs[199] and said that no decent man ought to read Shakespeare's sonnets because it was like listening at keyholes (besides, the relationship was not one that he approved).[200] No decent man ought to let his wife visit a deceased wife's sister.[201] Incredible! The only thing to do was to pelt him with sugared almonds—it was at dinner. But Clarissa sucked it all in; thought it so honest of him; so independent of him; Heaven knows if she didn't think him the most original mind she'd ever met!

That was one of the bonds between Sally and himself. There was a garden where they used to walk, a walled-in place, with rose-bushes and giant cauliflowers—he could remember Sally tearing off a rose, stopping to exclaim at the beauty of the cabbage leaves in the moonlight (it was extraordinary how vividly it all came back to him, things he hadn't thought of for years), while she implored him, half laughing of course, to carry off Clarissa, to save her from the Hughs and the Dalloways and all the other "perfect gentlemen" who would "stifle her soul" (she wrote reams of poetry in those days), make a mere hostess of her, encourage her worldliness. But one must do Clarissa justice. She wasn't going to marry Hugh anyhow. She had a perfectly clear notion of what she wanted. Her emotions were all on the surface. Beneath, she was very shrewd—a far better judge of character than Sally, for instance, and with it all, purely femi-

weekend spent at Lady Ottoline "Ott" Morrell's country estate in Garsington surrounded by public school types, Oxford boys with "perfect perfect clothes" and "nice socks" who presented with "the same clipped quick speech & politeness, & total insignificance." As peevish as she felt about Ottoline's guests, they inspired her in her writing of *Mrs. Dalloway*, as did her walk around the vegetable garden. "I am a great deal interested suddenly in my book," she wrote. "I want to bring in the despicableness of people like Ott: I want to give the slipperiness of the soul. I have been too tolerant often. The truth is people scarcely care for each other. They have this insane instinct for life. But they never become attached to anything outside themselves." The extended, dispersed, and highly sensual form of being that Woolf imagines for Clarissa and Septimus is distinctly opposed to the public school type's unfeeling rigidity.

199 Septimus's fear that the Skye terrier who climbs his leg is turning into a man on p. 100 is mined for comedy in Peter's memory of how Richard treated Clarissa's dog. Not only did Richard talk to the dog as if it were a human being, but he also talked to Clarissa as if she were a dog. Having addressed her so, his courtship of her must have been equally doggish, with him getting on his hind legs to discourage reading Shakespeare's sonnets. Woolf, who derived great pleasure from speaking of people as if they were animals, often used her imagination to ridicule and intimidate. But she also used it to create a sense of intimacy, fashioning animal nicknames for the people she loved. Leonard was her "mongoose," Vita Sackville-West her "donkey," then her "porpoise."

200 David Bradshaw suggests that Richard is likely referencing the first trial of Oscar Wilde in 1895, when prosecutors submitted as evidence of Wilde's homosexuality his 1889 essay "The Portrait of Mr. W. H.," which suggested that Shakespeare's sonnets were dedicated to a man, Willie Hughes. Asked by the prosecutor if he had ever "adored a young man madly," Wilde replied, "No, not madly; I prefer love—that is a higher form." "Then you have never had that feeling?" the prosecutor pressed. "No," Wilde answered. "The whole idea was borrowed from Shakespeare's sonnets."

201 The Deceased Wife's Sister's Marriage Act 1907 allowed a man to marry his dead wife's sister, a marital arrangement previously forbidden by British law. In 1921, the Deceased Brother's Widow's Marriage Act amended the 1907 act by also permitting a man to marry his dead brother's widow. "When the war took place many men, when they were called up,

nine; with that extraordinary gift, that woman's gift, of making a world of her own wherever she happened to be. She came into a room; she stood, as he had often seen her, in a doorway with lots of people round her. But it was Clarissa one remembered. Not that she was striking; not beautiful at all; there was nothing picturesque about her; she never said anything specially clever; there she was, however; there she was.

No, no, no! He was not in love with her any more! He only felt, after seeing her that morning, among her scissors and silks, making ready for the party, unable to get away from the thought of her; she kept coming back and back like a sleeper jolting against him in a railway carriage; which was not being in love, of course; it was thinking of her, criticising her, starting again, after thirty years, trying to explain her.[202] The obvious thing to say of her was that she was worldly; cared too much for rank and society and getting on in the world—which was true in a sense; she had admitted it to him. (You could always get her to own up if you took the trouble; she was honest.) What she would say was that she hated frumps, fogies, failures, like himself presumably; thought people had no right to slouch about with their hands in their pockets; must do something, be something; and these great swells, these Duchesses, these hoary old Countesses one met in her drawing-room, unspeakably remote as he felt them to be from anything that mattered a straw, stood for something real to her. Lady Bexborough, she said once, held herself upright (so did Clarissa herself; she never lounged in any sense of the word; she was straight as a dart, a little rigid in fact). She said they had a kind of courage which the older she grew the more she respected. In all this there was a great deal of Dalloway, of course; a great deal of the public-spirited, British Empire, tariff-reform, governing-class spirit, which had grown on her, as it tends to do. With twice his wits, she had to see things through his eyes—one of the tragedies of married life. With a mind of her own, she must always be quoting Richard—as if one couldn't know to a tittle what Richard

left their wives and families in the charge of their brothers," explained Lord Newton, who brought the act before Parliament. "Some of these men were killed, and in many instances an affection developed between the brother in-law and the widow." The act went on to specify that a man could not marry his brother's former wife if his brother was still alive.

202 The long stretch of Peter's thought that begins with his denial of his love proceeds to reveal just how in love he remains, and how willingly his memory betrays him.

thought by reading the *Morning Post*[203] of a morning! These parties, for example, were all for him, or for her idea of him (to do Richard justice he would have been happier farming in Norfolk[204]). She made her drawing-room a sort of meeting-place; she had a genius for it. Over and over again he had seen her take some raw youth, twist him, turn him, wake him up; set him going. Infinite numbers of dull people conglomerated round her, of course. But odd unexpected people turned up; an artist sometimes; sometimes a writer; queer fish in that atmosphere. And behind it all was that network of visiting, leaving cards, being kind to people; running about with bunches of flowers, little presents; So-and-so was going to France—must have an air-cushion; a real drain on her strength; all that interminable traffic that women of her sort keep up; but she did it genuinely, from a natural instinct.

Oddly enough, she was one of the most thorough-going sceptics he had ever met, and possibly (this was a theory he used to make up to account for her, so transparent in some ways, so

Reed bed on the Broads with boat shelter and windmill in distance, Norfolk, photograph, Peter Henry Emerson, 1886. *(Library of Congress)*

203 From 1772 to 1937, the *Morning Post* was a conservative newspaper known for paying close attention to the affairs of the aristocracy. "'Majesty' of every kind and from every clime was grist to the *Morning Post*'s sycophantic mill," explained historian W. H. Hindle of the articles that appeared faithfully each day detailing the car rides, the boat outings, the polo matches, the plays, parties, and operas where the rich mingled. While Woolf was writing *Mrs. Dalloway*, the editor of the *Morning Post* was H. A. Gwynne, a Welsh anti-Semite who wrote an introduction to *The Cause of World Unrest* (1920), a book that purportedly exposed a Jewish conspiracy to promote communism. Woolf read the *Morning Post* every day, partly to mine it for satire. "I have changed the Daily News for the Morning Post. The proportions of the world at once become utterly different. The M.P. has the largest letters & the double column devoted to the murder of Mrs Lindsay; anglo Indians, Anglo Scots, & retired old men & patriotic old ladies write letter after letter to deplore the state of the country; applaud the M.P., the only faithful standard bearer left." The *Morning Post* was acquired by the *Daily Telegraph* in 1937 and remains in circulation today.

204 Norfolk, one of the easternmost counties in the UK, was known for its agricultural production. Just before the First World War, a number of its fields were converted into airfields for the Royal Air Force (RAF).

The Serpentine, Hyde Park, George Sidney Shepherd. Oil on panel, mid-nineteenth century. *(Paul Mellon Collection, Yale Center for British Art)*

inscrutable in others), possibly she said to herself, As we are a doomed race, chained to a sinking ship (her favourite reading as a girl was Huxley[205] and Tyndall,[206] and they were fond of these nautical metaphors), as the whole thing is a bad joke, let us, at any rate, do our part; mitigate the sufferings of our fellow-prisoners (Huxley again); decorate the dungeon with flowers and air-cushions; be as decent as we possibly can. Those ruffians, the Gods, shan't have it all their own way—her notion being that the Gods, who never lost a chance of hurting, thwarting and spoiling human lives, were seriously put out if, all the same, you behaved like a lady. That phase came directly after Sylvia's death—that horrible affair. To see your own sister killed by a falling tree (all Justin Parry's fault—all his carelessness) before

205 Thomas Henry Huxley (1825–1895), an English biologist known as "Darwin's bulldog," began his career in 1846 as an assistant surgeon on board the HMS *Rattlesnake*. His passion was for marine invertebrates, the sea snails, jellyfish, and anemones that belonged to the class of animals he named "the oceanic hydrozoa," and to whose anatomy he would devote all his attention once the *Rattlesnake* arrived in Australia to survey the Great Barrier Reef. Upon his return to England in 1850, Huxley was elected a fellow of the Royal Society and, four years later, resigned from the navy to become professor of natural history at the Government School of Mines. Initially unpersuaded by "development theory," he changed his mind after Darwin befriended him following a lecture at the Royal Institution in 1855. ("How extremely stupid not to have thought of that!" was his famous response to the idea of natural selection.)

Huxley quickly anointed himself Charles Darwin's public champion and vowed to use evolutionary

your very eyes, a girl too on the verge of life, the most gifted of them, Clarissa always said, was enough to turn one bitter. Later she wasn't so positive, perhaps; she thought there were no Gods; no one was to blame; and so she evolved this atheist's religion of doing good for the sake of goodness.

And of course she enjoyed life immensely. It was her nature to enjoy (though, goodness only knows, she had her reserves; it was a mere sketch, he often felt, that even he, after all these years, could make of Clarissa). Anyhow there was no bitterness in her; none of that sense of moral virtue which is so repulsive in good women. She enjoyed practically everything. If you walked with her in Hyde Park now it was a bed of tulips, now a child in a perambulator, now some absurd little drama she made up on the spur of the moment. (Very likely she would have talked to those lovers, if she had thought them unhappy.) She had a sense of comedy that was really exquisite, but she needed people, always people, to bring it out, with the inevitable result that she frittered her time away, lunching, dining, giving these incessant parties of hers, talking nonsense, saying things she didn't mean, blunting the edge of her mind, losing her discrimination. There she would sit at the head of the table taking infinite pains with some old buffer who might be useful to Dalloway—they knew the most appalling bores in Europe—or in came Elizabeth and every thing must give way to *her.* She was at a High School, at the inarticulate stage last time he was over, a round-eyed, pale-faced girl, with nothing of her mother in her, a silent stolid creature, who took it all as a matter of course, let her mother make a fuss of her, and then said "May I go now?" like a child of four; going off, Clarissa explained, with that mixture of amusement and pride which Dalloway himself seemed to rouse in her, to play hockey. And now Elizabeth was "out",[207] presumably; thought him an old fogy, laughed at her mother's friends. Ah well, so be it. The compensation of growing old, Peter Walsh thought, coming out of Regent's Park, and holding his hat in hand, was simply this; that the passions remain as strong as ever, but one has gained—at last!—the power which adds the supreme flavour

theory like a "Whitworth gun in the armoury of liberalism," purging scientific education of religious dogma. His efforts culminated in his coinage in 1869 of the term "agnosticism." Writing in 1889, he described "agnosticism" as "the fundamental axiom of modern science [. . . .] In matters of the intellect, follow your reason as far as it will take you, without regard to any other consideration [. . . .] That I take to be the agnostic faith, which if a man keep whole and undefiled, he shall not be ashamed to look the universe in the face, whatever the future may have in store for him."

206 John Tyndall (1820–1893), an Irish physicist and a close friend of Thomas Henry Huxley, started his career studying the magnetic properties of crystals. A visit to the Alps in 1856 would give him his first sighting of the world's great glacier beds, of its highest and purest snow peaks, some hidden behind heavy cloud wreaths, others cutting straight into the bright blue sky. He became a mountaineer and one of the first men to summit the Weisshorn in 1861. There he started to study the heating effect of sunlight on snow, laying down the principles of radiant heat absorption that would prove the existence of the greenhouse effect.

Like Huxley, he was a defender of Darwin, an advocate for the separation of scientific from religious belief, and an atheist in all but name. "The problem of the connection of body and soul is as insoluble in its modern form as it was in the prescientific ages," he wrote in *Fragments of Science for Unscientific People* (1871). "But if the materialist is confounded and science rendered dumb, who else is prepared with a solution? To whom has this arm of the Lord been revealed? Let us lower our heads and acknowledge our ignorance, priest and philosopher, one and all."

207 The ritual of "coming out," whereby a young lady was presented at court, began during the reign of George III (1760–1820), but only emerged as a rite of passage during the reign of Queen Victoria (1837–1901). Debutantes dressed in full-skirted gowns of pure white muslin, silk, or crepe, with white kid gloves on their hands and ostrich feathers in their hair, came to court to curtsey before the queen. After coming out, young women would enter the London social season, an exhausting procession of afternoon teas, cocktail parties, and balls, all intended to find them suitable husbands. These presentations continued until 1958 when Queen Elizabeth II abolished the practice.

to existence—the power of taking hold of experience, of turning it round, slowly, in the light.

A terrible confession it was (he put his hat on again), but now, at the age of fifty-three, one scarcely needed people any more. Life itself, every moment of it, every drop of it, here, this instant, now, in the sun, in Regent's Park, was enough. Too much, indeed. A whole lifetime was too short to bring out, now that one had acquired the power, the full flavour; to extract every ounce of pleasure, every shade of meaning; which both were so

Debutante dress, c. 1890. *(State Library of Queensland)*

much more solid than they used to be, so much less personal. It was impossible that he should ever suffer again as Clarissa had made him suffer. For hours at a time (pray God that one might say these things without being overheard!), for hours and days he never thought of Daisy.

Could it be that he was in love with her, then, remembering the misery, the torture, the extraordinary passion of those days? It was a different thing altogether—a much pleasanter thing—the truth being, of course, that now *she* was in love with *him*. And that perhaps was the reason why, when the ship actually sailed, he felt an extraordinary relief, wanted nothing so much as to be alone; was annoyed to find all her little attentions—cigars, notes, a rug for the voyage—in his cabin. Every one if they were honest would say the same; one doesn't want people after fifty; one doesn't want to go on telling women they are pretty; that's what most men of fifty would say, Peter Walsh thought, if they were honest.

But then these astonishing accesses of emotion—bursting into tears this morning, what was all that about? What could Clarissa have thought of him? thought him a fool presumably, not for the first time. It was jealousy that was at the bottom of it—jealousy which survives every other passion of mankind, Peter Walsh thought, holding his pocket-knife at arm's length. She had been meeting Major Orde, Daisy said in her last letter; said it on purpose, he knew; said it to make him jealous; he could see her wrinkling her forehead as she wrote, wondering what she could say to hurt him; and yet it made no difference; he was furious! All this pother of coming to England and seeing lawyers wasn't to marry her, but to prevent her from marrying anybody else. That was what tortured him, that was what came over him when he saw Clarissa so calm, so cold, so intent on her dress or whatever it was; realising what she might have spared him, what she had reduced him to—a whimpering, snivelling old ass. But women, he thought, shutting his pocket-knife, don't know what passion is. They don't know the meaning of it to men. Clarissa was as cold as an icicle. There she would sit on the sofa by his side, let him take her hand, give him one kiss on the cheek—Here he was at the crossing.

A sound interrupted him; a frail quivering sound, a voice bubbling up without direction, vigour, beginning or end, running weakly and shrilly and with an absence of all human meaning into

ee um fah um so

foo swee too eem oo—

the voice of no age or sex, the voice of an ancient spring spouting from the earth; which issued, just opposite Regent's Park Tube Station, from a tall quivering shape, like a funnel, like a rusty pump, like a wind-beaten tree for ever barren of leaves which lets the wind run up and down its branches singing

ee um fah um so

foo swee too eem oo,

and rocks and creaks and moans in the eternal breeze.

Through all ages—when the pavement was grass, when it was swamp, through the age of tusk and mammoth, through the age of silent sunrise—the battered woman—for she wore a skirt—with her right hand exposed, her left clutching at her side, stood singing of love—love which has lasted a million years, she sang, love which prevails, and millions of years ago, her lover, who had been dead these centuries, had walked, she crooned, with her in May; but in the course of ages, long as summer days, and flaming, she remembered, with nothing but red asters, he had gone; death's enormous sickle had swept those tremendous hills, and when at last she laid her hoary and immensely aged head on the earth, now become a mere cinder of ice, she implored the Gods to lay by her side a bunch of purple heather, there on her high burial place which the last rays of the last sun caressed; for then the pageant of the universe would be over.[208]

As the ancient song bubbled up opposite Regent's Park Tube Station, still the earth seemed green and flowery; still, though it issued from so rude a mouth, a mere hole in the earth, muddy too, matted with root fibres and tangled grasses, still the old bubbling burbling song, soaking through the knotted roots of

208 The interlude of the battered woman looks back even further in time than the interlude of the solitary traveler, "through the age of tusk and mammoth, through the age of silent sunrise," before the rise of man. The battered woman is an androgynous figure, her femininity denoted only incidentally by her skirt. Yet even this detail misleads when one realizes that the battered woman is hardly a person at all and certainly not a member of modern civilization, with its motorcars and airplanes. She is a creature who has given herself to and has been absorbed by the land; a player in "the pageant of the universe." The history of the land is as inscrutable to us as her song, Woolf suggests, as the narrator hears the sound of the human voice mingled with the sound of the earth burbling—the battered woman's million years of enduring love indifferentiable from the million years the earth has endured mankind's existence, "the knotted roots of infinite ages, and skeletons and treasure." (In the manuscript of "The Hours," Woolf more explicitly confuses the "battered & rusty old pump" with the "battered old woman.")

This scene was likely inspired by Woolf's visit to the ruins of Bindon Abbey in Dorset with John Maynard Keynes and his wife Lydia in September 1923. In her diary, Woolf described Lydia as an earthbound woman, lying "in her pink jacket with the white fur in a Bishops tomb—a kind of shaped tank sunk in the earth on the way up to the Calvary." Later, she, Lydia, and Maynard "sat on the mound of the Calvary, the cross being gone, & Maynard talked about palaeolithic [*sic*] man & an interesting theory about the age of man—how the beginning of history about 5,000 B.C. is only the beginning of another lap in the race; others, many others, having been run previously & obliterated by ice ages." The novel's geological imagination of the battered woman orients its characters and the single day they are living to the largest possible scale of human time.

infinite ages, and skeletons and treasure, streamed away in rivulets over the pavement and all along the Marylebone Road,[209] and down towards Euston, fertilising, leaving a damp stain.

Still remembering how once in some primeval May she had walked with her lover, this rusty pump, this battered old woman with one hand exposed for coppers, the other clutching her side, would still be there in ten million years, remembering how once she had walked in May, where the sea flows now, with whom it did not matter—he was a man, oh yes, a man who had loved her. But the passage of ages had blurred the clarity of that ancient May day; the bright petalled flowers were hoar and silver frosted; and she no longer saw, when she implored him (as she did now quite clearly) "look in my eyes with thy sweet eyes intently,"[210] she no longer saw brown eyes, black whiskers or sunburnt face, but only a looming shape, a shadow shape, to which, with the bird-like freshness of the very aged, she still twittered "give me your hand and let me press it gently" (Peter Walsh couldn't help giving the poor creature a coin as he stepped into his taxi), "and if some one should see, what matter they?" she demanded; and her fist clutched at her side, and she smiled, pocketing her shilling, and all peering inquisitive eyes seemed blotted out, and the passing generations—the pavement was crowded with bustling middle-class people—vanished, like leaves, to be trodden under, to be soaked and steeped and made mould of by that eternal spring—

ee um fah um so
foo swee too eem oo.

"Poor old woman," said Rezia Warren Smith.

Oh poor old wretch! she said, waiting to cross.

Suppose it was a wet night? Suppose one's father, or somebody who had known one in better days had happened to pass, and saw one standing there in the gutter? And where did she sleep at night?

209 Named after "St. Mary Le Bon," a small church perched on the roadside, Marylebone Road is a large thoroughfare running east to west, from Regent's Park to Paddington.

210 As J. Hillis Miller has argued, the snatches of song attributed to the battered woman derive from Woolf's translation of Richard Strauss's "Allerseelen," or "All Souls' Day," "the day of a collective resurrection of spirits." "*Mrs. Dalloway* has the form of an All Souls' Day in which Peter Walsh, Sally Seton, and the rest rise from the dead to come to Clarissa's party," Miller writes. "As in the song the memory of a dead lover may on one day of the year become a direct confrontation of his or her risen spirit, so in *Mrs. Dalloway* the characters are obsessed all day by memories of the time when Clarissa refused Peter and chose to marry Richard Dalloway, and then the figures in those memories actually come back."

Cheerfully, almost gaily, the invincible thread of sound wound up into the air like the smoke from a cottage chimney, winding up clean beech trees and issuing in a tuft of blue smoke among the topmost leaves. "And if some one should see, what matter they?"

Since she was so unhappy, for weeks and weeks now, Rezia had given meanings to things that happened, almost felt sometimes that she must stop people in the street, if they looked good, kind people, just to say to them "I am unhappy"; and this old woman singing in the street "if some one should see, what matter they?" made her suddenly quite sure that everything was going to be right. They were going to Sir William Bradshaw; she thought his name sounded nice; he would cure Septimus at once. And then there was a brewer's cart, and the grey horses had upright bristles of straw in their tails; there were newspaper placards. It was a silly, silly dream, being unhappy.

So they crossed, Mr. and Mrs. Septimus Warren Smith, and was there, after all, anything to draw attention to them, anything to make a passer-by suspect here is a young man who carries in him the greatest message in the world, and is, moreover, the happiest man in the world, and the most miserable? Perhaps they walked more slowly than other people, and there was something hesitating, trailing, in the man's walk, but what more natural for a clerk, who has not been in the West End on a week-day at this hour for years, than to keep looking at the sky, looking at this, that and the other, as if Portland Place[211] were a room he had come into when the family are away, the chandeliers being hung in holland bags, and the caretaker, as she lets in long shafts of dusty light upon deserted, queer-looking arm-chairs, lifting one corner of the long blinds, explains to the visitors what a wonderful place it is; how wonderful, but at the same time, he thinks, how strange.

To look at, he might have been a clerk, but of the better sort; for he wore brown boots;[212] his hands were educated; so, too, his profile—his angular, big-nosed, intelligent, sensitive profile; but not his lips altogether, for they were loose; and his eyes (as

211 An exceptionally wide street in Marylebone, lined by opulent Georgian terrace houses and home to many professional bodies, charities, and embassies.

212 The manuscript of "The Hours" states that Septimus and Rezia are "both on the verge of the gentle class," for "the working class do not wear brown shoes."

eyes tend to be), eyes merely; hazel, large; so that he was, on the whole, a border case, neither one thing nor the other; might end with a house at Purley[213] and a motor car, or continue renting apartments in back streets all his life; one of those half-educated, self-educated men whose education is all learnt from books borrowed from public libraries, read in the evening after the day's work, on the advice of well-known authors consulted by letter.

As for the other experiences, the solitary ones, which people go through alone, in their bedrooms, in their offices, walking the fields and the streets of London, he had them; had left home, a mere boy, because of his mother; she lied; because he came down to tea for the fiftieth time with his hands unwashed; because he could see no future for a poet in Stroud;[214] and so, making a confidant of his little sister, had gone to London leaving an absurd note behind him, such as great men have written, and the world has read later when the story of their struggles has become famous.

London has swallowed up many millions of young men called Smith; thought nothing of fantastic Christian names like Septimus with which their parents have thought to distinguish them. Lodging off the Euston Road,[215] there were experiences, again experiences, such as change a face in two years from a pink innocent oval to a face lean, contracted, hostile. But of all this what could the most observant of friends have said except what a gardener says when he opens the conservatory door in the morning and finds a new blossom on his plant:—It has flowered; flowered from vanity, ambition, idealism, passion, loneliness, courage, laziness, the usual seeds, which all muddled up (in a room off the Euston Road), made him shy, and stammering, made him anxious to improve himself, made him fall in love with Miss Isabel Pole, lecturing in the Waterloo Road[216] upon Shakespeare.

Was he not like Keats?[217] she asked; and reflected how she might give him a taste of *Antony and Cleopatra*[218] and the rest; lent him books; wrote him scraps of letters; and lit in him such a fire as burns only once in a lifetime, without heat, flicker-

213 Located in the London Borough of Croydon, Purley is a suburban area that grew rapidly in the 1920s and 1930s. Until 1965, Purley was part of Surrey.

214 A textile town situated below the western escarpment of the Cotswold Hills in Gloucestershire.

215 A congested central road that runs from Marylebone Road to King's Cross.

View of Euston Road, looking west, undated. *(Wellcome Collection)*

216 Waterloo Road runs northwest and southeast between Westminster Bridge Road and Waterloo Bridge. In the early twentieth century, it was the site of Morley Memorial College for Working Men and Women, an institution where working-class adults could take evening classes. In 1905, Morley's principal, Miss Mary Sheepshanks, "a large kindly & rather able sort of woman," asked Virginia Stephen if she would start a women's club to "talk about books." From 1905 to 1907, Woolf taught classes on prose,

Shorthand class at Morley College, 1924. *(London Metropolitan Archives)*

ing a red gold flame infinitely ethereal and insubstantial over Miss Pole; *Antony and Cleopatra*; and the Waterloo Road. He thought her beautiful, believed her impeccably wise; dreamed of her, wrote poems to her, which, ignoring the subject, she corrected in red ink; he saw her, one summer evening, walking in a green dress in a square. "It has flowered," the gardener

Antony and Cleopatra, Act III, Scene XI, Georg Goldberg. Line engraving and etching, 1817–1901. *(Paul Mellon Collection, Yale Center for British Art)*

Greek history, and English composition, lectured on "The Dramatic in Life & Art," and led a Monday night "Reading Circle" on Keats, Shelley, and Browning.

217 English Romantic poet John Keats (1795–1821) served as the butt of several jokes Woolf would make about passionate literary men and their fanciful, disturbing attachments to women. When Woolf taught at Morley in 1907, she entertained a brief flirtation with a student named Cyril Zeldwyn, whom she called "my degenerate poet . . . rants and blushes, and almost seizes my hand when we happen to like the same lines . . . I can tell you the first sentence of my lecture: 'The poet Keats died when he was 25; and he wrote all his works before that.' Indeed, how very interesting, Miss Stephen." Keats would reappear in her 1924 essay "Indiscretions," about the feminist value of literary gossip. "[T]he divine poet was a little sultanic in his behavior; after the manly fashion of his time apt to treat his adored both as angel and cockatoo. A jury of maidens would ring in a verdict in Fanny's favor," she wrote. Her unpublished essay "Byron and Mr Briggs" would reassert her judgment of Keats as a misogynist: "'<E>every woman is in love with Keats' said <continued> Clarissa Dalloway, only to draw from Julia Hedge the unexpected ~~and obstinate~~ assertion ~~that she was entirely on Fanny's side~~, and no young woman of spirit could have been expected to tolerate for an instant his ~~exacting~~ conventional way with women."

218 Act 2, Scene 2 of Shakespeare's *Antony and Cleopatra* (1623) provides Septimus with the rich, fantastical language of ardor he uses to describe his love for Miss Isabel Pole: "The barge she sat in, like a burnished throne, / Burned on the water; the poop was beaten gold." Woolf admired Cleopatra's "method of baiting Antony." The manuscript of "The Hours" preserves Woolf's more explicit account of how Miss Pole might have used the play to bait Septimus: "She might give him a taste of Anthony & Cleopatra & the rest, emotions, ~~not only in the 1~~ only vaguely sexual."

might have said, had he opened the door;[219] had he come in, that is to say, any night about this time, and found him writing; found him tearing up his writing; found him finishing a masterpiece at three o'clock in the morning and running out to pace the streets, and visiting churches, and fasting one day, drinking another, devouring Shakespeare, Darwin, *The History of Civilisation*,[220] and Bernard Shaw.[221]

Something was up, Mr. Brewer knew; Mr. Brewer, managing clerk at Sibleys and Arrowsmiths,[222] auctioneers, valuers, land and estate agents; something was up, he thought, and, being paternal with his young men, and thinking very highly of Smith's abilities, and prophesying that he would, in ten or fifteen years, succeed to the leather arm-chair in the inner room under the skylight with the deed-boxes round him, "if he keeps his health," said Mr. Brewer, and that was the danger—he looked weakly; advised football, invited him to supper and was seeing his way to consider recommending a rise of salary, when something happened which threw out many of Mr. Brewer's calculations, took away his ablest young fellows, and eventually, so prying and insidious were the fingers of the European War, smashed a plaster cast of Ceres,[223] ploughed a hole in the geranium beds, and utterly ruined the cook's nerves at Mr. Brewer's establishment at Muswell Hill.[224]

Septimus was one of the first to volunteer. He went to France to save an England which consisted almost entirely of Shakespeare's plays and Miss Isabel Pole in a green dress walking in a square. There in the trenches the change which Mr. Brewer desired when he advised football was produced instantly; he developed manliness; he was promoted; he drew the attention, indeed the affection of his officer, Evans by name. It was a case of two dogs playing on a hearth-rug; one worrying a paper screw, snarling, snapping, giving a pinch, now and then, at the old dog's ear; the other lying somnolent, blinking at the fire, raising a paw, turning and growling good-temperedly. They had to be together, share with each other, fight with each other, quarrel with each other.[225] But when Evans (Rezia, who

219 In the manuscript of "The Hours," Woolf extends the metaphor of the flower blooming to portray Septimus as a character rooted in contradictions: "~~Septimus was~~ Sensitive, vain, callous, aspiring; a nervous man; mastered by impulses, <&> fears; proud of his temperament, affectionate; conscious of low birth & of gentle birth; at once a snob & a socialist . . . with more surface than usual exposed naked to the heats & colds of life—such were the seeds."

220 Leonard and Virginia Woolf's library housed two copies of *History of Civilisation in England* (1857–61), an unfinished work by Henry Thomas Buckle (1821–1862). He had a reputation as a reckless intellectual, a "self-styled historian" and prodigious chess player who suffered from "shattered nerves," according to Leslie Stephen's entry on Buckle in his *Dictionary of National Biography*. In *History of Civilisation in England*, Buckle set out to write a fourteen-volume work laying out the principles that governed human progress. The first volume was published in June 1857 and transformed Buckle into a London literary celebrity. His work on the second volume was interrupted by the death of his mother, after which he turned to writing about his philosophy of immortality. "Methinks, that in that moment of desolation, the best of us would succumb, but for the deep conviction that all is not really over; that we have as yet only seen a part; and that something remains behind," Buckle wrote in a review of John Stuart Mill's *On Liberty* (1859). "If this be a delusion, it is one which the affections have themselves created, and we must believe that the purest and noblest elements of our nature conspire to deceive us. So surely as we lose what we love, so surely does hope mingle with grief."

221 When Virginia Stephen and her brother Adrian rented 29 Fitzroy Square in Bloomsbury, they did so knowing that its former occupants were Irish playwright and critic George Bernard Shaw (1856–1950), his mother Bessie, and his sister Lucy. Upon meeting Shaw at lunch in 1932, Woolf wrote in her diary, "What life, what vitality! What immense nervous spring!"

222 An imaginary firm.

223 Ceres is the Roman goddess of the harvest, fertility, and motherhood.

224 Muswell Hill, a suburban neighborhood in north London, originally began as a scattering of country homes and turned into a suburban district at the turn of the nineteenth century.

225 Critics often describe the relationship between Septimus and Evans as homoerotic, pointing as evidence to Woolf's metaphor of the two romping

had only seen him once, called him "a quiet man," a sturdy red-haired man, undemonstrative in the company of women), when Evans was killed, just before the Armistice,[226] in Italy, Septimus, far from showing any emotion or recognising that here was the end of a friendship, congratulated himself upon feeling very little and very reasonably. The War had taught him. It was sublime. He had gone through the whole show, friendship, European War, death, had won promotion, was still under thirty and was bound to survive. He was right there. The last shells missed him. He watched them explode with indifference. When peace came he was in Milan, billeted in the house of an innkeeper with a courtyard, flowers in tubs, little tables in the open, daughters making hats, and to Lucrezia, the younger daughter,[227] he became engaged one evening when the panic was on him—that he could not feel.

For now that it was all over, truce signed, and the dead buried, he had, especially in the evening, these sudden thunder-claps of fear. He could not feel. As he opened the door of the room where the Italian girls sat making hats, he could see them; could hear them; they were rubbing wires among coloured beads in saucers; they were turning buckram shapes this way and that; the table was all strewn with feathers, spangles, silks, ribbons; scissors were rapping on the table; but something failed him; he could not feel. Still, scissors rapping, girls laughing, hats being made protected him; he was assured of safety; he had a refuge. But he could not sit there all night. There were moments of waking in the early morning. The bed was falling; he was falling. Oh for the scissors and the lamplight and the buckram shapes! He asked Lucrezia to marry him, the younger of the two, the gay, the frivolous, with those little artist's fingers that she would hold up and say "It is all in them." Silk, feathers, what not were alive to them.

"It is the hat that matters most," she would say, when they walked out together. Every hat that passed, she would examine; and the cloak and the dress and the way the woman held herself. Ill-dressing, over-dressing she stigmatised, not savagely, rather with impatient movements of the hands, like those of a painter

dogs on the hearthrug. Again, her animal imagery suggests intimacy, though the manuscript of "The Hours" played down the nature of this intimacy, depicting Septimus and Evans as two dogs seemingly unconcerned with each other: "Apparently paying each other little attention, ~~yet a yet~~ some very profound interest unites them, for they must be together even in their quarrels." Whereas Clarissa's relationship with Sally is often treated as an adolescent love, present now only as an absent sensation, Septimus's longing for Evans remains as urgent and consuming as the hallucinations that bring him back to life.

226 Woolf is surely referring to the armistice with Germany, signed on November 11, 1918. Though "The Hours" had Evans dying at Vimy Ridge, a battle fought in northern France in 1917, the timing was ill-suited to her novel's critique of war. She needed Evans to die later, once it had become clear that the cost of war had been irredeemably high. "Twenty-five minutes ago the guns went off, announcing peace," she wrote in her diary. "A siren hooted on the river. They are hooting still. A few people ran to look out of the windows. The rooks wheeled round, & were for a moment, the symbolic look of creatures performing some ceremony, partly of thanksgiving, partly of valediction over the grave." (The swooping rooks would appear near the beginning of *Mrs. Dalloway* on p. 5.) "A very cloudy still day, the smoke toppling over heavily towards the east; & that too wearing for a moment a look of something floating, waving, drooping." She judged the celebrations that followed as "sordid and depressing," "a servants festival," "got up to pacify & placate 'the people'" who had grown restless and discontented from the war.

227 A minor discrepancy in *Mrs. Dalloway*: While Rezia references her "sisters" on p. 94, here Septimus identifies her as the "younger daughter," implying she has only one older sister. The error is confirmed in the next paragraph, where Woolf writes that Lucrezia is "the younger of the two" sisters.

who puts from him some obvious well-meant glaring imposture; and then, generously, but always critically, she would welcome a shop-girl who had turned her little bit of stuff gallantly, or praise, wholly, with enthusiastic and professional understanding, a French lady descending from her carriage, in chinchilla, robes, pearls.

"Beautiful!" she would murmur, nudging Septimus, that he might see. But beauty was behind a pane of glass. Even taste (Rezia liked ices, chocolates, sweet things) had no relish to him. He put down his cup on the little marble table. He looked at people outside; happy they seemed, collecting in the middle of the street, shouting, laughing, squabbling over nothing. But he could not taste, he could not feel. In the tea-shop among the tables and the chattering waiters the appalling fear came over him—he could not feel. He could reason; he could read, Dante for example, quite easily ("Septimus, do put down your book," said Rezia, gently shutting the *Inferno*[228]), he could add up his bill; his brain was perfect; it must be the fault of the world then—that he could not feel.

"The English are so silent," Rezia said. She liked it, she said. She respected these Englishmen, and wanted to see London, and the English horses, and the tailor-made suits, and could remember hearing how wonderful the shops were, from an Aunt who had married and lived in Soho.[229]

It might be possible, Septimus thought, looking at England from the train window, as they left Newhaven;[230] it might be possible that the world itself is without meaning.

At the office they advanced him to a post of considerable responsibility. They were proud of him; he had won crosses.[231] "You have done your duty; it is up to us—" began Mr. Brewer; and could not finish, so pleasurable was his emotion. They took admirable lodgings off the Tottenham Court Road.[232]

Here he opened Shakespeare once more. That boy's business of the intoxication of language—*Antony and Cleopatra*—had shrivelled utterly. How Shakespeare loathed humanity—the putting on of clothes, the getting of children, the sordidity of the

228 Dante Alighieri's (ca. 1265–1321) *Inferno* is the first part of his fourteenth-century epic poem, *The Divine Comedy* (ca. 1308–21). Dante's journey through the nine circles of Hell allows him to recognize and to reject sin. Septimus's conviction that he has also sinned ("the sin for which human nature had condemned him to death," he thinks on p. 126) makes Dante's meditation on Hell easy reading for him.

229 Soho Square was laid out in the late 1680s in the hopes of attracting aristocratic residents to Soho, where the French Huguenots had settled in the seventeenth century, giving rise to its reputation as London's French Quarter. By the nineteenth century and through the twentieth, Soho was known for its prostitutes, music halls, theaters, and public houses.

230 A village in east Sussex, about four miles from Monk's House at the mouth of the River Ouse.

231 The British gallantry medals of the First World War were crosses or disks attached by a ribbon to a metal suspension bar. The material and design of the medal depended on the combatant's rank.

232 Tottenham Court Road, one of London's major roads, runs north from Euston Road to St Giles Circus and into the poorer outskirts of Bloomsbury. The slums of Tottenham Court Road appear in Woolf's description of another impoverished young writer, Henry Maitland, hero of Morley Roberts's novel *The Private Life of Henry Maitland*, which Woolf reviewed in 1923. Henry strove for dignity "with the shelf of classics, Greek, Latin, and English, bought with saved sixpences and lugged home volume by volume to a basement off the Tottenham Court Road," she wrote.

Wallas & Co. Pharmacy, 45 New Cavendish Street, London, artist unknown. Watercolor painting, c. 1900. *(Wellcome Collection)*

Soho Square, Fletcher Hanslip, undated. *(Wellcome Collection)*

mouth and the belly![233] This was now revealed to Septimus; the message hidden in the beauty of words. The secret signal which one generation passes, under disguise, to the next is loathing, hatred, despair. Dante the same. Aeschylus[234] (translated) the same. There Rezia sat at the table trimming hats. She trimmed hats for Mrs. Filmer's friends; she trimmed hats by the hour. She looked pale, mysterious, like a lily, drowned, under water, he thought.

"The English are so serious," she would say, putting her arms round Septimus, her cheek against his.

Love between man and woman was repulsive to Shakespeare. The business of copulation was filth to him before the end. But, Rezia said, she must have children. They had been married five years.

They went to the Tower[235] together; to the Victoria and Albert Museum;[236] stood in the crowd to see the King open Parliament.[237] And there were the shops—hat shops, dress shops, shops with leather bags in the window, where she would stand staring. But she must have a boy.

She must have a son like Septimus, she said. But nobody

Tottenham Court Road, 1927. *(Stockholm Transportation Museum)*

233 Septimus's sudden antipathy to Shakespeare's lack of humanity echoes Woolf's initial critique of "the great William," delivered to her brother Thoby while he was a student at Cambridge in 1901. "I shall want a lecture when I see you; to clear up some points about the Plays. I mean about the characters. Why aren't they more human? Imogen and Posthumous [*sic*] and Cymbeline—I find them beyond me—Is this my feminine weakness in the upper region?"

234 Described as the "father of tragedy," Aeschylus (ca. 525–ca. 456 BCE) was the author of the *Oresteia* (458 BCE), *Prometheus Bound* (n.d.), *The Suppliants* (458 BCE), *Seven Against Thebes* (467 BCE), and *The Persians* (472 BCE). While drafting *Mrs. Dalloway*, Woolf was reading Aeschylus in French and attempting to translate the *Agamemnon* (458 BCE), the second play of the *Oresteia*. The translation gave her a great deal of trouble. "The meaning is just on the far side of language," she wrote of Aeschylus in her essay "On Not Knowing Greek." Her frustration and admiration of how Aeschylus's meaning evades her attempts to render it into English echoes Septimus's feeling that there is a "message hidden in the beauty of words," but not reducible to them.

235 Built by William the Conqueror in the 1070s, the Tower of London sits on the north bank of the Thames. The fortress has served variously as an armory, a treasury, a prison, the location of the Royal Mint, and the home of the Crown Jewels of England.

236 The Victoria and Albert Museum, known as the "V&A," serves as one of the world's largest museums of applied and decorative arts. It was founded in 1852 after the co-organizers of the Crystal Palace Exhibition, Henry Cole and Prince Albert, decided to open an art museum that would continue to showcase the achievements of industry in Britain and its empire, while "extending taste and knowledge of the fine arts among the people." Originally called the Museum of Manufactures, it was renamed the South Kensington Museum, then the Victoria and Albert Museum at the laying of the foundation stone in 1899.

237 The State Opening of Parliament formally marks the beginning of a session of Parliament. It includes a speech from the throne known as the King's or Queen's Speech.

The Tower of London, Joseph Mallord William Turner. Etching with line engraving on paper, 1794. *(Paul Mellon Collection, Yale Center for British Art)*

could be like Septimus; so gentle; so serious; so clever. Could she not read Shakespeare too? Was Shakespeare a difficult author? she asked.[238]

One cannot bring children into a world like this. One cannot perpetuate suffering, or increase the breed of these lustful animals, who have no lasting emotions, but only whims and vanities, eddying them now this way, now that.

He watched her snip, shape, as one watches a bird hop, flit in the grass, without daring to move a finger. For the truth is (let her ignore it) that human beings have neither kindness, nor faith, nor charity beyond what serves to increase the pleasure of the moment. They hunt in packs. Their packs scour the desert and vanish screaming into the wilderness. They desert the fallen. They are plastered over with grimaces. There was Brewer at the office, with his waxed moustache, coral tie-pin, white slip, and pleasurable emotions—all coldness and clamminess within,—his geraniums ruined in the War—his cook's nerves destroyed; or Amelia Whatshername, handing round cups of tea punctually at five—a leering, sneering obscene little harpy; and the Toms and Berties in their starched shirt fronts oozing thick drops of vice. They never saw him drawing pictures of them naked at their antics in his notebook. In the street,

238 In a letter written in 1923, Woolf mocked Lydia Lopokova, her model for Rezia, for trying to learn Shakespeare. "Lydia has the soul of a squirrel: anything nicer you cant conceive: she sits by the hour polishing the sides of her nose with her front paws. Poor little wretch, trapped in Bloomsbury, what can she do but learn Shakespeare by heart? I assure you its tragic to see her sitting down to King Lear. Nobody can take her seriously."

vans roared past him; brutality blared out on placards; men were trapped in mines; women burnt alive; and once a maimed file of lunatics being exercised or displayed for the diversion of the populace (who laughed aloud), ambled and nodded and grinned past him, in the Tottenham Court Road, each half apologetically, yet triumphantly, inflicting his hopeless woe.[239] And would *he* go mad?

At tea Rezia told him that Mrs. Filmer's daughter was expecting a baby. *She* could not grow old and have no children! She was very lonely, she was very unhappy! She cried for the first time since they were married. Far away he heard her sobbing; he heard it accurately, he noticed it distinctly; he compared it to a piston thumping. But he felt nothing.

His wife was crying, and he felt nothing; only each time she sobbed in this profound, this silent, this hopeless way, he descended another step into the pit.

At last, with a melodramatic gesture which he assumed mechanically and with complete consciousness of its insincerity, he dropped his head on his hands. Now he had surrendered; now other people must help him. People must be sent for. He gave in.

Nothing could rouse him. Rezia put him to bed. She sent for a doctor—Mrs. Filmer's Dr. Holmes. Dr. Holmes examined him. There was nothing whatever the matter, said Dr. Holmes. Oh, what a relief! What a kind man, what a good man! thought Rezia. When he felt like that he went to the Music Hall, said Dr. Holmes. He took a day off with his wife and played golf.[240] Why not try two tabloids of bromide dissolved in a glass of water at bedtime? These old Bloomsbury houses, said Dr. Holmes, tapping the wall, are often full of very fine panelling, which the landlords have the folly to paper over. Only the other day, visiting a patient, Sir Somebody Something, in Bedford Square[241]—

So there was no excuse; nothing whatever the matter, except the sin for which human nature had condemned him to death; that he did not feel. He had not cared when Evans was killed; that was worst; but all the other crimes raised their heads and shook their fingers and jeered and sneered over the rail of the

239 The description echoes Woolf's diary entry from January 9, 1915, when Virginia and Leonard passed a "long line of imbeciles" while out for their daily walk. "The first was a very tall young man, just queer enough to look twice at, but no more; the second shuffled, & looked aside; & then one realised that every one in that long line was a miserable ineffective shuffling idiotic creature, with no forehead, or no chin, & an imbecile grin, or a wild suspicious stare. It was perfectly horrible. They should certainly be killed," she wrote. Hermione Lee connects Woolf's fear of mental illness and degeneracy—recall her insistence that Septimus would not be a "degenerate"—to her half-sister Laura, whom Woolf recalls as "a vacant-eyed girl whose idiocy was becoming daily more obvious, who could hardly read, who would throw scissors into the fire, who was tongue-tied and stammered and yet had to appear at the table with the rest of us."

240 Holmes cuts a more buffoonish character in the manuscript of "The Hours," where his descriptions of his habits, like playing golf, first appear as recommendations to Septimus. Hermione Lee suggests that this version of Holmes offered a more pointed caricature of Woolf's own doctors. "People <are> asleep when they think they're not asleep," says the manuscript Holmes. "<but> there's no harm in five grains of veronal. Don't get into the habit of course—~~Headaches are often caused by eye strain~~ As for this palpitation of the heart, ~~There's~~ nothing in that except nerves. Pressure on the top of the head, pain at the back of the neck & so on—why not go to see an oculist?" On his next visit, he tells Septimus, "Theres absolutely nothing whatever the matter with you. But if you lie here, thinking about your own symptoms, you'll only be fit for a lunatic asylum."

241 Bedford Square is a garden square in Bloomsbury. Built between 1775 and 1780, the square is surrounded by Georgian terrace homes, including 44 Bedford Square, the home of Lady Ottoline Morrell, lover of Bertrand Russell and friend to Woolf.

bed in the early hours of the morning at the prostrate body which lay realising its degradation; how he had married his wife without loving her; had lied to her; seduced her; outraged Miss Isabel Pole, and was so pocked and marked with vice that women shuddered when they saw him in the street. The verdict of human nature on such a wretch was death.

Dr. Holmes came again. Large, fresh-coloured, handsome, flicking his boots, looking in the glass, he brushed it all aside—headaches, sleeplessness, fears, dreams—nerve symptoms and nothing more, he said. If Dr. Holmes found himself even half a pound below eleven stone six,[242] he asked his wife for another plate of porridge at breakfast. (Rezia would learn to cook porridge.) But, he continued, health is largely a matter in our own control. Throw yourself into outside interests; take up some hobby. He opened Shakespeare—*Antony and Cleopatra*; pushed Shakespeare aside. Some hobby, said Dr. Holmes, for did he not owe his own excellent health (and he worked as hard as any man in London) to the fact that he could always switch off from his patients on to old furniture? And what a very pretty comb, if he might say so, Mrs. Warren Smith was wearing!

When the damned fool came again, Septimus refused to see him. Did he indeed? said Dr. Holmes, smiling agreeably. Really he had to give that charming little lady, Mrs. Smith, a friendly push before he could get past her into her husband's bedroom.

"So you're in a funk," he said agreeably, sitting down by his patient's side. He had actually talked of killing himself to his wife, quite a girl, a foreigner, wasn't she? Didn't that give her a very odd idea of English husbands? Didn't one owe perhaps a duty to one's wife? Wouldn't it be better to do something instead of lying in bed? For he had had forty years' experience behind him; and Septimus could take Dr. Holmes's word for it—there was nothing whatever the matter with him. And next time Dr. Holmes came he hoped to find Smith out of bed and not making that charming little lady his wife anxious about him.

Human nature, in short, was on him—the repulsive brute, with the blood-red nostrils. Holmes was on him. Dr. Holmes

242 "Eleven stone six" is 160 pounds.

came quite regularly every day. Once you stumble, Septimus wrote on the back of a postcard, human nature is on you. Holmes is on you. Their only chance was to escape, without letting Holmes know; to Italy—anywhere, anywhere, away from Dr. Holmes.

But Rezia could not understand him. Dr. Holmes was such a kind man. He was so interested in Septimus. He only wanted to help them, he said. He had four little children and he had asked her to tea, she told Septimus.

So he was deserted. The whole world was clamouring: Kill yourself, kill yourself, for our sakes. But why should he kill himself for their sakes? Food was pleasant; the sun hot; and this killing oneself, how does one set about it, with a table knife, uglily, with floods of blood,—by sucking a gaspipe? He was too weak; he could scarcely raise his hand. Besides, now that he was quite alone, condemned, deserted, as those who are about to die are alone, there was a luxury in it, an isolation full of sublimity; a freedom which the attached can never know. Holmes had won of course; the brute with the red nostrils had won. But even Holmes himself could not touch this last relic straying on the edge of the world, this outcast, who gazed back at the inhabited regions, who lay, like a drowned sailor, on the shore of the world.

It was at that moment (Rezia had gone shopping) that the great revelation took place. A voice spoke from behind the screen. Evans was speaking. The dead were with him.

"Evans, Evans!" he cried.

Mr. Smith was talking aloud to himself, Agnes the servant girl cried to Mrs. Filmer in the kitchen. "Evans, Evans!" he had said as she brought in the tray. She jumped, she did. She scuttled downstairs.

And Rezia came in, with her flowers, and walked across the room, and put the roses in a vase, upon which the sun struck directly, and went laughing, leaping round the room.

She had had to buy the roses, Rezia said, from a poor man in the street. But they were almost dead already, she said, arranging the roses.

So there was a man outside; Evans presumably; and the roses, which Rezia said were half dead, had been picked by him in the fields of Greece. Communication is health; communication is happiness. Communication, he muttered.

"What are you saying, Septimus?" Rezia asked, wild with terror, for he was talking to himself.

She sent Agnes running for Dr. Holmes. Her husband, she said, was mad. He scarcely knew her.

"You brute! You brute!" cried Septimus, seeing human nature, that is Dr. Holmes, enter the room.

"Now what's all this about," said Dr. Holmes in the most amiable way in the world. "Talking nonsense to frighten your wife?" But he would give him something to make him sleep. And if they were rich people,[243] said Dr. Holmes, looking ironically round the room, by all means let them go to Harley Street;[244] if they had no confidence in him, said Dr. Holmes, looking not quite so kind.

It was precisely twelve o'clock; twelve by Big Ben;[245] whose stroke was wafted over the northern part of London; blent with that of other clocks, mixed in a thin ethereal way with the clouds and wisps of smoke and died up there among the seagulls—twelve o'clock struck as Clarissa Dalloway laid her green dress on her bed, and the Warren Smiths walked down Harley Street. Twelve was the hour of their appointment. Probably, Rezia thought, that was Sir William Bradshaw's house with the grey motor car in front of it. (The leaden circles dissolved in the air.)[246]

Indeed it was—Sir William Bradshaw's motor car; low, powerful, grey with plain initials interlocked on the panel, as if the pomps of heraldry were incongruous, this man being the ghostly helper, the priest of science; and, as the motor car was grey, so to match its sober suavity, grey furs, silver grey rugs were heaped in it, to keep her ladyship warm while she waited. For often Sir William would travel sixty miles or more down into the country

243 In the manuscript of "The Hours," Woolf wrote: "They had & didn't mind paying three guineas [. . .] wh was what the great men of Harley Street payed for the same advice – They might go to see Dr. Bradshaw." She also wrote in the manuscript of *The Years* that one would require at least "three guineas" to see a doctor on Harley Street.

244 Named after Edward Harley, the 2nd Earl of Oxford and Mortimer, who developed the land in the early 1700s, Harley Street was famous for its large number of private medical practices. "What connection has the brain with the body? Nobody in Harley St could explain," wrote Woolf in her diary on January 15, 1933.

245 We arrive at the midpoint of the novel. Morning turns to afternoon; the characters begin to crowd one another. Now the novel's tracking of time offers itself as a technique for transitioning between many different points of view with order, with a sense of regularity. Big Ben chimes twelve as Septimus and Rezia arrive at Sir William's; the clock outside the department store Rigby and Lowndes chimes half past one as the thread of the story passes from Septimus and Rezia to Hugh Whitbread, arriving at Lady Bruton's home for lunch with her and Richard Dalloway; the bells sound at two as Lady Bruton falls asleep and the thread that binds her to Richard and Hugh snaps; Big Ben strikes three when Richard arrives at his home to try to tell Clarissa he loves her; it strikes the half hour and shifts from Clarissa at home to Miss Kilman in the street.

As Brian McHale argues, a novel's inability to represent simultaneity—a novel cannot, like a split screen in film or television, let the reader perceive two things happening at the same time—leads Woolf to "transition by triangulation." To create the illusion of simultaneity, the novel must deploy a "moment of parallel experience as a transition from one perceiving mind to another by way of a mutually-perceived sound," McHale writes. In the manuscript of "The Hours," Woolf imagined this simultaneity as a web, its thin lines connecting the characters to the narrator in the middle: "~~Spinning its <their> lovely web over the inner hollows, shop tossed, the glittering skein from [the] shop across the street; or hats, clothes, & diamonds; brittle as glass the filaments stretched, upon which the & the race balanced itself & the days traffic went forward, with music wrought into it, & a desperate energy.~~"

246 An echo from p. 7, and again on p. 71.

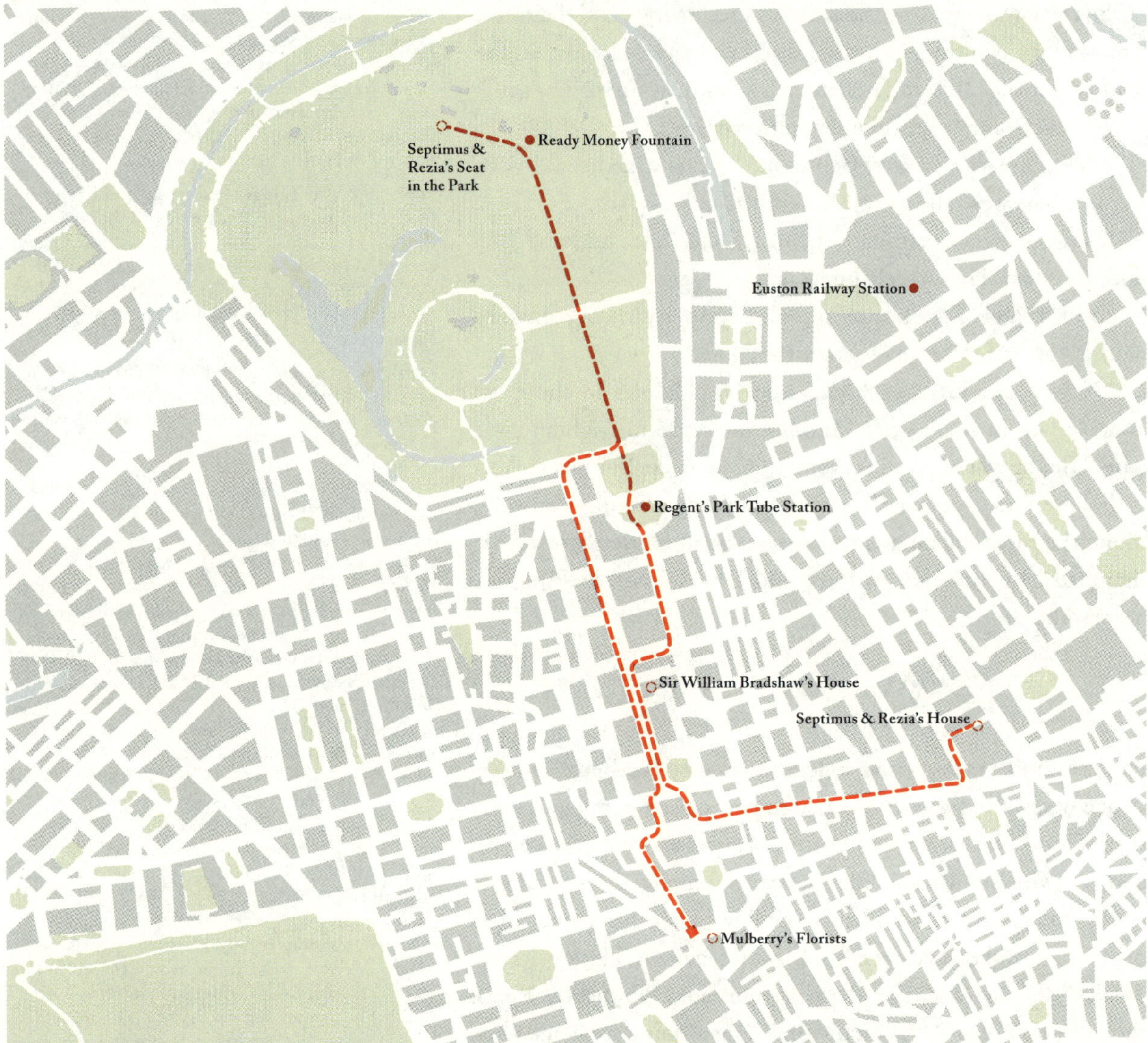

Septimus and Rezia's walk. *(Christian Nakarado)*

to visit the rich, the afflicted, who could afford the very large fee which Sir William very properly charged for his advice. Her ladyship waited with the rugs about her knees an hour or more, leaning back, thinking sometimes of the patient, sometimes, excusably, of the wall of gold, mounting minute by minute while she waited; the wall of gold that was mounting between them and all shifts and anxieties (she had borne them bravely; they had had their struggles) until she felt wedged on a calm ocean, where only spice winds blow; respected, admired, envied, with scarcely anything left to wish for, though she regretted her stoutness; large dinner-parties every Thursday night to the profession; an occasional bazaar to be opened; Royalty greeted; too little time, alas, with her husband, whose work grew and grew; a boy doing well at Eton;[247] she would have liked a daughter too; interests she had, however, in plenty; child welfare; the after-care of the epileptic, and photography, so that if there was a church building, or a church decaying, she bribed the sexton, got the key and took photographs, which were scarcely to be distinguished from the work of professionals, while she waited.

Sir William himself was no longer young. He had worked very hard; he had won his position by sheer ability (being the son of a shopkeeper); loved his profession; made a fine figurehead at ceremonies and spoke well—all of which had by the time he was knighted given him a heavy look, a weary look (the stream of patients being so incessant, the responsibilities and privileges of his profession so onerous), which weariness, together with his grey hairs, increased the extraordinary distinction of his presence and gave him the reputation (of the utmost importance in dealing with nerve cases) not merely of lightning skill and almost infallible accuracy in diagnosis, but of sympathy; tact; understanding of the human soul. He could see the first moment they came into the room (the Warren Smiths they were called); he was certain directly he saw the man; it was a case of extreme gravity. It was a case of complete breakdown—complete physical and nervous breakdown, with every symptom in an advanced stage, he ascertained in two or three minutes (writing answers to questions, murmured discreetly, on a pink card).

How long had Dr. Holmes been attending him?

Six weeks.

Prescribed a little bromide? Said there was nothing the matter? Ah yes (those general practitioners! thought Sir William.

247 Often referred to as "the chief nurse of England's statesmen," Eton is one of seven all-male boarding schools originally classed as a public school. Recall on p. 106 that Sally Seton describes Hugh Whitbread as "a perfect specimen of the public school type." One easily could imagine Hugh at Eton, lazing on the north bank of the Thames, proudly searching the horizon for the battlements of Windsor Castle. In her 1924 review of Arthur Christopher Benson's *Memories and Friends*, Woolf expressed her impatience for Etonian men in particular: "In order to appreciate Mr Benson's memories fully one should have been educated at Eton and Cambridge. One should have a settled income. One should have an armchair. One should have dined well."

It took half his time to undo their blunders. Some were irreparable).

"You served with great distinction in the War?"

The patient repeated the word "war" interrogatively.

He was attaching meanings to words of a symbolical kind. A serious symptom to be noted on the card.

"The War?" the patient asked. The European War—that little shindy of schoolboys with gunpowder? Had he served with distinction? He really forgot. In the War itself he had failed.[248]

"Yes, he served with the greatest distinction," Rezia assured the doctor; "he was promoted."

"And they have the very highest opinion of you at your office?" Sir William murmured, glancing at Mr. Brewer's very generously worded letter. "So that you have nothing to worry you, no financial anxiety, nothing?"

He had committed an appalling crime and been condemned to death by human nature.

"I have—I have," he began, "committed a crime——"[249]

"He has done nothing wrong whatever," Rezia assured the doctor. If Mr. Smith would wait, said Sir William, he would speak to Mrs. Smith in the next room. Her husband was very seriously ill, Sir William said. Did he threaten to kill himself?

Oh, he did, she cried. But he did not mean it, she said. Of course not. It was merely a question of rest, said Sir William; of rest, rest, rest; a long rest in bed. There was a delightful home down in the country where her husband would be perfectly looked after. Away from her? she asked. Unfortunately, yes; the people we care for most are not good for us when we are ill. But he was not mad, was he? Sir William said he never spoke of "madness"; he called it not having a sense of proportion. But her husband did not like doctors. He would refuse to go there. Shortly and kindly Sir William explained to her the state of the case. He had threatened to kill himself. There was no alternative. It was a question of law.[250] He would lie in bed in a beautiful house in the country. The nurses were admirable. Sir William would visit him once a week. If Mrs. Warren Smith was quite

248 Note the distinction between "the European War" and "the War itself." While the former is described as a "shindy," a minor commotion or disturbance caused by schoolboys playing with gunpowder, the latter is an "appalling crime." The idea of committing a crime with distinction—of winning medals for killing other human beings—appears perfectly reasonable to Sir William. It is unthinkable, unbearable to Septimus.

249 Septimus's inability to speak dramatizes Woolf's argument in her 1926 essay "On Being Ill" that illness defies easy expression, is hostile to literary representation. "The merest schoolgirl, when she falls in love, has Shakespeare, Donne, Keats to speak her mind for her; but let a sufferer try to describe a pain in his head to a doctor and language at once runs dry," Woolf wrote. "There is nothing ready made for him. He is forced to coin words himself, and, taking his pain in one hand, and a lump of pure sound in the other (as perhaps the inhabitants of Babel did in the beginning) so to crush them together that a brand new word in the end drops out."

250 Suicide was decriminalized in England and Wales by the passage of the Suicide Act of 1961. Prior to 1961, intentionally ending one's own life was a crime. Anyone who attempted it and failed could be prosecuted and imprisoned. Their property would be seized by the government and their family left destitute.

Woolf committed suicide by drowning herself in the Ouse on March 28, 1941, after a long, cold, black winter consumed by fear. It was the third year of the Second World War. Bombs were descending onto Sussex. Hitler's army and navy were devastating Europe. The morning before she died, Leonard wrote a letter to John Lehmann, managing director of the Hogarth Press, telling him that Virginia was at Monk's House, "on the verge of a complete nervous break down and is seriously ill." The next day, shortly before noon, she went to her writing lodge, then fetched her fur coat and walking stick from the house. She walked through the garden and down to the banks of the river. On the writer's block in the lodge, she left Leonard a note, which she had drafted several weeks earlier and edited a day or two before.

> Dearest,
> I want to tell you that you have
> given me complete happiness. No one
> could have done more than you have done.
> Please believe that.
> But I know I shall never get over
> this: & I am wasting your life. It is this madness.
> Nothing anyone says can persuade me.
> You can work, & you will be much
> better without me. You see I cant
> write this even, which shows I am right.

sure she had no more questions to ask—he never hurried his patients—they would return to her husband. She had nothing more to ask—not of Sir William.

So they returned to the most exalted of mankind; the criminal who faced his judges; the victim exposed on the heights; the fugitive; the drowned sailor; the poet of the immortal ode; the Lord who had gone from life to death; to Septimus Warren Smith, who sat in the arm-chair under the skylight staring at a photograph of Lady Bradshaw in Court dress,[251] muttering messages about beauty.

"We have had our little talk," said Sir William.

"He says you are very, very ill," Rezia cried.

All I want to say is that until this
disease came on we were perfectly
happy. It was all due to you.
No one could have been so good as
you have been. From the very
first day till now.
Everyone knows that,
V.

251 A ball gown, white or cream, glittering with jewels, medals, and decorations. Though feathers, veils, and trains were customary in the early twentieth century, they were banned in 1921 for being overly ostentatious. "The style of dress for ladies attending Courts is the same as they would wear at any official evening reception, with Jewels, Full-size Orders, Decorations and Medals," announced an updated edition of *Dress and Insignia Worn at His Majesty's Court, Issued with the Authority of the Lord Chamberlain*. Sketches showing the style of dresses expected were on view at the Ceremonial Office in St. James's Palace.

Court dress, 1923. *(Courtesy of the Elizabeth Sage Historic Costume Collection in the School of Art, Architecture, + Design at Indiana University, Bloomington)*

"We have been arranging that you should go into a home," said Sir William.

"One of Holmes's homes?" sneered Septimus.

The fellow made a distasteful impression. For there was in Sir William, whose father had been a tradesman, a natural respect for breeding and clothing, which shabbiness nettled; again, more profoundly, there was in Sir William, who had never had time for reading, a grudge, deeply buried, against cultivated people who came into his room and intimated that doctors, whose profession is a constant strain upon all the highest faculties, are not educated men.

"One of *my* homes, Mr. Warren Smith," he said, "where we will teach you to rest."

And there was just one thing more.

He was quite certain that when Mr. Warren Smith was well he was the last man in the world to frighten his wife. But he had talked of killing himself.

"We all have our moments of depression," said Sir William.

Once you fall, Septimus repeated to himself, human nature is on you. Holmes and Bradshaw are on you. They scour the desert. They fly screaming into the wilderness. The rack and the thumbscrew are applied. Human nature is remorseless.

"Impulses came upon him sometimes?" Sir William asked, with his pencil on a pink card.

That was his own affair, said Septimus.

"Nobody lives for himself alone," said Sir William, glancing at the photograph of his wife in Court dress.

"And you have a brilliant career before you," said Sir William. There was Mr. Brewer's letter on the table. "An exceptionally brilliant career."

But if he confessed? If he communicated? Would they let him off then, Holmes Bradshaw?

"I—I——" he stammered.

But what was his crime? He could not remember it.

"Yes?" Sir William encouraged him. (But it was growing late.)

Love, trees, there is no crime—what was his message?

He could not remember it.

"I—I——" Septimus stammered.

"Try to think as little about yourself as possible," said Sir William kindly. Really, he was not fit to be about.

Was there anything else they wished to ask him? Sir William would make all arrangements (he murmured to Rezia) and he would let her know between five and six that evening.

"Trust everything to me," he said, and dismissed them.

Never, never had Rezia felt such agony in her life! She had asked for help and been deserted! He had failed them! Sir William Bradshaw was not a nice man.

The upkeep of that motor car alone must cost him quite a lot, said Septimus, when they got out into the street.

She clung to his arm. They had been deserted.

But what more did she want?

To his patients he gave three-quarters of an hour; and if in this exacting science which has to do with what, after all, we know nothing about—the nervous system, the human brain—a doctor loses his sense of proportion, as a doctor he fails. Health we must have; and health is proportion; so that when a man comes into your room and says he is Christ (a common delusion), and has a message, as they mostly have, and threatens, as they often do, to kill himself, you invoke proportion; order rest in bed; rest in solitude; silence and rest; rest without friends, without books, without messages; six months' rest; until a man who went in weighing seven stone six comes out weighing twelve.[252]

Proportion, divine proportion, Sir William's goddess, was acquired by Sir William walking hospitals, catching salmon, begetting one son in Harley Street by Lady Bradshaw, who caught salmon herself and took photographs scarcely to be distinguished from the work of professionals.[253] Worshipping proportion, Sir William not only prospered himself but made England prosper, secluded her lunatics, forbade childbirth, penalised despair, made it impossible for the unfit to propagate their views until they, too, shared his sense of proportion—his,

252 "Seven stone six" is 104 pounds and "twelve" stone is 168 pounds.

253 "Proportion" is defined by the *Oxford English Dictionary* (*OED*) as "appropriate, fitting, or pleasing relation (of size, etc.) between things or parts of a thing; due relation of one part to another; balance, symmetry, harmony." The interlude on proportion is fascinating for how brazenly it challenges the novel's own art of proportion. It is hyperbolic, bloated with exaggeration and ironic exaltation: the mock-epic personification of Proportion and Conversion as goddesses; the awkward repetition of details from earlier in the novel ("caught salmon herself," "scarcely to be distinguished from the work of professionals"); the overwrought allegory of Sir William as a patriarchal empire builder. It exemplifies disproportion, lacking an appropriate relation to the rest of the novel's tone.

This disproportion of the interlude itself strikes readers more forcefully in a novel that, according to Dorothy M. Hoare, "represents the first complete triumph of technique." In *Mrs. Dalloway*, "Virginia Woolf is not so much at the mercy of urgent associations which clamour to be expressed at the expense of proportion," Hoare argued, satisfied with how Woolf had reined in the jumpy, ungainly, and excessive style of her earlier novels like *Jacob's Room*. Yet, in the interlude, Woolf's momentary sacrifice of formal proportion offers a powerful critique of proportion's dangerous ideological underpinnings: how proportion was used by cruel and powerful men to consolidate their control and tame unruly or asocial presences, ranging from ex-servicemen like Septimus to independent women like the young Lady Bradshaw. The critique bears a strong autobiographical charge. As Woolf noted in her diary, the doctors she saw for her manic-depressive episodes similarly urged her to practice "equanimity." She believed equanimity to be the privilege of the healthy, the well-socialized—the "soldiers in the army of the upright," she wrote in "On Being Ill." "In health, the genial pretence must be kept up and the effort renewed—to communicate, to civilise, to share, to cultivate the desert, educate the native, to work together by day and by night to sport," she continued. But in illness, people lost their sense of proportion. They became "deserters," moving "helter-skelter," "irresponsible and disinterested," but also capable of seeing the world for what it was.

Woolf's interlude maintains a different kind of proportion, all the same: a proportion between the time the clocks measure and the time it takes for the novel to tell its story. When Septimus and Rezia enter Sir William's office, it is twelve o'clock. Their visit lasts for forty-five minutes ("three-quarters of an hour"), after which the interlude on proportion extends until the clock strikes half past one—another forty-five minutes. The number of words devoted to the description of the doctor's visit and the interlude is roughly the same (give or take ten words, depending on where one starts and stops counting). The balance between time as measured by the clock and time as measured by the words in the novel is a more difficult art of proportion to master, or to perceive. Against the proportion championed by Sir William and the social system, the novel's art of proportion assimilates disproportion without suppressing it.

The deliberateness of Woolf's interlude becomes clearer when considered alongside the British Library notebooks. There, instead of her long meditation on Proportion and Conversion, we witness only a quick verbal exchange between Septimus and Sir William.

> You are the enemy, he said.
> No, no, said Sir William agreeably.
> Why not speak the truth? Septimus asked, for the last time?
> Why <is it> for the last time?" Sir William inquired, quite casually.
> "I shan't be here again.
> I hope to see you several times.
> Your car must cost a lot to keep up. That *was* your car at the door
> I have to visit patients all over England

Though this conversation more explicitly marks Sir William as the enemy, it does not use the novel's art of proportion to oppose everything Proportion and Conversion stand for: individual and national wealth greedily generated through institutionalization ("secluded her lunatics"), eugenics ("forbade childbirth"), censorship ("made it impossible for the unfit to propagate their views"), imperialism (Conversion, we are told, is a goddess engaged "in the heat and sands of India, the mud and swamp of Africa"), vanity ("adoring her own features stamped on the face of the populace"), and misogyny (as we learn, Lady Bradshaw's will has been colonized and oppressed by her husband). Before drafting this interlude on April 18, 1924, Woolf wrote at the top of the manuscript of "The Hours," "[A] delicious idea comes to me that I will write anything I want to write." The novel converts this feeling of freedom into form. The novelist is bound only by the rules of her art, the rules she has created and imposed.

254 The southeast corner of Hyde Park.

if they were men, Lady Bradshaw's if they were women (she embroidered, knitted, spent four nights out of seven at home with her son), so that not only did his colleagues respect him, his subordinates fear him, but the friends and relations of his patients felt for him the keenest gratitude for insisting that these prophetic Christs and Christesses, who prophesied the end of the world, or the advent of God, should drink milk in bed, as Sir William ordered; Sir William with his thirty years' experience of these kinds of cases, and his infallible instinct, this is madness, this sense; his sense of proportion.

But Proportion has a sister, less smiling, more formidable, a Goddess even now engaged—in the heat and sands of India, the mud and swamp of Africa, the purlieus of London, wherever in short the climate or the devil tempts men to fall from the true belief which is her own—is even now engaged in dashing down shrines, smashing idols, and setting up in their place her own stern countenance. Conversion is her name and she feasts on the wills of the weakly, loving to impress, to impose, adoring her own features stamped on the face of the populace. At Hyde Park Corner[254] on a tub she stands preaching; shrouds herself in white and walks penitentially disguised as brotherly love through factories and parliaments; offers help, but desires power; smites out of her way roughly the dissentient, or dissatisfied; bestows her blessing on those who, looking upward, catch submissively from her eyes the light of their own. This lady too (Rezia Warren Smith divined it) had her dwelling in Sir William's heart, though concealed, as she mostly is, under some plausible disguise; some venerable name; love, duty, self-sacrifice. How he would work—how toil to raise funds, propagate reforms, initiate institutions! But conversion, fastidious Goddess, loves blood better than brick, and feasts most subtly on the human will. For example, Lady Bradshaw. Fifteen years ago she had gone under. It was nothing you could put your finger on; there had been no scene, no snap; only the slow sinking, water-logged, of her will into his. Sweet was her smile, swift her submission; dinner in Harley Street, numbering eight or nine courses, feeding ten or fifteen guests of the professional classes, was smooth and urbane. Only as the evening wore on a very slight dulness, or uneasiness perhaps, a nervous twitch, fumble, stumble and confusion indicated, what it was[255] really painful to believe—that the poor lady lied. Once, long ago, she had caught salmon freely: now, quick to minister to the craving which lit her husband's eye so oilily for dominion, for power, she cramped, squeezed, pared, pruned, drew back, peeped through; so that without knowing precisely what made the evening disagreeable, and caused this pressure on the top of the head (which might well be imputed to the professional conversation, or the fatigue of a great doctor whose life, Lady Bradshaw said, "is not his own but his patient's"), disagreeable it was: so that guests, when the clock struck ten, breathed in the air of Harley Street even with rapture; which relief, however, was denied to his patients.

There in the grey room, with the pictures on the wall, and the valuable furniture, under the ground glass skylight, they learnt the extent of their transgressions; huddled up in armchairs, they watched him go through, for their benefit, a curious exercise with the arms, which he shot out, brought sharply back to his hip, to prove (if the patient was obstinate) that Sir William was master of his own actions, which the patient was not. There some weakly broke down; sobbed, submitted; others, inspired by Heaven knows what intemperate madness, called Sir William to his face a damnable humbug; questioned, even more impiously, life itself. Why live? they demanded. Sir William replied that life was good. Certainly Lady Bradshaw in ostrich feathers hung over the mantelpiece, and as for his income it was quite twelve thousand a year. But to us, they protested, life has given no such bounty. He acquiesced. They lacked a sense of proportion. And perhaps, after all, there is no God? He shrugged his shoulders. In short, this living or not living is an affair of our own? But there they were mistaken. Sir William had a friend in Surrey where they taught, what Sir William frankly admitted was a difficult art—a sense of proportion. There were, moreover, family affection; honor; courage; and a brilliant career. All of

255 In the manuscript of "The Hours," Woolf breaks this sentence by inserting a blank page, on which she scribbles the following note to herself.
"I do not wish to ~~labour~~ <press> the point,
for there is not time, but I believe
~~that nine <all> novels out of begin try to~~
~~with a character, & that if~~
~~thought each novelist treats~~
~~character differently~~. & that
it is for the purpose of giving character
that the form of the novel has been devised. For other
purposes it is obviously
too clumsy too verbose too little dramatic!
Her words would appear in a modified form in "Mr. Bennett and Mrs. Brown," which she was working on concurrent to *Mrs. Dalloway*: "I believe that all novels, that is to say, deal with character, and that it is to express character—not to preach doctrines, sing songs, or celebrate the glories of the British Empire, that the form of the novel, so clumsy, verbose, and undramatic, so rich, elastic, and alive, has been evolved."

these had in Sir William a resolute champion. If they failed, he had to support him police and the good of society, which, he remarked very quietly, would take care, down in Surrey, that these unsocial impulses, bred more than anything by the lack of good blood,[256] were held in control. And then stole out from her hiding-place and mounted her throne that Goddess whose lust is to override opposition, to stamp indelibly in the sanctuaries of others the image of herself. Naked, defenceless, the exhausted, the friendless received the impress of Sir William's will. He swooped; he devoured. He shut people up. It was this combination of decision and humanity that endeared Sir William so greatly to the relations of his victims.

But Rezia Warren Smith cried, walking down Harley Street, that she did not like that man.

Shredding and slicing, dividing and subdividing, the clocks of Harley Street nibbled at the June day, counselled submission, upheld authority, and pointed out in chorus the supreme advantages of a sense of proportion, until the mound of time was so far diminished that a commercial clock, suspended above a shop in Oxford Street, announced, genially and fraternally, as if it were a pleasure to Messrs. Rigby and Lowndes[257] to give the information gratis, that it was half-past one.

Looking up, it appeared that each letter of their names stood for one of the hours; subconsciously one was grateful to Rigby and Lowndes for giving one time ratified by Greenwich; and this gratitude (so Hugh Whitbread ruminated, dallying there in front of the shop window) naturally took the form later of buying off Rigby and Lowndes socks or shoes. So he ruminated. It was his habit. He did not go deeply. He brushed surfaces; the dead languages, the living, life in Constantinople, Paris, Rome; riding, shooting, tennis, it had been once. The malicious asserted that he now kept guard at Buckingham Palace, dressed in silk stockings and knee-breeches, over what nobody knew. But he did it extremely efficiently. He had been afloat on the cream of English society for fifty-five years. He had known Prime Ministers. His affections were understood to be deep. And if it were

256 The suggestion that shell shock is caused "by the lack of good blood" derives from the same eugenic ideology that motivates Lady Bruton's mission on p. 144 to send young people of respectable parentage to Canada to quell social unrest in its provinces.

257 Rigby and Lowndes is an imaginary shop. The narrator's observation that "each letter of their names stood for one of the hours" connects time as constructed by the clock (the hour) to time as constructed by the novel (the letter), bringing Septimus and Rezia's visit and the novel's disproportionate interlude on proportion to its end.

Anne Fernald notes that the last names are shared by suffrage activists: Edith Rigby (1872–1950), famous for throwing a black pudding at a Labour MP and placing a bomb that did not explode under the Liverpool Cotton Exchange; Marie Belloc Lowndes (1868–1947), a popular novelist and leader of the Women Writers' Suffrage League; and Mary Lowndes (1856–1929), a stained-glass artist and contributor to the feminist journal the *Englishwoman's Review*.

true that he had not taken part in any of the great movements of the time or held important office, one or two humble reforms stood to his credit; an improvement in public shelters was one; the protection of owls in Norfolk another; servant girls had reason to be grateful to him;[258] and his name at the end of letters to the *Times*, asking for funds, appealing to the public to protect, to preserve, to clear up litter, to abate smoke, and stamp out immorality in parks, commanded respect.

A magnificent figure he cut too, pausing for a moment (as the sound of the half-hour died away) to look critically, magisterially, at socks and shoes; impeccable, substantial, as if he beheld the world from a certain eminence, and dressed to match; but realised the obligations which size, wealth, health entail, and observed punctiliously even when not absolutely necessary, little courtesies, old-fashioned ceremonies which gave a quality to his manner, something to imitate, something to remember him by, for he would never lunch, for example, with Lady Bruton, whom he had known these twenty years, without bringing her in his outstretched hand a bunch of carnations and asking Miss Brush, Lady Bruton's secretary, after her brother in South Africa,[259] which, for some reason, Miss Brush, deficient though she was in every attribute of female charm, so much resented that she said "Thank you, he's doing very well in South Africa," when, for half-a-dozen years, he had been doing badly in Portsmouth.[260]

Lady Bruton herself preferred Richard Dalloway, who arrived at the same moment. Indeed they met on the doorstep.

Lady Bruton preferred Richard Dalloway of course. He was made of much finer material. But she wouldn't let them run down her poor dear Hugh. She could never forget his kindness—he had been really remarkably kind—she forgot precisely upon what occasion. But he had been—remarkably kind. Anyhow, the difference between one man and another does not amount to much. She had never seen the sense of cutting people up, as Clarissa Dalloway did—cutting them up and sticking them together again; not at any rate when one was sixty-two. She took Hugh's carnations with her angular grim smile. There

258 Why would servant girls have reason to be grateful to Hugh Whitbread? The comment recalls Woolf's dark aside in the manuscript that no servant girl of Hugh's would "lose her place in his household without being kept sight of <keeping his eye on her>." It also reassigns to Hugh a boast Woolf first placed in Richard Dalloway's mouth in *The Voyage Out*: "Well, when I consider my life, there is one fact I admit that I'm proud of; owing to me some thousands of girls in Lancashire—and many thousands to come after them—can spend an hour every day in the open air which their mothers had to spend over their looms."

259 As N. G. Garson observes, white-ruled, self-governing South Africa joined the First World War "not as an ally of Great Britain but as a subordinate part of the British Empire." The British declaration of war committed South Africa to supporting the empire, but the government had to decide whether to contribute people and resources to the war effort. It was a difficult decision. Fifteen years before, the Afrikaner leaders had united the South African Republic and the Orange Free State to fight against the British in the Boer War, or the Second War of Independence. Many Afrikaners hesitated to rush to the defense of the empire. However, white South African leaders also believed that their association with London could help to consolidate their domestic power, particularly over Black Africans. The desire for power prevailed, and South Africa dispatched troops to France to fight on the Western Front; to German South West Africa (now known as Namibia); to German East Africa (now Rwanda, Burundi, and the mainland of Tanzania); and to Palestine as part of the Egyptian Expeditionary Force. The decision to contribute forces to the war sparked a rebellion by ex-Boer generals and Afrikaner soldiers; 300 died.

260 A port city in the southeast of England and one of the British Empire's strategic naval ports during the First World War.

was nobody else coming, she said. She had got them there on false pretences, to help her out of a difficulty—

"But let us eat first," she said.

And so there began a soundless and exquisite passing to and fro through swing doors of aproned white-capped maids, handmaidens not of necessity, but adepts in a mystery or grand deception practised by hostesses in Mayfair[261] from one-thirty to two, when, with a wave of the hand, the traffic ceases, and there rises instead this profound illusion in the first place about the food—how it is not paid for; and then that the table spreads itself voluntarily with glass and silver, little mats, saucers of red fruit; films of brown cream mask turbot; in casseroles severed chickens swim; coloured, undomestic, the fire burns; and with the wine and the coffee (not paid for) rise jocund visions before musing eyes; gently speculative eyes; eyes to whom life appears musical, mysterious; eyes now kindled to observe genially the beauty of the red carnations which Lady Bruton (whose movements were always angular) had laid beside her plate, so that

261 Located on the eastern edge of Hyde Park, Mayfair is one of the most expensive and affluent districts in London. Though modern readers may think of Edwardian Mayfair as a neighborhood of boundless opulence, the area had been in decline since the turn of the twentieth century. According to the London County Council's *Survey of London*, falling property values and the fear of progressive legislation meant that old, aristocratic Mayfair was already being rebuilt for commercial and residential uses. Houses were demolished, private garages and stables cleared for garden space. Yet the governing classes attempted to mask their material decline by continuing to lead life with a luxury many of them could not afford. Hence the "profound illusion" that the food and coffee at Lady Bruton's luncheon is "not paid for," and that "the table spreads itself voluntarily."

Aldford House, 26 Park Lane, Mayfair, c. 1917–18. *(National Archives)*

Hugh Whitbread, feeling at peace with the entire universe and at the same time completely sure of his standing, said, resting his fork:

"Wouldn't they look charming against your lace?"

Miss Brush resented this familiarity intensely. She thought him an underbred fellow. She made Lady Bruton laugh.

Lady Bruton raised the carnations, holding them rather stiffly with much the same attitude with which the General held the scroll in the picture behind her; she remained fixed, tranced. Which was she now, the General's great-grand-daughter? great-great grand-daughter? Richard Dalloway asked himself. Sir Roderick, Sir Miles, Sir Talbot—that was it. It was remarkable how in that family the likeness persisted in the women. She should have been a general of dragoons herself. And Richard would have served under her, cheerfully; he had the greatest respect for her; he cherished these romantic views about well-set-up old women of pedigree, and would have liked, in his good-humoured way, to bring some young hot-heads of his acquaintance to lunch with her; as if a type like hers could be bred of amiable tea-drinking enthusiasts! He knew her country. He knew her people. There was a vine, still bearing, which either Lovelace[262] or Herrick[263]—she never read a word of poetry herself, but so the story ran—had sat under. Better wait to put before them the question that bothered her (about making an appeal to the public; if so, in what terms and so on), better wait until they have had their coffee, Lady Bruton thought; and so laid the carnations down beside her plate.

"How's Clarissa?" she asked abruptly.

Clarissa always said that Lady Bruton did not like her. Indeed, Lady Bruton had the reputation of being more interested in politics than people; of talking like a man; of having had a finger in some notorious intrigue of the eighties, which was now beginning to be mentioned in memoirs. Certainly there was an alcove in her drawing-room, and a table in that alcove, and a photograph upon that table of General Sir Talbot Moore, now deceased, who had written there (one evening in the eight-

262 Seventeenth-century English poet Richard Lovelace (1618–1657) was famous for his military service and Royalist politics. A lifelong supporter of King Charles I, he presented a Royalist petition to the House of Commons in 1642 and was imprisoned in the Gatehouse, London, where he wrote "To Althea, From Prison." "When (like committed linnets) I / With shriller throat shall sing / The sweetness, Mercy, Majesty, / And glories of my King," he wrote, pledging himself to his king first, his lover second. He was imprisoned again in 1648 and, immediately after his release, published his first volume of poetry, *Lucasta* (1649).

Lovelace in Prison, Francesco Bartolozzi RA. Stipple engraving and etching, 1788. *(Paul Mellon Collection, Yale Center for British Art)*

263 Seventeenth-century English poet Robert Herrick (1591–1674) was a cleric known for his poem of romantic persuasion, "To the Virgins, to Make Much of Time." Like Lovelace, his sympathies lay with the Crown. He was ejected from his vicarage for refusing to support the Parliamentarians in the English Civil War (1642–51) and, in 1648, published *Hesperides; or the Works both Human & Divine of Robert Herrick*, which he dedicated to the Prince of Wales.

ies) in Lady Bruton's presence, with her cognisance, perhaps advice, a telegram ordering the British troops to advance upon an historical occasion. (She kept the pen and told the story.) Thus, when she said in her offhand way "How's Clarissa?" husbands had difficulty in persuading their wives and indeed, however devoted, were secretly doubtful themselves, of her interest in women who often got in their husbands' way, prevented them from accepting posts abroad, and had to be taken to the seaside in the middle of the session to recover from influenza. Nevertheless her inquiry, "How's Clarissa?" was known by women infallibly to be a signal from a well-wisher, from an almost silent companion, whose utterances (half a dozen perhaps in the course of a lifetime) signified recognition of some feminine comradeship which went beneath masculine lunch parties and united Lady Bruton and Mrs. Dalloway, who seldom met, and appeared when they did meet indifferent and even hostile, in a singular bond.[264]

"I met Clarissa in the Park this morning," said Hugh Whitbread, diving into the casserole, anxious to pay himself this little tribute, for he had only to come to London and he met everybody at once; but greedy, one of the greediest men she had ever known, Milly Brush thought, who observed men with unflinching rectitude, and was capable of everlasting devotion, to her own sex in particular, being knobbed, scraped, angular, and entirely without feminine charm.[265]

"D'you know who's in town?" said Lady Bruton suddenly bethinking her. "Our old friend, Peter Walsh."

They all smiled. Peter Walsh! And Mr. Dalloway was genuinely glad, Milly Brush thought; and Mr. Whitbread thought only of his chicken.

Peter Walsh! All three, Lady Bruton, Hugh Whitbread, and Richard Dalloway, remembered the same thing—how passionately Peter had been in love; been rejected; gone to India; come a cropper;[266] made a mess of things; and Richard Dalloway had a very great liking for the dear old fellow too. Milly Brush saw that; saw a depth in the brown of his eyes; saw him hesitate;

264 In the manuscript of "The Hours," Woolf clarifies that Lady Bruton is a widow: "such an arrow being for Lady Bruton her husbands <the governors> untimely death, years ago. ~~shooting,~~ in the East."

265 Like the woman singing by the fountain, Miss Brush is another character of indeterminate sex—or rather, a character unsexed by the narrator, who dangles every convention of feminine charm ("a curl, smile, lip, cheek, nose") before Miss Brush only to deny her any trace of beauty. Unsexed, Miss Brush appears as a "detached spirit," "an uncorrupted soul whom life could not bamboozle." She sees Hugh Whitbread's greed, detests his unctuousness. She asks herself what Mr. Dalloway is thinking about Peter Walsh, and, answering her own question, her thoughts blend with the narrator's, offering the reader a preview of what will happen next in the novel: "That Peter Walsh had been in love with Clarissa; that he would go back directly after lunch and find Clarissa; that he would tell her, in so many words, that he loved her." The limit of her perception is her loyalty to Lady Bruton whose faults she cannot see, being in her employ and as enthralled by her as Lucy is by Clarissa.

266 "To come a cropper" is to fall over, as from a horse, or fail badly at a venture. The earliest use of the phrase came from sporting stories, such as those featured in *Jorrocks' Jaunts and Jollities* and *Soapy Sponge*, on display at Hatchards on p. 20.

consider; which interested her, as Mr. Dalloway always interested her, for what was he thinking, she wondered, about Peter Walsh?

That Peter Walsh had been in love with Clarissa; that he would go back directly after lunch and find Clarissa; that he would tell her, in so many words, that he loved her. Yes, he would say that.

Milly Brush once might almost have fallen in love with these silences; and Mr. Dalloway was always so dependable; such a gentleman too. Now, being forty, Lady Bruton had only to nod, or turn her head a little abruptly, and Milly Brush took the signal, however deeply she might be sunk in these reflections of a detached spirit, of an uncorrupted soul whom life could not bamboozle, because life had not offered her a trinket of the slightest value; not a curl, smile, lip, cheek, nose; nothing whatever; Lady Bruton had only to nod, and Perkins was instructed to quicken the coffee.

"Yes; Peter Walsh has come back," said Lady Bruton. It was vaguely flattering to them all. He had come back, battered, unsuccessful, to their secure shores. But to help him, they reflected, was impossible; there was some flaw in his character. Hugh Whitbread said one might of course mention his name to So-and-so. He wrinkled lugubriously, consequentially, at the thought of the letters he would write to the heads of Government offices about "my old friend, Peter Walsh," and so on. But it wouldn't lead to anything—not to anything permanent, because of his character.

"In trouble with some woman," said Lady Bruton. They had all guessed that *that* was at the bottom of it.

"However," said Lady Bruton, anxious to leave the subject, "we shall hear the whole story from Peter himself."

(The coffee was very slow in coming.)

"The address?" murmured Hugh Whitbread; and there was at once a ripple in the grey tide of service which washed round Lady Bruton day in, day out, collecting, intercepting, enveloping her in a fine tissue which broke concussions, mitigated interruptions, and spread round the house in Brook Street[267] a fine net

267 A street in Mayfair that runs from Grosvenor Square to Hanover Square, home to many wealthy and well-connected Londoners. Clarissa had stood on the corner of Brook and Bond Streets on p. 30.

where things lodged and were picked out accurately, instantly, by grey-haired Perkins, who had been with Lady Bruton these thirty years and now wrote down the address; handed it to Mr. Whitbread, who took out his pocket-book, raised his eyebrows, and slipping it in among documents of the highest importance, said that he would get Evelyn to ask him to lunch.

(They were waiting to bring the coffee until Mr. Whitbread had finished.)

Hugh was very slow, Lady Bruton thought. He was getting fat, she noticed. Richard always kept himself in the pink of condition. She was getting impatient; the whole of her being was setting positively, undeniably, domineeringly brushing aside all this unnecessary trifling (Peter Walsh and his affairs) upon that subject which engaged her attention, and not merely her attention, but that fibre which was the ramrod of her soul, that essential part of her without which Millicent Bruton would not have been Millicent Bruton; that project for emigrating young people of both sexes born of respectable parents and setting them up with a fair prospect of doing well in Canada. She exaggerated. She had perhaps lost her sense of proportion.[268] Emigration was not to others the obvious remedy, the sublime conception. It was not to them (not to Hugh, or Richard, or even to devoted Miss Brush) the liberator of the pent egotism, which a strong martial woman, well nourished, well descended, of direct impulses, downright feelings, and little introspective power (broad and simple—why could not every one be broad and simple? she asked) feels rise within her, once youth is past, and must eject upon some object—it may be Emigration, it may be Emancipation; but whatever it be, this object round which the essence of her soul is daily secreted becomes inevitably prismatic, lustrous, half looking-glass, half precious stone; now carefully hidden in case people should sneer at it; now proudly displayed. Emigration had become, in short, largely Lady Bruton.

But she had to write. And one letter to the *Times*, she used to say to Miss Brush, cost her more than to organise an expe-

268 Sir William's belief in "good blood" also informs Lady Bruton's project for emigrating young people "born of respectable parents" to Canada, a British dominion until 1931. Early twentieth-century Canadian eugenicists were quick to blame growing social and political unrest in the provinces on the mental deficiencies of British immigrants, particularly nonwhite, working-class men. In 1919, the British government started to give money to the Society for the Oversea Settlement of British Women. In May 1923, Charles Clarke, the first professor of psychiatry at the University of Toronto, gave a lecture to the Royal Medico-Psychological Association of England urging, according to the *Times*, "the introduction to Canada of the best Nordic types" to ensure the nation's successful development. The *Times* embraced Clarke's position in a piece published two days after his lecture, observing that his proposal to import Nordic types was "of great importance both to the Dominions and to the Mother Country."

Though Hugh, Richard, and even Miss Brush believe Lady Bruton has "perhaps lost her sense of proportion," her delusions are encouraged, allowed to fester, to gain in intensity and resolve, while Septimus's must be checked.

dition to South Africa (which she had done in the war). After a morning's battle beginning, tearing up, beginning again, she used to feel the futility of her own womanhood as she felt it on no other occasion, and would turn gratefully to the thought of Hugh Whitbread who possessed—no one could doubt it—the art of writing letters to the *Times*.

A being so differently constituted from herself, with such a command of language; able to put things as editors liked them put; had passions which one could not call simply greed. Lady Bruton often suspended judgement upon men in deference to the mysterious accord in which they, but no woman, stood to the laws of the universe; knew how to put things; knew what was said; so that if Richard advised her, and Hugh wrote for her, she was sure of being somehow right. So she let Hugh eat his soufflé; asked after poor Evelyn; waited until they were smoking, and then said,

"Milly, would you fetch the papers?"

And Miss Brush went out, came back; laid papers on the table; and Hugh produced his fountain pen; his silver fountain pen, which had done twenty years' service, he said, unscrewing the cap. It was still in perfect order; he had shown it to the makers; there was no reason, they said, why it should ever wear out; which was somehow to Hugh's credit, and to the credit of the sentiments which his pen expressed (so Richard Dalloway felt) as Hugh began carefully writing capital letters with rings round them in the margin, and thus marvellously reduced Lady Bruton's tangles to sense, to grammar such as the editor of the *Times*, Lady Bruton felt, watching the marvellous transformation, must respect. Hugh was slow. Hugh was pertinacious. Richard said one must take risks. Hugh proposed modifications in deference to people's feelings, which, he said rather tartly when Richard laughed, "had to be considered," and read out "how, therefore, we are of opinion that the times are ripe . . . the superfluous youth of our ever-increasing population . . . what we owe to the dead . . ." which Richard thought all stuffing and bunkum, but no harm in it, of course, and Hugh went on drafting sentiments in alphabetical order of the highest nobility, brushing the cigar ash from his waistcoat, and summing up now and then the progress they had made until, finally, he read out the draft of a letter which Lady Bruton felt certain was a masterpiece. Could her own meaning sound like that?

Hugh could not guarantee that the editor would put it in; but he would be meeting somebody at luncheon.

Whereupon Lady Bruton, who seldom did a graceful thing, stuffed all Hugh's carnations into the front of her dress, and flinging her hands out called him "My Prime Minister!" What she would have done without them both she did not know. They rose. And Richard Dalloway strolled off as usual to have a look at the General's portrait, because he meant, whenever he had a moment of leisure, to write a history of Lady Bruton's family.

And Millicent Bruton was very proud of her family. But they could wait, they could wait, she said, looking at the picture; meaning that her family, of military men, administrators, admirals, had been men of action, who had done their duty; and Richard's first duty was to his country, but it was a fine face, she said; and all the papers were ready for Richard down at Aldmixton[269] whenever the time came; the Labour Government[270] she meant. "Ah, the news from India!" she cried.[271]

And then, as they stood in the hall taking yellow gloves from the bowl on the malachite table and Hugh was offering Miss Brush with quite unnecessary courtesy some discarded ticket or other compliment, which she loathed from the depths of her heart and blushed brick red, Richard turned to Lady Bruton, with his hat in his hand, and said,

"We shall see you at our party to-night?" whereupon Lady Bruton resumed the magnificence which letter-writing had shattered. She might come; or she might not come. Clarissa had wonderful energy. Parties terrified Lady Bruton. But then, she was getting old. So she intimated, standing at her doorway; handsome; very erect; while her chow stretched behind her, and Miss Brush disappeared into the background with her hands full of papers.

269 An imaginary country estate.

270 Like all the novel's governing-class characters, Lady Bruton is bracing herself for the rise of the first Labour government in January 1924, following the elections of 1922 and 1923. Led by Prime Minister Ramsay MacDonald, the first MacDonald ministry lasted only until November 4, 1924, when the Conservative administration of Stanley Baldwin came into power.

271 The renewal of the fight for Indian independence was described in n. 6 on p. 5. As Alex Zwerdling documents, "the *Times* in June 1923 was full of 'news from India' sure to agitate" Lady Bruton: "imperial police 'overwhelmed and brutally tortured by the villagers' (2 June); 'Extremists Fomenting Trouble' (23 June); 'Punjab Discontent' (29 June)."

And Lady Bruton went ponderously, majestically, up to her room, lay, one arm extended, on the sofa. She sighed, she snored, not that she was asleep, only drowsy and heavy, drowsy and heavy, like a field of clover in the sunshine this hot June day, with the bees going round and about and the yellow butterflies. Always she went back to those fields down in Devonshire, where she had jumped the brooks on Patty, her pony, with Mortimer and Tom, her brothers. And there were the dogs; there were the rats; there were her father and mother on the lawn under the trees, with the tea-things out, and the beds of dahlias, the holly-hocks, the pampas grass; and they, little wretches, always up to some mischief! stealing back through the shrubbery, so as not to be seen, all bedraggled from some roguery. What old nurse used to say about her frocks!

Ah dear, she remembered—it was Wednesday in Brook Street. Those kind good fellows, Richard Dalloway, Hugh Whitbread, had gone this hot day through the streets whose growl came up to her lying on the sofa. Power was hers, position, income. She had lived in the forefront of her time. She had had good friends; known the ablest men of her day. Murmuring London flowed up to her, and her hand, lying on the sofa back, curled upon some imaginary baton such as her grandfathers might have held, holding which she seemed, drowsy and heavy, to be commanding battalions marching to Canada, and those good fellows walking across London, that territory of theirs, that little bit of carpet, Mayfair.

And they went further and further from her, being attached to her by a thin thread (since they had lunched with her) which would stretch and stretch, get thinner and thinner as they walked across London; as if one's friends were attached to one's body, after lunching with them, by a thin thread, which (as she dozed there) became hazy with the sound of bells, striking the hour or ringing to service, as a single spider's thread is blotted with rain-drops, and, burdened, sags down.[272] So she slept.

And Richard Dalloway and Hugh Whitbread hesitated at the corner of Conduit Street[273] at the very moment that Milli-

272 The single spider's thread that connects Millicent Bruton to Hugh Whitbread and Richard Dalloway, then Richard to Clarissa, is invisible, fragile, and light, liable to snap at any moment, on a whim. Compared to the alert, anxious connections forged by the crowds that watch the motorcar as it flows through the streets, or the airplane as it dives and swoops overhead, the ties that bind the governing class, oblivious to the lasting trauma of the war, are flimsy, easily broken. In his excellent study of modernism and war, *Tense Future*, Paul Saint-Amour compares the single spider's thread in *Mrs. Dalloway* to the spider's web in *The Years*, a spider's web that survives the wartime air raid, suggesting that the "social ties necessary to transcend war can only be formed in war, when . . . partitions of nation, class, and generation lose their 'surface hardness' enough to permit new combinations to form."

273 A street in Mayfair named after Conduit Mead, a large old field and meeting place for fox and hare hunts in the nineteenth century.

cent Bruton, lying on the sofa, let the thread snap; snored. Contrary winds buffeted at the street corner. They looked in at a shop window; they did not wish to buy or to talk but to part, only with contrary winds buffeting the street corner, with some sort of lapse in the tides of the body, two forces meeting in a swirl, morning and afternoon, they paused. Some newspaper placard went up in the air, gallantly, like a kite at first, then paused, swooped, fluttered; and a lady's veil hung. Yellow awnings trembled. The speed of the morning traffic slackened, and single carts rattled carelessly down half-empty streets. In Norfolk, of which Richard Dalloway was half thinking, a soft warm wind blew back the petals; confused the waters; ruffled the flowering

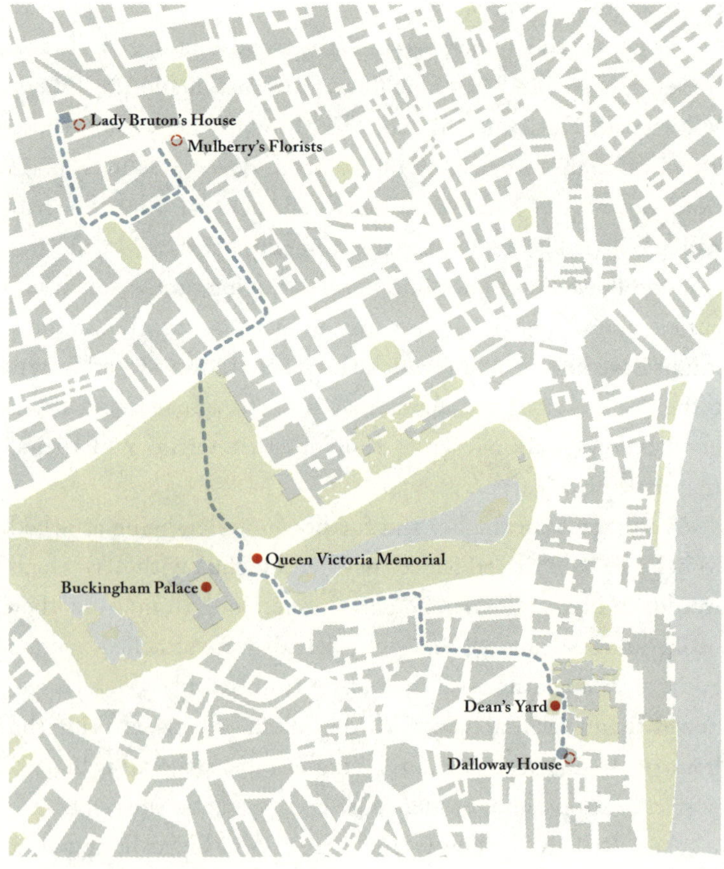

Richard Dalloway's walk. *(Christian Nakarado)*

grasses. Haymakers, who had pitched beneath hedges to sleep away the morning toil, parted curtains of green blades; moved trembling globes of cow parsley to see the sky; the blue, the steadfast, the blazing summer sky.

Aware that he was looking at a silver two-handled Jacobean mug, and that Hugh Whitbread admired condescendingly, with airs of connoisseurship, a Spanish necklace which he thought of asking the price of in case Evelyn might like it—still Richard was torpid; could not think or move. Life had thrown up this wreckage; shop windows full of coloured paste, and one stood stark with the lethargy of the old, stiff with the rigidity of the old, looking in.[274] Evelyn Whitbread might like to buy this Spanish necklace—so she might. Yawn he must. Hugh was going into the shop.

"Right you are!" said Richard, following.

Goodness knows he didn't want to go buying necklaces with Hugh. But there are tides in the body. Morning meets afternoon. Borne like a frail shallop[275] on deep, deep floods, Lady Bruton's great-grandfather and his memoir and his campaigns in North America were whelmed and sunk. And Millicent Bruton too. She went under. Richard didn't care a straw what became of Emigration; about that letter, whether the editor put it in or not. The necklace hung stretched between Hugh's admirable fingers. Let him give it to a girl, if he must buy jewels—any girl, any girl in the street. For the worthlessness of this life did strike Richard pretty forcibly—buying necklaces for Evelyn. If he'd had a boy he'd have said, Work, work. But he had his Elizabeth; he adored his Elizabeth.

"I should like to see Mr. Dubonnet," said Hugh in his curt worldly way. It appeared that this Dubonnet had the measurements of Mrs. Whitbread's neck, or, more strangely still, knew her views upon Spanish jewellery and the extent of her possessions in that line (which Hugh could not remember). All of which seemed to Richard Dalloway awfully odd. For he never gave Clarissa presents, except a bracelet two or three years ago, which had not been a success. She never wore it. It pained him to

274 Contrast Richard's lethargy and feelings of decrepitude in front of the jewelers with Clarissa's youthful extravagance on p. 9. Where Richard dismisses "this wreckage," the "shop windows full of coloured paste," Clarissa marvels at the sight of the shopkeepers "fidgeting in their windows with their paste and diamonds, their lovely old sea-green brooches in eighteenth-century settings to tempt Americans. . . ." In his walk back to their home, Richard will retrace much of Clarissa's morning route, thinking of her while his thoughts about the city, its people, its shops, its monuments, often diverge from hers.

275 A light sailing boat.

remember that she never wore it. And as a single spider's thread after wavering here and there attaches itself to the point of a leaf, so Richard's mind, recovering from its lethargy, set now on his wife, Clarissa, whom Peter Walsh had loved so passionately; and Richard had had a sudden vision of her there at luncheon; of himself and Clarissa; of their life together; and he drew the tray of old jewels towards him, and taking up first this brooch then that ring, "How much is that?" he asked, but doubted his own taste. He wanted to open the drawing-room door and come in holding out something; a present for Clarissa. Only what? But Hugh was on his legs again. He was unspeakably pompous. Really, after dealing here for thirty-five years he was not going to be put off by a mere boy who did not know his business. For Dubonnet, it seemed, was out, and Hugh would not buy anything until Mr. Dubonnet chose to be in; at which the youth flushed and bowed his correct little bow. It was all perfectly correct. And yet Richard couldn't have said that to save his life! Why these people stood that damned insolence he could not conceive. Hugh was becoming an intolerable ass. Richard Dalloway could not stand more than an hour of his society. And, flicking his bowler hat by way of farewell, Richard turned at the corner of Conduit Street eager, yes, very eager, to travel that spider's thread of attachment between himself and Clarissa; he would go straight to her, in Westminster.

But he wanted to come in holding something. Flowers? Yes, flowers, since he did not trust his taste in gold; any number of flowers, roses, orchids, to celebrate what was, reckoning things as you will, an event; this feeling about her when they spoke of Peter Walsh at luncheon; and they never spoke of it; not for years had they spoken of it; which, he thought, grasping his red and white roses together (a vast bunch in tissue paper), is the greatest mistake in the world. The time comes when it can't be said; one's too shy to say it, he thought, pocketing his sixpence or two of change, setting off with his great bunch held against his body to Westminster to say straight out in so many words (whatever she might think of him), holding out his flowers, "I love you." Why not? Really it was a miracle thinking of the war, and thousands of poor chaps, with all their lives before them, shovelled together, already half forgotten; it was a miracle. Here he was walking across London to say to Clarissa in so many words that he loved her. Which one never does say, he thought. Partly one's lazy; partly one's shy. And Clarissa—it was difficult to think of her; except in starts, as at luncheon, when he saw her quite distinctly; their whole life. He stopped at the crossing; and repeated—being simple by nature, and undebauched, because he had tramped, and shot; being pertinacious and dogged, having championed the down-trodden and followed his instincts in the House of Commons; being preserved in his simplicity yet at the same time grown rather speechless, rather stiff—he repeated that it was a miracle, that he should have married Clarissa; a miracle—his life had been a miracle, he thought; hesitating to cross. But it did make his blood boil to see little creatures of five or six crossing Piccadilly alone.[276] The police ought to have stopped the traffic at once. He had no illusions about the London police. Indeed, he was collecting evidence of their malpractices; and those costermongers,[277] not allowed to stand their barrows in the streets; and prostitutes, good Lord, the fault wasn't in

A police officer crossing the road with children, c. 1920.
(UK Photo and Social History Archive)

276 Traffic lights did not appear as regular fixtures of city life until 1926, when a series of manual electric lights was installed along Piccadilly. London streets were treacherous to cross. In a 1924 snippet in the *Nation and Athenaeum*, Woolf complained that "on the high road the procession of vehicles is irregular and chaotic, and the pedestrian has to depend upon the consideration and humanity of the motorist." While Woolf was drafting this section of the novel, her niece Angelica Bell was knocked down by a car in the streets of London and thought to have died. "My feeling was 'a pane of glass shelters me. I'm only allowed to look on at this.' at which I was half envious, half grieved," Woolf wrote of her attempt to conceal her fear and anguish in front of Vanessa. "Nothing was wrong with Angelica—it was only a joke this time." But the unfunny joke, as well as the suppression of emotion that attended it, would make its way into her description of stiff, speechless Richard Dalloway crossing the street.

277 A costermonger is a person who sells fruits and vegetables from a cart in the street.

them, nor in young men either, but in our detestable social system and so forth;[278] all of which he considered, could be seen considering, grey, dogged, dapper, clean, as he walked across the Park to tell his wife that he loved her.

For he would say it in so many words, when he came into the room. Because it is a thousand pities never to say what one feels, he thought, crossing the Green Park[279] and observing with pleasure how in the shade of the trees whole families, poor families, were sprawling; children kicking up their legs; sucking milk; paper bags thrown about, which could easily be picked up (if people objected) by one of those fat gentlemen in livery; for he was of opinion that every park, and every square, during the summer months should be open to children (the grass of the park flushed and faded, lighting up the poor mothers of Westminster[280] and their crawling babies, as if a yellow lamp were moved beneath). But what could be done for female vagrants like that poor creature, stretched on her elbow (as if she had flung herself on the earth, rid of all ties, to observe curiously, to speculate boldly, to consider the whys and the wherefores, impudent, loose-lipped, humorous), he did not know. Bearing his flowers like a weapon, Richard Dalloway approached her; intent he passed her; still there was time for a spark between them—she laughed at the sight of him, he smiled good humouredly, considering the problem of the female vagrant; not that they would ever speak. But he would tell Clarissa that he loved her, in so many words. He had, once upon a time, been jealous of Peter Walsh; jealous of him and Clarissa. But she had often said to him that she had been right not to marry Peter Walsh; which, knowing Clarissa, was obviously true; she wanted support. Not that she was weak; but she wanted support.

As for Buckingham Palace (like an old prima donna facing the audience all in white) you can't deny it a certain dignity, he considered, nor despise what does, after all, stand to millions of people (a little crowd was waiting at the gate to see the King drive out) for a symbol, absurd though it is; a child with a box of bricks could have done better, he thought; looking at the memo-

278 Though several critics have admired Conservative MP Richard Dalloway's ability to think structurally about costermongers, prostitutes, and vagrants, the phrase "in our detestable social system and so forth" is thrown off with a glibness that turns Richard's acknowledgment of the social system into a dismissal of it.

279 One of the Royal Parks of London, located between Hyde Park and St. James's Park. Thought to be a burial ground for lepers until 1668, the park rested on the outskirts of London for two hundred years, a haunt of miscreants and thieves. It was properly landscaped in the mid-nineteenth century, when it became a place for popular amusement, concerts, fireworks, and ballooning attempts.

280 Clarissa admires the mothers of Pimlico who "gave suck to their young" in the park on p. 14, while Richard sees the poor mothers of Westminster and thinks only of the government policy of keeping parks open during the summer.

LL London Postcard of Piccadilly, Green Park to the left-hand side, c. 1910.
(UK Photo and Social History Archive)

rial to Queen Victoria (whom he could remember in her horn spectacles driving through Kensington), its white mound, its billowing motherliness; but he liked being ruled by the descendant of Horsa;[281] he liked continuity; and the sense of handing on the traditions of the past.[282] It was a great age in which to have lived. Indeed, his own life was a miracle; let him make no mistake about it; here he was, in the prime of life, walking to his

281 Horsa (n.d.–ca. 455) and Hengist (n.d.–ca. 488) were legendary brothers, German exiles, and leaders of the first Anglo-Saxon settlers in Britain, according to Bede's eighth-century *Ecclesiastical History*. Horsa was killed in Aegelsthrep, in what is now modern-day Kent, after which Hengist began his reign. The kings of Kent consider themselves direct descendants of Hengist.

282 Again, we encounter the crowd waiting before the gates of Buckingham Palace; Queen Victoria billowing on her mound; the anticipation of royalty driving through the city. Richard's love for continuity is shared by the novel, which doubles back to the places and people encountered on pp. 9–33. The manuscript of "The Hours" offers an extended and more aggressively unflattering portrait of Buckingham Palace, which it describes as "<like a> prima donna, who has grown so stout that she can hardly waddle between the first violins on to the platform; & is seriously impeded by a bunch of carnations, & yet robes herself in white & stands out faces the audience, thought you may smile as its magnificence; & which is not so bad, if you reflect upon the courage of painting yourself white when you weigh twenty stone."

Queen Victoria Memorial, the Mall, c. 1911.
(UK Photo and Social History Archive)

house in Westminster to tell Clarissa that he loved her. Happiness is this, he thought.

It is this, he said, as he entered Dean's Yard. Big Ben was beginning to strike, first the warning, musical; then the hour, irrevocable. Lunch parties waste the entire afternoon, he thought, approaching his door.

The sound of Big Ben flooded Clarissa's drawing-room, where she sat, ever so annoyed, at her writing-table; worried;

Little Dean's Yard at Westminster, c. 1920. *(UK Photo and Social History Archive)*

annoyed. It was perfectly true that she had not asked Ellie Henderson to her party; but she had done it on purpose. Now Mrs. Marsham wrote: "She had told Ellie Henderson she would ask Clarissa—Ellie so much wanted to come".

But why should she invite all the dull women in London to her parties? Why should Mrs. Marsham interfere? And there was Elizabeth closeted all this time with Doris Kilman. Anything more nauseating she could not conceive. Prayer at this hour with that woman. And the sound of the bell flooded the room with its melancholy wave; which receded, and gathered itself together to fall once more, when she heard, distractingly, something fumbling, something scratching at the door. Who at this hour? Three, good Heavens! Three already! For with overpowering directness and dignity the clock struck three; and she heard nothing else; but the door handle slipped round and in came Richard! What a surprise! In came Richard, holding out flowers.[283] She had failed him, once at Constantinople;[284] and Lady Bruton, whose lunch parties were said to be extraordinarily amusing, had not asked her. He was holding out flowers—roses, red and white roses. (But he could not bring himself to say he loved her; not in so many words.)

But how lovely, she said, taking his flowers. She understood; she understood without his speaking; his Clarissa. She put them in vases on the mantelpiece. How lovely they looked! she said. And was it amusing, she asked? Had Lady Bruton asked after her? Peter Walsh was back. Mrs. Marsham had written. Must she ask Ellie Henderson? That woman Kilman was upstairs.

"But let us sit down for five minutes," said Richard.

It all looked so empty. All the chairs were against the wall. What had they been doing? Oh, it was for the party; no, he had not forgotten the party. Peter Walsh was back. Oh yes; she had had him. And he was going to get a divorce; and he was in love with some woman out there. And he hadn't changed in the slightest. There she was, mending her dress . . . .

"Thinking of Bourton," she said.

"Hugh was at lunch," said Richard. She had met him too!

283 Like Clarissa's morning walk, Richard's afternoon walk also ends with him bringing flowers to the house. Like the flowers that open the novel, these flowers—"roses, red and white roses"—are an ambivalent gift, the bearers of both Richard Dalloway's love and his inarticulacy. Later, Clarissa will express love for her already dying roses—"the only flowers she could bear to see cut," she thinks on p. 157—but none for the Albanians or Armenians whose lives have turned into a living death, "hunted out of existence, maimed, frozen, the victims of cruelty and injustice . . . no, she could feel nothing for the Albanians, or was it the Armenians?"

284 An echo from p. 52.

Well, he was getting absolutely intolerable. Buying Evelyn necklaces; fatter than ever; an intolerable ass.

"And it came over me 'I might have married you'," she said, thinking of Peter sitting there in his little bow-tie; with that knife, opening it, shutting it. "Just as he always was, you know."

They were talking about him at lunch, said Richard. (But he could not tell her he loved her. He held her hand. Happiness is this, he thought.) They had been writing a letter to the *Times* for Millicent Bruton. That was about all Hugh was fit for.

"And our dear Miss Kilman?" he asked. Clarissa thought the roses absolutely lovely; first bunched together; now of their own accord starting apart.

"Kilman arrives just as we've done lunch," she said. "Elizabeth turns pink. They shut themselves up. I suppose they're praying."

Lord! He didn't like it; but these things pass over if you let them.

"In a mackintosh with an umbrella," said Clarissa.

He had not said "I love you"; but he held her hand.[285] Happiness is this, is this, he thought.

"But why should I ask all the dull women in London to my parties?" said Clarissa. And if Mrs. Marsham gave a party, did *she* invite her guests?

"Poor Ellie Henderson," said Richard—it was a very odd thing how much Clarissa minded about her parties, he thought.

But Richard had no notion of the look of a room. However—what was he going to say?

If she worried about these parties he would not let her give them. Did she wish she had married Peter? But he must go.

He must be off, he said, getting up. But he stood for a moment as if he were about to say something; and she wondered what? Why? There were the roses.

"Some Committee?" she asked, as he opened the door.

"Armenians,"[286] he said; or perhaps it was "Albanians."[287]

And there is a dignity in people; a solitude; even between husband and wife a gulf; and that one must respect, thought Cla-

285 In the manuscript of "The Hours," Richard says, "I love you," and Clarissa does not respond: "~~Clarissa never said anything.~~ She never ~~said anything[.] But it was~~ all right."

286 Clarissa's confusion over the Armenians and the Albanians is a more naive and ethically reprehensible version of Woolf's own inability to imagine genocide: a practice of state-sponsored violence characterized by its extreme disproportion—the intent to destroy an entire race, religion, ethnic group, or nationality. "I laughed to myself over the quantities of Armenians," she confessed to her diary on May 12, 1919, upon learning about the massacre of some 1.5 million Armenians by the Turks during the First World War. "How can one mind whether they number 4,000 or 4,000,000? The feat is beyond me."

Prior to 1915, the Armenians, a Christian ethnic minority, had been allowed to maintain their religious and social structures so long as they paid extra taxes to the Ottoman authorities. Yet, as the sultanate crumbled during the war, the Armenians were left exposed to attacks by nationalists. When the Ottoman Empire entered the war on the side of Germany, the Young Turks, a movement of junior army officers committed to Turkish nationalism and pan-Islamism, accused the Armenians of helping the Russians defend their holdings in the Caucasus. On April 24, 1915, hundreds of Armenian intellectuals were arrested and executed, followed by the mass deportation of more than a million Armenians over the next several years—death marches across the Syrian desert, where countless men, women, and children died of starvation, exhaustion, and exposure. While the word "genocide" was not coined until 1943, its inventor, Polish-Jewish lawyer Raphael Lemkin, was first compelled to investigate the systematic extermination of ethnic minorities by accounts of the massacres of Armenians. Modern-day Turkish authorities continue to deny the appropriateness of the term "genocide," while most historians agree that this was the first genocide of the twentieth century.

British consular agents reported on the difficult conditions facing Armenians in Turkey during the dissolution of the Ottoman Empire, including the seizure of land plots and attacks on settlements. After 1915, the plight of the Armenians was frequently discussed by parliamentary committees dealing with the "Near East," though little was done to intervene or to help resettle the Armenians. "The whole Armenian matter . . . was abandoned in the aftermath of WWI, with the ascendancy of the Kemalist Turks, complications brought about by the Bolshevik Revolution, and imperial rivalries amongst the remaining Allied Powers," reports *British Parliamentary Debates on the Armenian Genocide, 1915–1918.*

rissa, watching him open the door; for one would not part with it oneself, or take it, against his will, from one's husband, without losing one's independence, one's self-respect—something, after all, priceless.[288]

He returned with a pillow and a quilt.

"An hour's complete rest after luncheon," he said. And he went.

How like him! He would go on saying "An hour's complete rest after luncheon" to the end of time, because a doctor had ordered it once. It was like him to take what doctors said literally; part of his adorable, divine simplicity, which no one had to the same extent; which made him go and do the thing while she and Peter frittered their time away bickering. He was already half-way to the House of Commons, to his Armenians, his Albanians, having settled her on the sofa, looking at his roses. And people would say, "Clarissa Dalloway is spoilt." She cared much more for her roses than for the Armenians. Hunted out of existence, maimed, frozen, the victims of cruelty and injustice (she had heard Richard say so over and over again)—no, she could feel nothing for the Albanians, or was it the Armenians? but she loved her roses (didn't that help the Armenians?)—the only flowers she could bear to see cut. But Richard was already at the House of Commons; at his Committee, having settled all her difficulties. But no; alas, that was not true. He did not see the reasons against asking Ellie Henderson. She would do it, of course, as he wished it. Since he had brought the pillows, she would lie down . . . . But—but—why did she suddenly feel, for no reason that she could discover, desperately unhappy? As a person who has dropped some grain of pearl or diamond into the grass and parts the tall blades very carefully, this way and that, and searches here and there vainly, and at last spies it there at the roots, so she went through one thing and another; no, it was not Sally Seton saying that Richard would never be in the Cabinet because he had a second-class brain (it came back to her); no, she did not mind that; nor was it to do with Elizabeth either and Doris Kilman; those were facts. It was a feeling,

287 Albania, which had been granted sovereignty by the European powers in 1913, was the site of persistent conflicts among Greek, Italian, and Yugoslav forces after the First World War and throughout the 1920s. Rising tensions between local Christians and former Ottoman officials, led by Prime Minister Ahmed Bey Zogu, resulted in several political assassinations. Zogu resigned as prime minister in 1924 to serve as president from 1925 to 1928 and, later, ascended to the throne as the nation's first king, Zog I, reigning from 1928 to 1939.

288 An echo of Clarissa's thoughts on marriage from p. 15.

some unpleasant feeling, earlier in the day perhaps; something that Peter had said, combined with some depression of her own, in her bedroom, taking off her hat; and what Richard had said had added to it, but what had he said? There were his roses. Her parties! That was it! Her parties! Both of them criticised her very unfairly, laughed at her very unjustly, for her parties. That was it! That was it!

Well, how was she going to defend herself? Now that she knew what it was, she felt perfectly happy. They thought, or Peter at any rate thought, that she enjoyed imposing herself; liked to have famous people about her; great names; was simply a snob in short. Well, Peter might think so. Richard merely thought it foolish of her to like excitement when she knew it was bad for her heart. It was childish, he thought. And both were quite wrong. What she liked was simply life.

"That's what I do it for," she said, speaking aloud, to life.[289]

Since she was lying on the sofa, cloistered, exempt,[290] the presence of this thing which she felt to be so obvious became physically existent; with robes of sound from the street, sunny, with hot breath, whispering, blowing out the blinds. But suppose Peter said to her, "Yes, yes, but your parties—what's the sense of your parties?" all she could say was (and nobody could be expected to understand): They're an offering; which sounded horribly vague. But who was Peter to make out that life was all plain sailing?—Peter always in love, always in love with the wrong woman? What's your love? she might say to him. And she knew his answer; how it is the most important thing in the world and no woman possibly understood it. Very well. But could any man understand what she meant either? about life? She could not imagine Peter or Richard taking the trouble to give a party for no reason whatever.

But to go deeper, beneath what people said (and these judgements, how superficial, how fragmentary they are!) in her own mind now, what did it mean to her, this thing she called life? Oh, it was very queer. Here was So-and-so in South Kensington; some one up in Bayswater; and somebody else, say, in May-

289 "But life, life! How I long to take you in my arms & crush you out!" Woolf wrote in her diary on March 6, 1923, speaking aloud to life just as Clarissa does, and thinking, too, of death, just as Clarissa will in the next several paragraphs. Woolf's rapture was prompted by the death of the writer Katherine Mansfield (1888–1923), an intimate, prickly friend and rival who had died from complications due to tuberculosis in January 1923. "Morgan Forster said that Prelude and The Voyage Out were the best novels of their time, & I said Damn Katherine! Why can't I be the only woman who knows how to write?" Woolf wrote in one of the few letters that the women exchanged. Along with the death of Kitty Maxse in 1922, Mansfield's death greatly affected Woolf as she was drafting *Mrs. Dalloway*. The novel's elegy for life is as much a personal commemoration of these friends as it is a national and historical memorialization of the wartime dead.

290 On June 9, 1924, Woolf stopped writing "The Hours" in the middle of this sentence and inserted a new page to plan the rest of the novel:
~~Whitmonday~~
~~June 9th~~
4 or 5 scenes more.
Kilman & Elizabeth.
The Warren Smiths.
Peter.
London.
The party.

fair. And she felt quite continuously a sense of their existence; and she felt what a waste; and she felt what a pity; and she felt if only they could be brought together; so she did it.[291] And it was an offering; to combine, to create; but to whom?

An offering for the sake of offering, perhaps.[292] Anyhow, it was her gift. Nothing else had she of the slightest importance; could not think, write, even play the piano. She muddled Armenians and Turks; loved success; hated discomfort; must be liked; talked oceans of nonsense: and to this day, ask her what the Equator was, and she did not know.

All the same, that one day should follow another; Wednesday, Thursday, Friday, Saturday; that one should wake up in the morning; see the sky; walk in the park; meet Hugh Whitbread; then suddenly in came Peter; then these roses; it was enough. After that, how unbelievable death was!—that it must end; and no one in the whole world would know how she had loved it all; how, every instant . . .

The door opened. Elizabeth knew that her mother was resting. She came in very quietly. She stood perfectly still. Was it that some Mongol[293] had been wrecked on the coast of Norfolk (as Mrs. Hilbery[294] said), had mixed with the Dalloway ladies, perhaps a hundred years ago? For the Dalloways, in general, were fair-haired; blue-eyed; Elizabeth, on the contrary, was dark; had Chinese eyes in a pale face; an Oriental mystery; was gentle, considerate, still. As a child, she had had a perfect sense of humour; but now at seventeen, why, Clarissa could not in the least understand, she had become very serious; like a hyacinth sheathed in glossy green, with buds just tinted, a hyacinth which has had no sun.[295]

She stood quite still and looked at her mother; but the door was ajar, and outside the door was Miss Kilman, as Clarissa knew; Miss Kilman in her mackintosh, listening to whatever they said.[296]

Yes, Miss Kilman stood on the landing, and wore a mackintosh; but had her reasons. First, it was cheap; second, she was over forty; and did not, after all, dress to please. She was poor,

291 "This social side is very genuine in me," Woolf wrote in her diary on June 28, 1923. "Nor do I think it reprehensible. It is a piece of jewellery I inherit from my mother—a joy in laughter, something that is stimulated, not selfishly wholly or vainly, by contact with my friends. And then ideas leap in me. Moreover, for my work now, I want freer intercourse, wider intercourse."

The connection Woolf makes between her social side and her intellectual side is echoed by the parallel she draws in *Mrs. Dalloway* between the work of the hostess and the work of the narrator. Both bring characters together. Both use the party as the device for doing so. The manuscript of "The Hours" made the parallels between the two much more explicit: "Life meant bringing together. An artist did the same sort of thing presumably . . . . And she did it because it was an offering. Just as somebody writes a book after all . . . . ~~Was it not perhaps her way of loving? Her way of giving as artists did when they painted, writers when they wrote?~~ It was her gift."

Both books and parties must be attentive to problems of timing, rhythm, and pace. How fitting, then, that Woolf's diary entry ends with a meditation on the proper length of parties: "Either we have arduous parties at long intervals, or I make my frenzied dashes up to London, & leave, guiltily, as the clock strikes 11." The party she creates in *Mrs. Dalloway*, through *Mrs. Dalloway*, is the perfect party. It is neither arduous nor abbreviated, but long enough to deliver Clarissa's social offering to her guests and Woolf's narrative offering to her readers.

292 In her first draft of Septimus's suicide in "The Hours," Woolf repeatedly referred to it as an "offering" to make the connection between his suicide and Clarissa's party clear: "'An offering' he murmured, with some idea of +thought+ ~~an altar~~ in ~~his~~ mind—the window sill was an altar; & so with in the belief that he was giving up to humanity what it asked of him he sprang vigorously, of his own free will. . . ." She would delete these sentences by the final version of the novel.

293 "Mongol" denoted the East Asian ethnic group native to Mongolia. It may be another ethnic descriptor that Woolf borrowed from the writings of Thomas Huxley, who popularized the use of the word to indicate "one of the five principal races of mankind." Though Clarissa cannot recall the difference between Albanians and Armenians, she can distinguish between the Mongol and the European elements in her daughter. Her anxious observation of Elizabeth's exotic looks, her dark hair and "Chinese eyes," distances mother from daughter, though, in sexuality and temperament, the two are more alike than Clarissa would care to admit.

moreover; degradingly poor. Otherwise she would not be taking jobs from people like the Dalloways; from rich people, who liked to be kind. Mr. Dalloway, to do him justice, had been kind. But Mrs. Dalloway had not. She had been merely condescending. She came from the most worthless of all classes—the rich, with a smattering of culture. They had expensive things everywhere; pictures, carpets, lots of servants. She considered that she had a perfect right to anything that the Dalloways did for her.

She had been cheated. Yes, the word was no exaggeration, for surely a girl has a right to some kind of happiness? And she had never been happy, what with being so clumsy and so poor. And then, just as she might have had a chance at Miss Dolby's school, the war came; and she had never been able to tell lies. Miss Dolby thought she would be happier with people who shared her views about the Germans. She had had to go. It was true that the family was of German origin; spelt the name Kiehlman in the eighteenth century; but her brother had been killed. They turned her out because she would not pretend that the Germans were all villains—when she had German friends, when the only happy days of her life had been spent in Germany! And after all, she could read history. She had had to take whatever she could get. Mr. Dalloway had come across her working for the Friends.[297] He had allowed her (and that was really generous of him) to teach his daughter history. Also she did a little Extension[298] lecturing and so on. Then Our Lord had come to her (and here she always bowed her head). She had seen the light two years and three months ago. Now she did not envy women like Clarissa Dalloway; she pitied them.

She pitied and despised them from the bottom of her heart, as she stood on the soft carpet, looking at the old engraving of a little girl with a muff. With all this luxury going on, what hope was there for a better state of things? Instead of lying on a sofa—"My mother is resting," Elizabeth had said—she should

294 A minor figure in *Mrs. Dalloway* but a major figure in *Night and Day*: the self-absorbed, eccentric mother of Katharine Hilbery, the novel's protagonist.

295 Elizabeth as a hyacinth, fresh, pale, serious, and quiet, contains echoes of T. S. Eliot's *The Waste Land* (1922): "'You gave me hyacinths first a year ago; / 'They called me the hyacinth girl.' / —Yet when we came back, late, from the Hyacinth garden, / Your arms full, and your hair wet, I could not / Speak, and my eyes failed, I was neither / Living nor dead, and I knew nothing, / Looking into the heart of light, the silence."

296 Virginia Stephen's own history of befriending older women—Janet Case, Violet Dickinson, Kitty Maxse, Nelly Cecil, Madge Vaughan, and Emma Vaughan—often makes its way into her writing as a source of dramatic tension. Her novels are full of erotically charged friendships between "a pragmatic, independent woman and a much younger, more confused, middle-class girl," observes Hermione Lee, who categorizes the relationship between Elizabeth and Miss Kilman as the most openly sexualized and distasteful version of this dynamic.

297 Founded during the English Civil War (1642–51), the Quakers, or the Religious Society of Friends, believe that one can have a direct experience of Christ without the intervening presence of the clergy. Most Quakers, having declared a commitment to peace in 1660, remained conscientious objectors during the First World War; however, they did form ambulance units and service committees to provide relief at the front and to help noncombatant communities.

Caroline Stephen (1834–1909), Woolf's paternal aunt, converted to Quakerism as an adult in the late nineteenth century. Woolf often called her aunt "the Quaker" or "the Nun." Despite Woolf's mocking, it was the £2,500 bequeathed to her by Aunt Caroline "the Quaker" in 1909 that allowed Woolf the financial freedom to pursue her writing.

298 Lecturing at universities, often after hours, as Isabel Pole does on p. 118, and as Woolf herself did at Morley Memorial College for Working Men and Women.

have been in a factory; behind a counter; Mrs. Dalloway and all the other fine ladies!

Bitter and burning, Miss Kilman had turned into a church two years three months ago. She had heard the Rev. Edward Whittaker preach; the boys sing; had seen the solemn lights descend, and whether it was the music, or the voices (she herself when alone in the evening found comfort in a violin; but the sound was excruciating; she had no ear), the hot and turbulent feelings which boiled and surged in her had been assuaged as she sat there, and she had wept copiously, and gone to call on Mr. Whittaker at his private house in Kensington. It was the hand of God, he said. The Lord had shown her the way. So now, whenever the hot and painful feelings boiled within her, this hatred of Mrs. Dalloway, this grudge against the world, she thought of God. She thought of Mr. Whittaker. Rage was succeeded by calm. A sweet savour filled her veins, her lips parted, and, standing formidable upon the landing in her mackintosh, she looked with steady and sinister serenity at Mrs. Dalloway, who came out with her daughter.

Elizabeth said she had forgotten her gloves. That was because Miss Kilman and her mother hated each other. She could not bear to see them together. She ran upstairs to find her gloves.

But Miss Kilman did not hate Mrs. Dalloway. Turning her large gooseberry-coloured eyes upon Clarissa, observing her small pink face, her delicate body, her air of freshness and fashion, Miss Kilman felt, Fool! Simpleton! You who have known neither sorrow nor pleasure; who have trifled your life away! And there rose in her an overmastering desire to overcome her; to unmask her. If she could have felled her it would have eased her. But it was not the body; it was the soul and its mockery that she wished to subdue; make feel her mastery. If only she could make her weep; could ruin her; humiliate her; bring her to her knees crying, You are right! But this was God's will, not Miss Kilman's. It was to be a religious victory. So she glared; so she glowered.

Clarissa was really shocked. This a Christian—this woman! This woman had taken her daughter from her! She in touch with invisible presences! Heavy, ugly, commonplace, without kindness or grace, she know the meaning of life!

"You are taking Elizabeth to the Stores?"[299] Mrs. Dalloway said.

Miss Kilman said she was. They stood there. Miss Kilman

299 The Army & Navy Co-operative Society Ltd., or the "Stores," originated in 1871 as low-price dealers of goods, drink, clothes, and articles of general use for military officers and their families. Located in an old distillery on Victoria Street, the Stores eventually opened to the public in 1918. To upper-class women like Clarissa Dalloway, its offerings would have seemed meager, haphazard, cheap. "The whole of the Stores would only produce one box of chocolates; its a most desolate sight," Woolf wrote to Vanessa Bell of her failed attempt to buy her nephew Julian a present.

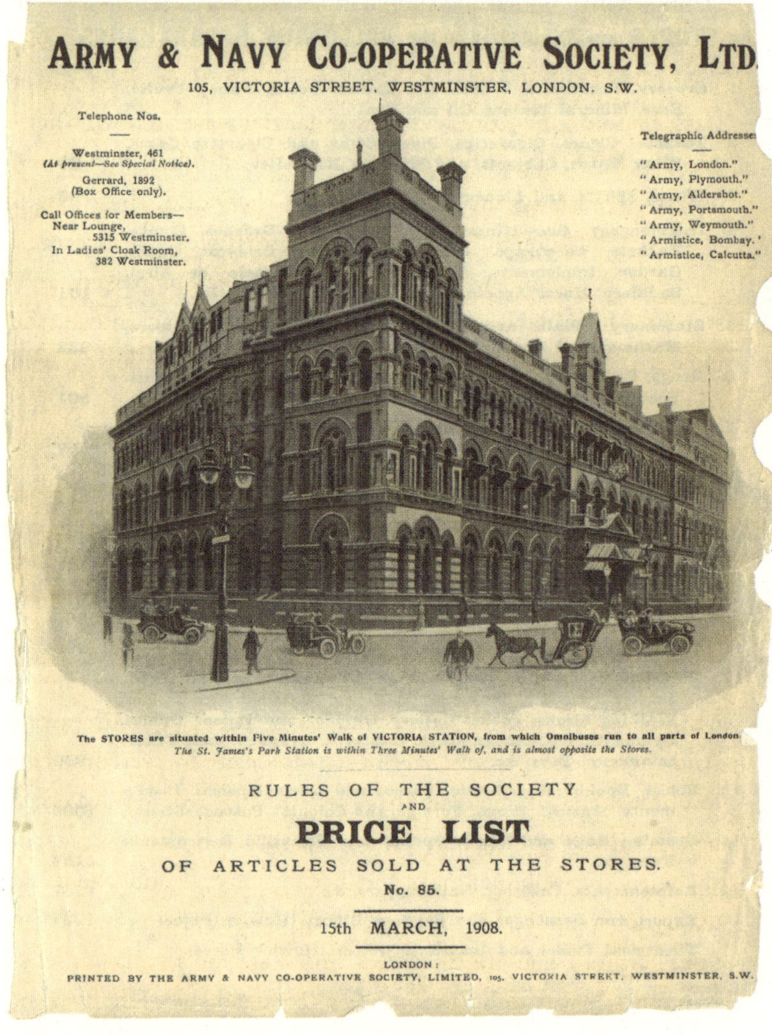

Army and Navy Stores UK magazine advertisement, 1924.
(John Frost Newspapers / Alamy)

was not going to make herself agreeable. She had always earned her living. Her knowledge of modern history was thorough in the extreme. She did out of her meagre income set aside so much for causes she believed in; whereas this woman did nothing, believed nothing; brought up her daughter—but here was Elizabeth, rather out of breath, the beautiful girl.

So they were going to the Stores. Odd it was, as Miss Kilman stood there (and stand she did, with the power and taciturnity of some prehistoric monster armoured for primeval warfare), how, second by second, the idea of her diminished, how hatred (which was for ideas, not people) crumbled, how she lost her malignity, her size, became second by second merely Miss Kilman, in a mackintosh, whom Heaven knows Clarissa would have liked to help.

At this dwindling of the monster, Clarissa laughed. Saying good-bye, she laughed.

Off they went together, Miss Kilman and Elizabeth, downstairs.

With a sudden impulse, with a violent anguish, for this woman was taking her daughter from her, Clarissa leant over the banisters and cried out, "Remember the party! Remember our party to-night!"[300]

But Elizabeth had already opened the front door; there was a van passing; she did not answer.

Love and religion! thought Clarissa, going back into the drawing-room, tingling all over. How detestable, how detestable they are! For now that the body of Miss Kilman was not before her, it overwhelmed her—the idea. The cruellest things in the world, she thought, seeing them clumsy, hot, domineering, hypocritical, eavesdropping, jealous, infinitely cruel and unscrupulous dressed in a mackintosh coat, on the landing; love and religion. Had she ever tried to convert any one herself? Did she not wish everybody merely to be themselves? And she watched out of the window the old lady opposite climbing upstairs. Let her climb upstairs if she wanted to; let her stop; then let her, as Clarissa had often seen her, gain her bedroom,

300 Notice Clarissa's pointed use of "our party" instead of "my party"—a small scratch at Miss Kilman; a reminder of her exclusion from Elizabeth's family life.

part her curtains, and disappear again into the background. Somehow one respected that—that old woman looking out of the window, quite unconscious that she was being watched. There was something solemn in it—but love and religion would destroy that, whatever it was, the privacy of the soul. The odious Kilman would destroy it. Yet it was a sight that made her want to cry.

Love destroyed too. Everything that was fine, everything that was true went.[301] Take Peter Walsh now. There was a man, charming, clever, with ideas about everything. If you wanted to know about Pope, say, or Addison,[302] or just to talk nonsense, what people were like, what things meant, Peter knew better than any one. It was Peter who had helped her; Peter who had lent her books. But look at the women he loved—vulgar, trivial, commonplace. Think of Peter in love—he came to see her after all these years, and what did he talk about? Himself. Horrible passion! she thought. Degrading passion! she thought, thinking of Kilman and her Elizabeth walking to the Army and Navy Stores.

Big Ben struck the half-hour.[303]

How extraordinary it was, strange, yes touching to see the old lady (they had been neighbours ever so many years)[304] move away from the window, as if she were attached to that sound, that string.[305] Gigantic as it was, it had something to do with her. Down, down, into the midst of ordinary things the finger fell making the moment solemn. She was forced, so Clarissa imagined, by that sound, to move, to go—but where? Clarissa tried to follow her as she turned and disappeared, and could still just see her white cap moving at the back of the bedroom. She was still there moving about at the other end of the room. Why creeds and prayers and mackintoshes? when, thought Clarissa, that's the miracle, that's the mystery; that old lady, she meant, whom she could see going from chest of drawers to dressing-table. She could still see her. And the supreme mystery which Kilman might say she had solved, or Peter might say he had solved, but Clarissa didn't believe either of them had

301 Is it, after all, Richard Dalloway's stiffness that stops him from telling Clarissa he loves her? For Richard, happiness is what he affirms when he holds his wife's hand. But in Clarissa's mind, love is antithetical to happiness, which demands privacy and peace, not conversation and passion.

302 Joseph Addison (1672–1719) was an English critic, poet, and playwright whose essays for the *Spectator* and the *Tatler* Woolf admired in her 1919 essay "Addison," first published in the *Times Literary Supplement* and later included in *The Common Reader*. While she warned that modern readers might find Addison's criticism "dull," or his "piety conventional," the clarity of his prose made "it possible for people of ordinary intelligence to communicate their ideas to the world," she wrote.

303 Big Ben strikes three-thirty. Half an hour has passed since Richard arrived at the house.

304 Virginia Stephen's family home in Kensington Gardens was on a dark, narrow street that allowed the Stephen children to observe people's lives in the houses opposite. For Hermione Lee, Woolf would work this "potent memory" into *Mrs. Dalloway* on three important occasions: first when Clarissa observes the old woman in the afternoon; second when Septimus observes the old man in the house opposite coming down the stairs on p. 131; and finally, when Clarissa observes the old woman going to bed on p. 227.

These sightings are opportunities to pay close attention to a strange human being while maintaining "the privacy of the soul," forgoing the pitiless exposure of self that love and religion demand. Observation at a distance is a form of respect, an offering of grace, one that echoes Woolf's notion of "character-reading" in "Mr. Bennett and Mrs. Brown." "You should insist that she is an old lady of unlimited capacity and infinite variety; capable of appearing in any place; wearing any dress; saying anything and doing heaven knows what," Woolf wrote of the imaginary Mrs. Brown. "But the things she says and the things she does and her eyes and her nose and her speech and her silence have an overwhelming fascination, for she is, of course, the spirit we live by, life itself."

305 Notice the equivalence Woolf draws between the sound of the clock and the string of the spider, the two connective fibers that run through this section of the narrative.

the ghost of an idea of solving, was simply this: here was one room; there another. Did religion solve that, or love?

Love—but here the other clock, the clock which always struck two minutes after Big Ben, came shuffling in with its lap full of odds and ends, which it dumped down as if Big Ben were all very well with his majesty laying down the law, so solemn, so just, but she must remember all sorts of little things besides—Mrs. Marsham, Ellie Henderson, glasses for ices—all sorts of little things came flooding and lapping and dancing in on the wake of that solemn stroke which lay flat like a bar of gold on the sea. Mrs. Marsham, Ellie Henderson, glasses for ices. She must telephone now at once.[306]

Volubly, troublously, the late clock sounded, coming in on the wake of Big Ben, with its lap full of trifles. Beaten up, broken up by the assault of carriages, the brutality of vans, the eager advance of myriads of angular men, of flaunting women, the domes and spires of offices and hospitals, the last relics of this lap full of odds and ends seemed to break, like the spray of an exhausted wave, upon the body of Miss Kilman standing still in the street for a moment to mutter "It is the flesh."

It was the flesh that she must control. Clarissa Dalloway had insulted her. That she expected. But she had not triumphed; she had not mastered the flesh. Ugly, clumsy, Clarissa Dalloway had laughed at her for being that; and had revived the fleshly desires, for she minded looking as she did beside Clarissa. Nor could she talk as she did. But why wish to resemble her? Why? She despised Mrs. Dalloway from the bottom of her heart. She was not serious. She was not good. Her life was a tissue of vanity and deceit. Yet Doris Kilman had been overcome.[307] She had, as a matter of fact, very nearly burst into tears when Clarissa Dalloway laughed at her. "It is the flesh, it is the flesh," she muttered (it being her habit to talk aloud), trying to subdue this turbulent and painful feeling as she walked down Victoria Street. She prayed to God. She could not help being ugly; she could not afford to buy pretty clothes. Clarissa Dalloway had laughed—but she would concentrate her mind

306 Another instance where the novel informs us exactly how the time measured by the clock (two minutes) relates to the time measured by the novel's fictional discourse (the stretch of prose from "How extraordinary" to "Love—").

307 Doris Kilman's strong, contradictory emotions for Clarissa mirror Clarissa's strong, contradictory emotions for Doris Kilman. So too does Miss Kilman's suspicion that her feelings for Clarissa are bound up with the desire for "self-love"—that she must resemble Clarissa to love herself, to embrace her flesh and sensuality. She is, along with Septimus, another one of Clarissa's queer doubles, enacting, in however tortured a manner, the political radicalism and lesbianism that Clarissa left behind.

The likely model for Doris Kilman was Louise Ernestine Matthaei (1880–1969), "a lanky gawky unattractive woman, about 35, with a complexion that blotches red & shiny suddenly," Woolf wrote in a diary entry dated April 9, 1918. Matthaei was a classics scholar and, until 1916, a classics fellow and director of studies at Newnham College, Cambridge. "She has left, we understand, 'under a cloud,'" Woolf noted. The "cloud" was her German origin, which she disclosed to Leonard when he offered her a place on the staff of the *Nation and Athenaeum*. Despite her "inconceivably stiff & ugly" manner of dress, she had "a quick mind," Woolf judged, though she entertained a strong revulsion for Matthaei's overall demeanor: "It is easy to see from her limp, apologetic attitude that the cloud has sapped her powers of resistance. We skirted round the war, but she edged away from it, & it seemed altogether odious that anyone should be afraid to declare her opinions—as if a dog used to excessive beating, dreading even the raising of a hand."

308 A freestanding postbox, usually a bright red cylinder with a cast-iron cap, first introduced in 1852 for the collection of letters by the Royal Mail.

upon something else until she had reached the pillar-box.[308] At any rate she had got Elizabeth. But she would think of something else; she would think of Russia; until she reached the pillar-box.

How nice it must be, she said, in the country, struggling, as Mr. Whittaker had told her, with that violent grudge against the world which had scorned her, sneered at her, cast her off, beginning with this indignity—the infliction of her unlovable body which people could not bear to see. Do her hair as she might, her forehead remained like an egg, bald, white. No clothes suited her. She might buy anything. And for a woman, of course, that meant never meeting the opposite sex. Never would she come first with any one. Sometimes lately it had seemed to her that, except for Elizabeth, her food was all that she lived for; her comforts; her dinner, her tea; her hot-water bottle at night. But one must fight; vanquish; have faith in God. Mr. Whittaker had said she was there for a purpose. But no one knew the agony! He said, pointing to the crucifix, that God knew. But why should she have to suffer when other women, like Clarissa Dalloway, escaped? Knowledge comes through suffering, said Mr. Whittaker.

She had passed the pillar-box, and Elizabeth had turned into the cool brown tobacco department of the Army and Navy Stores while she was still muttering to herself what Mr. Whittaker had said about knowledge coming through suffering and the flesh. "The flesh," she muttered.

What department did she want? Elizabeth interrupted her.

"Petticoats," she said abruptly, and stalked straight on to the lift.

Up they went. Elizabeth guided her this way and that; guided her in her abstraction as if she had been a great child, an unwieldy battleship. There were the petticoats, brown, decorous, striped, frivolous, solid, flimsy; and she chose, in her abstraction, portentously, and the girl serving thought her mad.

Elizabeth rather wondered, as they did up the parcel, what Miss Kilman was thinking. They must have their tea, said Miss Kilman, rousing, collecting herself. They had their tea.

Elizabeth rather wondered whether Miss Kilman could be hungry. It was her way of eating, eating with intensity, then looking, again and again, at a plate of sugared cakes on the table next them; then, when a lady and a child sat down and the child took the cake, could Miss Kilman really mind it? Yes, Miss Kilman did mind it. She had wanted that cake—the pink one. The pleasure of eating was almost the only pure pleasure left her, and then to be baffled even in that!

When people are happy they have a reserve, she had told Elizabeth, upon which to draw, whereas she was like a wheel without a tyre (she was fond of such metaphors), jolted by every pebble—so she would say staying on after the lesson, standing by the fire-place with her bag of books, her "satchel", she called it, on a Tuesday morning, after the lesson was over. And she talked too about the war. After all, there were people who did not think the English invariably right. There were books. There were meetings. There were other points of view. Would Elizabeth like to come with her to listen to So-and-so? (a most extraordinary-looking old man). Then Miss Kilman took her to some church in Kensington and they had tea with a clergyman. She had lent her books. Law, medicine, politics, all professions are open to women of your generation, said Miss Kilman. But for herself, her career was absolutely ruined, and was it her fault? Good gracious, said Elizabeth, no.

And her mother would come calling to say that a hamper had come from Bourton and would Miss Kilman like some flowers? To Miss Kilman she was always very, very nice, but Miss Kilman squashed the flowers all in a bunch, and hadn't any small talk, and what interested Miss Kilman bored her mother, and Miss Kilman and she were terrible together; and Miss Kilman swelled and looked very plain, but Miss Kilman was frightfully clever. Elizabeth had never thought about the poor. They lived with everything they wanted,—her mother had breakfast in bed every day; Lucy carried it up; and she liked old women because they were Duchesses, and being descended from some Lord. But Miss Kilman said (one of those Tuesday mornings when the lesson was over), "My grandfather kept an oil and colour shop in Kensington." Miss Kilman was quite different from any one she knew; she made one feel so small.

Miss Kilman took another cup of tea. Elizabeth, with her oriental bearing, her inscrutable mystery, sat perfectly upright; no, she did not want anything more. She looked for her gloves—her white gloves. They were under the table. Ah, but she must not go! Miss Kilman could not let her go! this youth, that was so beautiful! this girl, whom she genuinely loved! Her large hand opened and shut on the table.

But perhaps it was a little flat somehow, Elizabeth felt. And really she would like to go.

But said Miss Kilman, "I've not quite finished yet."

Of course, then, Elizabeth would wait. But it was rather stuffy in here.

"Are you going to the party to-night?" Miss Kilman said. Elizabeth supposed she was going; her mother wanted her to go. She must not let parties absorb her, Miss Kilman said, fingering the last two inches of a chocolate éclair.

She did not much like parties, Elizabeth said. Miss Kilman opened her mouth, slightly projected her chin, and swallowed down the last inches of the chocolate éclair, then wiped her fingers, and washed the tea round in her cup.

She was about to split asunder,[309] she felt. The agony was so terrific. If she could grasp her, if she could clasp her, if she could make her hers absolutely and for ever and then die; that was all she wanted. But to sit here, unable to think of anything to say; to see Elizabeth turning against her; to be felt repulsive even by her—it was too much; she could not stand it. The thick fingers curled inwards.

"I don't pity myself," she said. "I pity"—she meant to say

309 The image of being torn asunder was one Woolf often reached for to describe the shattering anguish of sexual desire: the agony of a beauty one could not possess. In "A Sketch of the Past," Woolf recalled sitting with her half-sister Stella's widower, Jack Hills, who tells her she cannot understand how "[i]t tears one asunder. . . ." "'Yes I can,' I murmured. Subconsciously, I knew that he meant his sexual desires tore him asunder." The phrase repeats in *Mrs. Dalloway*, in *Between the Acts* ("Love and hate— how they tore her asunder!" thinks Isa Oliver), and finally, in *A Room of One's Own*: "The beauty of the world, which is so soon to perish, has two edges, one of laughter, one of anguish, cutting the heart asunder."

"your mother," but no, she could not, not to Elizabeth. "I pity other people much more."

Like some dumb creature who has been brought up to a gate for an unknown purpose, and stands there longing to gallop away, Elizabeth Dalloway sat silent. Was Miss Kilman going to say anything more?

"Don't quite forget me," said Doris Kilman; her voice quivered. Right away to the end of the field the dumb creature galloped in terror.

The great hand opened and shut.

Elizabeth turned her head. The waitress came. One had to pay at the desk, Elizabeth said, and went off, drawing out, so Miss Kilman felt, the very entrails in her body, stretching them as she crossed the room, and then, with a final twist, bowing her head very politely, she went.

She had gone. Miss Kilman sat at the marble table among the éclairs, stricken once, twice, thrice by shocks of suffering. She had gone. Mrs. Dalloway had triumphed. Elizabeth had gone. Beauty had gone; youth had gone.

So she sat. She got up, blundered off among the little tables, rocking slightly from side to side, and somebody came after her with her petticoat, and she lost her way, and was hemmed in by trunks specially prepared for taking to India; next got among the accouchement sets and baby linen; through all the commodities of the world, perishable and permanent, hams, drugs, flowers, stationery, variously smelling, now sweet, now sour, she lurched; saw herself thus lurching with her hat askew, very red in the face, full length in a looking-glass;[310] and at last came out into the street.

The tower of Westminster Cathedral rose in front of her, the habitation of God.[311] In the midst of the traffic, there was the habitation of God. Doggedly she set off with her parcel to that other sanctuary, the Abbey,[312] where, raising her hands in a tent before her face, she sat beside those driven into shelter too; the variously assorted worshippers, now divested of social rank, almost of sex, as they raised their hands before their faces;

310 Miss Kilman is the third character now to observe herself in the looking glass at a moment of self-dissolution, a crisis as comic for its mingling of high emotion with low culture (éclairs, hams, drugs, stationery) as Peter's passionate retreat into babyhood on p. 82.

311 The red-and-white brick campanile of Westminster Cathedral soars over Victoria Street while the church squats down beside it: a large Byzantine sanctuary whose construction began in 1895 and was completed in 1903. Designed by John Francis Bentley, Westminster Cathedral remains the largest Roman Catholic church in England and Wales and the seat of the Archbishop of Westminster.

312 On or around 960, Westminster Abbey was founded as a small Benedictine monastery near the banks of the River Thames. Edward the Confessor (ca. 1003–1066) enlarged the monastery in 1042, and by 1052 had built a tremendous stone church that he dedicated to St. Peter the Apostle. The church became known as "west minster" to differentiate it from St Paul's Cathedral, the City of London's "east minster." Rebuilt by Henry III (1207–1272) in the Anglo-French Gothic style and consecrated in 1269, the new church was designed as the site for the coronation and burial of monarchs.

Westminster Abbey, Hospital, Etc., Thomas Shotter Boys. Lithograph with tint on card, c. 1842. *(Paul Mellon Collection, Yale Center for British Art)*

In her 1932 essay "Abbeys and Cathedrals," Woolf compared the old gray walls of Westminster Abbey to the glittering spires of St Paul's and declared the abbey "narrow and pointed, worn, restless and animated." The church seemed alive with the spirits of dead poets, "still musing, still pondering, still questioning the meaning of existence," their presence lighting the stone sanctuary from within. "Lights and shadows are changing and conflicting every moment. Blue, gold and violet pass, dappling, quickening, fading," she wrote. "Even the stone of the old columns

but once they removed them, instantly reverent, middle-class, English men and women, some of them desirous of seeing the wax works.[313]

But Miss Kilman held her tent before her face. Now she was deserted; now rejoined. New worshippers came in from the street to replace the strollers, and still, as people gazed round and shuffled past the tomb of the Unknown Warrior,[314] still she barred her eyes with her fingers and tried in this double darkness, for the light in the Abbey was bodiless, to aspire above the vanities, the desires, the commodities, to rid herself both of hatred and of love. Her hands twitched. She seemed to struggle. Yet to others

seems rubbed and chafed by the intensity of the life that has been fretting it all these centuries." Recall, too, Peter passing St Margaret's Church, just next to the abbey, on p. 73.

313 Funeral effigies of the monarchs were housed in the treasure museum of the abbey and are now held in the Queen's Diamond Jubilee Galleries. Some of their body parts were made of wax, others of painted wood. "There is not as much contrast as one would wish, perhaps, between the Museum at one end of Whitehall and the Abbey at the other," Woolf wrote in her 1928 essay "Waxworks at the Abbey," irritated by the large number of tourists and guides who milled about the abbey.

314 On November 11, 1920, a coffin containing an unidentified British soldier, whose remains had been

Westminster Abbey, west front, 1905. *(Library of Congress)*

Effigy of Mary, Queen of Scots, on her tomb in Westminster Abbey, 1859. *(Metropolitan Museum of Art)*

recovered from a French battlefield, was borne into Westminster Abbey on a horse-drawn carriage. He was followed by King George V, the royal family, the ministers of state, and one hundred guests of honor—all women, each one chosen because she had lost her husband and all her sons in the war. The coffin of the Unknown Warrior was interred in the western end of the nave, covered in soil from the major French battlefields, and shrouded with an embroidered silk funeral pall.

Tomb of the Unknown Warrior, Westminster Abbey, November 1920. *(Leonard Bentley)*

God was accessible and the path to Him smooth. Mr. Fletcher, retired, of the Treasury, Mrs. Gorham, widow of the famous K.C.,[315] approached Him simply, and having done their praying, leant back, enjoyed the music (the organ pealed sweetly), and saw Miss Kilman at the end of the row, praying, praying, and, being still on the threshold of their underworld, thought of her sympathetically as a soul haunting the same territory; a soul cut out of immaterial substance; not a woman, a soul.

But Mr. Fletcher had to go. He had to pass her, and being himself neat as a new pin, could not help being a little distressed by the poor lady's disorder; her hair down; her parcel on the floor. She did not at once let him pass. But, as he stood gazing about him, at the white marbles, grey window panes, and accumulated treasures (for he was extremely proud of the Abbey), her largeness, robustness, and power as she sat there shifting her knees from time to time (it was so rough the approach to her God—so tough her desires) impressed him, as they had impressed Mrs. Dalloway (she could not get the thought of her out of her mind that afternoon), the Rev. Edward Whittaker, and Elizabeth too.

And Elizabeth waited in Victoria Street for an omnibus. It was so nice to be out of doors. She thought perhaps she need not go home just yet. It was so nice to be out in the air. So she would get on to an omnibus. And already, even as she stood there, in her very well-cut clothes, it was beginning . . . . People were beginning to compare her to poplar trees, early dawn, hyacinths, fawns, running water, and garden lilies; and it made her life a burden to her, for she so much preferred being left alone to do what she liked in the country, but they would compare her to lilies, and she had to go to parties, and London was so dreary compared with being alone in the country with her father and the dogs.[316]

Buses swooped, settled, were off—garish caravans, glistening with red and yellow varnish. But which should she get on to? She had no preferences. Of course, she would not push her way. She inclined to be passive. It was expression she needed, but her eyes were fine, Chinese, oriental, and, as her mother said,

315 The suggestion is that Mr. Gorham was a member of the King's Counsel, a group of barristers of a higher status specially appointed by the lord chancellor to be the Crown's counsel.

316 The pastoral imagination of Clarissa's youth now belongs to Elizabeth, who resents how people at parties in the city pluck the language of country life—trees, dawn, water, flowers—to demand from her an absurd, awkward performance of womanhood. Recall the hyacinths on p. 159, which appear again here, and see p. 231.

Ambulatory, Westminster Abbey, Frederick Nash. Watercolor and graphite with pen and brown ink, c. 1800–1850. *(Paul Mellon Collection, Yale Center for British Art)*

Westminster Abbey and Bridge, Joseph Farington. Oil on canvas, 1794. *(Paul Mellon Collection, Yale Center for British Art)*

with such nice shoulders and holding herself so straight, she was always charming to look at; and lately, in the evening especially, when she was interested, for she never seemed excited, she looked almost beautiful, very stately, very serene. What could she be thinking? Every man fell in love with her, and she was really awfully bored. For it was beginning. Her mother could see that—the compliments were beginning. That she did not care more about it—for instance for her clothes—sometimes worried Clarissa, but perhaps it was as well with all those puppies and guinea pigs about having distemper, and it gave her a charm. And now there was this odd friendship with Miss Kilman. Well, thought Clarissa about three o'clock in the morning, reading Baron Marbot for she could not sleep, it proves she has a heart.

Suddenly Elizabeth stepped forward and most competently boarded the omnibus, in front of everybody. She took a seat on top. The impetuous creature—a pirate[317]—started forward, sprang away; she had to hold the rail to steady herself, for a pirate it was, reckless, unscrupulous, bearing down ruthlessly, circumventing dangerously, boldly snatching a passenger, or ignoring a passenger, squeezing eel-like and arrogant in between, and then rushing insolently all sails spread up Whitehall. And did Elizabeth give one thought to poor Miss Kilman who loved her without jealousy, to whom she had been a fawn in the open, a moon in a glade? She was delighted to be free. The fresh air was so delicious. It had been so stuffy in the Army and Navy Stores. And now it was like riding, to be rushing up Whitehall; and to each movement of the omnibus the beautiful body in the fawn-coloured coat responded freely like a rider, like the figure-head of a ship, for the breeze slightly disarrayed her; the heat gave her cheeks the pallor of white painted wood; and her fine eyes, having no eyes to meet, gazed ahead, blank, bright, with the staring incredible innocence of sculpture.

It was always talking about her own sufferings that made Miss Kilman so difficult. And was she right? If it was being on committees and giving up hours and hours every day (she hardly ever saw him in London) that helped the poor, her father did that,

317 The popular term for an unlicensed bus, as well as a metaphor for the bus as a ship, atop which Elizabeth will stand like its "figure-head," solitary and inscrutable, an almost inhuman presence.

goodness knows—if that was what Miss Kilman meant about being a Christian; but it was so difficult to say. Oh, she would like to go a little farther. Another penny was it to the Strand? Here was another penny, then. She would go up the Strand.[318]

She liked people who were ill. And every profession is open to the women of your generation, said Miss Kilman. So she might be a doctor. She might be a farmer. Animals are often ill. She might own a thousand acres and have people under her. She would go and see them in their cottages. This was Somerset House.[319] One might be a very good farmer—and that, strangely enough, though Miss Kilman had her share in it, was almost entirely due to Somerset House. It looked so splendid, so serious, that great grey building. And she liked the feeling of people working. She liked those churches, like shapes of grey paper, breasting the stream of the Strand. It was quite different here from Westminster, she thought, getting off at Chancery Lane.[320] It was so serious; it was so busy. In short, she would like to have a profession. She would become a doctor, a farmer, possibly go into Parliament if she found it necessary, all because of the Strand.

The feet of those people busy about their activities, hands

318 Recall Peter looking in the direction of the Strand on p. 77.

319 Great gray Somerset House sits on the south side of the Strand, overlooking the River Thames. Edward Seymour, Lord Protector and Duke of Somerset, began work on his palace in 1547; however, the building was seized by the Crown when the duke was overthrown and executed at the Tower of London in 1552. It became home to Princess Elizabeth one year later, who lived there until she was crowned Queen Elizabeth I in 1558.

Through the sixteenth and seventeenth centuries, Somerset House served myriad purposes: royal residence, storage facility, troop barracks. In 1775, the original structure was demolished after years of neglect, and the architect William Chambers was appointed to design its replacement. Four years later, Parliament passed an act for "erecting and establishing Publick Offices in Somerset House." The Royal Academy of Arts took up residence in the north wing and was soon followed by the Royal Society, the Society of Antiquaries, the Navy Board, and the Stamp Office. By the early twentieth century, the most important offices in Somerset House were the offices of Inland Revenue, responsible for tax services, and the General Register Office, responsible for births, marriages, and deaths.

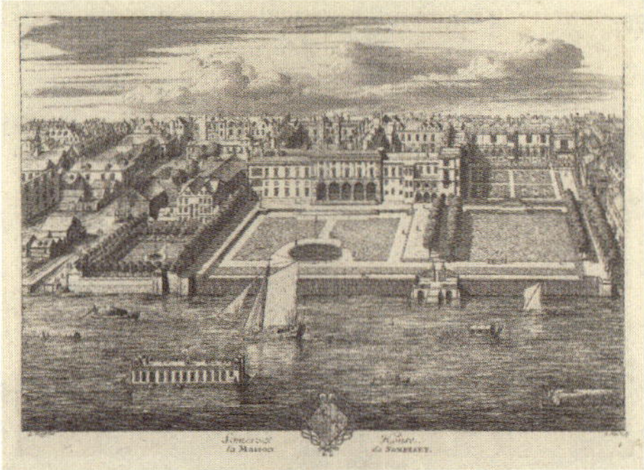

Somerset House, Johannes Kip. Engraving, undated. *(Paul Mellon Collection, Yale Center for British Art)*

320 The Knights Templar built Chancery Lane sometime in the mid-twelfth century to direct worshippers from their "old Temple" on High Holborn to their new temple on Fleet Street. In 1161, the old temple was acquired by Robert de Chesney, the Bishop of Lincoln, and turned into the High Court of Chancery, which had jurisdiction over trusts, land law, the estates of lunatics (a legal term at the time),

Waterloo Bridge and Somerset House. *(UK Photo and Social History Archive)*

Somerset House, London, Frederick Nash. Oil on artist's board, c. 1825.
(Paul Mellon Collection, Yale Center for British Art)

putting stone to stone, minds eternally occupied not with trivial chatterings (comparing women to poplars—which was rather exciting, of course, but very silly), but with thoughts of ships, of business, of law, of administration, and with it all so stately (she was in the Temple),[321] gay (there was the river), pious (there was the Church),[322] made her quite determined, whatever her mother might say, to become either a farmer or a doctor. But she was, of course, rather lazy.

And it was much better to say nothing about it. It seemed so silly. It was the sort of thing that did sometimes happen, when one was alone—buildings without architects' names, crowds of

and the guardianship of infants. Charles Dickens would lampoon the bureaucratic inefficiencies of the chancery in *Bleak House* (1853) and celebrate the quiet of Chancery Lane in the summer, when the lawyers and judges of England would scatter across the earth: "It is the long vacation in the regions of Chancery Lane. The good ships Law and Equity, those teak-built, copper-bottomed, iron-fastened, brazen-faced, and not by any means fast-sailing Clippers are laid up in ordinary . . . The courts are all shut up; the public offices lie in a hot sleep; Westminster Hall itself is a shady solitude where nightingales might sing, and a tenderer class of suitors than is usually found there, walk."

321 One of the main legal districts in London, the Temple is marked out by the Victoria Embankment to the south and the Strand and Fleet Street to the north. It consists of the Inner Temple and the Middle Temple, two of the four Inns of Court.

322 Built by the Knights Templar in the mid-twelfth century, Temple Church sits between Fleet Street and the River Thames. Famous for its romantic round nave and its heavy stone effigies, the church was consecrated in 1185.

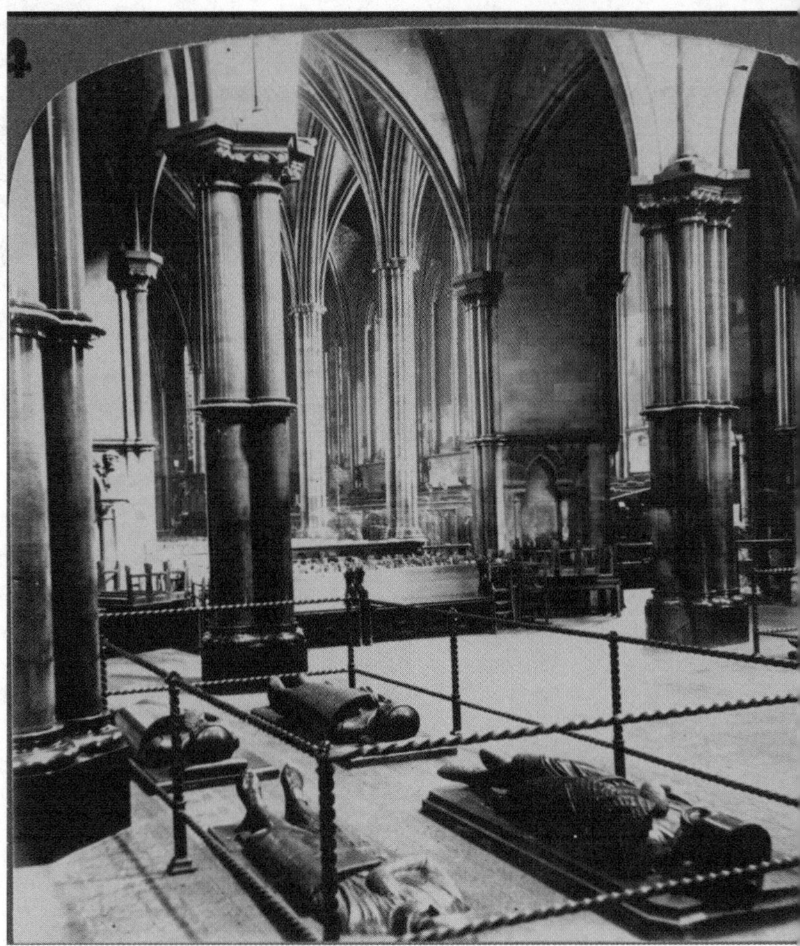

Tomb of Gallant Knights Templar in their old Temple Church, 1913. *(Library of Congress)*

people coming back from the city having more power than single clergymen in Kensington, than any of the books Miss Kilman had lent her, to stimulate what lay slumberous, clumsy, and shy on the mind's sandy floor, to break surface, as a child suddenly stretches its arms; it was just that, perhaps, a sigh, a stretch of the arms, an impulse, a revelation, which has its effects for ever, and then down again it went to the sandy floor. She must go home. She must dress for dinner. But what was the time?—where was a clock?

She looked up Fleet Street. She walked just a little way towards St. Paul's, shyly, like some one penetrating on tiptoe, exploring a strange house by night with a candle, on edge lest the owner should suddenly fling wide his bedroom door and ask her business, nor did she dare wander off into queer alleys, tempting by-streets, any more than in a strange house open doors which might be bedroom doors, or sitting-room doors, or lead straight to the larder. For no Dalloways came down the Strand daily; she was a pioneer, a stray, venturing, trusting.

In many ways, her mother felt, she was extremely immature, like a child still, attached to dolls, to old slippers; a perfect baby; and that was charming. But then, of course, there was in the Dalloway family the tradition of public service. Abbesses, principals, head mistresses, dignitaries, in the republic of women—without being brilliant, any of them, they were that. She penetrated a little farther in the direction of St. Paul's. She liked the geniality, sisterhood, motherhood, brotherhood of this uproar. It seemed to her good. The noise was tremendous; and suddenly there were trumpets (the unemployed) blaring, rattling about in the uproar; military music; as if people were marching; yet had they been dying—had some woman breathed her last, and whoever was watching, opening the window of the room where she had just brought off that act of supreme dignity, looked down on Fleet Street, that uproar, that military music would have come triumphing up to him, consolatory, indifferent.[323]

It was not conscious. There was no recognition in it of one's fortune, or fate, and for that very reason even to those dazed

323 The capacity for rapture Elizabeth has inherited from her mother lies dormant in her mind. Walking toward St Paul's and into the parade rouses it, carries her through the street on the roar of its sound. She shares her mother's sense of connectivity, "the geniality, sisterhood, motherhood, brotherhood" of the city, though she remains too immature to kindle it as her mother can—to stave off death. The manuscript of "The Hours" makes the resonance between the two women more explicit: "Never was she entirely without a sense of her mother's presence."

with watching for the last shivers of consciousness on the faces of the dying, consoling.

Forgetfulness in people might wound, their ingratitude corrode, but this voice, pouring endlessly, year in year out, would take whatever it might be; this vow; this van; this life; this procession, would wrap them all about and carry them on, as in the rough stream of a glacier the ice holds a splinter of bone, a blue petal, some oak trees, and rolls them on.

But it was later than she thought. Her mother would not like her to be wandering off alone like this. She turned back down the Strand.

A puff of wind (in spite of the heat, there was quite a wind) blew a thin black veil over the sun and over the Strand. The faces faded; the omnibuses suddenly lost their glow. For although the clouds were of mountainous white so that one could fancy hacking hard chips off with a hatchet, with broad golden slopes, lawns of celestial pleasure gardens, on their flanks, and had all the appearance of settled habitations assembled for the conference of gods above the world, there was a perpetual movement among them. Signs were interchanged, when, as if to fulfil some scheme arranged already, now a summit dwindled, now a whole block of pyramidal size which had kept its station inalterably advanced into the midst or gravely led the procession to fresh anchorage. Fixed though they seemed at their posts, at rest in perfect unanimity, nothing could be fresher, freer, more sensitive superficially than the snow-white or gold-kindled surface; to change, to go, to dismantle the solemn assemblage was immediately possible; and in spite of the grave fixity, the accumulated robustness and solidity, now they struck light to the earth, now darkness.[324]

Calmly and competently, Elizabeth Dalloway mounted the Westminster omnibus.

Going and coming, beckoning, signalling, so the light and shadow, which now made the wall grey, now the bananas bright yellow, now made the Strand grey, now made the omnibuses[325] bright yellow, seemed to Septimus[326] Warren Smith lying on

324 Like the battered woman singing outside Regent's Park Tube station, or the solitary traveler wandering in and out of Peter's dreams, the clouds above London give us a glimpse of a spiritual world beyond this moment, this place. In the clouds' shifting, dissolving surfaces, we see "the conference of gods" on the clouds—recall Woolf's fascination with *The Odyssey* on pp. xlv and n. 182 on p. 101—as well as the pyramids of Egypt and the celestial pleasure gardens of Buddhist paradise. ("Buddhism seems to me superior to all other religions," Leonard Woolf wrote in his autobiography *Growing*, about his years spent in Ceylon.) Woolf will bring us back to earth when, in the next paragraph, Elizabeth mounts the Westminster omnibus.

325 After the motorcar and the airplane, the omnibus appears as the third mode of transportation *Mrs. Dalloway* uses to "transition by triangulation," as Brian McHale described Woolf's technique of switching from one character's point of view to another's.

326 Perhaps foreshadowing the character whom she will create in *The Waves*, Woolf starts referring to Septimus as "Bernard" in the pages leading up to his suicide in "The Hours" manuscript.

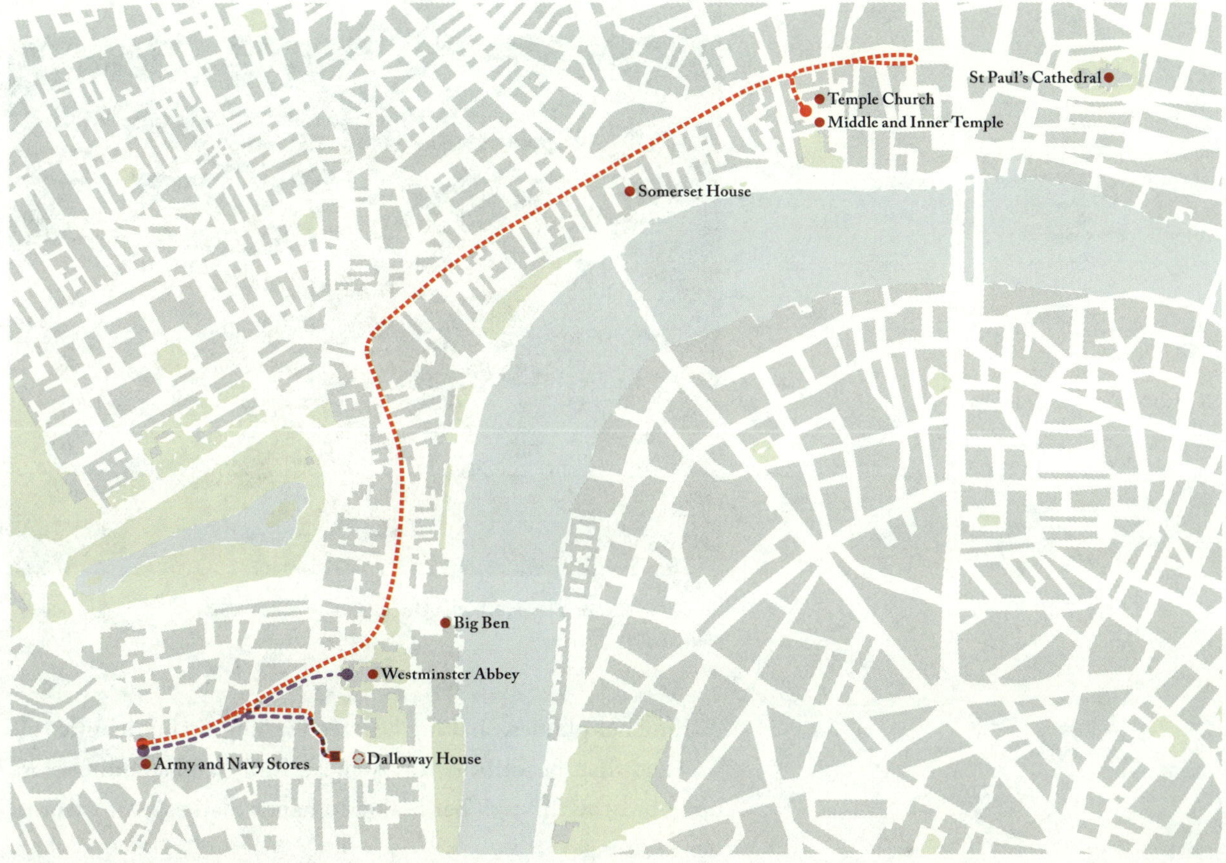

Elizabeth and Miss Kilman's walk. *(Christian Nakarado)*

the sofa in the sitting-room; watching the watery gold glow and fade with the astonishing sensibility of some live creature on the roses, on the wall-paper. Outside the trees dragged their leaves like nets through the depths of the air; the sound of water was in the room, and through the waves came the voices of birds singing. Every power poured its treasures on his head, and his hand lay there on the back of the sofa, as he had seen his hand lie when he was bathing, floating, on the top of the waves, while far away on shore he heard dogs barking and barking far away. Fear no more, says the heart in the body; fear no more.[327]

He was not afraid. At every moment Nature signified by some laughing hint like that gold spot which went round the wall—there, there, there—her determination to show, by bran-

327 Lying on the couch, Septimus concentrates all the thoughts and sensations he has experienced earlier in the novel: the light glimpsed through the trees; the leaves beckoning; the flap of the waves, the birdsong; and the Shakespearean refrain, urging bravery. The ecstasy of life surges and crests as death encroaches. As the moment of his suicide approaches, the novel begins to repeat itself with a tremendous sense of urgency, knitting together the visions of connectivity shared by Clarissa and Septimus.

Shoreham-on-Sea, Sussex, Charles Gogin. Oil on panel, 1889. *(Birmingham Museums Trust)*

dishing her plumes, shaking her tresses, flinging her mantle this way and that, beautifully, always beautifully, and standing close up to breathe through her hollowed hands Shakespeare's words, her meaning.

Rezia, sitting at the table twisting a hat in her hands, watched him; saw him smiling. He was happy then. But she could not bear to see him smiling. It was not marriage; it was not being one's husband to look strange like that, always to be starting, laughing, sitting hour after hour silent, or clutching her and telling her to write. The table drawer was full of those writings; about war; about Shakespeare; about great discoveries; how there is no death. Lately he had become excited suddenly for no reason (and both Dr. Holmes and Sir William Bradshaw said excitement was the worst thing for him), and waved his hands and cried out that he knew the truth! He knew everything! That man, his friend who was killed, Evans, had come, he said. He was singing behind the screen. She wrote it down just as he spoke it. Some things were very beautiful; others sheer nonsense. And he was always stopping in the middle, changing his mind; wanting to add something; hearing something new; listening with his hand up. But she heard nothing.

And once they found the girl who did the room reading one of these papers in fits of laughter. It was a dreadful pity. For that made Septimus cry out about human cruelty—how they tear each other to pieces. The fallen, he said, they tear to pieces. "Holmes is on us," he would say, and he would invent stories about Holmes; Holmes eating porridge; Holmes reading Shakespeare—making himself roar with laughter or rage, for Dr. Holmes seemed to stand for something horrible to him. "Human nature", he called him. Then there were the visions. He was drowned, he used to say, and lying on a cliff with the gulls screaming over him.[328] He would look over the edge of the sofa down into the sea. Or he was hearing music. Really it was only a barrel organ or some man crying in the street.[329] But "Lovely!" he used to cry, and the tears would run down his cheeks, which was to her the most dreadful thing of all, to see a man like Septimus, who had fought, who was brave, crying. And he would lie listening until suddenly he would cry that he was falling down, down into the flames! Actually she would look for flames, it was so vivid. But there was nothing. They were alone in the room. It was a dream, she would tell him, and so quiet him at last, but sometimes she was frightened too. She sighed as she sat sewing.

Her sigh was tender and enchanting, like the wind outside a wood in the evening. Now she put down her scissors; now she turned to take something from the table. A little stir, a little crinkling, a little tapping built up something on the table there, where she sat sewing. Through his eyelashes he could see her blurred outline; her little black body; her face and hands; her turning movements at the table, as she took up a reel, or looked (she was apt to lose things) for her silk. She was making a hat for Mrs. Filmer's married daughter, whose name was—he had forgotten her name.

"What's the name of Mrs. Filmer's married daughter?" he asked.

328 The image first appears in Woolf's short story "In the Orchard," published in *The Criterion* in 1922. Her protagonist Miranda drowses in an orchard, imagining that the earth might "carry me on its back as if I were a leaf, or a queen . . . or, Miranda went on, I might be lying on the top of a cliff with the gulls screaming above me."

329 Septimus's visions from from pp. 42 and 100 recalled from Rezia's unpoetic, uncomprehending point of view.

"Mrs. Peters," said Rezia. She was afraid it was too small, she said, holding it before her. Mrs. Peters was a big woman; but she did not like her. It was only because Mrs. Filmer had been so good to them—"She gave me grapes this morning," she said—that Rezia wanted to do something to show that they were grateful. She had come into the room the other evening and found Mrs. Peters, who thought they were out, playing the gramophone.

"Was it true?" he asked. She was playing the gramophone? Yes; she had told him about it at the time; she had found Mrs. Peters playing the gramophone.

He began, very cautiously, to open his eyes, to see whether a gramophone was really there. But real things—real things were too exciting. He must be cautious. He would not go mad. First he looked at the fashion papers on the lower shelf, then gradually at the gramophone with the green trumpet. Nothing could be more exact. And so, gathering courage, he looked at the sideboard; the plate of bananas; the engraving of Queen Victoria and the Prince Consort;[330] at the mantelpiece, with the jar of roses. None of these things moved. All were still; all were real.

"She is a woman with a spiteful tongue," said Rezia.

"What does Mr. Peters do?" Septimus asked.

"Ah," said Rezia, trying to remember. She thought Mrs. Filmer had said that he travelled for some company. "Just now he is in Hull,"[331] she said.

"Just now!" She said that with her Italian accent. She said that herself. He shaded his eyes so that he might see only a little of her face at a time, first the chin, then the nose, then the forehead, in case it were deformed, or had some terrible mark on it. But no, there she was, perfectly natural, sewing, with the pursed lips that women have, the set, the melancholy expression, when sewing. But there was nothing terrible about it, he assured himself, looking a second time, a third time at her face, her hands, for what was frightening or disgusting in her as she sat there in broad daylight, sewing? Mrs. Peters had a spiteful tongue. Mr. Peters was in Hull. Why then rage and prophesy? Why fly

330 The "Prince Consort" is Prince Albert. As Anne Fernald observes, until November 1924, the engraving showed a farmyard in Woolf's drafts.

331 Founded late in the twelfth century, Kingston upon Hull, generally abbreviated to Hull, developed into the foremost port on the east coast of England, exporting wool and woolen cloth, and importing wine and timber. A center for whaling and passenger shipping, its prosperity peaked just before the First World War, before it slipped into a rapid economic decline.

scourged and outcast? Why be made to tremble and sob by the clouds? Why seek truths and deliver messages when Rezia sat sticking pins into the front of her dress, and Mr. Peters was in Hull? Miracles, revelations, agonies, loneliness, falling through the sea, down, down into the flames, all were burnt out, for he had a sense, as he watched Rezia trimming the straw hat for Mrs. Peters, of a coverlet of flowers.

"It's too small for Mrs. Peters," said Septimus.

For the first time for days he was speaking as he used to do! Of course it was—absurdly small, she said. But Mrs. Peters had chosen it.

He took it out of her hands. He said it was an organ grinder's monkey's hat.[332]

How it rejoiced her that! Not for weeks had they laughed like this together, poking fun privately like married people. What she meant was that if Mrs. Filmer had come in, or Mrs. Peters or anybody, they would not have understood what she and Septimus were laughing at.

"There," she said, pinning a rose to one side of the hat. Never had she felt so happy! Never in her life!

But that was still more ridiculous, Septimus said. Now the poor woman looked like a pig at a fair. (Nobody ever made her laugh as Septimus did.)

What had she got in her work-box? She had ribbons and beads, tassels, artificial flowers. She tumbled them out on the table. He began putting odd colours together—for though he had no fingers, could not even do up a parcel, he had a wonderful eye, and often he was right, sometimes absurd, of course, but sometimes wonderfully right.

"She shall have a beautiful hat!" he murmured, taking up this and that, Rezia kneeling by his side, looking over his shoulder. Now it was finished—that is to say the design; she must stitch it together. But she must be very, very careful, he said, to keep it just as he had made it.

So she sewed. When she sewed, he thought, she made a sound like a kettle on the hob; bubbling, murmuring, always

332 Here, in the manuscript of "The Hours," Woolf inserts a fresh page and makes the following inexplicable, if charming, list of animals:
antelope,
zebra,
penguin,
pelican,
camel leopard
giraffe
lion, tiger
bison, buffaloe
monkey, hoopoe
ostrich marmot
madrill &
mongoose.

It is possible she is trying to come up with "pet names" (as she writes in a marginal note) for Septimus and Rezia to call each other. Or, as Diana Rose Newby has suggested to me, Woolf might be taking notes for her illustrated children's book *Nurse Lugton's Curtain*, written in 1924 but only published posthumously in 1965.

busy, her strong little pointed fingers pinching and poking; her needle flashing straight. The sun might go in and out, on the tassels, on the wall-paper, but he would wait, he thought, stretching out his feet, looking at his ringed sock at the end of the sofa; he would wait in this warm place, this pocket of still air, which one comes on at the edge of a wood sometimes in the evening, when, because of a fall in the ground, or some arrangement of the tress (one must be scientific above all, scientific), warmth lingers, and the air buffets the cheek like the wing of a bird.[333]

"There it is," said Rezia, twirling Mrs. Peters' hat on the tips of her fingers. "That'll do for the moment. Later . . ." her sentence bubbled away drip, drip, drip, like a contented tap left running.

It was wonderful. Never had he done anything which made him feel so proud. It was real, it was so substantial, Mrs. Peters' hat.

"Just look at it," he said.

Yes, it would always make her happy to see that hat. He had become himself then, he had laughed then. They had been alone together. Always she would like that hat.[334]

He told her to try it on.

"But I must look so queer!" she cried, running over to the glass and looking first this side, then that. Then she snatched it off again, for there was a tap at the door. Could it be Sir William Bradshaw? Had he sent already?

No! it was only the small girl with the evening paper.

What always happened, then happened—what happened every night of their lives. The small girl sucked her thumb at the door; Rezia went down on her knees; Rezia cooed and kissed; Rezia got a bag of sweets out of the table drawer. For so it always happened. First one thing, then another. So she built it up, first one thing and then another. Dancing, skipping, round and round the room they went. He took the paper. Surrey was all out, he read.[335] There was a heat wave. Rezia repeated: Surrey was all out. There was a heat wave, making it part of the

333 Septimus's gentle, loving observation of Rezia is darkened by the narrator's premonition of the fall to come. In her diaries, Woolf identified the party as the climax of the novel: the scene when all the seeds she had planted would suddenly bloom and tangle with one another. Yet Rezia and Septimus's brief and perfect happiness, the prelude to his suicide, seems the height of the novel's emotional drama. He kills himself not because life is unbearable, but because it is good and he does not want it to be otherwise.

334 Note the odd change of tense from the past to the past perfect, mingling the action of the novel with Rezia's remembrance of it—another omen of Septimus's death.

335 David Bradshaw notes that "Surrey was all out" refers to the cricket match between Surrey and Yorkshire, reported in a later edition of the newspaper Peter reads: "In 1923, Yorkshire's game against Surrey took place at Sheffield on Saturday 16, Monday 18, and Tuesday 19 June. Yorkshire won by 25 runs, but Surrey was not 'all out' twice in one day."

game she was playing with Mrs. Filmer's grandchild, both of them laughing, chattering at the same time, at their game. He was very tired. He was very happy. He would sleep. He shut his eyes. But directly he saw nothing the sounds of the game became fainter and stranger and sounded like the cries of people seeking and not finding, and passing farther and farther away. They had lost him!

He started up in terror. What did he see? The plate of bananas on the sideboard. Nobody was there (Rezia had taken the child to its mother; it was bedtime). That was it: to be alone for ever. That was the doom pronounced in Milan when he came into the room and saw them cutting out buckram shapes with their scissors; to be alone for ever.

He was alone with the sideboard and the bananas. He was alone, exposed on this bleak eminence, stretched out—but not on a hill-top; not on a crag; on Mrs. Filmer's sitting-room sofa. As for the visions, the faces, the voices of the dead, where were they? There was a screen in front of him, with black bulrushes and blue swallows. Where he had once seen mountains, where he had seen faces, where he had seen beauty, there was a screen.

"Evans!" he cried. There was no answer. A mouse had squeaked, or a curtain rustled. Those were the voices of the dead. The screen, the coal-scuttle, the sideboard remained him. Let him then face the screen, the coal-scuttle and the sideboard . . . but Rezia burst into the room chattering.

Some letter had come. Everybody's plans were changed. Mrs. Filmer would not be able to go to Brighton[336] after all. There was no time to let Mrs. Williams know, and really Rezia thought it very, very annoying, when she caught sight of the hat and thought . . . perhaps . . . she . . . might just make a little . . . . Her voice died out in contented melody.

"Ah, damn!" she cried (it was a joke of theirs, her swearing); the needle had broken. Hat, child, Brighton, needle. She built it up; first one thing, then another, she built it up, sewing.[337]

She wanted him to say whether by moving the rose she had improved the hat. She sat on the end of the sofa.

336 A resort city from the early 1700s onward, Brighton sits on the south coast of England, at the tip of Sussex. Woolf frequently accompanied Leonard to Brighton, where he would give talks and she would visit Vanessa, who liked to vacation there. Her diary entries about Brighton veer from amusement to horror at its "shell encrusted old women, rouged, decked, cadaverous." On one visit, she dined at the Sussex Grill, where, in the restroom, "p—ing as quietly as I could," she listened to the women chatting and noted the reek of fish. Later, she stopped in a bakery to observe large women stuffing themselves with cakes, "something scented, shoddy, parasitic about them," she wrote. "Where does the money come from to feed these fat white slugs? Brighton a love corner for slugs."

337 Clarissa's parties, Rezia's sewing, the spider's thread—the novel's figures of connection are all associated with women, with women's work, and especially the work of enchantment, domesticated by the hostess and the seamstress. "The hostess is our modern Sibyl," Woolf would write in *Orlando*. "She is a witch who lays her guests under a spell. In this house they think themselves happy; in that witty; in a third profound. It is all an illusion (which is nothing against it, for illusions are the most valuable and necessary of things, and she who can create one is among the world's greatest benefactors)."

Feminist critics have often described Woolf as a domestic modernist, a writer attentive to the home and the activities that take place therein. The spells cast by her novels are all the more powerful for transforming encounters with perfectly ordinary, feminized objects—Clarissa's torn dress, Rezia's hat—into extraordinary occasions for creative and critical thought.

Brighton from the west pier, c. 1920.*(Photo and Social History Archive)*

They were perfectly happy now, she said suddenly, putting the hat down. For she could say anything to him now. She could say whatever came into her head. That was almost the first thing she had felt about him, that night in the café when he had come in with his English friends. He had come in, rather shyly, looking round him, and his hat had fallen when he hung it up. That she could remember. She knew he was English, though not one of the large Englishmen her sister admired, for he was always thin; but he had a beautiful fresh colour; and with his big nose, his bright eyes, his way of sitting a little hunched, made her think, she had often told him, of a young hawk, that first evening she saw him, when they were playing dominoes, and he had come in—of a young hawk; but with her he was always very gentle. She had never seen him wild or drunk, only suffering sometimes through this terrible war, but even so, when she came in, he would put it all away. Anything, anything in the whole world, any little bother with her work, anything that struck her to say she would tell him, and he understood at once. Her own family even were not the same. Being older than she was and being so clever—how serious he was, wanting her to read Shakespeare before she could even read a child's story in

English!—being so much more experienced, he could help her. And she, too, could help him.

But this hat now. And then (it was getting late) Sir William Bradshaw.

She held her hands to her head, waiting for him to say did he like the hat or not, and as she sat there, waiting, looking down, he could feel her mind, like a bird, falling from branch to branch, and always alighting, quite rightly; he could follow her mind, as she sat there in one of those loose lax poses that came to her naturally, and, if he should say anything, at once she smiled, like a bird alighting with all its claws firm upon the bough.

But he remembered. Bradshaw said, "The people we are most fond of are not good for us when we are ill." Bradshaw said he must be taught to rest. Bradshaw said they must be separated.

"Must", "must", why "must"? What power had Bradshaw over him? "What right has Bradshaw to say 'must' to me?" he demanded.

"It is because you talked of killing yourself," said Rezia. (Mercifully, she could now say anything to Septimus.)

So he was in their power! Holmes and Bradshaw were on him! The brute with the red nostrils was snuffing into every secret place! "Must" it could say! Where were his papers? the things he had written?

She brought him his papers, the things he had written, things she had written for him. She tumbled them out on to the sofa. They looked at them together. Diagrams, designs, little men and women brandishing sticks for arms, with wings—were they?—on their backs; circles traced round shillings and sixpences—the suns and stars; zigzagging precipices with mountaineers ascending roped together, exactly like knives and forks; sea pieces with little faces laughing out of what might perhaps be waves: the map of the world. Burn them! he cried. Now for his writings; how the dead sing behind rhododendron bushes; odes to Time; conversations with Shakespeare; Evans, Evans, Evans—his messages from the dead; do not cut down trees; tell the Prime Minister. Universal love: the meaning of the world. Burn them! he cried.

But Rezia laid her hands on them. Some were very beautiful, she thought. She would tie them up (for she had no envelope) with a piece of silk.

Even if they took him, she said, she would go with him. They could not separate them against their wills, she said.

Shuffling the edges straight, she did up the papers, and tied the parcel almost without looking, sitting close, sitting beside him, he thought, as if all her petals were about her. She was a flowering tree; and through her branches looked out the face of a lawgiver, who had reached a sanctuary where she feared no one; not Holmes; not Bradshaw; a miracle, a triumph, the last and greatest.[338] Staggering he saw her mount the appalling staircase, laden with Holmes and Bradshaw, men who never weighed less than eleven stone six, who sent their wives to court, men who made ten thousand a year and talked of proportion; who differed in their verdicts (for Holmes said one thing, Bradshaw another), yet judges they were; who mixed the vision and the sideboard; saw nothing clear, yet ruled, yet inflicted. Over them she triumphed.

"There!" she said. The papers were tied up. No one should get at them. She would put them away.

And, she said, nothing should separate them. She sat down beside him and called him by the name of that hawk or crow which being malicious and a great destroyer of crops was precisely like him.[339] No one could separate them, she said.

Then she got up to go into the bedroom to pack their things, but hearing voices downstairs and thinking that Dr. Holmes had perhaps called, ran down to prevent him coming up.

Septimus could hear her talking to Holmes on the staircase.

"My dear lady, I have come as a friend," Holmes was saying.

"No. I will not allow you to see my husband," she said.

He could see her, like a little hen, with her wings spread barring his passage. But Holmes persevered.

"My dear lady, allow me . . ." Holmes said, putting her aside (Holmes was a powerfully built man).

Holmes was coming upstairs. Holmes would burst open the door. Holmes would say, "In a funk, eh?" Holmes would get him.

338 In gathering Septimus's papers, and judging his writings as beautiful and worth preserving, Rezia resembles the solitary traveler's vision of feminine justice from p. 85. A brave and uncompromising figure, she metamorphoses from a petulant child stamping her foot on p. 95 into a "flowering tree," "the face of a lawgiver" peeping out from behind her branches.

339 The narrator cedes the language of metamorphosis to Rezia, who now sees Septimus as the strong-beaked bird, the "hawk or crow," that the novel has compared him to since p. 26. It is touching and sorrowful that, as the moment of Septimus's death nears, Woolf endows Rezia with the clear, charitable, and exalting vision that has belonged to *Mrs. Dalloway*'s narrative consciousness all along. Husband and wife see each other with the greatest tenderness and sympathy just before death.

But no; not Holmes; not Bradshaw. Getting up rather unsteadily, hopping indeed from foot to foot, he considered Mrs. Filmer's nice clean bread-knife with "Bread" carved on the handle. Ah, but one mustn't spoil that. The gas fire? But it was too late now. Holmes was coming. Razors he might have got, but Rezia, who always did that sort of thing, had packed them. There remained only the window, the large Bloomsbury lodging-house window; the tiresome, the troublesome, and rather melodramatic business of opening the window and throwing himself out.[340] It was their idea of tragedy, not his or Rezia's (for she was with him). Holmes and Bradshaw liked that sort of thing. (He sat on the sill.) But he would wait till the very last moment. He did not want to die. Life was good. The sun hot. Only human beings? Coming down the staircase opposite an old man stopped and stared at him.[341] Holmes was at the door. "I'll give it you!" he cried, and flung himself vigorously, violently down on to Mrs. Filmer's area railings.

"The coward!" cried Dr. Holmes, bursting the door open. Rezia ran to the window, she saw; she understood. Dr. Holmes and Mrs. Filmer collided with each other. Mrs. Filmer flapped her apron and made her hide her eyes in the bedroom. There was a great deal of running up and down stairs. Dr. Holmes came in—white as a sheet, shaking all over, with a glass in his hand. She must be brave and drink something, he said. (What was it? Something sweet), for her husband was horribly mangled, would not recover consciousness, she must not see him, must be spared as much as possible, would have the inquest to go through, poor young woman. Who could have foretold it? A sudden impulse, no one was in the least to blame (he told Mrs. Filmer). And why the devil he did it, Dr. Holmes could not conceive.

It seemed to her as she drank the sweet stuff that she was opening long windows, stepping out into some garden. But where? The clock was striking—one, two, three; how sensible the sound was; compared with all this thumping and whispering; like Septimus himself. She was falling asleep. But the clock went on striking, four, five, six and Mrs. Filmer waving

340 An echo of Clarissa opening the window at the very beginning of the novel. Septimus's calculated, somewhat comic consideration of how to kill himself did not exist in the first proofs of *Mrs. Dalloway*, though they did in the manuscript of "The Hours." ("The gas tube? That was a long business," Septimus puns in "The Hours.") Woolf reinserted these sentences in late January 1925, typing them out by hand on a separate sheet of paper that she appended to the proofs.

341 An echo of Clarissa watching the old woman ascend the staircase on p. 163.

her apron (they wouldn't bring the body in here, would they?) seemed part of that garden; or a flag.[342] She had once seen a flag slowly rippling out from a mast when she stayed with her aunt at Venice. Men killed in battle were thus saluted, and Septimus had been through the War. Of her memories, most were happy.

She put on her hat, and ran through cornfields—where could it have been?—on to some hill, somewhere near the sea, for there were ships, gulls, butterflies; they sat on a cliff. In London, too, there they sat, and, half dreaming, came to her through the bedroom door, rain falling, whisperings, stirrings among dry corn, the caress of the sea, as it seemed to her, hollowing them in its arched shell and murmuring to her laid on shore, strewn she felt, like flying flowers over some tomb.[343]

"He is dead," she said, smiling at the poor old woman who guarded her with her honest light-blue eyes fixed on the door. (They wouldn't bring him in here, would they?) But Mrs. Filmer pooh-poohed. Oh no, oh no! They were carrying him away now. Ought she not to be told? Married people ought to be together, Mrs. Filmer thought. But they must do as the doctor said.

"Let her sleep," said Dr. Holmes, feeling her pulse. She saw the large outline of his body dark against the window. So that was Dr. Holmes.

ONE OF THE TRIUMPHS of civilisation, Peter Walsh thought.[344] It is one of the triumphs of civilisation, as the light high bell of the ambulance sounded. Swiftly, cleanly, the ambulance sped to the hospital, having picked up instantly, humanely, some poor devil; some one hit on the head, struck down by disease, knocked over perhaps a minute or so ago at one of these crossings, as might happen to oneself.[345] That was civilisation.[346] It struck him coming back from the East—the efficiency, the organisation, the communal spirit of London. Every cart or carriage of its own accord drew aside to let the ambulance pass. Perhaps it was morbid; or was it not touching rather, the respect

342 In its initial description of Rezia's reaction to Septimus's death, the manuscript of *Mrs. Dalloway* contained an explicit allusion to William Wordsworth, whose 1804 poem "Ode to Duty" described those who submitted like children to authority when faced with grievous loss: "~~&~~ the clock ~~struck~~ <strike> six. A rather austere sound. That Wordsworth had written with extreme ~~beauty~~ <beauty> about ~~Duty~~ it the stern daughter of the voice of God, she did not know or had forgotten." No longer the lawgiver, Rezia must obey Holmes's law, returning to her state of childlike innocence.

343 Woolf's childhood memory of waking up by the sea, first alluded to on p. 2, recurs as Rezia falls asleep.

344 In her diary entry of August 15, 1924, Woolf reported that, after writing Septimus's death, she would "go straight at the grand party & so end; forgetting Septimus, which is a very intense & ticklish business, & jumping Peter Walsh eating his dinner, which may be some obstacle too." What Woolf described as the "important intervening scene" of Peter seeing and hearing the ambulance was initially left out of her design for *Mrs. Dalloway*. It may have been written after she wrote the novel's end.

345 Unlike her use of the clock's chimes to shift from one character to another, Woolf does not use the sound of the ambulance to transition explicitly from Rezia to Peter. In the final version of the novel, the reader does not know if the ambulance Peter hears is carrying Septimus or someone else to the hospital. This is a choice made starker by the realization that, in the manuscript of "The Hours," Woolf specifies that the ambulance contains "Septimus, Dr. Holmes & two attendants," but removes this specification in *Mrs. Dalloway*.

The ambiguity that surrounds the ambulance's passengers reminds us that the story of Septimus, though known to us, remains a total mystery to Peter. The intimate knowledge one might spontaneously and mistakenly attribute to the two is a product of the narrator's consciousness, the "communal spirit of London" it has offered to us, and not the characters' awareness of each other. It is the narrator's choice to obscure and clarify that intimacy.

346 The extraordinary irony of the line ("That was civilisation"), at once tragic and maddening, prompts Rebecca Walkowitz to fix the passing ambulance, and not the party, as the novel's climax. Peter's interior monologue registers "both the cruelty and the kindness of civilization's triumph," she argues. The doctors and nurses in the ambulance deliver care to the ill and injured, but the ambulance also symbolizes war, the medical establishment, and

which they showed this ambulance with its victim inside—busy men hurrying home, yet instantly bethinking them as it passed of some wife; or presumably how easily it might have been them there, stretched on a shelf with a doctor and a nurse . . . Ah, but thinking became morbid, sentimental, directly one began conjuring up doctors, dead bodies; a little glow of pleasure, a sort of lust, too, over the visual impression warned one not to go on with that sort of thing any more—fatal to art, fatal to friendship.[347] True. And yet, thought Peter Walsh, as the ambulance turned the corner, though the light high bell could be heard down the next street and still farther as it crossed the Tottenham Court Road, chiming constantly, it is the privilege of loneliness; in privacy one may do as one chooses. One might weep if no one saw. It had been his undoing—this susceptibility—in Anglo-Indian society; not weeping at the right time, or laughing either. I have that in me, he thought, standing by the pillar-box, which could now dissolve in tears. Why, heaven knows. Beauty of some sort probably, and the weight of the day, which, beginning with that visit to Clarissa, had exhausted him with its heat, its intensity, and the drip, drip of one impression after another down into that cellar where they stood, deep, dark, and no one would ever know.[348] Partly for that reason, its secrecy, complete and inviolable, he had found life like an unknown garden, full of turns and corners, surprising, yes; really it took one's breath away, these moments; there coming to him by the pillar-box opposite the British Museum[349] one of them, a moment, in which things came together; this ambulance; and life and death. It was as if he were sucked up to some very high roof by that rush of emotion, and the rest of him, like a white shell-sprinkled beach, left bare. It had been his undoing in Anglo-Indian society—this susceptibility.

Clarissa once, going on top of an omnibus with him somewhere, Clarissa superficially at least, so easily moved, now in despair, now in the best of spirits, all aquiver in those days and such good company, spotting queer little scenes, names, people from the top of a bus, for they used to explore London and bring

Sir William's commitment to Proportion and Conversion—the aspects of civilization that led Septimus to commit suicide in the first place. Blinded by the "triumph" of civilization, Walkowitz argues, Peter cannot perceive "that the doctors who tend to the injured may be those who have driven Septimus to his death."

347 The conjoining of death and lust begins to prepare us for Clarissa's reaction to Septimus's death on p. 226. Unlike Peter, Clarissa risks sentimentality, risks abandoning herself to the "lust" of death by using it to feel the rapture and the ecstasy of life—an indulgence that Peter has criticized her for in the past, as she recalls it on p. 71 (see also n. 126 on p. 59).

348 The language describing Peter's consciousness, "the drip, drip of one impression after another," echoes the language used to describe Rezia's voice as it trails off on p. 186: "drip, drip, drip, like a contented tap left running."

349 It is fitting, if ironic, that Peter's mind would turn to "the triumphs of civilisation" in front of the British Museum, whose neoclassical facade colonizes an entire block of Great Russell Street in Bloomsbury. Founded in 1753 as the first public, national museum, the British Museum displays objects from around the world, particularly ancient Greek, Roman, and Egyptian artifacts. Notable objects include the Rosetta Stone, the Parthenon and Erechtheum Marbles (called the "Elgin Marbles" after Lord Thomas Elgin, their purveyor), and the colossal bust of Ramesses II, acquired from the British consul general in Egypt. The growth of the museum's collection throughout the eighteenth and nineteenth centuries was largely spurred by the expansion of the British Empire. In the mid-nineteenth century, it began to sponsor overseas excavations in modern-day Turkey and Iraq, and in the twentieth century augmented its collections with prehistoric artifacts donated by T. E. Lawrence and J. Pierpont Morgan. The economic pressures of the First World War caused the government to close all London museums in 1916. In 1917 and 1918, the threat of bombing forced the curators to relocate some of the antiquities from Bloomsbury to provincial libraries, a country house, and a station on the new Postal Tube Railway, but the museum reopened in 1919.

British Museum, London, c. 1890–1900. *(Library of Congress)*

back bags full of treasures from the Caledonian market[350]—Clarissa had a theory in those days—they had heaps of theories, always theories, as young people have. It was to explain the feeling they had of dissatisfaction; not knowing people; not being known. For how could they know each other? You met every day; then not for six months, or years. It was unsatisfactory, they agreed, how little one knew people. But she said, sitting on the bus going up Shaftesbury Avenue,[351] she felt herself everywhere; not "here, here, here"; and she tapped the back of the seat; but everywhere. She waved her hand, going up Shaftesbury Avenue.

350 Off Caledonia Road in north London, the Caledonian Market was a flea market that moved south of the Thames after the Second World War. Peter's description of his and Clarissa's retrieval of "treasures" offers a more playful and harmless version of treasure hunting than the British Museum's accumulation of antiquities.

351 Carved in 1886 to push slum dwellers out of the city center, Shaftesbury Avenue runs northeast from Piccadilly Circus to New Oxford Street, passing through Charing Cross Road at Cambridge Circus. Once the slums were cleared, theaters were built: the Lyric Theatre in 1888; the Apollo Theatre in 1901; the Hicks Theatre in 1906 (renamed the Globe Theatre in 1909); the Queens' Theatre in 1907. By the First

She was all that. So that to know her, or any one, one must seek out the people who completed them; even the places. Odd affinities she had with people she had never spoken to, some woman in the street, some man behind a counter—even trees, or barns. It ended in a transcendental theory which, with her horror of death, allowed her to believe, or say that she believed (for all her scepticism), that since our apparitions, the part of us which appears, are so momentary compared with the other, the unseen part of us, which spreads wide, the unseen might survive, be recovered somehow attached to this person or that, or even haunting certain places, after death. Perhaps—perhaps.[352]

Looking back over that long friendship of almost thirty years her theory worked to this extent. Brief, broken, often painful as their actual meetings had been, what with his absences and interruptions (this morning, for instance, in came Elizabeth, like a long-legged colt, handsome, dumb, just as he was beginning to talk to Clarissa), the effect of them on his life was immeasurable. There was a mystery about it. You were given a sharp, acute, uncomfortable grain—the actual meeting; horribly painful as often as not; yet in absence, in the most unlikely places, it would flower out, open, shed its scent, let you touch, taste, look about you, get the whole feel of it and understanding, after years of lying lost. Thus she had come to him; on board ship; in the Himalayas; suggested by the oddest things (so Sally Seton, generous, enthusiastic goose! thought of *him* when she saw blue hydrangeas). She had influenced him more than any person he had ever known. And always in this way coming before him without his wishing it, cool, lady-like, critical; or ravishing, romantic, recalling some field or English harvest. He saw her most often in the country, not in London. One scene after another at Bourton . . . .

He had reached his hotel. He crossed the hall, with its mounds of reddish chairs and sofas, its spike-leaved, withered-looking plants. He got his key off the hook. The young lady handed him some letters. He went upstairs—he saw her most often at Bourton, in the late summer, when he stayed there for a

World War, Shaftesbury Avenue had emerged as the main thoroughfare of the West End theater district.

352 Clarissa's "transcendental theory," born from her fear of death, offers Woolf's most elegant and concise summary of how the novel constructs its narrative consciousness. The scattering of one character's thoughts in another's, the precision with which characters retrace one another's steps are forms of attachment that persist despite—and indeed, because of—death. The idea is chalked up to Clarissa's youthful philosophizing, the momentary suspension of her "scepticism." Yet by elevating her transcendental theory into the organizing principle of *Mrs. Dalloway*, Woolf shows how the novel can turn life's terrors and its ecstasies into words, and, extending these words to others, ensure that its glow will never dim.

week, or fortnight even, as people did in those days. First on top of some hill there she would stand, hands clapped to her hair, her cloak blowing out, pointing, crying to them—She saw the Severn[353] beneath. Or in a wood, making the kettle boil—very ineffective with her fingers; the smoke curtseying, blowing in their faces; her little pink face showing through; begging water from an old woman in a cottage, who came to the door to watch them go. They walked always; the others drove. She was bored driving, disliked all animals, except that dog. They tramped miles along roads. She would break off to get her bearings, pilot him back across country; and all the time they argued, discussed poetry, discussed people, discussed politics (she was a Radical then); never noticing a thing except when she stopped, cried out at a view or a tree, and made him look with her; and so on again, through stubble fields, she walking ahead, with a flower for her aunt, never tired of walking for all her delicacy; to drop down on Bourton in the dusk. Then, after dinner, old Breitkopf would open the piano and sing without any voice,[354] and they would lie sunk in arm-chairs, trying not to laugh, but always breaking down and laughing, laughing—laughing at nothing. Breitkopf was supposed not to see. And then in the morning, flirting up and down like a wagtail[355] in front of the house . . . .

Oh it was a letter from her! This blue envelope; that was her hand. And he would have to read it. Here was another of those meetings, bound to be painful! To read her letter needed the devil of an effort. "How heavenly it was to see him. She must tell him that." That was all.

But it upset him. It annoyed him. He wished she hadn't written it. Coming on top of his thoughts, it was like a nudge in the ribs. Why couldn't she let him be? After all, she had married Dalloway, and lived with him in perfect happiness all these years.

These hotels are not consoling places. Far from it. Any number of people had hung up their hats on those pegs. Even the flies, if you thought of it, had settled on other people's noses. As for the cleanliness which hit him in the face, it wasn't cleanli-

353 The Severn, thought to derive from the name of the legendary Celtic princess *Sabrinnā*, meaning "of uncertain meaning," is the longest river in the UK, beginning in the Cambrian Mountains of Wales and running through Shropshire, Worcestershire, and Gloucestershire.

354 In the manuscript of "The Hours," the song Old Breitkopf sings is Robert Schumann's "Ich grolle nicht" ("I do not chide you").

355 A long-tailed, small, and nimble bird known for persistently wagging its tail up and down.

ness, so much as bareness, frigidity; a thing that had to be. Some arid matron made her rounds at dawn sniffing, peering, causing blue-nosed maids to scour, for all the world as if the next visitor were a joint of meat to be served on a perfectly clean platter. For sleep, one bed; for sitting in, one armchair; for cleaning one's teeth and shaving one's chin, one tumbler, one looking-glass. Books, letters, dressing-gown, slipped about on the impersonality of the horsehair like incongruous impertinences. And it was Clarissa's letter that made him see all this. "Heavenly to see you. She must say so!" He folded the paper; pushed it away; nothing would induce him to read it again!

To get that letter to him by six o'clock she must have sat down and written it directly he left her; stamped it; sent somebody to the post. It was, as people say, very like her. She was upset by his visit. She had felt a great deal; had for a moment, when she kissed his hand, regretted, envied him even, remembered possibly (for he saw her look it) something he had said—how they would change the world if she married him perhaps; whereas, it was this; it was middle age; it was mediocrity; then forced herself with her indomitable vitality to put all that aside, there being in her a thread of life which for toughness, endurance, power to overcome obstacles, and carry her triumphantly through he had never known the like of. Yes; but there would come a reaction directly he left the room. She would be frightfully sorry for him; she would think what in the world she could do to give him pleasure (short always of the one thing), and he could see her with the tears running down her cheeks going to her writing-table and dashing off that one line which he was to find greeting him . . . . "Heavenly to see you!" And she meant it.

Peter Walsh had now unlaced his boots.

But it would not have been a success, their marriage. The other thing, after all, came so much more naturally.

It was odd; it was true; lots of people felt it. Peter Walsh, who had done just respectably, filled the usual posts adequately, was liked, but thought a little cranky, gave himself airs—it was odd that *he* should have had, especially now that his hair was grey, a

356 The word "verandah" was originally introduced from India, as a derivative of the Hindi *varandā*, Bengali *bārāndā*, and modern Sanskrit *baranda*. It frequently appeared in Indian travelogues that described the verandah as the Indian term for a piazza or landing place.

contented look; a look of having reserves. It was this that made him attractive to women, who liked the sense that he was not altogether manly. There was something unusual about him, or something behind him. It might be that he was bookish—never came to see you without taking up the book on the table (he was now reading, with his bootlaces trailing on the floor); or that he was a gentleman, which showed itself in the way he knocked the ashes out of his pipe, and in his manners of course to women. For it was very charming and quite ridiculous how easily some girl without a grain of sense could twist him round her finger. But at her own risk. That is to say, though he might be ever so easy, and indeed with his gaiety and good-breeding fascinating to be with, it was only up to a point. She said something—no, no; he saw through that. He wouldn't stand that—no, no. Then he could shout and rock and hold his sides together over some joke with men. He was the best judge of cooking in India. He was a man. But not the sort of man one had to respect—which was a mercy; not like Major Simmons, for instance; not in the least, Daisy thought, when in spite of her two small children, she used to compare them.

He pulled off his boots. He emptied his pockets. Out came with his pocket-knife a snapshot of Daisy on the verandah;[356] Daisy all in white, with a fox-terrier on her knee; very charming, very dark; the best he had ever seen of her. It did come, after all, so naturally; so much more naturally than Clarissa. No fuss. No bother. No finicking and fidgeting. All plain sailing. And the dark, adorably pretty girl on the verandah exclaimed (he could hear her) Of course, of course she would give him everything! she cried (she had no sense of discretion), everything he wanted! she cried, running to meet him, whoever might be looking. And she was only twenty-four. And she had two children. Well, well!

Well indeed he had got himself into a mess at his age. And it came over him when he woke in the night pretty forcibly. Suppose they did marry? For him it would be all very well, but what about her? Mrs. Burgess, a good sort and no chatterbox, in whom he had confided, thought this absence of his in England, ostensibly to see lawyers, might serve to make Daisy reconsider, think what it meant. It was a question of her position, Mrs. Burgess said; the social barrier; giving up her children. She'd be a widow with a past one of these days, draggling about in the suburbs, or more likely, indiscriminate (you know, she said, what such women get like, with too much paint). But Peter Walsh pooh-poohed all that. He didn't mean to die yet. Anyhow, she must settle for herself; judge for herself, he thought, padding about the room in his socks, smoothing out his dress-shirt, for he might go to Clarissa's party, or he might go to one of the Halls, or he might settle in and read an absorbing book written by a man he used to know at Oxford. And if he did retire, that's what he'd do—write books. He would go to Oxford and poke about in the Bodleian.[357] Vainly the dark, adorably pretty girl ran to the end of the terrace; vainly waved her hand; vainly cried she didn't care a straw what people said. There he was, the man she thought the world of, the perfect gentleman, the fascinating, the distinguished (and his age made not the least difference to her), padding about a room in an hotel in Bloomsbury, shaving, washing, continuing, as he took up cans, put down razors, to poke about in the Bodleian, and get at the truth about one or two little matters that interested him. And he would have a chat with whoever it might be, and so come to disregard more and more precise hours for lunch, and miss engagements; and when Daisy asked him, as she would, for a kiss, a scene, fail to come up to the scratch[358] (though he was genuinely devoted to her)—in short it might be happier, as Mrs. Burgess said, that she should forget him, or merely remember him as he was in August 1922,[359] like a figure standing at the cross roads at dusk, which grows more and more remote as the dog-cart spins away, carrying her securely fastened to the back seat, though her arms are outstretched, and as she sees the figure dwindle and disappear, still she cries out how she would do anything in the world, anything, anything, anything . . . .

He never knew what people thought. It became more and more difficult for him to concentrate. He became absorbed;

357 The Bodleian Library at the University of Oxford is the second-largest library in England. Though its oldest room dates to 1488, it did not open as a library until 1602, under the patronage of Sir Thomas Bodley, a fellow of Merton College. Bodley married a rich widow whose late husband had made his fortune trading in sardines, and upon his retirement, he decided to "set up my Staffe at the Library doore in Oxford; being throughly perswaded, that in my solitude and surcease from the Common-wealth affaires, I could not busy my selfe to better purpose, then by reducing that place (which then in every part lay ruined and wast) to the publique use of Students."

358 To not be good enough.

359 Presumably the month and year when Peter and Daisy first met, as well as the month and year Woolf began writing *Mrs. Dalloway* in earnest.

he became busied with his own concerns; now surly, now gay; dependent on women, absent-minded, moody, less and less able (so he thought as he shaved) to understand why Clarissa couldn't simply find them a lodging and be nice to Daisy; introduce her. And then he could just—just do what? just haunt and hover[360] (he was at the moment actually engaged in sorting out various keys, papers), swoop and taste, be alone, in short, sufficient to himself; and yet nobody of course was more dependent upon others (he buttoned his waistcoat); it had been his undoing. He could not keep out of smoking-rooms, liked colonels, liked golf, liked bridge, and above all women's society, and the fineness of their companionship, and their faithfulness and audacity and greatness in loving which, though it had its drawbacks, seemed to him (and the dark, adorably pretty face was on top of the envelopes) so wholly admirable, so splendid a flower to grow on the crest of human life, and yet he could not come up to the scratch, being always apt to see round things (Clarissa had sapped something in him permanently), and to tire very easily of mute devotion and to want variety in love, though it would make him furious if Daisy loved anybody else, furious! for he was jealous, uncontrollably jealous by temperament. He suffered tortures! But where was his knife; his watch; his seals, his note-case, and Clarissa's letter which he would not read again but liked to think of, and Daisy's photograph? And now for dinner.

They were eating.

Sitting at little tables round vases, dressed or not dressed, with their shawls and bags laid beside them, with their air of false composure, for they were not used to so many courses at dinner; and confidence, for they were able to pay for it; and strain, for they had been running about London all day shopping, sightseeing; and their natural curiosity, for they looked round and up as the nice-looking gentleman in horn-rimmed spectacles came in; and their good nature, for they would have been glad to do any little service, such as lend a time-table or impart useful information; and their desire, pulsing in them, tugging at them subterraneously, somehow to establish connec-

360 The idea of haunting, which Clarissa's "transcendental theory" introduces to the novel, recalls us to Septimus's death and allows his character to linger at the reader's side even after his disappearance from the novel. The idea that the living may haunt one another also offers evidence for Alex Zwerdling's interpretation of Clarissa's party "as a kind of wake," an invitation to the living ghosts of British imperialism, still devoted to its smoking rooms and its colonels, its games of golf and bridge, to congregate and lament the empire's decline.

tions if it were only a birthplace (Liverpool,[361] for example), in common or friends of the same name; with their furtive glances, odd silences, and sudden withdrawals into family jocularity and isolation; there they sat eating dinner when Mr. Walsh came in and took his seat at a little table by the curtain.

It was not that he said anything, for being solitary he could only address himself to the waiter; it was his way of looking at the menu, of pointing his forefinger to a particular wine, of hitching himself up to the table, of addressing himself seriously, not gluttonously to dinner, that won him their respect; which, having to remain unexpressed for the greater part of the meal, flared up at the table where the Morrises sat when Mr. Walsh was heard to say at the end of the meal, "Bartlett pears."[362] Why he should have spoken so moderately yet firmly, with the air of a disciplinarian well within his rights which are founded upon justice, neither young Charles Morris, nor old Charles, neither Miss Elaine nor Mrs. Morris knew. But when he said, "Bartlett pears," sitting alone at his table, they felt that he counted on their support in some lawful demand; was champion of a cause which immediately became their own, so that their eyes met his eyes sympathetically, and when they all reached the smoking-room simultaneously, a little talk between them became inevitable.

It was not very profound—only to the effect that London was crowded; had changed in thirty years; that Mr. Morris preferred Liverpool; that Mrs. Morris had been to the Westminster flower-show,[363] and that they had all seen the Prince of Wales. Yet, thought Peter Walsh, no family in the world can compare with the Morrises; none whatever; and their relations to each other are perfect, and they don't care a hang for the upper classes, and they like what they like, and Elaine is training for the family business, and the boy has won a scholarship at Leeds,[364] and the old lady (who is about his own age) has three more children at home; and they have two motor cars, but Mr. Morris still mends the boots on Sunday: it is superb, it is absolutely superb, thought Peter Walsh, swaying a little backwards and forwards with his liqueur glass in his hand among the hairy red chairs and ash-

361 A port city on the eastern side of the Mersey River in northwest England's county of Lancashire. One of the country's main centers of growth during the Industrial Revolution, Liverpool emerged as a major port for the trading of tobacco, sugar, coal, and cotton, though its initial prosperity was due primarily to the slave trade in the eighteenth century.

362 The Williams' Bon Chrétien pear, known in England as the Williams pear and in America as the Bartlett pear, is a summer pear: bell-shaped, green- and golden-skinned. The scene recalls an invitation Woolf described in her diary on July 17, 1920: ". . . dinner at the Rubens Hotel, in the heart of a rich warm hearted British family, untouched in any way since 100 years ago. Civilization having produced that organism, stereotyped by it."

363 The Royal Horticultural Society held biweekly flower shows in the Royal Horticultural Halls on Vincent Square in Westminster. The buildings' glazed roofs bathed plants and flowers in natural light. The society's greatest shows were in the spring and autumn and featured flowers favored by the aristocracy: alpines, magnolias, rhododendrons, and camellias in the spring; leaves, berries, and fruits in the fall.

364 In 1925, the University of Leeds was a comparatively new university. It was established in 1874 as the Yorkshire College of Science, and its aim was to educate the children of middle-class industrialists and merchants. Unlike the classics-based education offered by Oxford and Cambridge, the college promised to teach progressive and practical skills: physics, mathematics, geology, mining, engineering, and textile technologies. It introduced the classics, modern literature, and history when it became Yorkshire College in the mid-1880s and combined with the Leeds School of Medicine. By 1904, the college received a royal charter as an independent body by King Edward VII and thenceforth began to operate as the University of Leeds.

trays, feeling very well pleased with himself, for the Morrises liked him. Yes, they liked a man who said "Bartlett pears." They liked him, he felt.

He would go to Clarissa's party. (The Morrises moved off; but they would meet again.) He would go to Clarissa's party, because he wanted to ask Richard what they were doing in India—the conservative duffers.[365] And what's being acted? And music . . . . Oh yes, and mere gossip.

For this is the truth about our soul, he thought, our self, who fish-like inhabits deep seas and plies among obscurities threading her way between the boles of giant weeds, over sun-flickered

365 According to the *Oxford English Dictionary*, "A person who is, or proves to be, without practical ability or capacity in a particular occupation or undertaking; an incompetent, inefficient, or useless person; (also) a person lacking in spirit or courage. Also more generally: a stupid or foolish person."

London, Evening, Childe Hassam. Pastel and crayon on paper mounted on paperboard, 1897. *(Hirshhorn Museum and Sculpture Garden, Smithsonian Institution, Washington, DC, Gift of Joseph H. Hirshhorn, 1966)*

spaces and on and on into gloom, cold, deep, inscrutable; suddenly she shoots to the surface and sports on the wind-wrinkled waves; that is, has a positive need to brush, scrape, kindle herself, gossiping. What did the Government mean—Richard Dalloway would know—to do about India?

Since it was a very hot night and the paper boys went by with placards proclaiming in huge red letters that there was a heat-wave, wicker chairs were placed on the hotel steps and there, sipping, smoking, detached gentlemen sat. Peter Walsh sat there. One might fancy that day, the London day, was just beginning. Like a woman who had slipped off her print dress and white apron to array herself in blue and pearls, the day changed, put off stuff, took gauze, changed to evening, and with the same sigh of exhilaration that a woman breathes, tumbling petticoats on the floor, it too shed dust, heat, colour; the traffic thinned; motor cars, tinkling, darting, succeeded the lumber of vans; and here and there among the thick foliage of the squares an intense light hung. I resign, the evening seemed to say, as it paled and faded above the battlements and prominences, moulded, pointed, of hotel, flat, and block of shops, I fade, she was beginning, I disappear, but London would have none of it, and rushed her bayonets into the sky, pinioned her, constrained her to partnership in her revelry.

For the great revolution of Mr. Willett's summer time[366] had taken place since Peter Walsh's last visit to England. The prolonged evening was new to him. It was inspiriting, rather. For as the young people went by with their despatch-boxes,[367] awfully glad to be free, proud too, dumbly, of stepping this famous pavement, joy of a kind, cheap, tinselly, if you like, but all the same rapture, flushed their faces. They dressed well too; pink stockings; pretty shoes. They would now have two hours at the pictures. It sharpened, it refined them, the yellow-blue evening light; and on the leaves in the square shone lurid, livid—they looked as if dipped in sea water—the foliage of a submerged city. He was astonished by the beauty; it was encouraging too, for where the returned Anglo-Indian sat by rights (he knew crowds of them) in the Oriental Club[368] biliously summing up

366 William Willett (1856–1915) was an English builder who published a 1907 pamphlet titled *The Waste of Daylight*. In it, he outlined a time-keeping scheme whereby clocks would be advanced by a sum total of 80 minutes in four incremental steps during April and reversed in September, thus extending daylight and saving millions of pounds in lighting costs. Willett campaigned tirelessly to see his scheme enacted by Parliament. However, "British Summer Time," or what Americans call "daylight savings time," was not adopted until the start of the First World War, when the need to save coal and spur production reinvigorated his proposal. On May 21, 1916, just over a year after Willett's death from influenza, clocks in Britain were advanced by an hour for the first time.

367 Recall Clarissa meeting Hugh with his despatch box on p. 12.

368 The Oriental Club is a London gentlemen's club that was located at 18 Hanover Square until it moved to its present location in Stratford Place and set up shop in what Lytton Strachey once described to Woolf as "a vast, hideous building . . . filled with vast hideous Anglo-Indians, very old and very rich." The club was founded in 1824 as a meeting place for "individuals of rank and talent" connected to the "Eastern empire," though it was not long before it admitted men who had simply traveled through Asia at one time or another. As reported in the April 1824 edition of *The Asiatic Journal and Monthly Miscellany*, "The British empire in the East is now so extensive, and the persons connected with it so numerous, that the establishment of an institution where they may meet on a footing of social intercourse, seems particularly desirable." The irony of Peter's disdain for "the returned Anglo-Indian" sitting in the Oriental Club, "biliously summing up the ruin of the world," is that he is going to Clarissa's party in part to gossip with Richard about what the government will do in India.

the ruin of the world, here was he, as young as ever; envying young people their summer time and the rest of it, and more than suspecting from the words of a girl, from a housemaid's laughter—intangible things you couldn't lay your hands on—that shift in the whole pyramidal accumulation which in his youth had seemed immovable. On top of them it had pressed; weighed them down, the women especially, like those flowers Clarissa's Aunt Helena used to press between sheets of grey blotting-paper with Littré's dictionary[369] on top, sitting under the lamp after dinner. She was dead now.[370] He had heard of her, from Clarissa, losing the sight of one eye. It seemed so fitting—one of nature's masterpieces—that old Miss Parry should turn to glass. She would die like some bird in a frost gripping her perch. She belonged to a different age, but being so entire, so complete, would always stand up on the horizon, stone-white, eminent, like a lighthouse marking some past stage on this adventurous,

369 The first edition of Emile Littré's *Dictionnaire de la langue française*, colloquially known as the *Littré*, was published in four large quarto volumes between 1863 and 1872. The dictionary was celebrated for its attention to philological, etymological, and historical detail, and for Littré's charmingly idiosyncratic practice of using quotations, some 250,000 in total, from seventeenth-century French literature to contextualize his definitions of words.

370 Aunt Helena is still alive. Peter encounters her at Clarissa's party on p. 220. Yet his certainty that she is dead, and his disbelief on discovering that she is not, marks her as one of the novel's living ghosts who are now rising as night falls.

A Cricket Match of the Royal Marine Artillery, London, Walter Paris. Watercolor, gouache, and graphite on paper, 1888. *(Paul Mellon Collection, Yale Center for British Art)*

long, long voyage, this interminable—(he felt for a copper to buy a paper and read about Surrey and Yorkshire (he had held out that copper millions of times) Surrey was all out once more)—this interminable life. But cricket was no mere game. Cricket was important. He could never help reading about cricket. He read the scores in the stop press first, then how it was a hot day; then about a murder case. Having done things millions of times enriched them, though it might be said to take the surface off. The past enriched, and experience, and having cared for one or two people, and so having acquired the power which the young lack, of cutting short, doing what one likes, not caring a rap what people say and coming and going without any very great expectations (he left his paper on the table and moved off), which however (and he looked for his hat and coat) was not altogether true of him, not to-night, for here he was starting to go to a party, at his age, with the belief upon him, that he was about to have an experience. But what?

Beauty anyhow. Not the crude beauty of the eye. It was not beauty pure and simple—Bedford Place leading into Russell Square.[371] It was straightness and emptiness of course; the symmetry of a corridor; but it was also windows lit up, a piano, a gramophone sounding; a sense of pleasure making hidden, but now and again emerging when, through the uncurtained window, the window left open, one saw parties sitting over tables, young people slowly circling, conversations between men and women, maids idly looking out (a strange comment theirs, when work was done), stockings drying on top ledges, a parrot, a few plants. Absorbing, mysterious, of infinite richness, this life. And in the large square where the cabs shot and swerved so quick, there were loitering couples, dallying, embracing, shrunk up under the shower of a tree; that was moving; so silent, so absorbed, that one passed, discreetly, timidly, as if in the presence of some sacred ceremony to interrupt which would have been impious. That was interesting. And so on into the flare and glare.[372]

His light overcoat blew open, he stepped with indescribable idiosyncrasy, leant a little forward, tripped, with his hands

371 A large garden square in Bloomsbury. Virginia and Leonard Woolf purchased their home at 52 Tavistock Square, just down the street from Russell Square, in 1924. Most of *Mrs. Dalloway* was written here.

372 The impersonal beauty of nature that Septimus perceives during his hallucinations, through Peter's homesick gaze, transformed into the impersonal beauty of London. The vitality of the city's social life transcends any individual perception of it. Its beauty is not "the crude beauty of the eye," Woolf clarifies, but inherent to the geometry of Russell Square: its "straightness and emptiness"; "the symmetry of a corridor"; the "windows lit up" and the sounds of the piano and gramophone drifting through them.

"London is enchanting," Woolf wrote in her diary on May 26, 1924. "I step out upon a tawny coloured magic carpet, it seems, & get carried into beauty without raising a finger. The nights are amazing, with all the white porticoes & broad silent avenues. And people pop in & out, lightly, divertingly like rabbits; & I look down Southampton Row, wet as a seal's back or red & yellow with sunshine, & watch the omnibus going and coming, & hear the old crazy organs. One of these days I will write about London, & how it takes up the private life & carries it on, without any effort."

behind his back and his eyes still a little hawk-like; he tripped through London, towards Westminster, observing.

Was everybody dining out, then? Doors were being opened here by a footman to let issue a high-stepping old dame, in buckled shoes, with three purple ostrich feathers in her hair. Doors were being opened for ladies wrapped like mummies in shawls with bright flowers on them, ladies with bare heads. And in respectable quarters with stucco pillars through small front gardens, lightly swathed, with combs in their hair (having run up to see the children), women came; men waited for them, with their coats blowing open, and the motor started. Everybody was going out. What with these doors being opened, and the descent and the start, it seemed as if the whole of London were embarking in little boats moored to the bank, tossing on the waters, as if the whole place were floating off in carnival. And Whitehall was skated over, silver beaten as it was, skated over by spiders, and there was a sense of midges[373] round the arc lamps; it was so hot that people stood about talking. And here in Westminster was a retired Judge, presumably, sitting four square at his house door dressed all in white. An Anglo-Indian presumably.

And here a shindy of brawling women, drunken women; here only a policeman and looming houses, high houses, domed houses, churches, parliaments, and the hoot of a steamer on the river, a hollow misty cry. But it was her street, this, Clarissa's; cabs were rushing round the corner, like water round the piers of a bridge, drawn together, it seemed to him because they bore people going to her party, Clarissa's party.

The cold stream of visual impressions failed him now as if the eye were a cup that overflowed and let the rest run down its china walls unrecorded. The brain must wake now. The body must contract now, entering the house, the lighted house, where the door stood open, where the motor cars were standing, and bright women descending: the soul must brave itself to endure. He opened the big blade of his pocket-knife.[374]

373 Though the festivities that Peter observes are pleasurable, rapturous even, the presence of "mummies," "spiders," and "midges" (small flies) suggests that the summer evening carries some pestilence, a feeling of decay.

374 Why should Peter enter a party armed with the "big blade of his pocket-knife"? We saw him wield it first on p. 66, when he conversed with Clarissa in her sitting room, pricking at her sense of pride. Now he reenters the house not as an "old buck," ready to wound the woman who spurned him, but as a subject of the British Empire, suddenly disillusioned by the offerings of civilization: "The cold stream of visual impressions failed him now." He takes out his knife, steadies himself. He is prepared to cut through civilization's false facades, its niceties, all of which converge on the party at the novel's end.

❦

Lucy came running full tilt downstairs, having just nipped in to the drawing-room to smooth a cover, to straighten a chair, to pause a moment and feel whoever came in must think how clean, how bright, how beautifully cared for, when they saw the beautiful silver, the brass fire-irons, the new chair-covers, and the curtains of yellow chintz: she appraised each; heard a roar of voices; people already coming up from dinner; she must fly![375]

The Prime Minister was coming, Agnes said: so she had heard them say in the dining-room, she said, coming in with a tray of glasses. Did it matter, did it matter in the least, one Prime Minister more or less? It made no difference at this hour of the night to Mrs. Walker among the plates, saucepans, cullenders,[376] frying-pans, chicken in aspic, ice-cream freezers, pared crusts of bread, lemons, soup tureens, and pudding basins which, however hard they washed up in the scullery, seemed to be all on top of her, on the kitchen table, on chairs, while the fire blared and roared, the electric lights glared, and still supper had to be laid. All she felt was, one Prime Minister more or less made not a scrap of difference to Mrs. Walker.

The ladies were going upstairs already, said Lucy; the ladies were going up, one by one, Mrs. Dalloway walking last and almost always sending back some message to the kitchen, "My love to Mrs. Walker," that was it one night. Next morning they would go over the dishes—the soup, the salmon; the salmon, Mrs. Walker knew, as usual underdone, for she always got nervous about the pudding and left it to Jenny; so it happened, the salmon was always underdone. But some lady with fair hair and silver ornaments had said, Lucy said, about the entrée, was it really made at home? But it was the salmon that bothered Mrs. Walker, as she spun the plates round and round, and pushed in dampers and pulled out dampers; and there came a burst of laughter from the dining-room; a voice speaking; then another burst of laughter—the gentlemen enjoying themselves when the ladies had gone. The

375 In her diary on September 7, 1924, Woolf announced that she had arrived at the party scene. She feared she was writing "sloppily, using nothing but present participles" in "my last lap of Mrs D." "There I am now—at last at the party, which is to begin in the kitchen, & climb slowly upstairs," she planned. "It is to be a most complicated spirited solid piece, knitting together everything & ending on three notes, at different stages of the staircase, each saying something to sum up Clarissa. Who shall say these things? Peter, Richard, & Sally Seton perhaps: but I don't want to tie myself down to that yet. Now I do think this might be the best of my endings, & come off, perhaps."

The party is an extraordinary device for bringing together not only the characters Woolf has created throughout *Mrs. Dalloway*, but their memories, feelings, and thoughts into a single concentrated space. Reading it closely, one can hear the novel repeating itself. The echoes of its past and its characters' pasts come through faintly at first; then grow louder and ever more insistent as it approaches Clarissa's ecstatic meditation on Septimus's death.

376 A rare spelling of "colander."

tokay, said Lucy running in. Mr. Dalloway had sent for the tokay, from the Emperor's cellars, the Imperial Tokay.[377]

It was borne through the kitchen. Over her shoulder Lucy reported how Miss Elizabeth looked quite lovely; she couldn't take her eyes off her; in her pink dress, wearing the necklace Mr. Dalloway had given her. Jenny must remember the dog, Miss Elizabeth's fox-terrier, which, since it bit had to be shut up and might, Elizabeth thought, want something. Jenny must remember the dog. But Jenny was not going upstairs with all those people about. There was a motor at the door already! There was a ring at the bell—and the gentlemen still in the dining-room, drinking tokay!

There, they were going upstairs; that was the first to come, and now they would come faster and faster, so that Mrs. Parkinson (hired for parties) would leave the hall door ajar, and the hall would be full of gentlemen waiting (they stood waiting, sleeking down their hair) while the ladies took their cloaks off in the room along the passage; where Mrs. Barnet helped them, old Ellen Barnet, who had been with the family for forty years, and came every summer to help the ladies, and remembered mothers when they were girls, and though very unassuming did shake hands; said "milady" very respectfully, yet had a humorous way with her, looking at the young ladies, and ever so tactfully helping Lady Lovejoy, who had some trouble with her underbodice. And they could not help feeling, Lady Lovejoy and Miss Alice, that some little privilege in the matter of brush and comb, was awarded them having known Mrs. Barnet—"thirty years, milady," Mrs. Barnet supplied her. Young ladies did not use to rouge, said Lady Lovejoy, when they stayed at Bourton in the old days. And Miss Alice didn't need rouge, said Mrs. Barnet, looking at her fondly. There Mrs. Barnet would sit, in the cloakroom, patting down the furs, smoothing out the Spanish shawls, tidying the dressing-table, and knowing perfectly well, in spite of the furs and the embroideries, which were nice ladies, which were not. The dear old body, said Lady Lovejoy, mounting the stairs, Clarissa's old nurse.

377 Tokay, or "Tokaji," refers to sweet wines from the Tokaj wine region of northeastern Hungary and southeastern Slovakia. Made from grapes infected by "noble rot," or *Botrytis cinerea*, a beneficial gray fungus, Tokay wines are sweet, topaz-colored, and potently alcoholic. Before 1918, the finest Tokaji wine was not sold but stored in the imperial cellars of the Habsburg monarchs—hence the name, Imperial Tokay.

And then Lady Lovejoy stiffened. "Lady and Miss Lovejoy," she said to Mr. Wilkins (hired for parties). He had an admirable manner, as he bent and straightened himself, bent and straightened himself and announced with perfect impartiality "Lady and Miss Lovejoy . . . Sir John and Lady Needham . . . Miss Weld . . . Mr. Walsh." His manner was admirable; his family life must be irreproachable, except that it seemed impossible that a being with greenish lips and shaven cheeks could ever have blundered into the nuisance of children.[378]

"How delightful to see you!" said Clarissa. She said it to every one. How delightful to see you! She was at her worst—effusive, insincere. It was a great mistake to have come. He should have stayed at home and read his book, thought Peter Walsh; should have gone to a music hall; he should have stayed at home, for he knew no one.

Oh dear, it was going to be a failure; a complete failure, Clarissa felt it in her bones as dear old Lord Lexham stood there apologising for his wife who had caught cold at the Buckingham Palace garden party. She could see Peter out of the tail of her eye, criticising her, there, in that corner. Why, after all, did she do these things? Why seek pinnacles and stand drenched in fire? Might it consume her anyhow! Burn her to cinders! Better anything, better brandish one's torch and hurl it to earth than taper and dwindle away like some Ellie Henderson! It was extraordinary how Peter put her into these states just by coming and standing in a corner. He made her see herself; exaggerate. It was idiotic. But why did he come, then, merely to criticise? Why always take, never give? Why not risk one's one little point of view? There he was wandering off, and she must speak to him. But she would not get the chance. Life was that—humiliation, renunciation. What Lord Lexham was saying was that his wife would not wear her furs at the garden party because "my dear, you ladies are all alike"—Lady Lexham being seventy-five at least! It was delicious, how they petted each other, that old couple. She did like old Lord Lexham. She did think it mattered, her party, and it made her feel quite sick to know that it was

378 The servants who open the penultimate section of the novel—Lucy, Agnes, Mrs. Walker, Jenny, Mrs. Barnet, and the two temporary workers, Mrs. Parkinson and Mr. Wilkins—have little on their minds other than the work at hand. What should we make of Woolf's choice to deny the servants the roving, nostalgic thoughts and memories that she allows even the morally bankrupt Hugh Whitbread?

One answer would be to accuse Woolf of snobbery, and to recall her long-suffering cook Nellie Boxall, "incurably fussy, nervy, insubstantial," whose presence lingers over Lucy and Clarissa's exchange on p. 61. Yet the snobbery she betrayed in life was precisely the snobbery she took aim at in her fiction. She knew that in the history of the novel, not all characters were imagined as having equally rich inner lives; that the characters excluded from the privilege of consciousness were often the poor and working class, the ill and injured. Her essays on character, like "Mr. Bennett and Mrs. Brown," decry the class politics of interiority, as do many of her novels. They do this not only by kindling the rich inner lives of characters who are not wealthy or powerful, but by showing how the emotional and psychological rigidity of the upper classes robs consciousness of its deep, lovely glow.

Woolf's critique of the politics of interiority is most pronounced at the party. By concentrating the energies of the governing class in a single place, the party seems to dull and flatten the thoughts of even upper- and middle-class characters who have been, up to this point in the novel, presented as psychologically complex. Clarissa is anxious and prone to exaggeration; Peter is bored and critical; Ellie Henderson, introduced on p. 210, worries about money. The sudden crudeness of these minds when forced to keep the company of Hugh Whitbread, Sir William, and the prime minister extends Woolf's critique of the social system on the level of style.

all going wrong, all falling flat. Anything, any explosion, any horror was better than people wandering aimlessly, standing in a bunch at a corner like Ellie Henderson, not even caring to hold themselves upright.

Gently the yellow curtain with all the birds of Paradise[379] blew out and it seemed as if there were a flight of wings into the room, right out, then sucked back. (For the windows were open.) Was it draughty, Ellie Henderson wondered? She was subject to chills. But it did not matter that she should come down sneezing to-morrow; it was the girls with their naked shoulders she thought of, being trained to think of others by an old father, an invalid, late vicar of Bourton, but he was dead now; and her chills never went to her chest, never. It was the girls she thought of, the young girls with their bare shoulders, she herself having always been a wisp of a creature, with her thin hair and meagre profile; though now, past fifty, there was beginning to shine through some mild beam, something purified into distinction by years of self-abnegation but obscured again, perpetually, by her distressing gentility, her panic fear, which arose from three hundred pounds income, and her weaponless state (she could not earn a penny) and it made her timid, and more and more disqualified year by year to meet well-dressed people who did this sort of thing every night of the season, merely telling their maids "I'll wear so and so," whereas Ellie Henderson ran out nervously and bought cheap pink flowers, half-a-dozen, and then threw a shawl over her old black dress. For her invitation to Clarissa's party had come at the last moment. She was not quite happy about it. She had a sort of feeling that Clarissa had not meant to ask her this year.

Why should she? There was no reason really, except that they had always known each other. Indeed, they were cousins. But naturally they had rather drifted apart, Clarissa being so sought after. It was an event to her, going to a party. It was quite a treat just to see the lovely clothes. Wasn't that Elizabeth, grown up, with her hair done in the fashionable way, in the pink dress? Yet she could not be more than seventeen. She was very, very

379 Native to New Guinea and Australia, birds of paradise are known for their astonishingly bright plumage, ruffs, and feathers. The term also refers to a South African flower sometimes called the "crane flower" or "crane lily" for its bright, beaked petals and blue tongue.

handsome. But girls when they first came out didn't seem to wear white as they used.[380] (She must remember everything to tell Edith.) Girls wore straight frocks, perfectly tight, with skirts well above the ankles. It was not becoming, she thought.

So, with her weak eyesight, Ellie Henderson craned rather forward, and it wasn't so much she who minded not having anyone to talk to (she hardly knew anybody there), for she felt that they were all such interesting people to watch; politicians presumably; Richard Dalloway's friends; but it was Richard himself who felt that he could not let the poor creature go on standing there all the evening by herself.

"Well, Ellie, and how's the world treating *you*?" he said in his genial way, and Ellie Henderson, getting nervous and flushing and feeling that it was extraordinarily nice of him to come and talk to her, said that many people really felt the heat more than the cold.

"Yes, they do," said Richard Dalloway. "Yes."

But what more did one say?

"Hullo, Richard," said somebody, taking him by the elbow, and, good Lord, there was old Peter, old Peter Walsh. He was delighted to see him—ever so pleased to see him! He hadn't changed a bit. And off they went together walking right across the room, giving each other little pats, as if they hadn't met for a long time, Ellie Henderson thought, watching them go, certain she knew that man's face. A tall man, middle aged, rather fine eyes, dark, wearing spectacles, with a look of John Burrows.[381] Edith would be sure to know.

The curtain with its flight of birds of Paradise blew out again. And Clarissa saw—she saw Ralph Lyon beat it back, and go on talking. So it wasn't a failure after all! it was going to be all right now—her party. It had begun. It had started. But it was still touch and go. She must stand there for the present. People seemed to come in a rush.

Colonel and Mrs. Garrod . . . Mr. Hugh Whitbread . . . Mr. Bowley[382] . . . Mrs. Hilbery . . . Lady Mary Maddox . . . Mr. Quin . . . intoned Wilkins. She had six or seven words

380 White coming-out dresses, symbols of wealth and purity, had become less popular by the twentieth century, when more relaxed dress codes allowed girls to wear pink and red frocks with high, tight skirts made of unforgiving georgette.

381 John Burrows, generally known as "Jack the Grinder," is a fictional murderer and thief whose case is tried in Anthony Trollope's novel *The Vicar of Bullhampton* (1870).

382 A reappearance of "Mr. Bowley who had rooms in the Albany" from p. 36.

383 An echo from p. 57.

with each, and they went on, they went into the rooms; into something now, not nothing, since Ralph Lyon had beat back the curtain.

And yet for her own part, it was too much of an effort. She was not enjoying it. It was too much like being—just anybody, standing there; anybody could do it; yet this anybody she did a little admire, couldn't help feeling that she had, anyhow, made this happen, that it marked a stage, this post that she felt herself to have become, for oddly enough she had quite forgotten what she looked like, but felt herself a stake driven in at the top of her stairs. Every time she gave a party she had this feeling of being something not herself, and that every one was unreal in one way; much more real in another. It was, she thought, partly their clothes, partly being taken out of their ordinary ways, partly the background; it was possible to say things you couldn't say anyhow else, things that needed an effort; possible to go much deeper. But not for her; not yet anyhow.

"How delightful to see you!" she said. Dear old Sir Harry! He would know every one.

And what was so odd about it was the sense one had as they came up the stairs one after another, Mrs. Mount and Celia, Herbert Ainsty, Mrs. Dakers—oh, and Lady Bruton!

"How awfully good of you to come!" she said, and she meant it—it was odd how standing there one felt them going on, going on, some quite old, some . . .

What name? Lady Rosseter? But who on earth was Lady Rosseter?

"Clarissa!" That voice! It was Sally Seton! Sally Seton! after all these years! She loomed through a mist. For she hadn't looked like *that*, Sally Seton, when Clarissa grasped the hot water can. To think of her under this roof, under this roof![383] Not like that!

All on top of each other, embarrassed, laughing, words tumbled out—passing through London; heard from Clara Haydon; what a chance of seeing you! So I thrust myself in—without an invitation . . . .

One might put down the hot water can quite composedly.

The lustre had left her. Yet it was extraordinary to see her again, older, happier, less lovely. They kissed each other,[384] first this cheek, then that, by the drawing-room door, and Clarissa turned, with Sally's hand in hers, and saw her rooms full, heard the roar of voices, saw the candlesticks, the blowing curtains, and the roses which Richard had given her.

"I have five enormous boys," said Sally.

She had the simplest egotism, the most open desire to be thought first always, and Clarissa loved her for being still like that. "I can't believe it!" she cried, kindling all over with pleasure at the thought of the past.

But alas, Wilkins; Wilkins wanted her; Wilkins was emitting in a voice of commanding authority, as if the whole company must be admonished and the hostess reclaimed from frivolity, one name:

"The Prime Minister,"[385] said Peter Walsh.

The Prime Minister? Was it really? Ellie Henderson marvelled. What a thing to tell Edith!

One couldn't laugh at him. He looked so ordinary. You might have stood him behind a counter and bought biscuits—poor chap, all rigged up in gold lace. And to be fair, as he went his rounds, first with Clarissa, then with Richard escorting him, he did it very well. He tried to look somebody. It was amusing to watch. Nobody looked at him. They just went on talking, yet it was perfectly plain that they all knew, felt to the marrow of their bones, this majesty passing; this symbol of what they all stood for, English society. Old Lady Bruton, and she looked very fine too, very stalwart in her lace, swam up, and they withdrew into a little room which at once became spied upon, guarded, and a sort of stir and rustle rippled through every one openly: the Prime Minister!

Lord, lord, the snobbery of the English! thought Peter Walsh, standing in the corner. How they loved dressing up in gold lace and doing homage! There! That must be—by Jove it was—Hugh Whitbread, snuffing round the precincts of the great, grown rather fatter, rather whiter, the admirable Hugh!

384 An echo from p. 58, though fainter. The kiss has lost its luster, the danger is safely consigned to memory. Though the rest of the paragraph finds Clarissa "kindling all over with pleasure at the thought of the past," that pleasure risks nothing in the present.

385 In June 1923, the time *Mrs. Dalloway* takes place, the prime minister was Stanley Baldwin. He was also the prime minister in November 1924 (when Woolf was retyping the novel), having recently replaced Ramsay MacDonald, whose first government lasted only nine months. Baldwin also appears in Woolf's 1927 essay "Street Haunting: A London Adventure" as "the aged Prime Minister": "Strolling sedately as if he were promenading a terrace beneath which the shires and counties of England lie sun-bathed, the aged Prime Minister recounts to Lady So-and-So with the curls and the emeralds the true history of some great crisis in the affairs of the land."

He looked always as if he were on duty, thought Peter, a privileged but secretive being, hoarding secrets which he would die to defend, though it was only some little piece of tittle-tattle dropped by a court footman which would be in all the papers to-morrow. Such were his rattles, his baubles, in playing with which he had grown white, come to the verge of old age, enjoying the respect and affection of all who had the privilege of knowing this type of the English public school man. Inevitably one made up things like that about Hugh; that was his style; the style of those admirable letters which Peter had read thousands of miles across the sea in the *Times*, and had thanked God he was out of that pernicious hubble-bubble if it were only to hear baboons chatter and coolies beat their wives.[386] An olive-skinned youth from one of the Universities stood obsequiously by. Him he would patronise, initiate, teach how to get on. For he liked nothing better than doing kindnesses, making the hearts of old ladies palpitate with the joy of being thought of in their age, their affliction, thinking themselves quite forgotten, yet here was dear Hugh driving up and spending an hour talking of the past, remembering trifles, praising the home-made cake, though Hugh might eat cake with a Duchess any day of his life, and, to look at him, probably did spend a good deal of time in that agreeable occupation. The All-judging, the All-merciful, might excuse. Peter Walsh had no mercy. Villains there must be, and, God knows, the rascals who get hanged for battering the brains of a girl out in a train do less harm on the whole than Hugh Whitbread and his kindness! Look at him now, on tiptoe, dancing forward, bowing and scraping, as the Prime Minister and Lady Bruton emerged, intimating for all the world to see that he was privileged to say something, something private, to Lady Bruton as she passed. She stopped. She wagged her fine old head. She was thanking him presumably for some piece of servility. She had her toadies, minor officials in Government offices who ran about putting through little jobs on her behalf, in return for which she gave them luncheon.[387] But she derived from the eighteenth century. She was all right.

386 Like Woolf, Peter is at once critical of English society ("that pernicious hubble-bubble") and racist toward the people of India. For a discussion of how Woolf's racism toward colonized peoples coexisted with her critique of empire, see n. 35 on p. 16.

387 Peter speculating about Hugh Whitbread, Lady Bruton, and the luncheons she hosts for her "toadies" inverts the conversation at Lady Bruton's luncheon on p. 153, where she and Hugh speculate about what has brought Peter back to Britain.

And now Clarissa escorted her Prime Minister down the room, prancing, sparkling, with the stateliness of her grey hair. She wore ear-rings, and a silver-green mermaid's dress. Lolloping on the waves and braiding her tresses she seemed, having that gift still; to be; to exist; to sum it all up in the moment as she passed; turned, caught her scarf in some other woman's dress, unhitched it, laughed, all with the most perfect ease and air of a creature floating in its element. But age had brushed her; even as a mermaid might behold in her glass the setting sun on some very clear evening over the waves.[388] There was a breath of tenderness; her severity, her prudery, her woodenness were all warmed through now, and she had about her as she said good-bye to the thick gold-laced man who was doing his best, and good luck to him, to look important, an inexpressible dignity; an exquisite cordiality; as if she wished the whole world well, and must now, being on the very verge and rim of things, take her leave. So she made him think. (But he was not in love.)[389]

Indeed, Clarissa felt, the Prime Minister had been good to come. And, walking down the room with him, with Sally there and Peter there and Richard very pleased, with all those people rather inclined, perhaps, to envy, she had felt that intoxication of the moment, that dilatation of the nerves of the heart itself till it seemed to quiver, steeped, upright;—yes, but after all it was what other people felt, that; for, though she loved it and felt it tingle and sting, still these semblances, these triumphs (dear old Peter, for example, thinking her so brilliant), had a hollowness; at arm's length they were, not in the heart; and it might be that she was growing old, but they satisfied her no longer as they used; and suddenly, as she saw the Prime Minister go down the stairs, the gilt rim of the Sir Joshua picture[390] of the little girl with a muff brought back Kilman with a rush; Kilman her enemy. That was satisfying; that was real. Ah, how she hated her—hot, hypocritical, corrupt; with all that power; Elizabeth's seducer; the woman who had crept in to steal and defile (Richard would say, What nonsense!). She hated her: she loved her.[391] It was enemies one wanted, not friends—not Mrs. Durrant and

388 As one might expect of a child raised near the sea, Woolf was dazzled by mermaids, exotic, mesmerizing creatures who embodied both the power and the danger of flinging oneself to the waves. "I'm a mermaid! I can swim," shouts Rachel Vinrace when, toward the end of Woolf's first novel, *The Voyage Out*, her lover Terence throws her to the floor. There they grapple with each other, "fighting for mastery, imagining a rock, and the sea heaving beneath them"—a scene that gains in significance when Rachel dies at the end of the novel.

In Woolf's stories and letters, the otherworldly beauty of the mermaid is usually cut by her vulnerability to nature, especially to time. "I was so much overcome by her beauty that I really felt as if I'd suddenly got into the sea, and heard the mermaids fluting on their rocks," Woolf wrote of Ottoline Morrell. "How it was done I cant think; but she has red-gold hair in masses, cheeks as soft as cushions with a lovely deep crimson on the crest of them, and a body shaped more after my notion of a mermaids [*sic*] than I've ever seen; not a wrinkle or blemish—swelling, but smooth." One suspects she knew that Ottoline's beauty would not last, at least not in its unadulterated form.

389 An echo from p. 109.

390 Sir Joshua Reynolds (1723–1792) was an English portraitist and history painter who served as the first president of the Royal Academy of Arts upon its creation in 1768. He is known for promoting the "grand manner" in painting, which he describes in his lecture series *Discourses on Art* as the "great style": a transformation of imperfect realities into the ideal forms of the ancient Greeks and Romans and the Italian Renaissance masters. Recall that in *The Voyage Out*, Clarissa is described as standing over the ship's passengers like "a Reynolds."

391 As on p. 54, where the moment is figured as pleasurable and pestilent, here the "intoxication of the moment" mingles Clarissa's love and hate for Miss Kilman as "Elizabeth's seducer." In the morning, Clarissa, determined to set aside her hate for Miss Kilman, thinks on p. 24, "She would have loved Miss Kilman! But not in this world. No." The evening finds Clarissa embracing both her undisguised repulsion and her undisguised attraction to the "hot, hypocritical, corrupt" and "real" sensations of Miss Kilman's seduction of her daughter.

Elizabeth Gunning, Duchess of Hamilton and Argyll, Sir Joshua Reynolds RA. Oil on canvas, c. 1760. *(Paul Mellon Collection, Yale Center for British Art)*

Private View of the Royal Academy, William Payne. Watercolor and graphite on paper, 1858. *(Paul Mellon Collection, Yale Center for British Art)*

Clara,[392] Sir William and Lady Bradshaw, Miss Truelock and Eleanor Gibson (whom she saw coming upstairs). They must find her if they wanted her. She was for the party!

There was her old friend Sir Harry.

"Dear Sir Harry!" she said, going up to the fine old fellow who had produced more bad pictures than any other two Academicians[393] in the whole of St. John's Wood (they were always of cattle, standing in sunset pools absorbing moisture, or signifying, for he had a certain range of gesture, by the raising of one foreleg and the toss of the antlers, "the Approach of the Stranger"—all his activities, dining out, racing, were founded on cattle standing absorbing moisture in sunset pools).

"What are you laughing at?" she asked him. For Willie Titcomb and Sir Harry and Herbert Ainsty were all laughing. But no. Sir Harry could not tell Clarissa Dalloway (much though he liked her; of her type he thought her perfect, and threatened

392 Mrs. Durrant and Clara first appear in *Jacob's Room* as the mother and sister of Timothy Durrant, one of Jacob's friends at the University of Cambridge.

393 An Academician is a member of the Royal Academy of Arts, an institution that Woolf mocked in "A Society," a short story that appeared in *Monday or Tuesday*. A group of seven women infiltrate the all-male cultural societies of the early twentieth century and find them ridiculous, insufferable. At the Royal Academy, one of the women must recite "her report upon the pictures": "O! for the touch of a vanished hand and the sound of a voice that is still. Home is the hunter, home from the hill . . ." But the other women interrupt before she finishes, incapable of listening to any more of "this gibberish."

to paint her) his stories of the music hall stage. He chaffed her about her party. He missed his brandy. These circles, he said, were above him. But he liked her; respected her, in spite of her damnable, difficult, upper-class refinement, which made it impossible to ask Clarissa Dalloway to sit on his knee. And up came that wandering will-o'-the-wisp, that vagous[394] phosphorescence, old Mrs. Hilbery, stretching her hands to the blaze of his laughter (about the Duke and the Lady), which, as she heard it across the room, seemed to reassure her on a point which sometimes bothered her if she woke early in the morning and did not like to call her maid for a cup of tea: how it is certain we must die.

"They won't tell us their stories," said Clarissa.

"Dear Clarissa!" exclaimed Mrs. Hilbery. She looked to-night, she said, so like her mother as she first saw her walking in a garden in a grey hat.

And really Clarissa's eyes filled with tears. Her mother, walking in a garden! But alas, she must go.

For there was Professor Brierly, who lectured on Milton,[395] talking to little Jim Hutton (who was unable even for a party like this to compass both tie and waistcoat or make his hair lie flat), and even at this distance they were quarrelling, she could see. For Professor Brierly was a very queer fish. With all those degrees, honours, lectureships between him and the scribblers, he suspected instantly an atmosphere not favourable to his queer compound; his prodigious learning and timidity; his wintry charm without cordiality; his innocence blent with snobbery; he quivered if made conscious, by a lady's unkempt hair, a youth's boots, of an underworld, very creditable doubtless, of rebels, of ardent young people; of would-be geniuses, and intimated with a little toss of the head, with a sniff—Humph!—the value of moderation; of some slight training in the classics in order to appreciate Milton. Professor Brierly (Clarissa could see) wasn't hitting it off with little Jim Hutton (who wore red socks, his black being at the laundry) about Milton. She interrupted.

394 An obsolete word meaning "wandering" or "unsettled."

395 John Milton (1608–1674) was an English poet famous for his epic poem *Paradise Lost* (1667) and his pamphlet *Areopagitica* (1644), which defended the right to freedom of speech and expression. He was one of Leslie Stephen's favorite authors, as Woolf recalled in her memoirs: "Milton of old writers was the one he knew best; he specially loved the 'Ode on the Nativity,' which he said to us regularly on Christmas night."

Yet she would return to Milton more critically in her book-length essay *A Room of One's Own* (1929), urging women writers to find a way to escape from "Milton's bogey": Milton's influence on the masculinist literary culture of her father's England, as well as Milton's portrait of God as the ultimate patriarch. In wondering what the legacy of five hundred pounds per year she has inherited from her Quaker aunt might allow her to achieve as a writer, Woolf concludes that she has the "freedom to think of things in themselves," not through the accepted thoughts of men. "That building, for example, do I like it or not?" she asks. "Is that picture beautiful or not? Is that in my opinion a good book or a bad? Indeed my aunt's legacy unveiled the sky to me, and substituted for the large and imposing figure of a gentleman, which Milton recommended for my perpetual adoration, a view of the open sky."

She said she loved Bach. So did Hutton. That was the bond between them, and Hutton (a very bad poet) always felt that Mrs. Dalloway was far the best of the great ladies who took an interest in art. It was odd how strict she was. About music she was purely impersonal. She was rather a prig. But how charming to look at! She made her house so nice, if it weren't for her Professors. Clarissa had half a mind to snatch him off and set him down at the piano in the back room. For he played divinely.

"But the noise!" she said. "The noise!"

"The sign of a successful party." Nodding urbanely, the Professor stepped delicately off.

"He knows everything in the whole world about Milton," said Clarissa.

"Does he indeed?" said Hutton, who would imitate the Professor throughout Hampstead:[396] the Professor on Milton; the Professor on moderation; the Professor stepping delicately off.

But she must speak to that couple, said Clarissa, Lord Gayton and Nancy Blow.

Not that *they* added perceptibly to the noise of the party. They were not talking (perceptibly) as they stood side by side by the yellow curtains. They would soon be off elsewhere, together; and never had very much to say in any circumstances. They looked; that was all. That was enough. They looked so clean, so sound, she with an apricot bloom of powder and paint, but he scrubbed, rinsed, with the eyes of a bird, so that no ball could pass him or stroke surprise him. He struck, he leapt, accurately, on the spot. Ponies' mouths quivered at the end of his reins. He had his honours, ancestral monuments, banners hanging in the church at home. He had his duties; his tenants; a mother and sisters; had been all day at Lord's,[397] and that was what they were talking about—cricket, cousins, the movies—when Mrs. Dalloway came up. Lord Gayton liked her most awfully. So did Miss Blow. She had such charming manners.

"It is angelic—it is delicious of you to have come!" she said. She loved Lord's; she loved youth, and Nancy, dressed at enormous expense by the greatest artists in Paris, stood there looking

396 A district of north London associated with young intellectuals, poets, artists, and musicians, and a frequent target of Woolf's satire. In a 1916 letter to Vanessa Bell, Woolf described her visit to the Hampstead house of Janet Case and her sister Emphie as an experience of pure aesthetic vulgarity: "She [Janet] is still more or less bedridden, and keeps her disease in the dark, though she was writing an article upon illegitimacy in Sweden for a newspaper. Downstairs, Emphie was playing very badly on the violin to a party of wounded soldiers. The house is crowded with photographs of old pupils, deceased parents and the Elgin Marbles, and they have covers to all the po's. Does this convey any of the spirit of Hampstead to you?" Later, in a letter to Ethel Smyth, she described the journalist Kingsley Martin and his wife as living "in a high airy brainy room at Hampstead, where there's nuts on a check table cloth and autotypes from Albert Durer on a mud coloured wall."

397 An echo from p. 9.

as if her body had merely put forth, of its own accord, a green frill.

"I had meant to have dancing," said Clarissa.

For the young people could not talk. And why should they? Shout, embrace, swing, be up at dawn; carry sugar to ponies; kiss and caress the snouts of adorable chows; and then, all tingling and streaming, plunge and swim. But the enormous resources of the English language, the power it bestows, after all, of communicating feelings (at their age, she and Peter would have been arguing all the evening), was not for them. They would solidify young. They would be good beyond measure to the people on the estate, but alone, perhaps, rather dull.

"What a pity!" she said. "I had hoped to have dancing."

It was so extraordinarily nice of them to have come! But talk of dancing! The rooms were packed.

There was old Aunt Helena in her shawl. Alas, she must leave them—Lord Gayton and Nancy Blow. There was old Miss Parry, her aunt.

For Miss Helena Parry was not dead: Miss Parry was alive.[398] She was past eighty. She ascended staircases slowly with a stick. She was placed in a chair (Richard had seen to it). People who had known Burma in the 'seventies were always led up to her. Where had Peter got to? They used to be such friends. For at the mention of India, or even Ceylon,[399] her eyes (only one was glass) slowly deepened, became blue, beheld, not human beings—she had no tender memories, no proud illusions about Viceroys, Generals, Mutinies—it was orchids she saw, and mountain passes, and herself carried on the backs of coolies in the 'sixties over solitary peaks; or descending to uproot orchids (startling blossoms, never beheld before) which she painted in water-colour; an indomitable Englishwoman, fretful if disturbed by the war, say, which dropped a bomb at her very door, from her deep meditation over orchids and her own figure journeying in the 'sixties in India—but here was Peter.

"Come and talk to Aunt Helena about Burma," said Clarissa.

And yet he had not had a word with her all the evening!

398 Recall on p. 204 when Peter declares that Miss Parry is dead. She is not dead. But Woolf's sketch of her reveals a certain insensateness, an incapacity to register human life or feeling. Through her blue-glazed eye, she sees only the beauty of her orchids, her watercolors, "not human beings." As Anne Fernald notes, Woolf's Aunt Anne Thackery Ritchie suffered from a similar numbness to the activity of mankind after the war. She "had a bomb drop on the Lodge opposite her house in November 1917," Woolf wrote, killing her neighbor and blowing in all the windows of her house. "Her granddaughter wrote that, afterward, 'Grandmama lay on a sofa in the dark looking tired and bored.'"

399 Ceylon, or modern-day Sri Lanka, was part of the British Empire from 1815 to 1948. Leonard Woolf worked as a colonial administrator in Ceylon from 1904 to 1911.

"We will talk later," said Clarissa, leading him up to Aunt Helena, in her white shawl, with her stick.

"Peter Walsh," said Clarissa.

That meant nothing.

Clarissa had asked her. It was tiring; it was noisy; but Clarissa had asked her. So she had come. It was a pity that they lived in London—Richard and Clarissa. If only for Clarissa's health it would have been better to live in the country. But Clarissa had always been fond of society.

"He has been in Burma," said Clarissa.

Ah! She could not resist recalling what Charles Darwin had said[400] about her little book on the orchids of Burma.

(Clarissa must speak to Lady Bruton.)

No doubt it was forgotten now, her book on the orchids of Burma, but it went into three editions before 1870, she told Peter. She remembered him now. He had been at Bourton (and he had left her, Peter Walsh remembered, without a word in the drawing-room that night when Clarissa had asked him to come boating).

400 Charles Darwin's *On the Various Contrivances by Which British and Foreign Orchids Are Fertilised by Insects, and on the Good Effects of Intercrossing* was first published in 1862 and detailed the coevolution of the orchids and the insects that Darwin had observed in Cudham Valley, outside the English village of Downe. "I have found the study of orchids eminently useful in showing me how nearly all parts of the flower are coadapted for fertilisation by insects, & therefore the result of n. selection,—even most trifling details of structure," Darwin wrote in a letter to Joseph Dalton Hooker on March 14, 1862. After the book achieved great success in botanical circles, botanists from around the world started corresponding with Darwin about local species of orchids.

Leonard Woolf standing next to a horse, Sri Lanka, undated. *(Virginia Woolf Monk's House photograph album, MH-1, MS Thr 557, [127b]. Houghton Library, Harvard College Library)*

"Richard so much enjoyed his lunch party," said Clarissa to Lady Bruton.

"Richard was the greatest possible help," Lady Bruton replied. "He helped me to write a letter. And how are you?"

"Oh, perfectly well!" said Clarissa. (Lady Bruton detested illness in the wives of politicians.)[401]

"And there's Peter Walsh!" said Lady Bruton (for she could never think of anything to say to Clarissa; though she liked her. She had lots of fine qualities; but they had nothing in common—she and Clarissa. It might have been better if Richard had married a woman with less charm, who would have helped him more in his work. He had lost his chance of the Cabinet). "There's Peter Walsh!" she said, shaking hands with that agreeable sinner, that very able fellow who should have made a name for himself but hadn't (always in difficulties with women),[402] and, of course, old Miss Parry. Wonderful old lady!

Lady Bruton stood by Miss Parry's chair, a spectral grenadier, draped in black, inviting Peter Walsh to lunch; cordial; but without small talk, remembering nothing whatever about the flora or fauna of India. She had been there, of course; had stayed with three Viceroys; thought some of the Indian civilians uncommonly fine fellows; but what a tragedy it was—the state of India! The Prime Minister had just been telling her (old Miss Parry, huddled up in her shawl, did not care what the Prime Minister had just been telling her), and Lady Bruton would like to have Peter Walsh's opinion, he being fresh from the centre, and she would get Sir Sampson to meet him, for really it prevented her from sleeping at night, the folly of it, the wickedness she might say, being a soldier's daughter. She was an old woman now, not good for much. But her house, her servants, her good friend Milly Brush—did he remember her?—were all there only asking to be used if—if they could be of help, in short. For she never spoke of England, but this isle of men, this dear, dear land,[403] was in her blood (without reading Shakespeare), and if ever a woman could have worn the helmet and shot the arrow, could have led troops to attack, ruled with indomitable

401 An echo from pp. 141–42.

402 An echo from pp. 144–45.

403 Though Lady Bruton claims to have never read Shakespeare, her invocation of England as a "dear, dear land" mimics John of Gaunt's famous deathbed speech in Act 2, Scene 1 of *Richard II* (1623). With his last breath, John of Gaunt bids farewell to his nation, a historically global power now in a state of decline, rotted by the corruption of its leaders: "This land of such dear souls, this dear dear land, / Dear for her reputation through the world, / Is now leased out—I die pronouncing it— / Like to a tenement or pelting farm. / England, bound in with the triumphant sea, / Whose rocky shore beats back the envious siege / Of wat'ry Neptune, is now bound in with shame, / With inky blots and rotten parchment bonds. / That England that was wont to conquer others / Hath made a shameful conquest of itself."

justice barbarian hordes and lain under a shield noseless in a church, or made a green grass mound on some primeval hillside, that woman was Millicent Bruton. Debarred by her sex, and some truancy, too, of the logical faculty (she found it impossible to write a letter to the *Times*), she had the thought of Empire always at hand, and had acquired from her association with that armoured goddess her ramrod bearing, her robustness of demeanour, so that one could not figure her even in death parted from the earth or roaming territories over which, in some spiritual shape, the Union Jack had ceased to fly. To be not English even among the dead—no, no! Impossible![404]

But was it Lady Bruton? (whom she used to know). Was it Peter Walsh grown grey? Lady Rosseter asked herself (who had been Sally Seton). It was old Miss Parry certainly—the old aunt who used to be so cross when she stayed at Bourton. Never should she forget running along the passage naked, and being sent for by Miss Parry![405] And Clarissa! oh Clarissa! Sally caught her by the arm.

Clarissa stopped beside them.

"But I can't stay," she said. "I shall come later. Wait," she said, looking at Peter and Sally. They must wait, she meant, until all these people had gone.

"I shall come back," she said, looking at her old friends, Sally and Peter, who were shaking hands, and Sally, remembering the past no doubt, was laughing.

But her voice was wrung of its old ravishing richness; her eyes not aglow as they used to be, when she smoked cigars, when she ran down the passage to fetch her sponge bag without a stitch of clothing on her, and Ellen Atkins asked, What if the gentlemen had met her? But everybody forgave her. She stole a chicken from the larder because she was hungry in the night; she smoked cigars in her bedroom; she left a priceless book in the punt. But everybody adored her (except perhaps Papa). It was her warmth; her vitality—she would paint, she would write. Old women in the village never to this day forgot to ask after "your friend in the red cloak who seemed so bright". She accused Hugh Whitbread,

404 Lady Bruton's association of herself with the "armoured goddess" of empire, an association that persists even in death, mocks the patriotic poetic trope of the corpse embodying the nation. Woolf likely had in mind Rupert Brooke's (1887–1915) popular poem "The Soldier": "If I should die, think only this of me: / That there's some corner of a foreign field / That is forever England." The poem, published after Brooke died of septicemia while sailing to the siege of Gallipoli, presents the corpse at once as an insular and a colonizing entity. It gives "spiritual shape" (as Woolf puts it) to the grotesquerie of nationalism's aims better than any living person could.

405 An echo from p. 56.

406 An echo from p. 232.

of all people (and there he was, her old friend Hugh, talking to the Portuguese Ambassador), of kissing her in the smoking-room to punish her for saying that women should have votes.[406] Vulgar men did, she said. And Clarissa remembered having to persuade her not to denounce him at family prayers—which she was capable of doing with her daring, her recklessness, her melodramatic love of being the centre of everything and creating scenes, and it was bound, Clarissa used to think, to end in some awful tragedy; her death; her martyrdom; instead of which she had married, quite unexpectedly, a bald man with a large buttonhole who owned, it was said, cotton mills at Manchester. And she had five boys!

She and Peter had settled down together. They were talking: it seemed so familiar—that they should be talking. They would discuss the past. With the two of them (more even than with Richard) she shared her past; the garden; the trees; old Joseph Breitkopf singing Brahms without any voice; the drawing-room wallpaper; the smell of the mats. A part of this Sally must always be; Peter must always be. But she must leave them. There were the Bradshaws, whom she disliked.

She must go up to Lady Bradshaw (in grey and silver, balancing like a sea-lion at the edge of its tank, barking for invitations, Duchesses, the typical successful man's wife), she must go up to Lady Bradshaw and say . . .

But Lady Bradshaw anticipated her.

"We are shockingly late, dear Mrs. Dalloway; we hardly dared to come in," she said.

And Sir William, who looked very distinguished, with his grey hair and blue eyes, said yes; they had not been able to resist the temptation. He was talking to Richard about that Bill probably, which they wanted to get through the Commons. Why did the sight of him, talking to Richard, curl her up? He looked what he was, a great doctor. A man absolutely at the head of his profession, very powerful, rather worn. For think what cases came before him—people in the uttermost depths of misery; people on the verge of insanity; husbands and wives. He had to decide questions of appalling difficulty. Yet—what she felt was, one wouldn't like Sir William to see one unhappy. No; not that man.

"How is your son at Eton?" she asked Lady Bradshaw.

He had just missed his eleven,[407] said Lady Bradshaw, because of the mumps. His father minded even more than he did, she thought, "being," she said, "nothing but a great boy himself."

Clarissa looked at Sir William, talking to Richard. He did not look like a boy—not in the least like a boy.

She had once gone with some one to ask his advice. He had been perfectly right; extremely sensible. But Heavens—what a relief to get out to the street again! There was some poor wretch sobbing, she remembered, in the waiting-room. But she did not know what it was about Sir William; what exactly she disliked. Only Richard agreed with her, "didn't like his taste, didn't like his smell." But he was extraordinarily able. They were talking about this Bill. Some case Sir William was mentioning, lowering his voice. It had its bearing upon what he was saying about the deferred effects of shell shock. There must be some provision in the Bill.[408]

Sinking her voice, drawing Mrs. Dalloway into the shelter of a common femininity, a common pride in the illustrious qualities of husbands and their sad tendency to overwork, Lady Bradshaw (poor goose—one didn't dislike her) murmured how, "just as we were starting, my husband was called up on the telephone, a very sad case. A young man (that is what Sir William is telling Mr. Dalloway) had killed himself. He had been in the army." Oh! thought Clarissa, in the middle of my party, here's death, she thought.

She went on, into the little room where the Prime Minister had gone with Lady Bruton. Perhaps there was somebody there. But there was nobody. The chairs still kept the impress of the Prime Minister and Lady Bruton, she turned deferentially, he sitting four-square, authoritatively. They had been talking about India. There was nobody. The party's splendour fell to the floor, so strange it was to come in alone in her finery.

407 The cricket team of his boardinghouse.

408 The bill is unnamed and likely fictitious, but it recalls the presentation in August 1922 of the *Report of the War Office Committee of Enquiry into "Shell-Shock."* See n. 178 on p. 98.

What business had the Bradshaws to talk of death at her party? A young man had killed himself. And they talked of it at her party—the Bradshaws talked of death. He had killed himself—but how? Always her body went through it, when she was told, first, suddenly, of an accident; her dress flamed, her body burnt. He had thrown himself from a window. Up had flashed the ground; through him, blundering, bruising, went the rusty spikes. There he lay with a thud, thud, thud in his brain, and then a suffocation of blackness. So she saw it. But why had he done it? And the Bradshaws talked of it at her party!

She had once thrown a shilling into the Serpentine,[409] never anything more. But he had flung it away. They went on living (she would have to go back; the rooms were still crowded; people kept on coming). They (all day she had been thinking of Bourton, of Peter, of Sally), they would grow old. A thing there was that mattered; a thing, wreathed about with chatter, defaced, obscured in her own life, let drop every day in corruption, lies, chatter. This he had preserved. Death was defiance. Death was an attempt to communicate, people feeling the impossibility of reaching the centre which, mystically, evaded them; closeness drew apart; rapture faded; one was alone. There was an embrace in death.

But this young man who had killed himself—had he plunged holding his treasure? "If it were now to die, 'twere now to be most happy,"[410] she had said to herself once, coming down, in white.

Or there were the poets and thinkers. Suppose he had had that passion, and had gone to Sir William Bradshaw, a great doctor, yet to her obscurely evil, without sex or lust, extremely polite to women, but capable of some indescribable outrage—forcing your soul, that was it—if this young man had gone to him, and Sir William had impressed him, like that, with his power, might he not then have said (indeed she felt it now), Life is made intolerable; they make life intolerable, men like that?[411]

Then (she had felt it only this morning) there was the terror; the overwhelming incapacity, one's parents giving it into

409 An echo from p. 18.

410 An echo from p. 57.

411 Is Clarissa's reaction to Septimus's death sympathetic? Or is it an extension of her snobbery? In his very moving reading of the novel's end in *Time and Narrative*, Paul Ricoeur suggests that Clarissa's intuition of Septimus's motivations for his suicide joins three voices—hers, his, and the narrator's—in a single voice that judges and condemns English civilization in times of war and peace: "Life is made intolerable; they make life intolerable, men like that." This voice places Clarissa "on a crest between the two extremes" of temporal existence: life and death. Yet she redeems Septimus's death by continuing to live, instead of killing herself, as Woolf initially had planned for her to do. "Septimus's death, understood and in some way shared, gives to the instinctive love that Clarissa holds for life a tone of defiance and of resolution," Ricoeur concludes.

Against Ricoeur's politically and ethically redemptive reading, Julia Briggs wonders if Clarissa's reaction to Septimus's death is more complacent than defiant. Given her refusal to think of the Armenians (or Albanians), her contempt for Miss Kilman and poor Ellie Henderson, it is very possible that Clarissa is merely accepting "his death as the sacrifice that enables the party to go on—as if the millions of war deaths have served only to guarantee the continuance of her way of life." By Briggs's account, the Clarissa of *Mrs. Dalloway* has not changed as dramatically from the Clarissa of "Mrs. Dalloway in Bond Street" as one might imagine.

one's hands, this life, to be lived to the end, to be walked with serenely; there was in the depths of her heart an awful fear. Even now, quite often if Richard had not been there reading the *Times*, so that she could crouch like a bird and gradually revive, send roaring up that immeasurable delight, rubbing stick to stick, one thing with another, she must have perished. She had escaped. But that young man had killed himself.

Somehow it was her disaster—her disgrace. It was her punishment to see sink and disappear here a man, there a woman, in this profound darkness, and she forced to stand here in her evening dress. She had schemed; she had pilfered. She was never wholly admirable. She had wanted success, Lady Bexborough and the rest of it. And once she had walked on the terrace at Bourton.

Odd, incredible; she had never been so happy. Nothing could be slow enough; nothing last too long. No pleasure could equal, she thought, straightening the chairs, pushing in one book on the shelf, this having done with the triumphs of youth, lost herself in the process of living, to find it, with a shock of delight, as the sun rose, as the day sank. Many a time had she gone, at Bourton when they were all talking, to look at the sky; or seen it between people's shoulders at dinner; seen it in London when she could not sleep. She walked to the window.

It held, foolish as the idea was, something of her own in it, this country sky, this sky above Westminster. She parted the curtains; she looked. Oh, but how surprising!—in the room opposite the old lady stared straight at her![412] She was going to bed. And the sky. It will be a solemn sky, she had thought, it will be a dusky sky, turning away its cheek in beauty. But there it was—ashen pale, raced over quickly by tapering vast clouds. It was new to her. The wind must have risen. She was going to bed, in the room opposite. It was fascinating to watch her, moving about, that old lady, crossing the room, coming to the window. Could she see her? It was fascinating, with people still laughing and shouting in the drawing-room, to watch that old woman, quite quietly, going to bed alone. She pulled the blind now. The

412 Recall that the first minor character we met in the novel was Scrope Purvis, who stared at Clarissa as she stood on the curb, perceiving her as an old, ailing woman. Recall, too, that Clarissa did not see him. Now, as we near the novel's end, the final minor character we meet, the unnamed old lady across the street, stares straight ahead at Clarissa, but does not see her. The shifting of Clarissa's role, from observed old lady to observer of an old lady, ties beginning to end. But it also reveals to us the utter ordinariness, the contingency, of Clarissa's character. The novel could very well have been about the life of the woman across the street. Why Clarissa as opposed to her? According to Woolf's philosophy of character, there is no good answer to this question.

Westminster Night—From My Studio Window, Joseph Pennell. Mezzotint on paper, 1908.
(Smithsonian American Art Museum, Gift of Jane Fowler Bassett)

clock began striking. The young man had killed himself; but she did not pity him; with the clock striking the hour, one, two, three, she did not pity him, with all this going on. There! the old lady had put out her light! the whole house was dark now with this going on, she repeated, and the words came to her, Fear no more the heat of the sun.[413] She must go back to them. But what an extraordinary night! She felt somehow very like him—the young man who had killed himself. She felt glad that he had done it; thrown it away while they went on living. The clock was striking.[414] The leaden circles dissolved in the air. [415] He made her feel the beauty; made her feel the fun.[416] But she must go back. She must assemble. She must find Sally and Peter. And she came in from the little room.

"BUT WHERE IS CLARISSA?" said Peter. He was sitting on the sofa with Sally. (After all these years he really could not call her "Lady Rosseter".) "Where's the woman gone to?" he asked. "Where's Clarissa?"

Sally supposed, and so did Peter for the matter of that, that there were people of importance, politicians, whom neither of them knew unless by sight in the picture papers, whom Clarissa had to be nice to, had to talk to.[417] She was with them. Yet there was Richard Dalloway not in the Cabinet. He hadn't been a success, Sally supposed? For herself, she scarcely ever read the papers. She sometimes saw his name mentioned. But then—well, she lived a very solitary life, in the wilds, Clarissa would say, among great merchants, great manufacturers, men, after all, who did things. She had done things too!

"I have five sons!" she told him.

Lord, lord, what a change had come over her! the softness of motherhood; its egotism too. Last time they met, Peter remembered, had been among the cauliflowers in the moonlight, the leaves "like rough bronze" she had said, with her literary turn; and she had picked a rose. She had marched him up and down

413 An echo from p. 19 of the refrain of *Cymbeline*, as well as from p. 51 when Septimus finds consolation in these same words: "Fear no more, says the heart in the body; fear no more. He was not afraid."

414 In the manuscript of "The Hours," Woolf clarified that the clock was striking midnight and elaborated Clarissa's decision to return to the party as an act of resistance: & she would go back & she would fight Sir William Bradshaw; & she would take that rose, ~~& she would~~ Richards rose—she would be & she would never, ~~submit~~ <submit>, never for an ~~a~~ instant! ~~give up!~~ Eight, ~~said~~ Big Ben, nine; ten; eleven; & then with a sort of finality, the ~~pes~~ presumably the strokes were accurately placed, & the last was no more empathic than the first, Twelve."

415 An echo from pp. 7, 71, and 129.

416 Most British editions of *Mrs. Dalloway* omit this sentence, which Woolf struck from the British proofs but kept in the American proofs, slightly amending its original form: "He made her feel the beauty; the fun." Any editor must choose whether to include the line, in its original or altered form, or to omit it entirely.

To omit it is to leave the precise nature of Clarissa's communion with Septimus indistinct. Though she may feel "very like him," his death does not necessarily restore her to the fun and beauty of living. Indeed, it may make her feel admiration for his choice to die in order to affirm life. To include it is to articulate the nature of the connection between Clarissa and Septimus in no uncertain terms, as Paul Ricoeur does in n. 411 on p. 226. Both are on the side of life, committed to beauty and feeling, defiant of authority. But including the line also risks portraying Clarissa as someone who treats the suicide of a stranger as an occasion for aesthetic bliss and sentimental reverie, or even worse, as a necessity for her way of life.

417 "The amusing thing about a party is to watch the people—coming and going, coming and going," Woolf wrote in *Jacob's Room*. The parties in her fiction, from *The Voyage Out* to *Mrs. Dalloway*, always feature one or two observers who stand at a safe, skeptical distance from the action, the guests and the gossip.

that awful night, after the scene by the fountain; he was to catch the midnight train. Heavens, he had wept!

That was his old trick, opening a pocket-knife, thought Sally, always opening and shutting a knife when he got excited. They had been very, very intimate, she and Peter Walsh, when he was in love with Clarissa, and there was that dreadful, ridiculous scene over Richard Dalloway at lunch. She had called Richard "Wickham." Why not call Richard "Wickham?" Clarissa had flared up! and indeed they had never seen each other since, she and Clarissa, not more than half-a-dozen times perhaps in the last ten years. And Peter Walsh had gone off to India, and she had heard vaguely that he had made an unhappy marriage, and she didn't know whether he had any children, and she couldn't ask him, for he had changed. He was rather shrivelled-looking, but kinder, she felt, and she had a real affection for him, for he was connected with her youth, and she still had a little Emily Brontë[418] he had given her, and he was to write, surely? In those days he was to write.

418 Emily Brontë (1818–1848) was an English novelist and poet famous for her Gothic romance *Wuthering Heights* (1847). Woolf complimented Brontë's "genius" in *The Common Reader* and deemed her "a greater poet" than her sister Charlotte Brontë.

Jacket for *The Common Reader*, Hogarth Press, Vanessa Bell, 1925. *(Smith College, Mortimer Rare Book Collection)*

"Have you written?" she asked him, spreading her hand, her firm and shapely hand, on her knee in a way he recalled.

"Not a word!" said Peter Walsh, and she laughed.[419]

419 Recall that the "Solitary Traveller" interlude on p. 86 offers a brief vision of a man who will not finish the book he is writing. That vision is more firmly tethered to Peter here, when he confesses to Sally that he has not written a word.

She was still attractive, still a personage, Sally Seton. But who was this Rosseter? He wore two camellias on his wedding day—that was all Peter knew of him. "They have myriads of servants, miles of conservatories," Clarissa wrote; something like that. Sally owned it with a shout of laughter.

"Yes, I have ten thousand a year"—whether before the tax was paid or after, she couldn't remember, for her husband, "whom you must meet," she said, "whom you would like," she said, did all that for her.

And Sally used to be in rags and tatters. She had pawned her great-grandfather's ring which Marie Antoinette had given him—had he got it right?—to come to Bourton.

Oh yes, Sally remembered; she had it still, a ruby ring which Marie Antoinette had given her great-grandfather. She never had a penny to her name in those days, and going to Bourton always meant some frightful pinch. But going to Bourton had meant so much to her—had kept her sane, she believed, so unhappy had she been at home. But that was all a thing of the past—all over now, she said. And Mr. Parry was dead; and Miss Parry was still alive. Never had he had such a shock in his life! said Peter. He had been quite certain she was dead. And the marriage had been, Sally supposed, a success? And that very handsome, very self-possessed young woman was Elizabeth, over there, by the curtains, in red.

(She was like a poplar, she was like a river, she was like a hyacinth, Willie Titcomb was thinking.[420] Oh how much nicer to be in the country and do what she liked![421] She could hear her poor dog howling, Elizabeth was certain.) She was not a bit like Clarissa, Peter Walsh said.

"Oh, Clarissa!" said Sally.

What Sally felt was simply this. She had owed Clarissa an enormous amount. They had been friends, not acquaintances, friends, and she still saw Clarissa all in white going about the house with her hands full of flowers—to this day tobacco plants made her think of Bourton. But—did Peter understand?—she lacked something. Lacked what was it? She had charm; she had extraordinary charm. But to be frank (and she felt that Peter was an old friend, a real friend—did absence matter? did distance matter? She had often wanted to write to him, but torn it up, yet felt he understood, for people understand without things being said, as one realises growing old, and old she was, had been that afternoon to see her sons at Eton, where they had the mumps), to be quite frank, then, how could Clarissa have done it?—married Richard Dalloway? a sportsman, a man who cared only for dogs. Literally, when he came into the room he smelt of the stables. And then all this? She waved her hand.

Hugh Whitbread it was, strolling past in his white waistcoat, dim, fat, blind, past everything he looked, except self-esteem and comfort.

"He's not going to recognise *us*," said Sally, and really she hadn't the courage—so that was Hugh! the admirable Hugh!

420 Amid the intensity of the party, Willie Titcomb offers a moment of necessary comic relief. Elizabeth's worry on p. 159 that people have started comparing her to hyacinths is confirmed, but one can hardly respect the opinions of a man called "Willie Titcomb."

421 An echo from p. 172.

422 Just as it does not occur to Peter on p. 88 that Clarissa might be putting on a show for Sally, it does not occur to Sally that Clarissa might not come for reasons other than snobbery—namely, her fear of resurrecting the strong feelings of the past.

"And what does he do?" she asked Peter.

He blacked the King's boots or counted bottles at Windsor, Peter told her. Peter kept his sharp tongue still! But Sally must be frank, Peter said. That kiss now, Hugh's.

On the lips, she assured him, in the smoking-room one evening. She went straight to Clarissa in a rage. Hugh didn't do such things! Clarissa said, the admirable Hugh! Hugh's socks were without exception the most beautiful she had ever seen—and now his evening dress. Perfect! And had he children?

"Everybody in the room has six sons at Eton," Peter told her, except himself. He, thank God, had none. No sons, no daughters, no wife. Well, he didn't seem to mind, said Sally. He looked younger, she thought, than any of them.

But it had been a silly thing to do, in many ways, Peter said, to marry like that; "a perfect goose she was," he said, but, he said, "we had a splendid time of it," but how could that be? Sally wondered; what did he mean? and how odd it was to know him and yet not know a single thing that had happened to him. And did he say it out of pride? Very likely, for after all it must be galling for him (though he was an oddity, a sort of sprite, not at all an ordinary man), it must be lonely at his age to have no home, nowhere to go to. But he must stay with them for weeks and weeks. Of course he would; he would love to stay with them, and that was how it came out. All these years the Dalloways had never been once. Time after time they had asked them. Clarissa (for it was Clarissa of course) would not come. For, said Sally, Clarissa was at heart a snob—one had to admit it, a snob. And it was that that was between them, she was convinced.[422] Clarissa thought she had married beneath her, her husband being—she was proud of it—a miner's son. Every penny they had he had earned. As a little boy (her voice trembled) he had carried great sacks.

(And so she would go on, Peter felt, hour after hour; the miner's son; people thought she had married beneath her; her five sons; and what was the other thing—plants, hydrangeas, syringas, very very rare hybiscus lilies that never grow north of the Suez Canal,[423] but she, with one gardener in a suburb near Manchester, had beds of them, positively beds! Now all that Clarissa had escaped, unmaternal as she was.)

A snob was she? Yes, in many ways. Where was she, all this time? It was getting late.

"Yet," said Sally, "when I heard Clarissa was giving a party, I felt I couldn't *not* come—must see her again (and I'm staying in Victoria Street, practically next door). So I just came without an invitation. But," she whispered, "tell me, do. Who is this?"

It was Mrs. Hilbery, looking for the door. For how late it was getting! And, she murmured, as the night grew later, as people went, one found old friends; quiet nooks and corners; and the loveliest views. Did they know, she asked, that they were surrounded by an enchanted garden? Lights and trees and wonderful gleaming lakes and the sky. Just a few fairy lamps, Clarissa Dalloway had said, in the back garden! But she was a magician! It was a park . . . . And she didn't know their names, but friends she knew they were, friends without names, songs without words, always the best. But there were so many doors, such unexpected places, she could not find her way.

"Old Mrs. Hilbery," said Peter; but who was that? that lady standing by the curtain all the evening, without speaking? He knew her face; connected her with Bourton. Surely she used to cut up underclothes at the large table in the window? Davidson, was that her name?

"Oh, that is Ellie Henderson," said Sally. Clarissa was really very hard on her. She was a cousin, very poor. Clarissa *was* hard on people.

She was rather, said Peter. Yet, said Sally, in her emotional way, with a rush of that enthusiasm which Peter used to love her for, yet dreaded a little now, so effusive she might become—how generous to her friends Clarissa was! and what a rare quality one found it, and how sometimes at night or on Christmas Day, when she counted up her blessings, she put that friendship first. They were young; that was it. Clarissa was pure-hearted; that was it. Peter would think her sentimental. So she was. For she

423 Built by the Suez Canal Company between 1859 and 1869, the Suez Canal is an artificial waterway that extends from Port Said in northeast Egypt to the Suez Port (sometimes called Port Tewfik) on the Gulf of Suez. The opening of the Suez Canal had a dramatic effect on world trade. It reduced the journey from London to the Arabian Gulf by almost half its distance and allowed the world to be circled in record time. Though the canal came under attack by the combined German-Ottoman forces during the First World War, the British, Indians, and Egyptians fended them off. The canal was jointly operated by the United Kingdom and France until 1956 when Egyptian president Gamal Abdel Nasser nationalized the canal—a move that led to the Suez Crisis: a military and political confrontation with Egypt that lasted for one week and two days in the fall of that year.

had come to feel that it was the only thing worth saying—what one felt. Cleverness was silly. One must say simply what one felt.

"But I do not know," said Peter Walsh, "what I feel."

Poor Peter, thought Sally. Why did not Clarissa come and talk to them? That was what he was longing for. She knew it. All the time he was thinking only of Clarissa, and was fidgeting with his knife.

He had not found life simple, Peter said. His relations with Clarissa had not been simple. It had spoilt his life, he said. (They had been so intimate—he and Sally Seton, it was absurd not to say it.) One could not be in love twice, he said. And what could she say? Still, it is better to have loved (but he would think her sentimental—he used to be so sharp). He must come and stay with them in Manchester. That is all very true, he said. All very true. He would love to come and stay with them, directly he had done what he had to do in London.

And Clarissa had cared for him more than she had ever cared for Richard, Sally was positive of that.

"No, no, no!" said Peter (Sally should not have said that—she went too far). That good fellow—there he was at the end of the room, holding forth, the same as ever, dear old Richard. Who was he talking to? Sally asked, that very distinguished-looking man? Living in the wilds as she did, she had an insatiable curiosity to know who people were. But Peter did not know. He did not like his looks, he said, probably a Cabinet Minister. Of them all, Richard seemed to him the best, he said—the most disinterested.

"But what has he done?" Sally asked. Public work, she supposed. And were they happy together? Sally asked (she herself was extremely happy); for, she admitted, she knew nothing about them, only jumped to conclusions, as one does, for what can one know even of the people one lives with every day? she asked. Are we not all prisoners? She had read a wonderful play about a man who scratched on the wall of his cell,[424] and she had felt that was true of life—one scratched on the wall. Despairing of human relationships (people were so difficult), she often went

424 Anne Fernald suggests that the play is likely to be *Richard II*, to which Lady Bruton also alludes on p. 222. In Richard's soliloquy in Act 5, Scene 5, delivered from the prison of Pomfret Castle, he contemplates scratching through the walls of his cell: "Thoughts tending to ambition they do plot / Unlikely wonders; how these vain weak nails / May tear a passage through the flinty ribs / Of this hard world, my ragged prison walls; / And, for they cannot, die in their own pride."

into her garden and got from her flowers a peace which men and women never gave her. But no; he did not like cabbages; he preferred human beings, Peter said.[425] Indeed, the young are beautiful, Sally said, watching Elizabeth cross the room. How unlike Clarissa at her age! Could he make anything of her? She would not open her lips. Not much, not yet, Peter admitted. She was like a lily, Sally said, a lily by the side of a pool. But Peter did not agree that we know nothing. We know everything, he said; at least he did.

But these two, Sally whispered, these two coming now (and really she must go, if Clarissa did not come soon), this distinguished-looking man and his rather common-looking wife who had been talking to Richard—what could one know about people like that?

"That they're damnable humbugs," said Peter, looking at them casually. He made Sally laugh.

But Sir William Bradshaw stopped at the door to look at a picture. He looked in the corner for the engraver's name. His wife looked too. Sir William Bradshaw was so interested in art.

When one was young, said Peter, one was too much excited to know people. Now that one was old, fifty-two to be precise (Sally was fifty-five, in body, she said, but her heart was like a girl's of twenty);[426] now that one was mature then, said Peter, one could watch, one could understand, and one did not lose the power of feeling, he said. No, that is true, said Sally. She felt more deeply, more passionately, every year. It increased, he said, alas, perhaps, but one should be glad of it—it went on increasing in his experience. There was some one in India. He would like to tell Sally about her. He would like Sally to know her. She was married, he said. She had two small children. They must all come to Manchester, said Sally—he must promise before they left.

"There's Elizabeth," he said, "she feels not half what we feel, not yet." "But," said Sally, watching Elizabeth go to her father, "one can see they are devoted to each other." She could feel it by the way Elizabeth went to her father.

425 An echo from p. 6.

426 Like Peter, who denies that he is old, Sally is also resistant to admitting her age. The irony of the line is that, as Lady Rosseter with her five boys at Eton, her "heart" is no longer "like a girl's of twenty."

For her father had been looking at her, as he stood talking to the Bradshaws, and he had thought to himself who is that lovely girl? And suddenly he realised that it was his Elizabeth, and he had not recognised her, she looked so lovely in her pink frock! Elizabeth had felt him looking at her as she talked to Willie Titcomb. So she went to him and they stood together, now that the party was almost over, looking at the people going, and the rooms getting emptier and emptier, with things scattered on the floor. Even Ellie Henderson was going, nearly last of all, though no one had spoken to her, but she had wanted to see everything, to tell Edith. And Richard and Elizabeth were rather glad it was over, but Richard was proud of his daughter. And he had not meant to tell her, but he could not help telling her. He had looked at her, he said, and he had wondered, who is that lovely girl? and it was his daughter! That did make her happy. But her poor dog was howling.

"Richard has improved. You are right," said Sally. "I shall go and talk to him. I shall say good-night. What does the brain matter," said Lady Rosseter, getting up, "compared with the heart?"

"I will come," said Peter, but he sat on for a moment. What is this terror? what is this ecstasy? he thought to himself. What is it that fills me with extraordinary excitement?

It is Clarissa, he said.

For there she was.[427]

427 Instead of following her initial plan to allow three characters, Peter, Sally, and Richard, to say something about Clarissa, Woolf gave *Mrs. Dalloway*'s concluding moment to Peter. Perhaps she realized that neither Richard's stoicism nor Sally's exuberance could deliver the complexity of emotion she sought. She wrote the novel's final line on October 8, 1924. "It is disgraceful," she recorded in her diary one week later. "I did run up stairs thinking I'd make time to enter that astounding fact—the last words of the last page of Mrs Dalloway; but was interrupted. Anyhow I did them a week ago yesterday. 'For there she was.'"

Her four simple words remind the reader of Peter's inability on p. 73 to describe Clarissa's effect on him, as well as of Woolf's playful hint on p. 227 that one could never explain or justify why this novel is about Clarissa as opposed to any other "old lady" one might see standing on a curb or in a window in Westminster. The novel's final words sum up Woolf's commitment to her character's irreducibility, her singularity. In inviting the reader to wonder where, precisely, Clarissa is, the only definitive place we can point to is the novel; its beginning and its end; its title. For there she is—*Mrs. Dalloway*, in our hands, moments away from expiring.

Like Peter, Woolf felt she had run out of words to describe Clarissa Dalloway by the end. "I felt glad to be quit of it," she wrote when she finished the novel. "It has been a strain the last weeks, yet fresher in the head; with less I mean of the usual feeling that I've shaved through, & just kept my feet on the tight rope. I feel indeed rather more fully relieved of my meaning than usual—whether this will stand when I re-read is doubtful." Going back to the beginning to revise confirmed her sense that she had accomplished more in this novel than in any of her previous ones. It also reacquainted her with her character. Rewriting the first section toward the end of October 1924, she discovered possibilities she had missed, a richer and more fascinating inner life for Clarissa. One could imagine Woolf asking us, at the end, to follow her lead: to go back to the beginning and read again; to refuse to close the door on Mrs. Dalloway's party.

Portrait of Virginia Woolf, Vanessa Bell. Oil on board, 1912. *(Steve Vidler / Alamy)*

ACKNOWLEDGMENTS

THANK YOU, ALIA. Thank you, Dan and Haley. Thank you, Sarah, Gloria, Rachel, Karen, Kamran, Priya, and Mike. Thank you, Anne and Elaine and the late David Bradshaw for being such extraordinary predecessors.

For saving me from myself, I am grateful to Danielle Gilman, Katherine Kruger, and Pamela Weidman. For making the writing and illustration of this book possible in the middle of a pandemic, thank you to the librarians and archivists at the New York Public Library, British Library, Library of Congress, State Library of Queensland, Houghton Library, Smith College Library, Washington State University Library, Metropolitan Museum of Art, Yale Center for British Art, London Metropolitan Archive, UK Photo and Social History Archive, Wellcome Collection, Dean & Chapter of Westminster, The Keep, Monk's House, and the Society of Authors.

To Daniel DiCamillo, who gave me permission to tell a small part of our story here: thank you for twenty-five years of friendship—for fighting and for forgiving.

To Christian and Aydin and Altan: I adore you. Thank you for making me feel the fun.

WORKS CONSULTED

BY VIRGINIA WOOLF

Between the Acts. Penguin, 1992.

Collected Essays, ed. Leonard Woolf, 5 vols. Chatto & Windus, 1966–67.

The Common Reader. Penguin, 1992.

The Common Reader: Second Series. Hogarth Press, 1932.

The Diary of Virginia Woolf, ed. Anne Oliver Bell and Andrew McNeillie, 5 vols. Harcourt, 1979–85.

The Essays of Virginia Woolf, ed. Andrew McNeillie, 3 vols., 1904–12.

Jacob's Room. Penguin, 1992.

The Letters of Virginia Woolf, ed. Nigel Nicolson and Joanne Traumann, 6 vols. Mariner Books, 1978–82.

The Moment and Other Essays. Hogarth Press, 1947.

Moments of Being: A Collection of Autobiographical Writing, ed. Jeanne Schulkind. Sussex University Press, 1985.

Monday or Tuesday. Penguin, 1993.

Mrs. Dalloway, ed. Anne Fernald. Cambridge, 2015; ed. David Bradshaw. Oxford, 1992.

Night and Day. Penguin, 1992.

Orlando: A Biography. Penguin, 1993.

A Passionate Apprentice: The Early Journals of Virginia Woolf, ed. Mitchell A. Leaska. Harcourt, 1991.

A Room of One's Own. Penguin, 1993.

Three Guineas. Hogarth Press, 1938.

The Voyage Out. Penguin, 1992.

The Waves. Penguin, 1992.

ABOUT VIRGINIA WOOLF

Abel, Elizabeth. *Virginia Woolf and the Fictions of Psychoanalysis*. Chicago University Press, 1989.

Auerbach, Erich. *Mimesis: The Representation of Reality in Western Literature*. Princeton University Press, 1953.

Barrett, Ellen, and Patricia Cramer, eds. *Virginia Woolf: Lesbian Readings*. New York University Press, 1997.

Beer, Gillian. *Virginia Woolf: The Common Ground*. Edinburgh University Press, 1996.

Bell, Quentin. *Bloomsbury Recalled*. Columbia University Press, 1995.

———. *Virginia Woolf: A Biography*. Harcourt Brace, 1972.

Berman, Jessica, ed. *A Companion to Virginia Woolf*. John Wiley & Sons, 2016.

Black, Naomi. *Virginia Woolf as Feminist*. Cornell University Press, 2004.

Briggs, Julia. *Virginia Woolf: An Inner Life*. Penguin, 2006.

Childs, Donald J. *Modernism and Eugenics: Woolf, Eliot, Yeats, and the Culture of Degeneration*. Cambridge University Press, 2009.

Dalgarno, Emily. *Virginia Woolf and the Visible World*. Cambridge University Press, 2007.

DiBattista, Maria. *Virginia Woolf's Major Novels: The Fables of Anon*. Yale University Press, 1980.

Dunn, Jane. *A Very Close Conspiracy: Vanessa Bell and Virginia Woolf*. Jonathan Cape, 1990.

Forrester, Viviane. *Virginia Woolf: A Portrait*. Columbia University Press, 2015.

Froula, Christine. *Virginia Woolf and the Bloomsbury Avant-Garde: War, Civilization, Modernity*. Columbia University Press, 2005.

Glendinning, Victoria. *Leonard Woolf: A Biography*. Free Press, 2006.

Gordon, Lyndall. *Virginia Woolf: A Writer's Life*. Virago, 2006.

Haffey, Kate. "Exquisite Moments and the Temporality of the Kiss in *Mrs. Dalloway* and *The Hours*." *Narrative* 18, no. 2 (2010): 137–62.

Lee, Hermione. *Virginia Woolf*. Vintage, 1997.

Light, Alison. *Mrs. Woolf and the Servants: An Intimate History of Domestic Life in Bloomsbury*. Bloomsbury, 2008.

McHale, Brian. *Constructing Postmodernism*. Routledge, 1992.

Mepham, John. *Virginia Woolf: A Literary Life*. Palgrave Macmillan, 1991.

Miller, J. Hillis. *The J. Hillis Miller Reader*, ed. Julian Wolfreys. Edinburgh University Press, 2005.

Outka, Elizabeth. *Viral Modernism: The Influenza Pandemic and Interwar Literature*. Columbia University Press, 2019.

Ricoeur, Paul. *Time and Narrative, Volume 2*. Chicago University Press, 1985.

Saint-Amour, Paul K. *Tense Future: Modernism, Total War, Encyclopedic Form*. Oxford University Press, 2015.

Sherry, Vincent. *The Great War and the Language of Modernism*. Oxford University Press, 2003.

Strachey, Lytton. *Eminent Victorians*. 1918.

Stockton, Kathryn Bond. *The Queer Child, or Growing Sideways in the Twentieth Century*. Duke University Press, 2009.

Sutton, Emma. *Virginia Woolf and Classical Music: Politics, Aesthetics, Form*. Edinburgh University Press, 2013.

Thornbury, Walter. *Old and New London: The City Ancient and Modern*. Cassell, Petter & Galpin, 1873.

Walkowitz, Rebecca L. *Cosmopolitan Style: Modernism Beyond the Nation*. Columbia University Press, 2006.

Wicke, Jennifer. "*Mrs. Dalloway* Goes to Market: Woolf, Keynes, and Modern Markets." *NOVEL: A Forum on Fiction* 28, no. 1 (1994): 5–23.

Wussow, Helen. *New Essays on Virginia Woolf*, ed. Helen Wussow. Contemporary Research Press, 1995.

———. *The Hours: The British Museum Manuscript of Mrs. Dalloway*. Pace University Press, 2010.

Zwerdling, Alex. *Virginia Woolf and the Real World*. University of California Press, 1986.